DEAD WATER

Simon Toyne is the international bestselling author of the Sanctus trilogy – *Sanctus*, *The Key* and *The Tower* – and the Solomon Creed series. He wrote *Sanctus* after quitting his job as a TV executive and it became the biggest selling debut thriller of 2011 in the UK. His books have been translated into 29 languages and published in over 100 countries. *Dead Water* is the third book in a new series featuring Dr Laughton Rees and DCI Tannahill Khan, following *Dark Objects* and *Blood Traces*.

www.simontoyne.net

𝕏 @simontoyne
🄵 @simon.toyne.writer
🄾 @simontoyne

Also by Simon Toyne

THE SANCTUS TRILOGY
Sanctus
The Tower
The Key

THE SOLOMON CREED SERIES
Solomon Creed
The Boy Who Saw
Broken Promise

THE LAUGHTON REES AND TANNAHILL KHAN SERIES
Dark Objects
Blood Traces (Previously published as *The Clearing*)

SIMON TOYNE

Dead Water

HEMLOCK
PRESS

Hemlock Press
An imprint of HarperCollins*Publishers*
1 London Bridge Street,
London SE1 9GF

www.harpercollins.co.uk

HarperCollins*Publishers*
Macken House, 39/40 Mayor Street Upper
Dublin 1, D01 C9W8, Ireland

Published by HarperCollins*Publishers* Ltd 2025
1

A catalogue copy of this book is available from the British Library.

ISBN: 9780007551712 (HB)
ISBN: 9780007551729 (TPB)

Set in Sabon LT Std by HarperCollins*Publishers* India

Printed and bound in the UK using 100% Renewable
Electricity at CPI Group (UK) Ltd

To my editors, Julia Wisdom, David Highfill, and Tessa James, for all the guidance and support

FOREWORD

The River Thames that snakes through the heart of London is believed to be named after the Old English word 'Tamesis', meaning 'Dark One'. This may be in reference to its cloudy, silted waters, or it could be for other reasons. For the same murky waters have also provided an effective and convenient mode of body disposal for murderers from pre-Roman times to the present. Even today an average of one body a week is pulled from the surprisingly cold and fast-flowing river.

In the Victorian era, when the Port of London was at its busiest, most congested, and – arguably – most dangerous, the watermen who plied their various trades on Old Father Thames knew the river by other names.

The Black Highway.

The Devil's Sluice.

Dead Water Way.

DAY ONE

1

The red evening sky and sharp lines of London reflect in the warped liquid mirror of the Thames; steel, glass, ancient stone, captured in a river far older than any of it. It looks like one of those heavily filtered images from a travel blog, or a tourist website – or it would, if not for the corpse in the foreground.

The dead man lies on his back close to the river's edge, his tailored suit still somehow managing to look good despite the foul black mud that has smeared and soaked deep into the pale blue of the waterlogged wool. The man's shoes are good quality too, not quite as good as the suit but definitely not the sort of thing some desolate street-suicide would wear, the type who regularly jumped in the river to end it all. The quality of the clothes suggests that this man falls into the other main category of river victim – the tragic accident: a drunken dare and a leap from a jetty or a party boat that quickly turned fatal, a sneaky piss into the river that ended with a slip, a bang to the head, cold-water shock, and death by drowning. But that is not what happened here: even from his position high on the embankment DCI Tannahill Khan can see that much.

He works quickly, wriggling and rustling his way into a fresh paper suit as the rest of the CSI team busy themselves on the muddy bank below, arranging temporary lights to push back the

rapid advance of night and setting up screens to hide the body from the swelling crowd on the embankment. There's an added feeling of urgency with this one, not just because of the fading daylight, or the exposed and public nature of the crime scene, but because the floater – the blunt name the river police call all bodies found in the Thames whether they are floating or not – has been discovered at low tide, and the dead, mirrored water of the Thames is already starting to buckle with the force of the current as that tide begins to turn. In less than half an hour the spot where the body is now lying will be submerged again, along with any evidence that might still be found around it.

Tannahill fastens the paper suit at the neck, wiggles his fingers into a fresh pair of blue Nitrile gloves and powers up the digital camera ready to record the scene. He'll only get one look at this, and whatever images and footage he now captures will be his only record and point of future reference.

He sets the camera running and heads down a set of steep stone steps to the riverbank below, being careful to capture into evidence every worn stone stair, though he's pretty sure neither killer nor victim would have used them. Floaters were called that for a reason and the spot a body was pulled from the river was rarely the same place it had entered.

Tannahill reaches the muddy, gravel and litter-choked slope of the upper bank and tilts the camera upwards, holding for a slow count of ten on a big, wide shot of the whole scene: the darkening London skyline with Tower Bridge looming to his left, a fast-response MPU boat idling beneath it ready to transport the body if needed, and the corpse lying on the river's edge in the centre of it all.

Tannahill zooms in on the paper-suited forms surrounding it: the principal Scene of Crime Officer, the forensic pathologist, the SOCO hunched over the body and taking initial measure-ments – lividity, core body temperature – trying to establish a rough time of death to help work out how long the body has been in the water. Getting useful post-mortem readings from

a floater is notoriously difficult, the near-freezing waters of the Thames chilling the body rapidly and ruining all the usual scales of measurement. Even so, murder scene protocol needs to be followed, and the SOCO has to finish doing their thing before Tannahill can start doing his.

He studies the paper-suited figure standing over the SOCO, trying to figure out which of the five pathologists is on duty tonight, and therefore how speedy this process is likely to be. The figure moves, almost as if sensing his scrutiny, and a darkly made-up Cleopatra eye flashes briefly in his direction then returns to the corpse. Even with the surgical mask covering most of her face Tannahill recognizes Dr Evelyn Prior, one of the more senior forensic pathologists on the roster with a reputation for being incredibly thorough and utterly uncompromising. It won't matter to her that the tide is rising, or that he is waiting for them to finish the primary examination. She'll take as long as she needs then immediately start leaning on him to release the body so she can take it away to conduct the autopsy.

Tannahill stops recording and taps his fingers against the side of the camera, anxious to get on with his work but powerless to speed things up. He takes a deep breath, the rot and algae-salted tang of the river catching unpleasantly at the back of his throat. He pulls his phone from his pocket, calls a recently dialled number and looks up at the darkening sky as the phone starts to ring, the reds now deepening into bruise purples and slate greys.

'Hey.' Laughton Rees answers on the second ring. She sounds breathless, like she's hurrying home for the evening that he is about to torpedo.

'Hey,' Tannahill says. 'Listen . . . something's come up.'

'Oh.' He hears the disappointment in her voice. 'Are we talking slight delay or total write-off?'

'Hard to say. A body washed up down the river from you.'

There's a brief pause. 'On the north side, by Tower Bridge?'

Tannahill looks around and frowns. 'Yes, how did you know...?'

'Loads of bodies wash up at that spot,' Laughton cuts him off. 'It's something to do with the particular curve of the river-bank and the way the currents flow into it. When they built Tower Bridge they actually incorporated a temporary mortuary in the foundations so they could leave the washed-up bodies there on public display to try and help identify them. It's called Dead Man's Hole.'

Tannahill smiles. They have been seeing each other for nearly eight months now, ever since that business in the Forest of Dean, and he is still constantly surprised and impressed by the depth of her macabre knowledge. 'Can you imagine if they still did that today?' he says, 'just lined up murder victims on the side of the road for people to gawp at.'

'They do,' Laughton replies. 'It's called the internet. If Dead Man's Hole was still a thing today, someone would stick a webcam on the place and live-stream it with the hashtag *doyou-knowthisperson?*'

Tannahill glances up at the crowd on the embankment, phones held aloft as everyone tried to get a glimpse of the body. 'Yeah well, that would not be much help in this case.'

'Really!' Laughton asks. 'How so?'

Tannahill turns back to the river where Dr Evelyn Prior and the SOCO finally stand up and away from the body, giving him his first close and clear view of it, lying in the mud in its expensive suit and decent shoes – with no head, and no hands.

2

'Oh shit!' Laughton Rees pushes her way through the heavy front door of her apartment building and earns a surprised look from the white-haired security guard. She shoots him an apologetic smile then lowers her voice as she makes her way over to the bank of mailboxes opposite the main door. 'What are you thinking, gang-related? Contract killing maybe?'

'Actually, my first thought was that it's totally ballsed up our evening.' Tannahill sounds weary and distant, though Laughton knows he's barely a three-minute walk away.

'Oh, don't worry, we can talk to Gracie another time about us. You could still come over once you're done if it's not too late, get her more used to you being around. I can cook something and keep it warm.' She separates a small key, fits it into a mailbox marked *Penthouse* and retrieves a thick bundle of mail, mostly official looking and addressed to Dr Laughton Rees.

'Yeah, maybe,' Tannahill says.

'I'm not promising it will be edible.'

'That's OK, I'm not promising I'll eat it.'

Laughton smiles. One of the many things she likes about Tannahill is that, unlike most men she encounters in the male-dominated world of law enforcement, he is neither patron-

7

izing nor intimidated by her. She heads over to the lift, shoots another smile at the security guard, then presses the 'P' button to take her up to her flat.

'Listen,' Tannahill says, 'as appealing as a warmed-up mystery meal under the withering gaze of your teenage daughter sounds, I honestly don't know how long this is going to take. Identifying the victim is obviously going to take a while, unless by some miracle he has some ID on him.'

'Unlikely,' Laughton murmurs. 'Why remove the head and hands if you then leave a driving licence behind?'

'Exactly, though he does look like the type of person who's liable to be missed. Could be that he's already been reported missing and I'll get an ID from that, though of course then I'll have to deal with the bereaved. Whichever way you look at it, it's not going to be quick. The FP hasn't even finished doing their initial exam yet.'

'Who's the pathologist?'

'Evelyn Prior.'

'Oooo, nice.'

Laughton, along with a large section of the Metropolitan Police force, has a tiny bit of a crush on Dr Evelyn Prior, an aggressively stylish woman in a famously grey profession. Her glossy black hair and impressive cosmetic perfection make her look more like an old-fashioned film star than a pathologist. She also has a reputation of bagging the most unusual and interesting cases, so a headless, handless corpse washed up on the banks of the River Thames is right up her street.

'Looks like she's finishing up,' Tannahill says. 'I'll call you later when I have more of an idea how long this is going to take.'

'OK. Don't worry. There'll be other nights.'

'Yeah, but there'll be other bodies too.'

Laughton smiles. 'I love it when you talk dirty to me.'

'Ha!' the phone disconnects as the lift doors slide open.

Laughton heads out into the expensively hushed quiet of the

eighth-floor corridor of the Brannigan building and she feels the usual sensation of being in the wrong place. After years spent variously on the streets, in rehab centres, and in shabby rentals all over the city, the fact that she now lives in this slice of prime riverside real estate still doesn't seem possible. She slides the numbered security key into the lock of her front door and opens it on to a wide entrance hall lined with hardwood panelling with hidden lighting, and a pale marble floor that sweeps away to full-length windows framing the London skyline, and the darkening sky beyond.

She shrugs off her coat, hangs it in the small cloakroom hidden behind one of the panels then drops her keys into a bowl beneath a photo of a stern, athletic-looking man in his sixties wearing a well-tailored police dress uniform. The uniform belongs to the commissioner of police of the metropolis and the man wearing it is John Rees, Laughton's late father, who is the reason she is now living here. She touches his face, an automatic ritual and act of remembrance but also of penance, because he had left her this apartment by doing the very thing she had spent most of her adult life wishing for – namely, dying.

She heads across the marble expanse of floor towards the kitchen, lured by the sound of slightly too loud music that suggests her daughter Gracie has taken up residence there.

Gracie doesn't look up as Laughton enters, her blonde high-lighted hair falling over her face, her attention switching between her laptop and a patchwork of papers spread across the entire surface of the large kitchen island in the centre of the room.

'Hi!' Laughton balances the stack of mail on the one corner of work surface not covered by whatever it is her daughter is working on. 'What's this?'

'History project,' Gracie replies, her frowning attention still fixed on the overlapping documents.

'How come you're doing it in here?'

'Because my desk is too small,' Gracie murmurs in an *isn't it obvious?* tone of voice. She picks up some of the papers and moves them around as if trying to conjure some sort of order from the chaos.

'You could spread everything out on the floor.' Laughton pulls an already opened bottle of white from the wine-chiller, uncorks it and pours a healthy glug into a wine glass Gracie has thoughtfully and uncharacteristically left out for her. 'That's what I did when I was doing my PhD.'

'My floor's covered in clothes,' Gracie says in the same *are you stupid?* tone.

Laughton thinks momentarily about suggesting that maybe she tidy her room but opts instead for taking a long, welcome sip of the crisp, chilled wine instead.

She studies her daughter, hunched over her assignment with the same kind of fierce and blinkered work focus she recognizes in herself. She sees so much of herself in her daughter, especially now she's growing up, but there's so much of her that remains a mystery too. The older she gets, and the further she moves away from the little girl she had once been, the more that mystery seems to deepen.

Gracie looks up as if sensing her mother's scrutiny. 'What time's *he* coming round?'

Laughton notes the emphasis and her deliberate choice not to use Tannahill's name. It was the cause of increasing frustration for her that, the more her relationship with Tannahill warmed up, the frostier Gracie became towards him. This evening had been set up as an attempt to spend some informal, domestic time together, in the hope that Gracie might soften toward Tannahill and the idea of him being around more. They had started discussing the possibility of him moving in, which was a big step for her and would be an even bigger one for Gracie. Apart from Laughton's very few, very brief, and uniformly disastrous attempts at dating, it had only ever been the two of them, which was going to be a hard dynamic to

break. Judging by her daughter's mood, however, it seemed that the headless corpse that had washed up to ruin the evening maybe hadn't been such a bad thing after all.

'He's not coming now,' Laughton says. 'Something came up. A work thing.'

Gracie rolls her eyes. 'Doesn't it always.' She looks back down and frowns at the mess of paperwork in front of her.

Laughton picks up the sheet of paper closest to her, recognizing the familiar format of a parish record, with columns of names and dates listing marriages. 'So, what's the project?' She scans the document, a list of marriages that had taken place three decades earlier, and comes to a sudden halt halfway down the page. She looks up and finds Gracie's steady gaze now fixed firmly on her.

'This is my mum and dad's wedding day,' Laughton says, holding up the sheet of paper.

Gracie nods and slides a large piece of paper over to her. 'We've got to research our own family tree,' she says.

Laughton looks down at the new page, the lines of a tree pre-drawn on it with branches connecting blank boxes for parents, grandparents and so on, going back five generations. Gracie's name and date of birth are written in the box at the bottom, Laughton's is written above it next to an empty space where her father's name should be. 'I was hoping you could help me . . . fill in some of the blanks.'

Laughton stares at the empty space for 'father', realizing now what this is: the homework publicly spread out on the kitchen island instead of tucked away in Gracie's bedroom, the wine glass strategically left out for her, and Gracie at the centre of it all, watching her now with a kind of clenched stillness. It was a trap, carefully set specifically for her, and Laughton had walked right into it.

Gracie has never really asked about her father before, or seemed to want to know anything about him, which has suited Laughton just fine. She had expected her to become curious at

11

some point, especially now she was deep in the tangled weeds of teenagehood, trying to find a pathway through to her own sense of identity, but she had not expected the conversation to be prompted by a school history assignment. She slid the piece of paper back over to Gracie.

'You could just do my side of the family to keep it simple. Presumably this is more a test of your research skills than anything, no one's going to be actually fact-checking it.'

Gracie shakes her head. 'Only doing one side of the family would be weird.'

'Why?'

'Because these are all going up on the classroom wall when they're done, so everyone will see I haven't got a dad and it'll be really cringe.'

Laughton takes another sip of wine then shrugs. 'Lots of people don't have dads.'

'*Everyone* has a dad.'

'No, they don't, not in the old traditional sense at least. You could say it was a sperm donor, that's pretty close to the truth anyway.'

'Eww, I am *not* going to say that. It's not true anyway. You knew my dad and I didn't just come along because of some . . . gross clinical procedure. Why won't you tell me about him?'

Laughton sits down on a stool by the island, her energy suddenly drained by the prospect of dredging all this up. 'I do want to tell you about him, honestly I'm happy to, but . . .' She looks down at the papers spread across the island. 'Not for this. This feels like the wrong reason to be having this particular conversation.'

'Why though? You always said if I'm old enough to ask the question I'm old enough to hear the answer. Well, I'm asking you – who is my dad?'

Laughton meets her daughter's gaze, fierce and immovable. In her own work as a criminologist and sometime expert witness in criminal trials she has been variously described – generally

by the opposing counsel – as 'dogged', 'relentless', and 'annoyingly persistent'. Clearly her daughter has inherited the same traits. But Gracie has also artfully manipulated this situation, carefully staging the scene in order to corner her and raise a sensitive and difficult question. That is a different skill entirely, and one, Laughton realizes, that she probably inherited from her father. Maybe it was time to open that door after all.

She leans forward, picks up a pencil from the mess of paperwork and reluctantly adds a name to the blank space next to hers, letter by individual letter, like she's writing out a spell to summon an unpleasant and unwanted spirit.

Gracie tilts her head so she can read it. 'Shelby Facer.' She says it out loud, and Laughton clenches a little inside at the sound of his name spoken in the safe, personal space of her kitchen. Gracie looks up at her. 'Who is he?'

Laughton shakes her head and takes a deep breath as she mentally opens a door in her mind that has been kept locked for as long as Gracie has been alive.

'Someone who happened to float by at a time in my life when I was drowning. He was older. Wiser, I thought, and he had a kind of confidence that was . . . seductive. So I grabbed on to him and clung on. I thought he'd saved me. And he did, I suppose, but not in the way I thought.'

'How then?'

Laughton smiles. 'He gave me you. You were the one who saved me.' She downs the wine in her glass then reaches for the bottle.

'Listen, I really don't know that much about him, I was only with him for a few months and that was over sixteen years ago, but I'll tell you what I do know and then you can decide what to do with that information – deal?'

Gracie nods. 'OK.'

'But before I get into all that,' Laughton uncorks the bottle and refills her glass. 'I'm definitely going to need more wine.'

3

Bright white light from two portable LED arrays washes over the black mud, illuminating both the headless body and the vaguely spectral figure of Dr Evelyn Prior walking away from it in her white paper suit. Even in this setting and wearing her crime scene attire she still manages to move as if she's walking down the red carpet at a West End premiere.

'Find anything useful?' Tannahill asks as soon as she's close enough to hear over the constant background hum of London.

Evelyn Prior pushes back the hood and shakes loose a waterfall of black hair.

'Skin maceration is minimal, so he hasn't been in the water for long. No sign of lividity, which suggests that the body has only recently washed up – the movement of the water prevents the blood from settling, though there is also a deep wound to the chest, which I'm guessing will turn out to be the cause of death. I'll need to have a proper look, but exsanguination would also explain the lack of lividity.'

'You think he bled out?'

'He didn't die from the beheading, if that's what you're asking. There's no sign of bruising around the neck or wrists, suggesting that both head and hands were removed post-mortem. The cuts through the bone are also too neat to have

been aggravated, they definitely weren't hacked off by someone in a homicidal frenzy using something like an axe or a cleaver. The killer must have employed an instrument specific to the task, a surgical saw or similar, and they were careful and apparently not in any rush. The cuts are very controlled and deliberate. I can confirm all this once the body has been removed to the morgue and I've had time to carry out a proper examination, but I think it's extremely unlikely that he was killed here, so hopefully you can do all your due process and release the body to me fairly quickly.'

Tannahill glances past her to where the river is already lapping at the feet of the headless body. 'I don't think the tide is going to give me much option.'

Evelyn Prior pulls off her blue gloves, folding one inside the other in a practised movement. 'Spring tide, too,' she says.

Tannahill continues nodding, though he has no idea what a spring tide is.

'Full moon,' Dr Prior explains, picking up on his confusion. 'It's when the tidal range is at its most extreme, low tide is extra low then it *springs* back fast.' She glances back at the body. 'I'd guess you have around ten minutes or so before he starts floating away again.'

She looks back and studies Tannahill for a moment in a way that makes him feel suddenly uncomfortable and hot, then she moves past and heads away up the muddy bank, leaving him alone with the body and the rising tide. He glances up at the crowd on the embankment, bigger now, and with the glow of phones illuminating a line of eager faces still trying to get a glimpse of the body behind the temporary screens. The crowd is another compelling reason to hurry things along.

He takes a deep breath and sets his camera running again, moving towards the body, filming his approach and scanning the mud for something, anything, that might be worth recording into evidence before the river steals it away. He pans slowly across the dark mud surrounding the body first. It is embedded

with stones, worn bricks and driftwood, clear plastic fragments turned milky, and a thousand other bits of rubbish collected and churned together by the restless river. He spots a bright white object half-submerged in the black slime next to the stump of the right hand and stoops down for a closer look, thinking it might be a bone fragment. The focus shifts on the camera as he reaches out and levers the object out of the mud with the tip of his gloved finger. It is longer than it had first appeared and bent slightly at one end, a clay pipe, Victorian probably, dropped or thrown into the Thames like an old-fashioned cigarette maybe a hundred years earlier and only now being given up again by the river. He returns it to the mud and pans the camera slowly along the whole length of the body, capturing it as it was found.

Even from a cursory examination he can tell Dr Prior was right. The victim did not meet his end here. Apart from the spot where Dr Prior and the SOCO had stood while they examined the body, the mud is undisturbed. Small piles of litter and river muck have collected along the upstream side of the victim, showing how the water flowed around him after he finally snagged to a halt on the bank. Tannahill might not be familiar with spring tides but he knows the tidal flow in the Thames is strong enough to transport a body several miles up or downstream, depending on where it entered the water. And because the tide has been steadily going out for the last five or six hours, this person could have been killed pretty much anywhere upstream, possibly to the west of London itself where thick trees screen miles of the riverbank and there are fewer witnesses.

He shifts his position and zooms in on the empty space where the victim's right hand should be. Bone and flesh have been cut cleanly through just as Dr Prior had said, no ragged edges, no bone splinters, as neat as a leg of pork hanging in a butcher's window. He moves on to record details of the neck and notes the same neat, clean cuts. There is something chilling

about this precision; clear evidence that whoever did this was calmly capable of doing something most people would find stomach-churning and horrific.

Next he moves on to the left wrist and spots something, a blue line, possibly part of a tattoo, visible on the skin at the edge of the shirt cuff.

He leans in and tries pushing the cuff back with his gloved finger but it barely moves; the waterlogged cotton cinched too tight around equally waterlogged and swollen flesh. Tannahill leaves it for now, shifting the camera over to the man's chest to focus on what Dr Prior had said was the probable cause of death. The wound sits in the centre of a bloom of dirty pink cotton that was probably once white. There had been a lot of blood, he can still see that, even though the Thames has done its best to rinse most of it from the shirt.

He reaches out and parts the slit in the cotton with his fingers. The stab wound beneath is about three centimetres long and as neat as the slit in the shirt, the sliced edges rinsed pale by the Thames and gaping slightly. It's in the exact spot where the heart is, and judging by the amount of blood soaked into the man's shirt, deep enough to puncture it.

Single stab wound.

Strong enough to pierce the heart.

That took strength, not only physical but mental. No one accidentally stabs someone in the heart, they have to really mean it. Whoever killed this man had *meant* to do it. He – and it was almost certainly a 'he' going by the strength needed to deliver such a mortal wound – had intended to kill this person and done so with one powerful blow. Afterwards he had calmly sawn off the victim's head and hands using tools he had brought along specifically for the task, then he had transported the body to the river's edge and dumped it in the water.

Tannahill thinks about this.

Most homicides are messy and accidental and therefore easily solved, not least because the killer gives themselves up

17

ninety-nine per cent of the time. Premeditated murders are generally a little harder because actual murderers try to cover their tracks, although, unlike in the TV shows and films, most of them are neither thorough nor clever enough to succeed.

But not in this case.

This killer is different, and the murder has been very carefully planned and prepared. Nothing seems accidental or opportunistic about it, and that's the thing that is puzzling him. Because the killer could easily have weighed the body down before dumping it in the Thames, filled the pockets with rocks or wrapped a chain around it to make sure it sank and stayed hidden until the river broke it up and carried away the parts. Or he could have disposed of the body somewhere else, somewhere remote and anonymous: a pre-dug grave in woodland, or in the freshly poured concrete of a building under construction.

But he hasn't done any of these things.

What he has actually done is go to the trouble of concealing the body's identity by removing the head and hands, then dumped it in a river so famous for giving up its dead that they'd even built a morgue into the foundations of one of its most famous bridges to display them all. And the only reason Tannahill can think of for him to do this is because the killer *wanted* the body to be found, he *wanted* someone like Tannahill to stand here, asking himself these questions.

He looks at the body as a whole again, the nice suit and shoes, the ruined shirt with the single slit showing where the victim's life had gushed out of him, and notices something else. The jacket, though grey and mired from the river water, has almost no blood on it. He reaches down and opens it to look at the lining, an expensive-looking, dark blue silk. Apart from a few stains where it has rested against the ruined shirt, the lining is relatively clean. This suggests two things: one, the victim wasn't wearing the jacket when he was killed, because if he had been it would have been as soaked with blood as the

shirt; and two, the killer must have put the jacket back on to the body after he had killed him, possibly even after he had removed the head and hands, like he had been dressing the body ready for inspection.

Tannahill shuts off the camera and slides it into the front pocket of his paper suit, leaving both hands free to search the body more thoroughly. He checks the jacket first, patting each pocket before sliding his gloved hand inside. They all come up empty. He looks back at the stump of the victim's right hand where the blue line of the tattoo peeks out from under the cuff. A tattoo can help identify a body if it is distinct enough.

'Anything?'

The voice makes Tannahill jump and he turns to find Detective Sergeant John Baker looming over him, the hiss of the evening traffic having masked the paper whisper of his approach.

'Maybe.' Tannahill turns back to the corpse and uses both hands to pull the sleeve of the jacket back, revealing more of the dress shirt cuff beneath. It is held in place by a silver cufflink with a red rose design enamelled on to it.

'When do you reckon we can release the body?' Baker says, looking back up at the embankment. 'Only I'm already getting earache from her majesty and we're starting to attract a bit of a crowd.'

'Give me one second.' Tannahill twists the cufflink and grey river water squeezes out of the saturated fabric before it pops loose. He hands it to Baker. 'Bag that for me, would you?'

Behind him he hears the rustle of an evidence bag being pulled from a pocket then he leans forward and pulls the sleeve back to reveal the rest of the tattoo.

Only it isn't a tattoo.

Tannahill pulls the camera from his pocket, sets it recording then zooms in on the letters, hastily scrawled on the inside of the man's wrist in marker pen.

'P. Brannigan,' Baker says, peering over Tannahill's shoulder.

'Do you think that could be the name of our man here, or maybe the geezer he was going to meet?'

Tannahill pans the camera along the letters, recording them in to evidence. 'I think the killer would probably have noticed his own name written on the arm he was sawing a hand off, don't you?'

'Oh yeah, good point. I'll still run it, though, see if anything pops up.'

Tannahill stops recording and stares at the writing. Out on the river a large party boat cruises past, close enough to the shore to send a wash of water over the lower legs of the victim and reminding Tannahill of the rising tide.

'Tell Dr Prior she can have the body now,' he says, still staring at the writing on the dead man's arm. Something about it feels disturbingly familiar. Something so . . .

The muscles in his face tighten as he realizes in a rush what it is. He fumbles his phone from his pocket, adrenaline making his fingers tremble now, finds a recently dialled number and calls it.

4

Gracie stares at her father's name, sitting on the lower branches of her family tree.

'So, what do you want to know?' Laughton settles back on to the stool and places a freshly charged wine glass in front of her like a tiny liquid shield.

Gracie shakes her head gently. 'I don't know, I mean – who was he? How did you meet? What was he like? . . . Everything.'

Laughton takes a deep breath like she's about to jump off a high cliff into deep water.

'Shelby Facer,' she exhales his name, her forehead furrowed with the challenge of where to begin and how much she should say.

'You've got to understand that I was utterly lost when I met him. My mother, your grandmother, had been murdered and my life was in pieces. I was fifteen, a tiny bit younger than you are now, and I totally blamed my dad for what had happened. The man who killed my mum was someone he had arrested but who had been let go because of a legal technicality, a mistake in the investigation basically, an investigation my dad had been in charge of. He was supposed to be the big protector, the big bad copper battling evil guys out on the streets of London to keep us all safe. Only he'd ended up bungling it

and bringing evil to our door instead – and my mum had died because of it.'

Laughton stares at the cold liquid in her wine glass, as if her past is contained in it.

'After Mum died I didn't feel safe any more. I felt terrified and . . . angry. I had such rage, at my dad, at Mum too for abandoning me. It was grief really, a vast and bottomless grief.' She shakes her head as she remembers. 'Not the ideal cocktail of emotions to fuel the best life decisions.

'Anyway, in the wake of Mum's death and my incandescent rage at my father for letting it happen, for *causing* it to happen as far as I could see, I ran away, from him, from my home, from everything. I wasn't thinking about where I was going or what might happen to me. I didn't care.'

The furrow between Laughton's eyebrows deepens as she forces herself to remember.

'I don't think I actively wanted to die or anything like that, I wasn't suicidal, I just stopped looking after myself, couldn't see the point in preserving myself for some future I could no longer imagine. So I ran, from everything I had been, and fell into a self-destructive spiral, fuelled by grief and shame, because on some level I thought *I* had let my mum down too. She had died saving me and the thought that someone I loved so much was now dead because of me is a hell of a burden to carry. It drags you down. It dragged me down at least.

'I can't remember too much about that time. It's all a blur of being cold, sleeping rough, scavenging food, begging on the streets, and doing whatever I could to numb the pain. I was on a journey down to the very bottom of my grief, I think, trying to see how deep it went. And somewhere near the bottom, maybe at the very bottom itself, is where I met Shelby Facer.'

A sudden buzz sounds in the heavy silence of the kitchen and Laughton's phone lights up amid the patchwork of papers. Tannahill's name flashes up on the screen. Laughton grabs it and rejects the call to silence it.

'Work?' Gracie says in a flat, weary tone.

'No, it's . . .' Laughton places the phone back on the worktop. 'It's not important.' She looks back at Gracie, keen to get to the end of this road now she's started down it but also wary about how much to reveal. She had only realized how predatory and manipulative Shelby had been in retrospect. And though Gracie had said she wanted to know about her father, what benefit would it do her to be told that he was no better than a grooming paedophile, preying on young girls no older than Gracie was now? Surely, it was better to spare her the painful details of exactly who and what he was. Laughton takes another sip of wine and picks her next words carefully, thinking about how much light she should shine into this darkest corner of her past.

'I met Shelby in a squat off Deptford High Street, a boarded-up electronics shop that had been taken over by a group of homeless people and turned into a kind of commune. Shelby seemed to be the leader of the group, at least he was the one with the most authority. He was very charming, well-spoken, definitely an unusual presence among the rest of that crowd of derelicts and runaways. He seemed apart from it all somehow, like he was there by choice, living on the margins of society because he wanted to, rather than because something terrible had happened in his life to drive him there, which was pretty much the story for everyone else. He also had a confidence about him no one else had, like he knew things you didn't, like you'd be safe if you stuck by him.'

'How come he was there?' Gracie's voice is soft, almost tentative.

Laughton shakes her head, remembering. 'There were all kinds of stories swirling around about who he was: that he was an aristocrat who'd been disowned because of some terrible scandal, that he'd been a successful child actor who'd lost his way as he grew up, that he'd been a singer in a band who'd had one hit before slipping into obscurity. He never confirmed

or denied any of them, he'd just smile that smile he had, like he knew something you didn't and change the subject. Looking back now, I wouldn't be surprised if he had actually been the source of all the rumours, building his own legend.

'He was also a bit older than most of the others, certainly much older than me, maybe even as old as my dad, which I'm sure a psychiatrist would have plenty to say about. I guess I had a raw and ragged empty space that my father, the main authority figure in my life, had once occupied, and Shelby Facer happened to come along to fill it. And I was actually happy that he did, for a time at least. He was glamorous and charismatic, and I was flattered by his attention, and he made me feel . . . wanted.'

Laughton glances back up at Gracie, who is watching her with a stillness so unnerving she has to look away again. Shelby had also got her hooked on drugs to make her more dependent on him, should she share that too?

'So how long were you together?' Gracie's voice drags Laughton back to the present.

'Oh God, no more than a few weeks, just long enough for me to fall pregnant with you. I actually found out by accident. There was a raid on the squat and a bunch of arrests, including me. When they were booking me at the station I didn't give my real name because I didn't want my dad to find out where I was, but, now I know how police informants work, I realize he probably knew where I was the whole time and it was him who arranged the raid in the first place.' She shakes her head sadly. 'I never got the chance to ask him about any of this before he died.'

Her phone buzzes – Tannahill. Again Laughton rejects the call to silence it.

'After my arrest I was examined by a police medic. My father might have been behind that too, because it wasn't standard protocol back then, especially as I hadn't complained about an assault or anything. This was how I discovered I was pregnant: pregnant, malnourished and clinically dependent on Temazepam.'

Her eyes flick up at Gracie then she looks away again. She had never told her this little piece of her personal history before.

'You have to realize that everybody self-medicates in a situation like that. It's actually quite logical. If your reality is grim and painful it makes sense to do whatever you can to escape or alter it. Temazepam was cheap and plentiful, and seemed way less scary than other options.' She frowns as a thought strikes her. 'I suppose I must have still had some functioning element of self-preservation to choose that over some of the alternatives.'

Another unpleasant memory surfaces of Shelby trying to get her to try other things to 'expand her mind' and 'broaden her consciousness', like he was talking about going somewhere nice on holiday rather than injecting heroin or smoking crack. Shelby had always been the one with the stash and the freebies, another reason why everybody liked him. If she had been with him for longer maybe he would have worn her down. Fortunately, the raid had saved her.

She looks up at Gracie and smiles. 'I remember being told I was pregnant by a kind-voiced nurse. There was a WPC in the room as well. She asked if there was anyone I could call, family or friends. I told her there was no one. I imagine that also got back to my father, which is . . . awful to think about. I never got to ask him about that either.

'Falling pregnant with you was what pulled me out of the nose-dive. All of a sudden I was responsible for someone other than myself and, because in my mind I had already been partly responsible for the death of one person I loved, I couldn't bear the thought of it happening again. And even though at that point I still didn't really care what happened to me, I cared very deeply about what happened to you. And you were inside me, part of me, so I had to start looking after myself in order to look after you. And I did. I got clean, went back to school, and then you came along.'

Gracie frowns as a thought strikes her. 'Was I born in prison?'

'No, I was in care, not prison – different deal but equally scary. I knew they would try to take you from me because I was so young but I wasn't going to let that happen. Not a chance. I read up on family law in a local library while I was pregnant and worked out how I could keep you. Usually, you have to be an adult before you can exercise responsibility for a child, which, legally speaking, means being eighteen or over. But as a sixteen-year-old you can also petition the court to declare you as an adult and, as long as you can demonstrate an acceptable level of responsibility and there's no evidence that the child in your care is at risk of harm or neglect, social services can't take a baby from its mother. I argued all this myself in court, because I couldn't afford a lawyer and getting legal aid would have taken too long.' She looks up and smiles at her daughter. 'So, I guess you also helped me find my career.'

'And what about my dad?' Gracie says quietly. 'What happened to him?'

'I honestly don't know. After the raid I was taken straight into care and I went willingly because I knew they'd help me get clean so I could look after you. Shelby never tried to contact me, never made sure I was OK or tried to help me in any way.' Laughton looks up and catches the hurt clouding Gracie's face. 'I don't think that was a rejection of you, I'm not sure he even knew you existed. Shortly after we parted ways he got caught up in some big drug-related bust in Florida and went down for thirty years. I genuinely don't know anything more about him than that and I've never felt the need to find out more. I'm sorry if that sounds cold, but he really is a stranger to me. He may be your father biologically speaking, but in every other sense of the word, in every *meaningful* sense, he's a stranger to you too.'

Gracie shakes her head. 'He's still a part of me. I've got *his* blood in my veins as well as *yours*.'

Laughton looks at Gracie and catches a brief glimpse of Shelby in her daughter's face which makes her pause.

26

When she was about Gracie's age, she had chosen to remove herself from her father's life and now wished she hadn't. There was so much about him she didn't know and would probably never know now he was gone. So, if Gracie wanted to find out about her father, what right did she have to stop her? Shelby might even be dead now for all she knew.

'There were a few articles written around the time of his arrest,' Laughton says. 'I'm sure they're probably online somewhere. They might have some more info about him, his background or whatever.'

The phone buzzes a third time. Tannahill again. Laughton moves to silence it but stops. It's unlike him to be this persistent, normally he leaves a message and waits for her to call back. 'I should probably take this,' she says, screwing up her face in apology.

Gracie nods, her attention already turned to the laptop in front of her.

Laughton turns away before answering the call. 'Hey,' she says, 'what's up?'

'What are you doing right now?' Tannahill's voice sounds low and serious.

Laughton glances back at Gracie already speed-reading something on her laptop. 'Nothing, why?'

'That body that washed up downriver from you, I found something weird on it.'

'Weird like how?'

'Weird like . . .' He pauses. 'Like the victim might be somehow connected to you. Why don't you come down and take a look?'

Gracie's face creases into a deep frown as she reaches the end of whatever she's reading. She looks up at Laughton.

'He's not in prison,' she says, turning the screen round so Laughton can see the news article displayed on it. 'Shelby Facer was released four days ago and extradited back to the UK. He's here.'

27

5

Laughton's mind buzzes like a broken fridge as she hurries along the embankment. She had thought Shelby Facer was safely buried in her past, locked in some foreign prison, but he wasn't. He was here. In the UK. Probably back in London for all she knew. She could turn a corner and bump into him right now. Or he could be lying on a slab with his head and his hands missing for reasons unknown.

The victim might be somehow connected to you – Tannahill had said but wouldn't say why he thought that.

Ordinarily an evening with a headless corpse and a mystery at the heart of it was Laughton's idea of heaven, but tonight she could have done without it. She could have done without all of it. She had expected this evening to be tricky, but introducing the idea of Tannahill moving in now seemed like nothing compared to how things had actually turned out.

She arrives at the one-storey, white-and-blue building that houses the Metropolitan Police Marine Support Unit and presses a buzzer by the small, almost apologetic sign by the entrance. A uniformed officer answers, nods when she flashes her Met ID badge then leads her down a hallway lined with framed photographs of boats to the floating jetty at the back of the building. Four Targa fast-response boats bob up and down with

the movement of the river. One is being hosed down by two crew wearing the black ninja-like uniforms of the river police.

'Over there at the body bath,' Laughton's escort points to a square structure the size of a standard garage with a blue tarpaulin draped over it.

Laughton smiles her thanks and heads across the jetty towards a gap in the tarp where bright light spills out on to the deck. The crew washing down the response boat glance over at her as she walks past, intrigued by her civilian clothes and the late hour. They will have been the team who transported the body here, so knew exactly what awaited her behind the tarpaulin screens. Laughton hears a low murmur of voices as she draws closer, clears her throat, then pushes her arm through the gap and follows it inside.

The blue tent is headache-bright after the dark of the London night and Laughton has to narrow her eyes to take in the assortment of people gathered around the stainless-steel bath dominating the centre of the space. The bath is both larger and shallower than a regular domestic bath and sits on a frame of metal poles that raise it up to a workable height. Tannahill stands on the far side of it, his eyes lighting up above the surgical mask covering most of his face the moment he sees Laughton. The other people – a mortuary technician, a police photographer, a detective sergeant acting as exhibits officer, and a SOCO – all have their backs to her, their attention fixed on the corpse lying in the centre of the shallow bath. The body has been stripped and the harsh lighting accentuates the deathly pallor of the waterlogged skin. The folded remains of a suit lie by the corpse's feet next to a pair of shoes which are being slid into an evidence bag by the DS. The bag has 'DB18' written in marker pen in the section where a name should be. DB18 stands for 'Dead Body 18' and tells Laughton two things: one, that they still haven't identified the victim; and two, this is the eighteenth body to be fished out of the Thames this year, though it is barely even spring.

'This is Dr Laughton Rees from London Metro,' Tannahill says, addressing the person opposite him. 'She's a consultant criminologist who's helped us out on a few cases. I asked her to come take a look and share her opinion.'

'Forgive me if I don't shake hands,' a woman replies, her voice unusually low and instantly recognizable as belonging to Dr Evelyn Prior. She continues to stare down at the corpse, her gloved hands holding a probe that is currently inserted into a small but nasty-looking wound in the centre of the dead man's chest. 'As I was saying before your *guest* arrived,' she continues with the vaguest hint of annoyance. 'I believe this horizontal incision to be the most likely cause of death. It's sited in the third left intercostal space beside the sternum, directly above the heart.' She pulls out the probe and studies it. 'Roughly nine centimetres deep, which is enough to have pierced the cardiac sac and possibly severed the aorta. I'll have to open him up before I can ascertain exactly how he died, but there are no other obvious injuries and no defensive injuries on the forearms either. This suggests the victim was either taken completely by surprise by a swift and sudden blow, or they were unconscious when the fatal blow was delivered, quite possibly drugged. I'll run a full toxicology screen when I get the body to the morgue and put all the findings in my report.'

Laughton studies the headless body, trying to work out what it is about it that made Tannahill think it might be connected to her. Even without the head she can tell the man was of a certain age – fifty, maybe older. An unwanted image flashes in her mind of Shelby walking naked across the old office they'd called their bedroom in the Deptford squat. She blinks it away and looks back at the body. It could be him, though she can't see how Tannahill could have made that connection.

'Any guess as to time of death?' Tannahill asks.

'I'm not in the business of guessing,' Dr Prior retorts sharply. 'I deal only in facts and evidence. What I *can* tell you is that the body has not been in the water for very long as there are

minimal abrasions on the extensor surfaces of the skin. An inert body in water generally assumes what we call "the drowning position" where the anterior aspect of the individual faces downward with their back towards the surface. As the body is carried along by the current the lower extremities, the arms and legs, hang down and bash against the riverbed creating post-mortem injuries.'

She picks up the victim's left wrist and points at the area around the stump.

'Here both the epidermis and subcutaneous tissue appear mostly intact, and the feet were protected by the victim's shoes. There are also minimal signs of post-mortem animal predation, even around the main wounds, which would be the first places fish would feed, drawn by the faint blood trail in the water.'

Dr Prior holds the arm up higher. 'The skin exhibits signs of mild *cutis anserina*, or goose flesh, which is caused by rigor of the arrector pilli muscles.' She runs her gloved finger along the inner arm. 'The epidermis itself still retains integrity. There's some wrinkling, which is normal both pre- and post-mortem, but there's no sign of marbling or sloughing, showing that the victim cannot have been submerged for a significant amount of time. Judging by the level of decomposition, or lack thereof, I would say the victim hasn't been dead long either, though they might have been refrigerated between death and being deposited in the river. However, the lack of lividity suggests to me that is probably not the case here. Again, I'll give you a more accurate and definitive appraisal once I've had time to conduct a proper post-mortem. I'll harvest DNA as well to help you with the identification process, seeing as we have no fingerprints or dental records to go on.'

'Actually,' Tannahill says, looking up at Laughton. 'I was hoping Dr Rees might be able to help us with that.'

Laughton looks up at him, feeling the attention of the room suddenly shift entirely on to her. 'Why do you think I might recognize him?'

31

'Why don't you take a look,' Tannahill says, holding her gaze. 'I don't want to influence your reaction, just look and see if there's anything that strikes you as familiar or noteworthy about him.'

Laughton holds his gaze for a moment longer, narrowing her eyes at him, then she looks at Baker. 'Do you have a spare mask I can use, I don't want to . . .'

Dr Prior produces a surgical mask from somewhere with a flourish, like it's a trick she's been waiting to perform. She also takes the opportunity to finally turn round and scrutinize Laughton. Her eyes are remarkable, a deep blue that teeter on the edge of violet, made all the more dramatic by the heavy but perfectly applied make-up that frames them.

'Thanks.' Laughton takes the mask and fits the loops over her ears as Evelyn Prior proceeds to study her, like she is something of academic interest lying on her slab.

'I knew your father,' Evelyn says, her low voice sounding strangely intimate, like maybe there had been more to their relationship than just work. 'He was a good man, could be a bit of a dick at times but he was management, so I suppose that went with the job. I can see a bit of him in you,' she continues, still studying Laughton with cold interest. 'But not much.'

'I look more like my mother,' Laughton says, adjusting the mask over her nose and mouth before stepping up to the stainless-steel bath, reciting in her mind the mantra she wrote about how to process evidence at a murder scene.

You must notice the things that seem unremarkable
You must never be distracted by the obvious

As the body is the most obvious thing, she ignores it at first and looks at the folded pile of clothes instead, the clean, straight cuts visible in the blue material where it has been sliced away from the body. The shirt is separate from the suit, the washed-out blood looking purplish grey under the harsh lighting. She notices the neat incision at the centre of the blood bloom and the single rose cufflink in one of the sleeves, red with a white centre.

She imagines the victim carefully threading them through the shirt's cuffs, taking care with his appearance, maybe wanting to make a good impression on whoever it was he was about to meet, the person who would end his life then dump him in the dirty river. Whoever this person was, he had not been dressing for a fight, that seemed clear, and whatever he had been expecting it was certainly not this.

She looks at the body now, the skin glowing under the examination lights. It is very pale, almost as if the victim had been drained not only of blood but also of colour. The only things that have any tint at all are the chest wound, which is a pale, purplish grey, and the frilled edges of the stumps where the hands and head have been removed.

Removed – she thinks – not hacked off or severed.

Laughton tries to imagine this man as he was in life based on what she can see of him now. He is tall, or was before several inches had been stolen from him. He also looks like someone who was once in fairly decent shape but whose arms and chest have softened slightly with age. Somewhere between mid-forties and early sixties seems about right and again she thinks of Shelby Facer. He would be in that age range now. She mentally runs through everyone else she knows who might be a physical and age match and comes up blank.

Next, she scans the body, starting from the toes and working her way up to the neck, looking for any distinguishing features. He has bunions on both feet, indicating a lifetime of wearing tight shoes, and a small scar on his right side above the hip, which looks old and more surgical than violent, an appendix scar maybe, which might help with identification. She tries to remember if Shelby had an appendix scar but can't. Her eyes shift across and briefly linger on his penis, shrivelled and pale under the lights. He is uncircumcised, as was Shelby, but her intimate knowledge of him pretty much ends there. Their historic fumblings had generally been quick and had usually taken place in the dark.

She moves on, scanning his upper body for more scars, tattoos, birthmarks, anything that might trigger a memory, and spots something on the inner forearm of his right arm, a blue line that might be a tattoo. She leans forward in order to see it and something shrieks like a siren in her head the moment she reads what's written there.

'What?' Tannahill says, spotting her reaction.

Laughton stares down at the writing on the dead man's arm – *P. Brannigan.*

She realizes now why Tannahill had wanted to see if she made the same connection without any hints or prompts.

'Where exactly was this body found?' She asks, keeping her voice as calm as she can.

'By London Bridge,' Baker replies. 'On the north bank.'

Laughton nods slowly. 'Close to where I live,' she says, staring at the writing on the dead man's arm. 'The Penthouse of the Brannigan building.'

She looks up at Tannahill and sees the recognition in his eyes. 'P. Brannigan is not a name,' Laughton says for the benefit of Dr Prior and everyone else present. 'P. Brannigan is my address.'

6

Laughton bursts out of the tarpaulin tent, speed-dialling Gracie. She stops at the edge of the jetty and stares out at the creeping black water of the Thames as she listens to the ringing tone purr in her ear. Tannahill emerges from the tent behind her but she doesn't look at him. She's way too angry right now so she keeps her attention focused on the ringing tone, fingers tapping out patterns of three on the safety rail as she wills it to connect.

'Hey,' Gracie answers finally, sounding vague and distracted.

'Hi, it's me. Are you OK?'

'Yeah, why?' Gracie's voice changes as she picks up the stress in her mother's voice.

'I was just . . . It's nothing . . . I was checking you were all right.'

'Yeah, all good. I was about to order a pizza.'

'NO!' The word comes out with far more force than Laughton intended. 'I mean, I'll pick something up on my way home.'

There's a long pause. 'Are *you* OK?'

Laughton thinks about the headless corpse lying in the shallow stainless-steel bath behind her with her address scrawled on what's left of its right arm, the address where her daughter is currently home alone. 'Yes, I'm . . . don't answer the door to anyone, not even a delivery. I won't be long, I promise.'

'What's up, Mum?' Gracie sounds a little nervous now, which is maybe not a bad thing.

'I'll fill you in on everything when I get home. Sorry to be mysterious. I'm probably over-reacting but . . . please, sit tight and I'll tell you all about it when I get home. I won't be long. I'll bring pizzas from Vapianos.'

'OK.'

'Love you.'

Another pause. 'Love you too.'

Laughton hangs up and takes a deep breath of cold night air that tastes of rank river water and diesel fumes.

'You OK?' Tannahill asks, his tentative tone suggesting he already knows the answer.

Laughton wheels on him. 'In what world did you think it was a sensible idea to make me leave my teenage daughter alone at an address that appears to have been written on the arm of a headless corpse?'

Tannahill opens his mouth to speak but closes it again. He looks out at the river and nods slowly, his lips pressed into a thin line. 'I'm sorry, I didn't think. I needed a second opinion and wanted to see your unguarded reaction when you saw the body, which I wouldn't have got if I'd described it to you over the phone. But you're right, I was only thinking about the case, I wasn't thinking about . . .' He shakes his head as he tries to find the right words. 'I just wasn't thinking. I'm sorry.'

Laughton turns away to face the river again, too angry to look at him. Maybe him moving in wasn't such a great idea after all if this was his general level of domestic responsibility.

'I can send someone round to your flat if you like,' Tannahill says. 'Get someone to check in on Gracie, make sure she's OK.'

Laughton shakes her head. 'Don't bother. There's a permanent security guard on reception and she won't answer the door to anyone now anyway.'

Tannahill nods. 'OK. I'm really sorry.'

Laughton continues her staring contest with the river. Night

has fallen fully now and the water glistens with the reflected lights of London, glossy and black, more like oil than water. She's angry at Tannahill for dragging her here but there's something bigger that's bothering her too. Could the headless body be Shelby?

'I presume you've run the name P. Brannigan through missing persons?' she murmurs.

'Yes. No one with that name is on file as missing. We also ran a check using a physical description, or as much of one as we can establish, and the only middle-aged men reported missing recently are either too large or too short. Hopefully the DNA will throw up something, but there's going to be a delay on that as all the labs are now closed for the night. Our best hope is that someone comes forward and reports him missing, which in this case I'm pretty sure they will. He's too well-dressed to be a nobody. Anyone wearing a suit like that is going to have a house, a life, people who are close who I assume will miss him sooner rather than later.'

'Never assume.' Laughton continues to stare into the oil-black river. 'When archaeologists first started digging up bodies from early burial sites they would often find brooches in amongst the bones. They assumed that the number of brooches must be an indicator of how rich and important the person had been and that was accepted theory for decades. But a recent paper by Dr Hugh Willmott from the university of Sheffield argued that the brooches are actually nothing to do with status at all, they're simply indicators of what time of year the person was buried.' She turns to Tannahill and sees his confusion.

'Early man did not have buttons,' she explains. 'They wore animal skins and roughly woven cloaks fastened together by brooches. Dr Willmott had been researching customs and traditions in early settlements and discovered that the common funeral practice was to bury people quickly in the clothes they had died in, which made sense because it helped stop the spread of disease. So, if someone died in winter they would be wearing

more clothes, and therefore have more brooches than if they'd died in summer.'

Tannahill nods slowly, then frowns. 'How does any of that apply to our DB?'

'Status,' Laughton replies. 'The point is the brooches had nothing to do with status and everything to do with circumstance. So just because our man in there was wearing a decent suit when he died, doesn't necessarily mean he was somebody who'd be missed in life.'

She cocks her head to one side as something new occurs to her then she turns and walks straight past Tannahill, heading back to the bright slash of light leaking from inside the tarpaulin tent.

Dr Prior and DS Baker both look up as Laughton bursts through the gap. Evelyn Prior has already removed her paper suit and mask and transformed into such an unexpected vision of glamour that it causes Laughton to pause for a moment and stare at her, standing against the industrial blue of the tarp in a bottle-green cocktail dress that makes her look even more like an old-school Italian film star.

'I was on my way to the opera when the call came in,' Dr Prior explains, holding her arms out in an elegant flourish. 'I don't usually dress like this for work.'

'Right,' Laughton says, 'you look . . . amazing.'

'Thank you. Though I'm assuming you didn't charge back in here just to pay me a compliment.'

'No, I wanted to take another look at the exhibits before they get sent off if that's OK?'

'Knock yourself out,' Baker says, and goes back to unrolling a body bag next to the stiffening corpse, aided by a couple of river police officers.

Laughton steps over to the foot of the stainless-steel bath where the clothes taken from the body now lie inside individual evidence bags. Behind her she is aware that Tannahill has also re-entered the tent but ignores him.

She crouches down, bringing her eyes level with the evidence

bags and studies the shoes first, her eye running along the edge where the stitching binds the upper to the sole. They're well-made but also slightly worn, the heels on both shoes show signs of wear on the outstep, the leather bulges slightly around the big toe, matching the slight bunions she had noticed earlier. There are also scuff marks on the toes, though these look fresh and most likely occurred when the body was floating in the water with the feet hanging down and scraping along the bottom.

'What is it?' Tannahill murmurs behind her.

'Old shoes,' Laughton murmurs. 'Good quality but not new, not fashionable either, at least not any more.'

Tannahill leans in to look at them as Laughton turns her attention to the suit, folded over itself to fit inside the evidence bag. It's waterlogged and grimy, but she can still see the bright blue of the material, particularly around the fresh cuts where it was removed from the body.

'Same with the suit,' she says. 'Well-made but old-fashioned: narrow lapels, and double-breasted, more like something you'd find in the back of a wardrobe, or in a charity or vintage shop.'

She studies the cuff of the jacket where the paler interfacing material is starting to show through the blue of the wool at the edge. 'It's also distressed in a way you would expect to see in an older suit that's been well-worn.' She switches her attention to the final bag containing the bloodstained shirt, turns it slightly so she can see the label. 'This shirt is newer than the other items,' she says. 'It's not as good quality either, it's a standard off-the-peg shirt from Marks and Spencer. The fact that he chose to wear this type of dress shirt complete with cufflinks, rather than something more casual, suggests our victim may have been trying to impress whoever he was meeting, but maybe didn't have much in the way of means to do it. The suit is better quality, possibly even bespoke, but it's old.'

She stands up and looks down at the whole outfit, somebody's Sunday best now cut up and river-soiled, folded and labelled in plastic bags. She shakes her head.

'I don't necessarily think this is the kind of person who might be missed. He's wearing clothes that were at their best ten to fifteen years ago.'

She turns to the river police officer who is about to zip the body inside the bag. 'Hold on one sec,' she looks down at the corpse again, half in and half out of the bag. Without its head the body is grotesquely anonymous, a pale sack of flesh and bone, but even so, the body type does match, and so does the profile of someone who might have had money to buy himself a decent suit more than a decade earlier but was now on a budget.

'There's a chance I might know who this is,' she whispers. 'I could be wrong, I hope I am, but it's worth checking out.'

She turns to Tannahill. 'The name is Shelby Facer. He was released from a Florida penitentiary four days ago and extradited back here.'

Tannahill pulls his phone from his pocket. 'Who's Shelby Facer?'

'He's . . .' Laughton hesitates, thinking about whether she really wants to tell Tannahill who Shelby Facer is or his connection to her. An hour ago she would have done so gladly, well, maybe not gladly, but now, the thought of getting into all that with him in this depressing tent with strangers around makes her feel intensely uncomfortable. 'He's the only person I can think of who's the right age, could be wearing clothes that were fashionable fifteen years ago, *and* who might have my address scrawled on his arm,' she says, sticking to the relevant details and avoiding the backstory.

Tannahill unlocks his phone, ready to note the name down but frowns at something on the screen instead. He taps it to open a message then blows out a weary breath and shakes his head.

'What is it?'

Tannahill holds his phone out for Laughton to see and she peers at the headline on the screen:

HEADLESS CORPSE FOUND BY TOWER BRIDGE
AND THAT'S NOT ALL THEY FOUND . . .

Below it is a grainy photograph taken before the crime-scene screens went up, clearly showing a body lying at the water's edge.

A deep line forms between Laughton's eyebrows. 'What else *did* we find and how does this news site know about it already?'

Tannahill scrolls quickly through the article and shakes his head. 'Nothing, it's click-bait. Someone posted the photo on Reddit and it's been picked up and repackaged by one of the nationals, which is why I got this alert. I'd better prepare a statement before this snowballs.' He looks up at Laughton. 'Looks like this evening is a total write-off after all. Sorry again about . . . all this.' Tannahill gestures at the brightly lit tent.

Laughton stares at him coldly for a beat then turns to Evelyn Prior, still a vision of glamour in her green cocktail dress. 'Hope your evening is still salvageable,' she says.

Dr Prior raises an eyebrow. 'Unfortunately not. The Queen of the Night will have sung "*Der Hölle Rache*" by now and *The Magic Flute* is pretty much all downhill from there.' She glances down at the body as Baker zips it inside the bag. 'The dead are so inconsiderate.' She looks over at Tannahill, still frowning down at his phone. 'Maybe I can find something else to do instead.'

'What was that name again?' Tannahill asks, oblivious to Evelyn Prior's scrutiny.

'Shelby as in *Peaky Blinders*,' Laughton replies, feeling suddenly territorial. 'Facer as in "Face" with an "R" on the end.'

'And who is he?'

'Someone I used to know,' Laughton says, still unwilling to get into the details. Then she turns and slips out of the tent, already calling Gracie again as she hurries back to the Penthouse of the Brannigan Building as fast as she possibly can.

7

News about the headless body spreads quickly, the irresistible combination of the gruesome image and an eyeball-grabbing headline drawing clicks and shares from all the online ghouls.

On most of the posts, the photo is pixelated, a digital veil drawn over the goriest parts to protect the sensitive but which only serves to send the gore-vultures fluttering to the darker corners of the internet in search of an uncensored version. The lack of a head also elevates this 'Body found in River Thames' story above the run-of-the-mill suicides that regularly wash up on the muddy shores. Suicides are depressing, don't sell very well and are therefore hardly newsworthy. Exotic murders, however, are big box office.

Because of this, the image spreads steadily and widely, first through individual posts and shares on social media, then via niche crime forums until finally it is picked up by the more sensational mainstream news sites, amplifying it a thousand-fold and bringing it to the attention not only of Tannahill as he stands over the actual body, but also the battalions of conspiracy theorists who immediately start speculating wildly about who the headless person might be, throwing out the names of every high-profile scoundrel with recent, well-publicized troubles as possibilities. The front runners are quickly established as a

Russian steel magnate who'd fallen out of favour with the Kremlin, a daytime TV presenter recently sacked from his decades-long job after child porn was found on his laptop, and a disgraced Tory MP, deselected after losing an expensive libel case against a national newspaper that had accused him of being in the pocket of an international drug cartel, and actually had the evidence that he was. The MP is the one most people have their money on, mainly because he is the closest physical match to the body in the picture and because beheading and behanding – *is that even a word?* people wonder in the chat groups – sounds more like a cartel type of thing.

And so it spreads, shared by the shocked, the outraged, the blood-thirsty ghouls but always, always shared until, by the time it reaches the man standing in the shelter of a bus stop – flat cap pulled low over his eyes, shoulders hunched inside his coat against the evening chill – it has been seen by over fifteen million people in well over a dozen countries.

The phone buzzes in his pocket in response to the news alert he'd set up earlier using the keywords 'Headless', 'Body' and 'Thames' but he doesn't look at it, not yet. Instead, he stares unblinking down the street, as if awaiting the arrival of a bus, when in fact he is watching the woman standing in the pizza place on the other side of the road.

Laughton Rees obsessively checks her phone while a skinny kid with face tattoos and a nose-ring boxes up her overpriced, artisanal, wood-fired, sourdough pizza. From where he's standing it looks like she only ordered one, which is good. One pizza means no visitors.

The kid with the face tatts hands the pizza to Laughton and she steps out into the street holding the box in front of her like a tray as she heads back towards the river. He waits for a few seconds then glances down at his phone to read the news alert:

HEADLESS CORPSE FOUND BY TOWER BRIDGE
AND THAT'S NOT ALL THEY FOUND . . .

The headline makes him want to read the rest but he hasn't got time, so he slips the phone back in his pocket, steps out from the bus shelter and follows Laughton down the road at an amble.

He stays on the opposite side of the street, matching her pace to maintain the distance between them. The evening crowd has thinned now, driven home early by the cold, and the dark, and the lingering urge to hibernate which clings like dirty snow to the tail end of the winter blues.

Ahead of him Laughton disappears around the corner and he ups his pace a little, just another office worker hurrying home after working late. He slows again as he reaches the corner then moves around it on to the broad, open space of the Thames embankment.

She is closer now, close enough that he can smell the garlic and oregano vapour-trail of her pizza. His stomach growls in response. Should have eaten something earlier.

Ahead of him she turns sharply and springs up a wide set of marble steps, taking them two at a time before tapping in a code and pushing open the heavy front door of her apartment building. He isn't close enough to catch the code, and is too far away to slip through the door behind her so he carries on walking, heading to a bench on the embankment. From the corner of his eye he can see her inside the lobby. She says something to the security guard behind the desk on her way over to the lift and he smiles in response. The guard has white hair and grey skin, probably ex-military, or maybe ex-police, topping up his pension with this nice cushy, part-time security job in an air-conditioned building. He's clearly there to make the residents feel safer, rather than for any serious, practical use. They might as well stick a cardboard cut-out behind the desk. But then the guard is never the problem in a building like this, it's the button under his desk he can press to bring real security running. It's also the cameras fitted above every entrance and exit that are backed up remotely so you can't even swipe the tapes and junk them like you could back in the good old days.

He reaches the bench and sits down, turning to his side so he can still see the building as he pulls his phone from his pocket, tilting his head down so his cap covers his face.

From where he is sitting he can see two cameras over the front door – one pointing straight down, one pointing out at the pavement in front of the building – and two more in the lobby, one above the reception desk and one above the lifts where Laughton now waits, pizza in hand.

The doors open and she disappears inside.

The ancient security guard watches the doors close then looks down at his lap to continue reading his book, or playing Candy Crush, or whatever it is he does to while away the hours. The guard picks up a mug of tea from beneath the desk, takes a long swig and chases it with a chocolate biscuit which makes his stomach growl again. He smiles as he remembers something he read once about how hunger makes you sharper and more alert, something to do with our caveman ancestors and how being hungry made them better hunters. It made sense. When you were hungry there was more at stake; if you killed something, you ate, if you didn't, well – you died.

And he has a hunger. Oh yes, he has a hunger, and he has used it to sharpen himself over sixteen long years, honing himself to a razor-sharp instrument of revenge. It's a particular hunger born of rage and injustice that requires something more than regular food to feed it.

He pulls his phone from his pocket and re-reads the headline, the wording sensational, blunt, and deliberately designed to make you click on the link to find out more:

AND THAT'S NOT ALL THEY FOUND . . .

He clicks to read the article and frowns when he discovers it doesn't tell him anything at all.

Not that it matters.

He doesn't need any third-party article to tell him what else

45

was on the body because he already knows.

He deletes the message, slides the phone back into his pocket and looks back at the building. A man in a long coat stops in front of it, looking up at the building like he's contemplating whether to climb it or not.

Up on the top floor the light in the corridor turns on in response to movement, probably from the lift door opening. He pictures her now heading to the front door of the Penthouse flat. He knows exactly what it looks like because he's seen photos of it in the sales brochure he found online from when the building was first completed. He imagines her opening the front door and heading across all that marble to the huge kitchen with the massive island in the centre. And there she will sit, eating her overpriced pizza in her overpriced apartment while he sits out here on this hard bench feeling hungry and cold.

He imagines her taking a slice of pizza out of the box, the tomato sauce thick like blood, the stringy mozzarella stretching like tendons and his stomach rumbles in response.

Definitely should have eaten something earlier.

Then again, he doesn't need hunger to sharpen his ability to hunt.

All he needs is an opportunity.

As if in answer, a Deliveroo driver on a bike pulls to a stop in front of the building and hurries up to the entrance holding a paper bag. The security guard glances up, buzzes him in and turns his attention back to his book or whatever is helping him through the night. The delivery driver heads to the lifts then, just like that, a total stranger is inside the building.

8

Tannahill enters the fourth floor of NoLMS headquarters, a seventies-style office block in a scruffy area of no man's land running along the railway lines leading to King's Cross station. The North London Murder Squad, along with a couple of other North London divisions, moved here 'temporarily' when their beautiful stone building was sold to developers in a bid to cut costs and raise revenue following the last public spending review. The 'new' offices – all strip lighting, vertical blinds, and open plan with cubicle partitions – are noisy and depressing, the combined activity of the various teams creating a kind of hive din that is constant and distracting. It also means everyone knows you're in the building the moment you step out of the lift.

'Hey Khan,' someone calls across the open-plan office, 'need a *hand* with your new case?'

This raises chuckles and high-fives from the officers surrounding the joker.

'No, but I'll give you a shout if I need any dad jokes,' Tannahill shouts back as he makes his way over to his desk. News travels fast in the Murder Squad and a handless, headless corpse was always going to bring out the comedians.

He reaches the far side of the office and collapses into his

faded threadbare office chair, sending a puff of foam dust exploding from various rips along the edges of the seat cover. Tannahill logs on to his computer and does his best to zone out the office noise as he quickly types up the press release he drafted in his head on the journey over: *Male between fifty and sixty-five years of age, white, five feet ten to six feet one in height.* He adds details of where the body was found but avoids spelling out that it was missing its head and hands, saying instead that identification was proving difficult. He also describes the suit and shoes hoping they might jog someone's memory, and debates with himself whether to leave out the detail about the rose cufflinks but adds it anyway, figuring he's more interested in identifying the body quickly than holding back information that could help filter out potential time-wasters further down the line. Finally, he adds an incident number for people to call, proofreads it, then sends it over to the press office for immediate release.

He sits back in his lumpy chair and stares up at the water-stained ceiling tiles above his desk. Before it had become home to various police departments, the office block had been the headquarters of an insurance company that had gone out of business, and the depressing character of that company's slow demise had somehow managed to bleed into the very fabric of the building. Almost all of the ceiling tiles on the fourth floor bear water stains, suggesting that the sprinklers were tripped at some point and there clearly hadn't been enough money to repair the damage. The carpet is ruined too, so worn and ingrained with a kind of sticky black filth that it had taken Tannahill a good couple of months to realize that it wasn't actually lino.

He studies the water stain above his head, undecided whether it looks more like an upside-down pear or a badly drawn map of Africa, and thinks about calling Laughton, goes so far as to pull his phone from his pocket then decides against it. He puts his phone down, clicks on a shortcut to open the National

48

Crime Database instead, and inputs his username and password. He enters the name Laughton had given him, 'Shelby' as in *Peaky Blinders*, 'Facer' as in Face with an 'R' on the end, and hits *Return*. An extensive charge sheet comes back charting the criminal career of one Shelby Andrew Facer, born 1962 in Peterborough, Cambridgeshire.

He reads through it, the chronology of arrests charting the usual trajectory of the career criminal, starting with small-time stuff – shoplifting, minor drug dealing and possession offences that earned him suspended, non-custodial sentences; then, once he'd used up his goodwill and eventually pissed off a judge enough with his repeat offending, progressing inevitably to prison time. Once inside he clearly met and mixed with older career criminals, who, judging by the more serious charges he started collecting after he was released, had encouraged him both by example and introduction, to move on to bigger things. The next charges on his record were way more serious than his earlier efforts – possession of controlled substances with intent to supply, bank and credit card fraud, handling stolen goods, selling stolen goods – until eventually he flew too close to the sun and it all came crashing down.

His undoing had taken the form of a multi-million-dollar, international drug deal that would have propelled him into the major leagues had it not been infiltrated on the US side by an undercover DEA officer. His intel had resulted in a large, dual-agency operation between the Met in London and the DEA working out of Miami, Florida. They'd called it 'Operation Henry 8', maybe because the main guy had a big red beard or something. Tannahill opens the attached case files and reads through the cover sheet listing the various files associated with the case – witness statements, requisition documents, charge sheets etc.

He clicks on the top link, hoping he might be able to find something useful in it, the name of a known associate or an

officer who worked the case who might be able to help him track Shelby down, but gets back an 'Access Denied' message. He clicks on the next link – same response. He works through every link in turn but nearly all of the documents are either unavailable or so heavily redacted that what they do contain is practically unreadable. Even sixteen years after it was closed, the case that sent Shelby Facer to a US prison is still classified, which only makes Tannahill want to read everything it contained even more.

He taps his fingers on the scarred surface of his desk. Finding information about Shelby Facer was proving way harder than it should be. He could maybe get permission to declassify the files but that would mean petitioning someone higher up the chain of command, which will be time-consuming and will probably result in a 'No'. Still, he quickly types an email to his chief superintendent, copying in the case file numbers and requesting they be reopened. He hits *send* then reads through the few documents that still have some information in them, just about managing to piece together the story of what happened.

Shelby Facer had been the bag man for a consortium of six people in the UK – Shelby, a man named William 'Billy' Carver, and four others whose names were all redacted. They had been attempting to set up a major new drug importation route with four Miami-based representatives of the Sinaloa Cartel in Mexico – names also redacted. To secure the shipment, Shelby had flown to Miami with what he thought was thirty million dollars' worth of uncut diamonds and Billy Carver acting as security. The diamonds were a down payment on the first of what they clearly hoped to be many shipments of cocaine along a container ship transportation route from the Port of Miami directly to the Port of London. Except one of the people involved on the US side was a DEA informant and instead of promoting Shelby Facer to the big leagues the job had landed him and Billy Carver in jail for a thirty-year stretch. It would have been

even more only the diamonds had turned out to be fakes and the smuggling charges dropped.

Tannahill writes down 'Billy Carver', then clicks back to the main page of Shelby Facer's record and opens the most recent addition, Shelby's extradition paperwork.

His phone buzzes on the desk and he peers at the screen, hoping it's Laughton. He blows out a long, weary breath when he sees who it actually is, considers letting it go to voicemail but relents and answers it anyway.

'Hey Mam.' He traps the phone between his chin and his shoulder and resumes scrolling through the release documents, looking for an address or a contact number.

'What you doin' answering your phone?' His mother sounds somewhere between surprised and cross.

Tannahill frowns. 'You rang me.'

'Yes, but I didn't expect you to answer. I was going to leave you a message.'

'OK, do you want me to hang up?'

'No, no – there's no point now, I was going to ask you how your evening went with your lady friend but the fact that you're answering your phone and I can hear that godawful noise of your office in the background tells me everything I need to know.'

'Something came up,' he says.

'Doesn't it always! Ah, Tanny, you're a lost cause.'

'Thanks, Mam.'

Tannahill has endeavoured to keep as much distance between his mother and what generally passes as his private life as possible, mainly because his very traditional, very Irish mother's idea of small talk with any prospective partner is to ask things like how many children they want and how soon they want to get married.

'You need to start putting your life before your work or you'll end up old and alone,' his mother says, playing a well-worn record. 'Did you manage to talk to her at all?'

Tannahill thinks back to the frosty conversation he'd had with Laughton on the jetty. 'Yes,' he says, 'we talked a bit.'

'And what did she say?'

'Not much, really. Nothing was decided. It wasn't really the right time.'

He hears a loud snort. 'Sure, when is it ever?'

'Mam, I can't help it if a dead body turns up. I don't have the kind of job where you can leave things in an in-tray and deal with them the following morning.'

'I know, Tanny, but there's always going to be something getting in the way until you change your priorities and visualize what it is you really want.'

Tannahill closes his eyes. His mam has recently discovered self-help podcasts which she listens to obsessively while walking the dog or cleaning – also obsessively – and her language has become peppered with therapy speak.

'So, what was it this time?' his mother asked. 'A fight in a pub? Some kind of domestic that ended up with a bread knife sticking out of some poor soul?'

'Mam, you know I can't discuss the specifics of ongoing cases.'

He hears another long sigh, which may be exasperation at his hopeless love life or frustration at the fact that he never gave her any juicy details of the murders he's working on.

'Tanny,' his mother says in her all too familiar *I'm-not-cross-I'm-disappointed* voice. 'You can't keep going on like this. I bet you haven't eaten a scrap of food today either.'

'I'll grab something later.'

'It's always later with you. I'll eat later, I'll come round and see you later, I'll sort my life out later. I'll get married and settle down later. You always think there'll be a later, but the only time that really counts is now. Yesterday is history, tomorrow a mystery, but today is a gift, that's why it's called the present.'

Tannahill smiles. His mother has also started collecting and

dispensing these kinds of fridge-magnet philosophies in the same way she had once done with passages from the Bible.

'I promise I'll eat something, OK, Mam? But I need to get back to work now.'

'All right, son. I just worry about you is all. And by the way, a packet of crisps out of a machine doesn't count as food.'

'I'll get something on my way home, I promise.'

'Ah, but when might that be?'

'It'll be a lot sooner if you let me get on with some work.'

Another heavy sigh. 'All right, son. You look after yourself.'

'I will, Mam. Night.'

He hangs up and scrolls to the end of the PDF of Shelby Facer's extradition paperwork, signed and filled in with the details of the contact address where he intended to stay after he returned to the UK. Tannahill copies the scrawled address into Google – 13 Barrie Avenue, London NW1 – and hits *Return*.

He gets results for Barrie Avenues in Kidderminster, Dunstable, and Dumfries as well as a Barrie House in Lancaster Gate W2, but no Barrie *Avenue* in NW1. He tries Barrie Road and Barrie Street but there's nothing in London NW1 for those either. He looks across the nest of desks to where his colleague Bob Chamberlain is framed by neat towers of files and frowning at his own monitor.

'Hey Bob, you ever hear of a Barrie Avenue in NW1?'

'Jesus,' Chamberlain says, settling back into his chair and folding his hands over his expansive tummy as he looks off into the middle distance. 'Haven't heard that one in a while.'

Tannahill waits for him to elaborate but he continues to stare into space like he's remembering happier times.

Sergeant Bob Chamberlain is the best detective on Tannahill's team who isn't actually a detective. Grey hair, grey suit, grey demeanour, he's like a man made from gunmetal and about as hard and inflexible. He has been flying a desk ever since a carjacker ran over his leg while he was still in uniform and he

knows the streets of the capital almost as well as his London cabbie father had done.

'So . . .' Tannahill prompts. 'What's the deal with Barrie Avenue?'

'Oh,' Chamberlain says, snapping out of his reverie. 'It's nothing, or rather, no*where*. It's a fake address that used to get flung about back in the day by anyone who didn't want to give us a real address. The NW stands for 'Nowhere' and Barrie Avenue is, I think, a reference to J. M. Barrie. You know, the guy who wrote *Peter Pan* and thus created Neverland, the original one, not the nonce-palace Michael Jackson lived in. Basically, it means Neverland in Nowhere, so whoever gave you that address, good luck finding them because they're in the wind, my friend.'

Tannahill nods. 'Great.' Nothing about this case was straight-forward.

'Who gave you that address?' Chamberlain asks. 'Has to be someone old-school, I might remember them.'

'Suspect's name is Shelby Facer, recently released from US prison and now back in the UK.'

The twin caterpillars of Chamberlain's eyebrows move closer together as if convening an emergency meeting. 'Facer, yeah, that rings a bell,' the caterpillars draw even closer as his mind rapidly shuffles through decades of old cases.

'He was arrested just over sixteen years ago in a UK/US co-agency operation,' Tannahill prompts, trying to jog his memory further. 'The operation was codenamed "Henry 8".'

Chamberlain's eyebrows fly up. 'Yes, I do remember that one, it was called Henry 8 because there were six people involved, the same number as Henry the Eighth's wives, though from memory I think they only caught two of them.'

'Yes, one was this Shelby Facer character who gave the false address, the other was' – Tannahill checks the note he'd made earlier – 'Billy Carver.'

Chamberlain's face darkens instantly. 'Him I *do* know. Nasty

piece of work. Proper nutter. Worked security for the Gallaghers out of East Ham. Really lived up to his name. I questioned him once about a shooting in a pub car park. He had shark eyes, nothing behind them. Gave you the impression that he could just as happily slit your throat as peel an orange. He was looking at thirty years to life for that one but didn't even break sweat. Sat there and stared at me like a crocodile waiting to feel hungry. We had to release him in the end after the two witnesses who'd originally placed him in the area at the time of the shooting suddenly changed their minds about what they'd seen. I remember when they finally nicked him and he got sent down for this Henry 8 case, everyone breathed a huge sigh of relief. One less psycho on our streets, one more problem for the Yanks to deal with. Not many people make my blood run cold, but Billy Carver did.' Chamberlain frowns as something occurs to him. He looks up at Tannahill, his eyes magnified slightly behind his glasses. 'You said this Shelby Facer who gave the bogus address was recently released?'

'Yes, four days ago.'

Chamberlain looks down at his keyboard and quickly taps something on it. He looks up at his monitor, his eyes darting back and forth behind his glasses as he reads whatever is displayed there.

'Bollocks!' he says flatly, sitting back in his chair and seeming to deflate a little. He looks back at Tannahill through the teetering twin towers of his caseload. 'Carver got out four days ago too.' He takes his glasses off and pinches the bridge of his nose. 'Well isn't that just great!'

Tannahill enters Billy Carver's name in his own terminal and another charge sheet pops up, even longer than Shelby Facer's. He opens a mugshot of Billy Carver taken at the time of his arrest and studies him. He looks solid, mean, light brown hair and blank eyes, and with an unsettling aura about him, exactly the kind of person you would not want to encounter on a dark night, or even in broad daylight for that matter. He looks back

up at Chamberlain. 'You said Carver lived up to his name.'

Chamberlain stops pinching the bridge of his nose and fits his glasses back in place. 'Yes, that's right. I told you he worked for the Gallaghers. He was muscle in their loan-sharking business: collecting bad debts, making an example of those who didn't or couldn't pay, that sort of thing. Carver by name, Carver by nature they used to say about him because he was a blade artist. He had a reputation for chopping things off – fingers, toes, sometimes whole hands if the debts were big enough. No one ever testified on the record, of course, probably because they wanted to keep hold of the bits they still had. And Carver was always careful, surgical even.'

Tannahill feels the skin tighten on the back of his neck. 'What do you mean, surgical?'

'I mean like he knew what he was doing. He'd worked for his old man when he was younger. William Carver Senior had been a butcher in the East End, at least he was when he wasn't in the boozer or the bookies. Little Billy Carver had been his apprentice for a while, before he'd realized he could earn more from chopping bits off people instead of animals. He was a trained butcher too.'

9

Laughton enters her flat and is greeted again by the muffled sound of Gracie's music coming from the kitchen. She touches the photo of her father, closes the door and heads towards the mournful music, holding the pizza in front of her like a peace offering. Gracie is sitting in exactly the same position she was when Laughton left over an hour earlier, staring intently down at the patchwork of documents in front of her. Laughton dumps the pizza on top of it.

'Hey!!' Gracie grabs the box and pushes the papers out from under it. 'This is my homework.'

'It's also the kitchen.' Laughton opens a wall cabinet and takes a clean glass from inside, pulls the open bottle of wine from the chiller, half fills her glass then opens the pizza box and takes a large, stringy slice. Gracie watches her take a bite, walks over to the fridge and returns with a squeezy bottle of mayonnaise. She squirts some into the cardboard lid, takes a slice herself and dips the tip into the mayo before taking a bite.

They eat in silence, Laughton enjoying the food despite the night she was having and Gracie's grim music groaning away in the background.

'Elodie thinks it's weird eating pizza with mayo,' Gracie pulls

off a chunk of crust and dips it in the mayo. 'But she leaves the crusts, which I think is even weirder.'

Laughton pulls the crust off her own slice. 'I used to leave the crusts too until I was working late one night, we ordered pizza and I saw someone doing this.' She dips her crust in the mayo, pops it in her mouth and chews contentedly.

Gracie nods. 'Everything's better with mayo.'

They chew on in satisfied silence for a moment then Gracie reaches for a second slice. 'What was all that about on the phone earlier?' she asks, folding the slice in half and pausing it in front of her mouth like she's talking into a microphone. 'You sounded flustered.'

Laughton pictures the headless body shining under the harsh examination lights, her address written on the arm, a body that might possibly belong to Gracie's father. She thinks about telling her everything that has happened including what she suspects, but quickly decides not to, not until she has more information at least. No point in getting her worried about nothing if the headless corpse turns out to be some random stranger.

'It's nothing,' she says, helping herself to a second slice. 'There was something about the case I was called out to that spooked me a little. Sorry if I freaked you out. I'm just tired I think – long day.' She nods at Gracie's laptop. 'What about you?' she asks, keen to change the subject, 'You manage to find anything new?'

'Not much. I found a few articles written around the time he was sentenced but they all say the exact same things – name, age, nationality. I did find this though.' She spins the laptop around so Laughton can see the screen.

Shelby Facer stares back at her, his blank expression and height-lines behind his head showing that the photo is a mug shot. It's the first time she's seen his face in sixteen years and her reaction surprises her.

She doesn't feel anything.

Nothing at all.

It's as if the person she had been back then, the lost little girl so desperate for someone to cling to that she had been taken in by this man, was someone else entirely. She thinks about that girl now, naïve and vulnerable, and feels protective towards her, like she is now the parent that little girl was always searching for.

'Do you think I look like him?' Gracie asks.

Laughton cringes inwardly at the question but studies the photo anyway, forcing herself to compare the most precious thing in her life with one she values not at all.

'Not really,' she says. 'You look more like me at your age. I can see more of my mother in you than your father.'

Gracie spins the laptop back round and studies the photo. 'I was trying to find a more recent picture to see what he looks like now but there aren't any. There's nothing before his arrest either. That was all pre-internet and I'm guessing he wasn't high-profile enough to make the press. It's all very skimpy, so I was wondering if maybe . . .'

Her voice trails off and Laughton looks up to discover Gracie staring at her with her mouth screwed over to one side, which normally means she wants something but is afraid to ask.

'What?'

'Well, I was wondering if you could maybe look him up on one of your work databases.'

'The National Crime Database? No!' The 'No' comes out way more firmly than she'd intended so she adds a laugh to try and soften it a little. 'I can't do that.'

'Why can't you?'

'Because the NCD is not Wikipedia, it's not a public resource and it's definitely not meant for personal use. Every search is logged and has to be justified as being strictly work related. They're incredibly rigorous about it, they have to be, otherwise everyone with access would be looking up their daughter's boyfriend, or the guy they met online to see if they had a criminal record or not.'

'But couldn't you say it was for something you were working on?'

'No, hun, I couldn't, and I won't. Apart from the fact that it's not ethical I'm also not prepared to risk my job for what is effectively just a school project.'

Gracie looks down at the paperwork spread out around the pizza box. 'It's not *just* a school project,' she murmurs. 'Not to me.'

The dirgy background music chooses this exact instant to stop, the sudden silence adding extra drama to the moment. They both sit in the muffled hiss of a London silence, mother and daughter, weighed down by the heaviness of what hangs between them. In the end it is Laughton who cracks. She picks up the sheet of paper with the family tree drawn on it and stares down at Shelby's name written in the box next to hers, as if their relationship, such as it was, was this easy to define. Her eyes drift over the blank spaces above his name.

'You could always make up stuff about his side of the family,' she says, feeling the single parent's urge to immediately fix anything that's broken in her child's life. 'No one's going to check. You could invent a whole family tree for him and, as long as you keep it sensible and don't make out like he's descended from royalty or anything, who's going to know the difference?'

'I'll know,' Gracie says. 'And I don't want to make stuff up, I want to find out the truth. This is not just a school project – this is about me and who I am. It's about my family and my past. It's actually about your family too.' She looks back down at the laptop and taps something on the keyboard. 'I found something in one of the longer articles written at the time Dad was sentenced.'

Laughton winces at the word 'Dad' but Gracie is too distracted to catch it, her full attention fixed on whatever she is now scrolling through.

'It was the only thing that gave any extra details about the

operation leading to his arrest and included the name of the officer in charge of everything on the UK side of things.' She turns the laptop around and Laughton speed-reads the article until her eyes virtually trip up over the name buried in the text. DCI John Rees. Her father. Gracie's grandfather. The man whose framed picture she touches every time she enters or exits the flat that had once been his home.

'When I saw that I started thinking,' Gracie says tentatively. 'If your dad was running the whole operation, maybe he kept copies of the case files. I mean, given the fact that this would obviously have been more personal to him than most of the cases he worked, he might have kept some kind of record, don't you think? So, if they were like on an old computer or something, you wouldn't need to look anything up at work.'

Laughton continues staring at her father's name, a fresh realization dawning.

Her father had been the one in charge of the operation that had removed Shelby from her life.

Of course he had.

When they had reconciled shortly before his death she'd discovered that her dad had always watched over her, like a guardian angel, respecting her desire for distance but looking after her all the same. Even at the very beginning, when she had first run away from home and blamed him for causing her mother's death, he had still been there, making sure she was OK, maintaining the illusion of her escape and only intervening at arm's length, sending his officers into the squat where she was living with Shelby Facer and making it look like a routine raid rather than a personal intervention.

She had been wrong about her father her entire adult life and when he lay dying in a hospital bed there had been so many things she had wanted to ask as she sat by his side, but the fog of morphine had never cleared long enough for them to talk. Even after he was gone and she had inherited the flat and all it contained, she had hoped she might learn more about

61

him through what he left behind. But, it turned out, she had been wrong about that too.

She remembered unlocking the door for the first time and entering alone. She had told Gracie to stay away because she hadn't known what she might find or how she would react. She had hoped it would be filled with all kinds of personal things, photo albums, drawers filled with scraps of a life she'd been removed from, that she'd removed herself from. But there was nothing. It felt like no one had really lived here at all. There weren't even any books, only a battered old copy of *The Lion, the Witch and the Wardrobe* that had made her cry when she found it, not because it held any great emotional meaning for her but precisely because it didn't. He must have kept it for a reason, presumably because he had read it to her when she was a child, but she had no memory of that at all.

The only other thing she had found that was remotely personal was a photo of her and her mother, taken when Laughton had been about ten years old. She was sitting on her mother's knee and they were both smiling at whoever was taking the picture. She assumed the photographer had been her dad. You only smile at someone like that if you love them. There had been another photo tucked into the frame, taken on a camera with a long lens, like the type you use in a covert surveillance operation. It showed Gracie playing on the swings in a park with Laughton in the background, pushing her. She could physically see how far away her father was from them both in that picture, and the thought that he had put it in the same frame as the one of her and her mother, bringing his broken family together the only way he could, had made her cry again. And *she* had done that to him. She had pushed him away, and by the time she had realized that she had got it all wrong, it was too late and there was no time left to change it, or ever put it right.

'There are no case files,' she says flatly, turning the laptop away. 'There was nothing personal here at all, only that photo

of me as a kid that's on my desk. Your grandfather was obviously not the sentimental type.'

The hiss of another London silence stretches between them for a long moment.

'Would you do things differently, if you had the chance?' Gracie asks, her voice barely more than a whisper. 'Would you have spent more time with him, if you could?'

Laughton nods, 'Of course, I would give anything to be able to spend . . .' She looks up, realizing too late that she's stepped into another trap. 'Your situation is totally different from mine.'

'How? How is it different?'

'Well, your dad is dangerous, for one thing.'

'Is he?'

'Yes, he has spent a large chunk of his life in prison.'

'Not for anything violent, though. Not for anything dangerous. And he only got caught because *your* dad wanted to get rid of him.'

'It wasn't because of my dad, it was because of *Shelby* and what *he* did, because of who *he* is.'

'How do you know who he is or what he's like? The last time you saw him was, like, sixteen years ago. You don't know him any more. Maybe he's changed.'

'Yes, and maybe he hasn't.'

'Shouldn't we at least give him a chance, though? Would it be so terrible to at least try and find out where he is, maybe make contact with him and get to know him a little?'

'No.'

'Why not? You just said you regret not spending more time with your dad and having a chance to get to know him better, so how come you won't even entertain the idea of me wanting to spend some time with mi—'

The knock on the door makes both of their heads whip round. It is so soft and hesitant that Laughton wonders if she heard it at all. She turns back to Gracie and mouths. 'Was that the door?'

63

Gracie shakes her head uncertainly. 'I think so,' she whispers, both of them instinctively remaining quiet.

Laughton turns back. Listens again.

Visitors from outside can only gain access to the building by calling the video entry-phone at the front door and then being buzzed in. A knock on the door must therefore come from a neighbour or someone already in the building but the only other flat on the top floor belonged to a man who worked for a Hong Kong bank and he was almost never there. Maybe it wasn't a knock after all, maybe it was some other noise that had sounded like a—

The knock comes again.

Tap. Tap.

Gentle but distinct and undeniable.

Laughton glances back at Gracie then rises from her stool and heads out into the hallway, instinctively keeping her foot-steps light so she can listen out for further sounds as she draws closer to the front door.

10

Tannahill stares hard at his monitor, a feeling of growing unease expanding in his chest as he speed-reads the extensive criminal record of William 'Billy' Carver: multiple arrests for violence, grievous bodily harm, actual bodily harm, attempted murder, possession of an unlicensed firearm – plenty of arrests but not many convictions, charges usually dropped for unspecified reasons, though based on what Chamberlain told him earlier, he can pretty much guess why.

'You said Carver had a reputation for chopping bits off people?' Tannahill says as he scrolls down to the bottom of the file. 'Fingers, hands, that kind of thing.'

'A reputation, yes,' Chamberlain replies, 'nothing ever proven.'

He finds Carver's extradition paperwork and opens it. 'Did you ever hear any rumours of him decapitating anyone?'

'No, but it wouldn't surprise me if he had. Are you thinking your headless floater might have something to do with Carver?'

'Maybe.'

Chamberlain nods. 'Wouldn't surprise me. He's a vindictive bastard with a memory like an elephant. I imagine he'll have spent the last sixteen years fantasizing about all the things he'd like to do to the people who put him inside.'

Tannahill reaches the bottom of the page where Carver wrote his contact address in the UK and copies it into the maps app on his phone: Albion House, Jamaica Street, Stepney, E1. The screen refreshes, showing a section of East London. He taps the button for directions and a blue line appears linking Khan's current location at NoLMS HQ to the address. Forty minutes by car, ten minutes quicker by tube. He puts his phone down and opens the PNC – the Police National Computer – taps Billy Carver's contact address into it then clicks on the tab to bring up the electoral roll. He finds the details for the address and nods.

'He's gone home,' he murmurs. 'The East End address Carver gave on his extradition documents is registered to a Mrs Elizabeth Mary Carver, who, judging by her DOB is most probably his mother, or maybe an auntie.'

Chamberlain smiles. 'Well fancy that, little Billy Carver, running home to Mummy. It's a shame John Rees isn't still around to see all this.'

Tannahill looks up at the mention of his old boss's name. 'Why?'

'Because he'd get a kick out of it. I mean, he wouldn't welcome the return of Billy Carver, not after everything he did to get rid of him, but he'd get a big laugh out of the fact that big, tough, scary Billy Carver has ended up running home to his mum. John Rees was in charge of the UK side of it. He was the one who set it all up.'

For a moment Tannahill feels like he has stepped off a cliff and the information he's just learned is the ground rushing up towards him – *John Rees responsible for putting Billy Carver away, Billy Carver who liked chopping bits off his enemies, the headless corpse with John Rees's address written on the arm.*

He leaps out of his seat, snatching his phone from the desk.

'Send a squad car round to John Rees's old address,' he says, searching for Laughton's number on his phone. Chamberlain

looks up at him, shocked into stillness by Tannahill's sudden change of tone. 'It's the Penthouse of the Brannigan building by Tower Bridge.'

Chamberlain continues to stare up at him, his large eyebrows knitted together in confusion.

'Do it NOW!' Tannahill says, turning for the door, phone clamped to his ear, listening to the dialling tone and willing Laughton to answer.

11

Laughton stops at the end of the hallway and stares at the solid front door, wishing there was a peephole in it so she could see who was standing on the other side.

She listens out for any noise in the corridor beyond.

Nothing.

She thinks about saying something, asking who's there. Maybe it's best to remain silent, see what happens. She settles in for a period of stillness and listening when her phone rings suddenly and loudly in her pocket, shattering the silence. She fumbles for it, feeling suddenly exposed, pulls it from her pocket and glances at the screen. Tannahill! She fumbles to silence it but a voice calls out from the other side of the door which makes her freeze.

'Hello! . . . Laughton?'

That voice. Even though she hasn't heard it in almost sixteen years, she recognizes it instantly and knows exactly who is standing on the other side of her door.

Her phone buzzes again in her hand and she silences it without answering. Her head whips round to a noise behind her and she finds Gracie standing by the kitchen door. Laughton raises a finger to her lips to keep her quiet. If they can both remain silent and still, maybe he'll go away. Gracie doesn't

know it's her father standing on the other side of this door and Laughton wants to keep it that way.

'Hello!?' the voice comes again. He sounds different somehow, less self-assured, which only makes Laughton more suspicious. Because of course he would want to appear meek, he was standing on the wrong side of a very solid door that he wanted to persuade her to open.

She maintains eye contact with Gracie, her mind a tumble of thoughts.

Why is he here?

What does he want?

How the hell did he get past the security guard on the front desk?

But though she wants answers to all these questions, what she wants even more is for him to leave. If she can wait it out long enough for him to go away, she can find out the answers later, in her own time and on her own terms, not like this, ambushed in her home with her daughter standing behind her.

She wills Gracie to stay quiet, to remain oblivious to who has come to visit. All they have to do is stay still and he will eventually go away and leave them in peace.

Her phone rings again. Way, way too loud. She glares at the screen, sees Tannahill's name and feels like smashing her phone against the wall. The voice in the hall calls out again, muffled slightly by the heavy door but loud enough for Gracie to hear.

'Laughton, is that you?' it says, sounding almost pathetic. 'It's me. It's Shelby.'

Gracie's eyes double in size and Laughton knows that her plan to play possum is not going to work. He knows she's there and now Gracie knows he's there too. Her father. Entirely absent for every one of her fifteen years of life but now standing a few feet away from her, as if the very act of mentioning his name earlier had been enough to summon him.

Laughton silences the buzzing phone. She doesn't want to

talk to Tannahill but she'll have to talk to Shelby now. There's no way of avoiding it.

She reaches for the security bolt on the side of the door and notices her fingers are trembling slightly. She hates the fact that he still has the power to unsettle her, even after so many years. She takes a breath to gather herself then slowly moves the bolt across, trying not to make a noise as she does it.

'What are you doing here?' she asks, forcing her voice to stay low and controlled despite the chaos of emotions inside her.

There's a pause and she pictures Shelby standing in the corridor outside, leaning in, listening, probably close enough to reach out and touch her if the door wasn't in the way, and the thought makes Laughton take a small, involuntary step backward.

'I need your help,' Shelby says, his voice quiet and diminished somehow, a lesser version of what she remembers, like it has been hollowed out. 'I'm sorry to surprise you like this,' he continues, his voice still low and cautious, 'but I'm in danger, real danger, and there's a chance you might be able to help me.'

Laughton feels her anger grow. How dare he come here asking for help and potentially bringing danger with him.

'It's to do with your dad,' Shelby adds, and Laughton glances across at the framed photo of her father by the door, his face appearing to frown slightly as if he's listening in to the conversation.

'My father is dead,' Laughton says flatly.

'I know. I saw it in the news and I'm sorry for your loss, genuinely, but . . . this *is* where he used to live, right?'

Laughton's skin tightens as she recalls her father's address, *her* address now, scrawled on the pale skin of the headless body earlier. 'What's that got to do with anything?'

'I'd rather not talk about this while standing in a public corridor,' he says, his voice even quieter now. 'Give me five minutes and I can explain everything. Five minutes is all I ask.'

Laughton can't believe he has the balls to turn up like this after sixteen years of nothing and expect her to let him back

into her life. She hates him for it, resents the hold he still has over her and impulsively acts to reject that power by doing the one thing she never had the courage to do when she'd been a little lost girl of fifteen. She reaches for the lock, twists it, and yanks the door open to confront him.

Shelby jumps back and flinches at the loud bang as the security bolt engages. He stares at Laughton through the narrow gap, eyes wide with shock. He looks thin and wary, like a stray dog caught sniffing at something he shouldn't. He attempts a smile and reveals a broken front tooth.

'You're looking well,' he says in his familiar but hollowed-out voice.

Laughton takes him in: the broken tooth, the skin on his face and around his mouth loose and grey, his head tilted down slightly, the overhead lights throwing his eyes into deep shadow and illuminating the fact that his sandy hair, cut prison short and receding at the temples, has turned more salt than pepper. He's wearing an overcoat that looks a size too big over a Miami Dolphins sweatshirt, and a pair of faded black jeans that don't match the brown brogues on his feet. He looks exactly like his voice sounds, recognizable but diminished, a faded copy of the man he had once been. But she sees something else too, something in his face that she had never noticed before because she had never had cause to look for it. She can see hints of Gracie.

'Tell me why you're here,' Laughton says, moving on from this uncomfortable realization.

Shelby glances behind him at the empty hallway, as if concerned someone might be listening. He turns back, his face looking genuinely haunted, opens his mouth to speak but before he can say anything Laughton sees a change in his face and realizes too late what has caused it. She turns to find Gracie, standing right behind her, staring through the narrow gap at the man in the hallway, an expression on her face somewhere between shock and wonder. Laughton wants to slam the door and press a reset button to erase the last five minutes. She

hadn't even wanted to talk about Shelby earlier and now here he was, in the flesh, staring at the daughter she never wanted him to meet.

'Well,' Shelby says softly. 'Don't you look *exactly* like your mother.'

Laughton turns and steps between them. 'You need to leave,' she hisses.

'Please,' Shelby says, the desperation back in his voice. 'Listen to what I have to say first.'

'No,' Laughton says. 'You need to go.' She moves to slam the door in his face but feels the light touch of a hand on her shoulder. She looks back at Gracie and can see in her eyes without her having to say a word, that she wants her to open the door and let him in. And for her, she might, she actually might. Despite her fierce maternal desire to protect her daughter from this man she doesn't trust, this man who was nothing but trouble in her life, she also knows that by getting between him and her daughter she might only succeed in alienating herself, like her father had done with her. She turns back to Shelby standing hopefully in the hallway.

'Five minutes,' she says, 'but the door stays closed.'

'OK, OK.' Shelby holds his hands up in a pantomime of surrender, his eyes flitting between her and Gracie. He takes one more look over his shoulder and steps forward, his face now filling the narrow gap left by the security bolt, reminding Laughton of Jack Nicholson in *The Shining*. 'Five minutes then I'm gone,' he says, 'I swear to God.'

Laughton glances at her phone. 'Four minutes and fifty seconds,' she says.

'OK, OK. So, there are people looking for me and they might come here, because your dad used to live here.'

'What people and why would they come here?'

Shelby rubs his face with his hand and Laughton notices scars on the back of it. 'It's a long story,' he says, 'but basically your dad was responsible for me getting put away. It's fine, I

don't blame him, I know it wasn't personal as such, I mean not really, he did it to get me away from you, so I suppose it was personal, but personal to do with you rather than personal against me, if you see what I mean. Either way, I don't hold it against him, but there are other people involved and they're maybe not so forgiving.'

Laughton glances down at her phone. 'Four minutes left. What other people?'

'I don't know. Not all of them. It was all very secretive, but one of them was working with the police. The only other person I knew is the one I'm worried about. He was arrested and imprisoned at the same time as me, a guy named Billy Carver. He's dangerous. Vindictive. He blames me for what happened, even though I went to prison the same as him, but he also blames your dad because he was the one in charge of the operation that made sure I was arrested and locked up in the US. It was a drug deal basically – raw diamonds in exchange for a shipment of cocaine. I was the courier and Carver was my security.'

Laughton checks the time on her phone. 'You have three minutes left. What do I have to do with any of this?'

'Billy Carver is out for revenge. On you, your father, and everyone else involved in the operation that put him away. In the court documents it said the diamonds I was carrying were fakes, but they weren't – not initially, at least. I had to get them authenticated first and Carver was there when it happened. I know he thinks I swapped them, or if not me then somebody else on the UK side. He was released four days ago, same day as me, so he'll be looking for me now, and for the names of all the other people involved. It was all on a need-to-know basis. And your dad will have known.'

'My father is dead,' Laughton says. 'You got two minutes forty left, by the way.'

'I know, but surely he kept copies of some of his case files, especially the ones that meant the most to him.'

Something cold slides down Laughton's spine as she realizes this is almost exactly what Gracie had said minutes earlier.

'There were no files,' she says flatly. 'And why are you so sure this Billy Carver is going to come here anyway?'

'Because I think he's started tracking down the others and he may already have found one. There's a guy, the only other person apart from Billy Carver who I knew was involved in all this. His name's Malcolm Fowler, though everyone calls him Minty. He kept in touch with me while I was in prison and offered me a place to stay when I got out. That's where I've been crashing since I got back to England, till I can get back on my feet. Only yesterday he went out for a few hours to see someone about a job and now he's not answering his phone. I'm worried something may have happened to him.'

Shelby looks over his shoulder again, takes a step closer, pressing his face into the gap in the door and dropping his voice to a whisper.

'Billy Carver is dangerous, Laughton. So, if there *are* any old case files you need to find them and make sure *he* doesn't get hold of them. Because everyone who was remotely involved with that operation is now in danger. And that includes you.'

Laughton's phone buzzes in her hand. Tannahill again. She rejects the call and checks the time. 'Time's up,' she says.

Shelby steps back from the door, both hands raised in mock surrender. 'You need to be careful,' he says. 'If I can find my way right to your door then so can he.' He looks past her at Gracie and smiles. 'Take care of yourselves.'

He turns to walk away but the soft bong of the lift makes him stop. Then the doors slide slowly open, revealing the silhouette of a large, powerfully built man inside.

74

12

'Oh come ON!' Tannahill yanks his phone from his ear and glares at the screen as Laughton rejects his call again.

Outside the car window, London whips past in a blur, the wail of the siren clearing the way ahead as much as it can, though not nearly enough. They slow down again as they approach another junction clogged with traffic and Tannahill squeezes his phone, willing the traffic to vanish and the car to go faster.

'How long?' he asks the driver.

'Four minutes, sir. Maybe less.'

Tannahill glares out of the window. Outside, the London evening flows slowly past in complete indifference. No one even looks his way despite the noise of the siren and the flashing blue lights.

He had been lucky to find the squad car parked outside NoLMS HQ but he wasn't feeling especially fortunate now. Why didn't Laughton pick up? Even if she was still mad at him she must realize he needed to talk to her. It made him worry that maybe there was another reason she wasn't answering.

He looks ahead at the solid wall of traffic, edging slowly apart to try and let them through but taking way too long to do it.

She had been heading home the last time he had seen her. That was almost an hour ago now. Not long really, but long enough for something bad to have happened.

Ahead of him a narrow channel appears in the traffic as the cars pull on to the pavement and the squad car squeezes through and starts speeding up again.

Four minutes.

Maybe less.

Tannahill dials another number and presses the phone to his ear.

Please, *please* let it be less.

13

Laughton stares past Shelby at the large figure in the lift. Nobody moves.

Then a man's voice shatters the silence.

'MOVE AWAY FROM THE DOOR,' it says, loud and serious. 'HANDS WHERE I CAN SEE THEM!'

The figure surges into the corridor, the reflective strips on his high-vis vest flashing under the overhead lights as he passes beneath them. Behind him another uniformed officer appears, eyes on Shelby, handcuffs in hand.

Shelby looks back at Laughton, a hurt look on his face. 'You called the police,' he says, stepping away from the door.

'No,' Laughton replies, looking back at Gracie. 'I didn't.' Gracie is watching wide-eyed at the scene unfolding outside her front door. 'I didn't call anyone,' Laughton says, more to her than to Shelby.

Out in the corridor the hulking lead officer grabs Shelby by the arm and pushes him hard against the opposite wall, twisting his arm behind him and extracting a shout of pain.

'Leave him alone,' Gracie shouts through the gap.

The officer ignores her and twists Shelby's other hand behind his back so he can fit the cuffs on.

'Are you arresting me?' Shelby says, his voice sounding shocked.

'We're bringing you in for questioning, sir.'

'Questioning about what? I haven't done anything.'

'LEAVE HIM ALONE!' Gracie shouts again.

Laughton puts a hand on her shoulder. 'It's OK,' she says, her voice low and controlled. 'He'll be OK.'

Gracie whirls round and fixes her with large, angry eyes. 'But he hasn't done anything. Tell them he hasn't done anything. Tell them you're OK that he's here. Tell them you invited him.' She glares at her mother, waiting for her to act, waiting for her to *say* something, then her face twists in disgust when she realizes she's not going to do anything.

'HEY,' she shouts out into the corridor. 'LEAVE HIM ALONE. HE'S WITH US! HE'S OUR GUEST.'

The two officers ignore her. They grab Shelby's shoulders, pull him away from the wall then turn him towards the lift and start leading him away. Shelby glances over his shoulder at Gracie and manages to shoot her a smile.

'Eyes front,' the lead officer says, shoving him in the back and making him stumble and look forward.

'HEY!!!' Gracie shouts at the policeman's broad back. 'LET HIM GO!!'

Laughton puts her hand on Gracie's shoulder and attempts to pull her away from the door. 'Leave it for now,' she says. 'I'll find out where they're taking him and then we can figure out our next move.'

Gracie squirms free from her grip. 'Why are the police even here? Who called them?'

Outside in the corridor the policemen and Shelby reach the lift just as the soft bonging sounds again and the doors slide open revealing the answer to Gracie's question.

Tannahill locks eyes with Shelby then looks at Laughton and steps out of the lift to allow the officers to bundle Shelby into it. Gracie glares at Tannahill, then at her mother, then

turns and stomps away into the apartment, slamming her bedroom door so violently it echoes out in the hall like a gunshot.

Tannahill appears at the door. 'She OK?'

'Not really,' Laughton looks up at him for a long beat, trying not to let her anger overwhelm her. 'Did you send those two officers round here?'

'Yes.' He glances at the security bolt, expecting her to unhook it and let him in. 'I had reason to believe an ex-con called Billy Carver might be heading here with less than friendly intentions. I tried calling but you didn't answer your phone, which made me worried, so I called the nearest squad car and told them to get here as fast as they could and apprehend anyone who wasn't you or Gracie.'

Laughton nods. 'Thanks,' she says, sounding not the least bit thankful. 'But the person you arrested is not Billy Carver.'

'Oh.' Tannahill glances back in the direction of the lift as the doors close on the two officers and the man in cuffs who is looking directly at him with a curious expression. He turns back to Laughton. 'Who was it?'

Laughton stares at him for a beat then lets out a long, weary breath. 'That – is Shelby Facer.'

'Really? What's he doing here?'

'He came to warn me about Billy Carver.'

Tannahill frowns as he struggles to join the dots. 'Why would he do that?'

Laughton holds his gaze for a beat, his bright blue eyes seeming to shine in the soft lighting of the corridor. This was definitely not how their evening was supposed to turn out. She takes another deep breath and lets it out slowly.

'Shelby Facer is Gracie's father,' she says.

Tannahill takes a small step back like he's been shoved. 'Does Gracie know?'

Laughton nods then looks back down the corridor at the closed door of Gracie's bedroom. 'Listen,' she says, turning

back to Tannahill. 'I should probably go and check she's OK. It's been a bit of a . . . well, it's a lot to take in.'

'Yes, sure. Of course.' Tannahill looks down at the security bolt again. 'Listen, if you want . . . I could stay here tonight.'

'No!' Laughton's response is hard and immediate.

'You sure? I mean, a recently released criminal did just turn up at your door'

'And it was a good job I was home, wasn't it?'

Tannahill catches the loaded comment and looks down at the floor. 'Yes, look, I'm sorry about earlier, I didn't think, I shouldn't have called you away. At least let me put a police guard outside.'

Laughton shakes her head. 'You haven't got the spare manpower and you can't afford the overtime. Just tell the desk security guard to be extra vigilant and give him a recent picture of this Billy Carver character. I'll be fine. We can look after ourselves. We're pretty secure up here.'

Tannahill nods in the direction of the lift. 'He got in though. And when I got here a Domino's delivery guy was stepping out of the lift into reception, so it's not exactly Fort Knox.'

'He didn't get into the flat, though, did he?'

Tannahill looks at the security bolt then back at Laughton. She can see the mild hint of hurt on his face as it dawns on him that he is getting the same treatment as her ex. 'So, what did he say to you?'

'He told me to be careful and he also gave me a name: Malcolm Fowler. He thinks Billy Carver might have got to him already. He might be your DB.'

'Malcolm Fowler,' Tannahill repeats, fixing the name in his memory. 'Did he say who he was or how he was connected?'

Laughton looks at him for a long beat, the pull of her furious daughter strengthening behind her and fuelling her own mild fury at Tannahill. 'Why don't you go and ask Shelby yourself,' she says, 'seeing as you went to all that trouble of apprehending him.'

Then she closes the door and locks it behind her.

14

Laughton listens through the door to the sound of the corridor outside. The carpet is too thick to hear footsteps so she waits until she hears the bonging of the lift again, then walks down the hallway and stops outside Gracie's door. She leans in and listens for a moment, not quite sure what she's expecting to hear: muffled sobs, the clicks of a furious WhatsApp message being composed, the sound of things breaking? What she hears is worse than all of them – silence.

She raises her hand, pauses for a moment before tapping her knuckle gently on the door three times.

'Hon,' she says, her voice reflecting back off the wooden door. 'You OK? You want to talk?'

'Go away.'

Laughton relaxes a little at the sound of her daughter's voice, muffled slightly and coming from the far side of the room where her bed is. She sounds more angry than upset, which, on the sliding scale of teenage emotions, is preferable. Angry she can deal with. She's had a lot of practice with angry.

She gently lays her hand on the door, holds it there for a moment then steps away, treading softly across the marble floor and into the kitchen.

She looks down at the mess of paperwork covering the island,

her wine glass rising like a lighthouse from the sea of documents. She picks it up and notices the wet circle on the page it has been standing on. She'll be in trouble for that, she thinks, taking a sip of wine and making a face. It's gone warm, another example of her ruined evening.

She tips the remains of the wine into the sink, rips a sheet of kitchen paper off the roll and uses it to blot at the glass ring on the document, fragments of the evening replaying in her mind – Shelby, Tannahill, the headless body, her address written on the pale skin of the inner arm. It wasn't exactly the evening she'd had planned, but at least it hadn't been boring. The kitchen roll starts smearing the ink on Gracie's homework so she abandons the task and tidies the documents instead, stacking them in a neat pile and hiding the spoiled page in the middle of the deck so at least its discovery might happen when Gracie is at school and Laughton is safely out of range.

She places the document with the family tree on top and stares down at Shelby's name written next to hers. Now he's a physical entity and not just some abstract concept, Gracie will be more intrigued about him. And if she was honest, she was right, if she had the chance to go back to when *she* was fifteen and spend time with *her* father she would do it in a heartbeat, so she couldn't really deny her daughter an opportunity to do the same. And Gracie was smart. Laughton had to trust that she wouldn't be taken in by Shelby's bullshit, like she had been at the same age.

She leaves the stack of documents on the island and picks up the pile of post she had abandoned earlier. She opens the kitchen drawer she and Gracie refer to as 'The Drawer of Power' and flicks through the letters, dumping most of them unopened into the already overstuffed drawer. 'The Drawer of Power' is where the mail lives and only gets emptied and sorted when it's no longer possible to close it, which happens about once a month. She flicks through the usual collection of bills, offers of credit cards, and estate agency introductions, checking

there's nothing really important in there that can't wait until the monthly purge. She reaches the final envelope and stops.

Ghost post.

When she first moved here, one of the more painful elements of settling in had been having to deal with the steady stream of her dead father's mail, informing everyone of his passing as she tied up the loose ends of a life that had ended too soon and too abruptly for him to tie them himself. Gracie, who had a knack for coining phrases that instantly stuck, had called it 'ghost post'. She hadn't had any for a while. Ghost post never went in the 'Drawer of Power', another of Gracie's inventions.

Laughton pushes the drawer shut with her hip and tears the envelope open. She pulls out a letter with an acid yellow letterhead, and quickly reads the contents. It's from a storage facility informing her father that his annual payment had failed.

She looks at the address of the storage place, somewhere out in the East End of London, which strikes her as odd. There are plenty of closer facilities he could have used.

The letter mentions a figure outstanding, a number to call to settle it, and a notification that the company has the legal right to confiscate the contents of the storage unit and auction them off to pay the debt if it is not settled within fourteen days.

She re-reads the section about confiscating the contents thinking only one, single thought.

What contents? What secretive things from her father's past could possibly be contained in this storage unit?

SIXTEEN YEARS EARLIER

JOHN REES

'John!'

Rees opens his eyes. Commander Thorpe is peering at him from beneath the raised visor of his Tac helmet. 'You good?'

Rees stares at him. He is not good, not even close – but he's not going to say that.

After the murder of his wife he'd been told to take as much time off as he needed, as if that was going to help. But time off had meant silent hours alone in his now empty house, trying to avoid the places where the blood had been – the stairs, the hallway, the landing outside the bedroom where the worst of it had taken place. He had often found himself, with no memory of how he came to be there, looking down at that spot on the floor. Despite the new carpet and the best efforts of the clean-up team, he was still able to see it all. Time off had also meant listening to the heavy hush that had so recently been filled by the sound of his wife singing along to the radio

in the kitchen, or his daughter clumping down the stairs, always so noisy for such a tiny thing. But now his wife was dead and his daughter was gone. No amount of time off was going to fix that.

What he needed, he had realised, was time off from his life. Work was actually an escape, a responsibility beyond himself, the only thing left that kept him tethered to something solid. Work was a useful distraction, his penance and salvation.

Commander Fairweather had swung it for him to tag along with SO-19 after dropping in to see how Rees was doing and finding him standing in the rain in his back garden, staring up at the house with no shoes or coat on. He had offered him a longer leave of absence and specialist counselling, but Rees had asked to go back to active duty instead, somewhere he could be useful and where the focus of the job would stop him thinking about other things. Given his training and background, Fairweather had suggested SO-19. 'SO' stood for Special Operations with the number identifying which division. 19 was firearms and, as Rees was fully certified and they were short on staff and long on need, here he was, swapping therapy for jumping out of vans and kicking in doors. But everyone knew what he'd been through, and not everyone was happy he was here.

'I'm good,' Rees said, flicking the safety off his MP5 assault rifle and keeping the muzzle pointed at the ground. Thorpe regarded him for a beat longer, then nodded and walked away to resume his position at the front of the six-man team lined up along the blackened brick wall of the warehouse. Rees looked along the line. Every man cradled a weapon, H and K standard issue, the same dull black as the body armour each wore. He could feel the tension coming off them, the sharpness of their focus, tight and hard like a spear. This was what he needed. To be part of something. To be of use.

The alert had come in twenty minutes earlier, a sudden and unexpected culmination of the long and careful surveillance of a radical terror cell known as 'Black Sceptre'. They were repre-

sentatives of UNITA, a rebel force from Angola who had been shopping around London's less well-known marketplaces for a large consignment of weapons. The place they came from was diamond rich and the rebels were offering to pay top dollar to whoever might supply them with the arms they needed. SO-19 had been working with SO-15 – counter-terrorism command – keeping a close eye on their progress, ready to scoop up both the Angolans and whoever came forward to trade with them – two birds, one stone. Somewhere inside the warehouse, the deal was going down right now. The moment it concluded, and the sellers drove away, they would make their move. On the other side of the warehouse, another unit was covering the only other entrance and would pick the sellers up as they left the location. Nice and quiet. Divide and rule. Quick and clean. That was the plan.

But then the gunfire started.

It sounded like firecrackers, sharp snaps muffled by the thick brick, but every man tensed when they heard it. Thorpe's voice cut through the pops, sounding close because of the headsets. 'On my mark!'

Two men surged past him and took up ready positions either side of the door, rifles aimed inward, one high, one low.

Thorpe held up three fingers, two, one . . .

A third man stepped forward and kicked the door hard, sending it flying open with a loud BOOM!. He jumped aside and the two men by the door pointed their rifles through the now open space, sweeping the barrels in opposite directions to cover the blind spots.

'Clear!' murmured through the headsets and everyone moved as one, pouring through the door with their rifle sights leading the way.

Rees went last, followed by Thorpe.

The gunfire was louder inside the building, sharp sporadic cracks ricocheting off painted brick walls. It was coming from behind a set of double doors at the end of a short corridor.

There were voices too, some angry, one clearly in pain, Portuguese spoken with African accents. The shouts and the exchange of gunfire suggested there was some kind of a standoff. Something had gone wrong with the buy and now they were trying to kill each other, or get away, or both.

More gunfire punctuated the shouts and the two men on point took positions either side of the double doors, their rifles pointing inward. Rees checked behind him, though it was unlikely anyone would be coming from that direction. All the action was clearly in front of them.

Thorpe's voice rumbled through the headsets.

'Hold.'

Rees wondered if Thorpe was going to announce their presence, give the men inside at least the chance to give themselves up but he said nothing, letting the people with guns focus on each other rather than turning on them.

More intermittent gunfire cracked and popped beyond the doors. Whoever had been crying out in pain was silent now. A deep boom thundered inside the warehouse, a shotgun blast by the sound of it, then everything fell silent.

Thorpe waited for a beat longer then finally called out, 'POLICE!'

Rees braced himself for more gunfire in response but none came.

'We have the building surrounded,' Thorpe continued. 'Drop your weapons and raise your hands above your heads, we're coming in.'

There was the sound of movement inside the warehouse, muffled conversation, then rapid footsteps. They were running away, towards the other exit.

'GO!' Thorpe said and the doors flew open. Rees raised his rifle and braced himself for gunfire as the men either side of the door covered the next two who moved into the warehouse in a crouch, rifles leading the way.

The warehouse beyond was a maze, stacked pallets forming

tunnels and towers. Lots of blind spots. The smell of cordite hung in the air, mingling with the bitter smell of cigarettes, burnt coffee and body odour. A white van was parked in the centre of the space, the rear doors hanging open and bullet holes dotting the side panels. A man lay on the ground beside it. He wasn't moving.

The first two men reached the van and one of them tapped a gloved finger on the man's open eye, then looked back at Thorpe, shook his head. He moved past the dead body and tucked in beside the van, scoping the other side of the warehouse over the barrel of his rifle.

'POLICE!' A voice called out from deep in the other side of the building. 'DROP YOUR WEAPONS.'

The command was met with gunfire.

Rees dropped lower and looked in the direction of the gunshots but could not see anything. The shootout was taking place in what looked like a loading bay beyond the abandoned van. The fleeing suspects had run straight into the second armed response unit. If they doubled back, the two point men were in position and ready to engage. The suspects had nowhere to go, meaning it was pretty much over, but that didn't mean Rees could relax. The location wasn't secure yet.

He looked around his side of the warehouse, watching for any movement, scoping out any place where someone might be hiding. Over to the right were two open doors leading to what looked like small offices. Thorpe had seen them too. He pointed at Rees then at the nearest of the two open doors.

Rees nodded and moved quickly across the floor, taking up a position to the left of the door while Thorpe moved into a mirror position on the right. They paused for a second, listening for any sound. Thorpe nodded and Rees swept his rifle up and through the door, quick-scanning the small office beyond for anything or anyone. It was messy inside, bookshelves crammed with paperwork and a cluttered desk in the centre with two large, green, canvas bags dumped on top of it. There was a

pot of coffee in the corner, a handgun next to it and two thick bundles of banknotes next to that. A broken mug on the floor showed that someone had left in a hurry. The room was deserted now and there was nowhere a man could hide. Rees nodded at Thorpe who stepped into the room and moved towards the green bags. Rees swung round to the second open door, took a breath, then swept his rifle into the office.

It was the same size as the first – messy, cramped, dirty. There were a couple of bedrolls with sleeping bags bunched up on top and empty beer bottles on the floor next to them. Rees stepped into the room and poked the sleeping bags with the toe of his boot, stamping down on the lumps in case something was concealed inside them. On the second one he felt something hard beneath the sole of his boot. He crouched down, picked up the sleeping bag and shook it. A small plastic Ziploc bag fell onto the ground. He picked it up and held it to the light. Inside was a handful of small, cloudy-coloured stones, fifty or so, maybe more. There was a small tear in the plastic bag, possibly from where he had stepped on it, and he shook a stone through it, grabbed one of the empty beer bottles and scratched the surface, making a deep gouge in the glass. Uncut diamonds, a lot of them, probably payment for the guns. The buyers obviously hadn't trusted the sellers and had hidden them in here. Given the way things had panned out, their instincts had been right.

Rees took an evidence bag from his pocket, shook it out and dropped the bag of diamonds and the loose rock inside then closed it up and stuffed it inside his armoured vest to leave both hands free for his rifle. He took one last look around the room and stepped back outside, glancing to his left to check on Thorpe. Through the gap in the office door he saw him by the coffee pot. He had his back to the door and was stuffing the bundles of cash into his pockets, no evidence bag, no attempt to preserve them as exhibits.

Rees had heard the rumours about Thorpe – a good cop but

certainly no saint, and definitely someone you did not want to get on the wrong side of. He was well-liked, funny, chummy with all the top brass and acted like he was untouchable. Maybe he was. There were also whispers that he was equally pally with the higher-ups on the other side of the criminal street. Everybody's friend, it seemed – not someone you wanted as an enemy.

Thorpe turned and their eyes locked. Thorpe smiled.

'Nice little donation for the widows and orphans fund,' he said, patting his pocket and not even pretending he'd taken the cash for anything other than himself. 'You find anything?'

Rees could feel the diamonds pressing against his ribs. He wondered how many of them would make it into evidence if he handed them over to Thorpe? Half? A quarter? None at all?

'Nothing,' he said, then turned away from the door and headed over to the van to wait with the others for the order to stand down.

DAY TWO

15

Interview room 7 at Whitechapel police station smells like a toilet and looks more like a set from a period drama than a room real-life police might use. Green and cream ceramic tiles line the walls, and bars that look like a blacksmith might have made them block narrow, high windows that let light dribble in from the pavement above through three-feet-thick walls. The steel table bolted to one wall is newer, as are the two chairs either side of it, but the room they stand in has changed little since the station was first built in 1889 as a direct response to the exploits of Jack the Ripper, still the most infamous local criminal and someone who the police had famously failed to catch. Ironically, it was also down to this same historical association that the building had managed to escape the rapacious clutch of the modern London property developer. As Whitechapel police station featured on all the Ripper walks that led hundreds of thousands of tourists each year around the most famous crime scene locations in history, it had been listed as a building of historical importance and so could not be turned into flats. It was also still a working police station with interview rooms and, crucially, holding cells, which was something the temp offices at NoLMS HQ did not have, and was why Tannahill had told the squad car to bring Shelby Facer directly here.

Tannahill looks at Shelby now across the dull, scarred surface of the table, the recorder sitting between them, bolted to the wall and seeming out of place in this antique room. Shelby appears to be exhausted, his shoulders slumped, his gaze angled down at the table. Tannahill presses the record button and leans into the microphone, also bolted to the table.

'Time is twelve-oh-three a.m. on Wednesday the fifteenth of March. Place is interview room seven at Whitechapel police station, present are DCI Tannahill Khan and Shelby Facer, who is being questioned following his apprehension outside the penthouse flat of the Brannigan building, a private and security-protected residence.' He leans back and looks up at Shelby. 'Mr Facer, would you mind telling me what you were doing at that address?'

Shelby continues to stare down at the battered surface of the table, the lack of focus in his eyes suggesting his mind is elsewhere. 'March fifteenth,' he murmurs. 'You know what that is?'

Tannahill waits for him to continue but Shelby carries on staring through, the table and says nothing.

'I know you've been out of circulation for a while,' Tannahill prompts, 'but the way this is supposed to work is that I ask the questions.'

Shelby's eyes flick up and Tannahill notices a brightness to them that seems at odds with the rest of his worn-out appearance. 'March fifteenth is the "Ides" of March,' Shelby says, as if explaining something to a slow child, 'the ones Julius Caesar was told to beware of. And you know what happened to him?'

Shelby's accent and delivery carry some of the taint of his time in a Florida jail, still mostly English but with a slight American flavour.

'Wasn't he stabbed in the back by his friends?' Tannahill says. 'I can see why you might relate.'

Shelby regards him for a beat as if trying to figure him out and the beginnings of a smile appears on his face.

'You know who told me March fifteenth was the Ides of March?' He pauses for a moment then the smile spreads wider, revealing the sharp edge of a broken front tooth. 'Laughton Rees told me that. Fifteen years old and already the smartest person I'd ever met.' He shakes his head and looks down at the table again as if conjuring some golden, cherished memory in his mind. 'God knows what she ever saw in me. That's why I was at that address. In answer to your question, I was there to see Laughton Rees, an old friend of mine and also,' his eyes flick back up to Tannahill's in time to catch his reaction, 'mother of my child.'

Tannahill forces himself to hold Shelby's gaze and focuses hard on keeping his breathing level and steady. Shelby Facer had obviously managed to pick up on the personal connection between him and Laughton in the brief moments the three of them were in the corridor. Now he was trying to needle him about it and was doing a pretty good job. And though part of him wanted to reach over the table, grab Shelby by his baggy Miami Dolphins sweatshirt and smash his broken-toothed, smiling face down hard on the table, another part of him, the greater part, was intrigued as to why he was bothering to try and get under his skin like this, especially given the fact that he had lied on his extradition forms about where he was staying in the UK and was now in police custody.

'Tell me why you wanted to see Laughton Rees so urgently,' Tannahill asks. 'It's a little late to make an unwanted house call.'

Shelby's smile holds steady. 'What makes you think my visit was unwanted?'

'Well, we found you outside the flat not inside it and there was a security bolt in place on the door to make sure things stayed that way. Also, when you were being apprehended, your old friend Laughton Rees did nothing to stop you being hauled away, so I would say, given all that evidence, your presence at this *private* address was clearly not welcome, whatever your relationship with the owner used to be.'

Shelby regards Tannahill coldly for a beat, the smile still in place but with less confidence behind it. 'Well, aren't you a proper little boy scout?' he says.

There it was again, the needle. It was like he wanted to be arrested and thrown in the cells.

'I'm not a boy scout,' Tannahill says flatly, 'I'm a detective chief inspector of the London Metropolitan Police concerned about a recently released felon breaking into a private residence late at night. I'm also quite tired and very much in two minds about whether we continue this conversation now or I call it a day and leave you in the cells overnight – which, in the spirit of openness and honesty, I should inform you are the same vintage as this room and every bit as unpleasant.' He reaches out and his finger hovers over the record button. 'So, Shelby, which is it going to be?'

Shelby studies him for a moment then his smile grows wider, revealing the sharp edge of his broken tooth again. 'All right, Detective Chief Inspector, consider my ass to have been spanked. I'll play ball. What do you want to know?'

Tannahill pulls his hand away from the record button and leans back in his chair. 'Tell me about Malcolm Fowler.'

'Minty,' Shelby corrects him. 'Everybody calls him Minty. Lovely bloke but terrible breath. Sucks on Polos all the time, hence the name, though it might also explain the state of his teeth and therefore his ongoing breath problem. Anyway, Minty was one of the six people involved in the deal that ended up with me spending an extended holiday in Florida. When I knew I was going to be released, I called him and he said I could stay with him until I could get myself sorted, only now he's gone missing and I'm worried something might have happened to him.'

'Why?'

'Because of his involvement in Operation Henry 8.'

'Why do you think something bad might have happened to him because of that?'

'Because anyone who was involved back then has a target on their back now.' Shelby leans forward and holds up three fingers on both hands. 'There were six people involved, right? Three on the front end of the deal, and three in the back who set it all up, provided the seed money and had the connections to shift the product once it got shipped.'

He holds his right hand higher. 'The three on the front end were me, Minty Fowler, and a guy called Billy Carver who was working security. When the deal went sour, me and Billy were the only ones who got hung out to dry and Carver is convinced we were sold out by someone. Now he's out of prison he's looking for payback and is trying to track down the other three, only he doesn't know their names. Minty didn't go to prison so Carver will probably think there's a reason for that. He'll probably think he struck a deal and will try and squeeze him for info, and Carver has a reputation for being quite persuasive in the way he obtains information.'

'Do *you* think Minty knew the names of the other people involved?'

Shelby shakes his head. 'I asked him straight up and he said he didn't. Never had direct contact with anyone on the back end; everything was set up through anonymous calls.'

'Do you believe him? I mean, if he did set you up he's not likely to tell you is he?'

'No, I believe him. Minty was only low-key involved, there was no reason for him to know who he was dealing with, and it was always better for someone in his line of work not to know.'

'What was his role?'

'He was the quartermaster. Minty's always been the guy who could get you what you needed – money, tickets, fake IDs, credit cards. He also operated a number of safe houses, places to stash things and sometimes people whenever needed.'

'And what was your role?'

'I knew a guy in London who was connected to the cartels –

not in any business capacity, only social. We partied together a few times and he must have really enjoyed the parties because he offered my name up to his bosses as someone they could trust. Also, *yo hablo español*. The Mexicans don't like to conduct business of this scale in English, they consider it to be bad luck, apparently, and don't want anything to be lost in translation. So I got the job because I speak Spanish.'

'What's the name of this guy who vouched for you?'

Shelby shakes his head. 'I'm not going to give you his name. It's a dead end anyway, literally. He was killed while I was in prison. Life expectancy is pretty low in that line of work.'

'So you, Minty and Billy Carver are hired to operate the front end of this deal.'

'Yes.'

'Minty is the fixer, you're the negotiator and Carver is the muscle.'

'Yes. I'm the bag man too. I'm carrying thirty million dollars' worth of uncut diamonds hidden in my luggage to give to the cartel guys in exchange for a shipping container full of cocaine. If that had made it to these shores it would have changed the drug trade in this country. But the whole operation was compromised and everyone ran for the hills. Everyone except me and Billy.'

'Could Minty have been the one who betrayed you?'

'No, it wasn't him.'

'How can you be so sure?'

'Because I know him. Because he's not that type of guy. Because I asked him and I believed what he told me.'

'When did he go missing?'

'Today sometime. I saw him this morning around ten, then I was out all day and got back around six thirty, seven.'

'So he hasn't been missing for that long. Why do you think something might have happened to him?'

'Because we were both being very careful. We knew Billy Carver was back in town and I knew he was on the warpath

because of all the things he'd said to me when we were on trial. He thought *he'd* been set up, despite the fact that I got arrested too and ended up spending the same amount of time in prison as him. He's a psychopath, a total narcissist, everything was always about him. I'd never met him before this job, only knew him by reputation, and spending a couple of days with him on the plane and in Florida made me wish it had stayed that way. He's an all-round unpleasant human being. When we were awaiting trial he told me he was going to find out who stitched him up, make them all pay, and get what he was owed, and he definitely included me in that.'

'What do you think he meant by making them pay?'

Shelby looks at Tannahill like he's an idiot. 'What do you think he meant? Billy Carver is a well-known headcase, he's out to kill everyone who crossed him. That's why I think something bad has happened to Minty.'

Shelby shifts forward in his chair and leans on the table. 'The thing is, Minty is still doing what he's always done, getting things for people as and when required, and last night he got an order for something that required him to go and see one of his suppliers.'

'What was the item?'

Shelby glances at the recorder with the red record light glowing. 'That's not important, what is important is that he left the house this morning and I haven't seen him since.'

Tannahill nods. 'Maybe this "particular item" proved harder for him to get hold of than he thought.'

Shelby shakes his head. 'Minty could get hold of anything within a few hours. He was also a very cautious guy. Had to be. You don't get much business in his line of work if you have a reputation for being reckless or sloppy. So, because we knew Billy Carver was out there looking for us, Minty suggested we call each other every two hours, to check in. The last time I spoke to Minty was noon. He called me. When I didn't hear from him at two I called him but it rang out. That's when I

cleared out of the house. I figured if Carver had caught up with Minty he would have beaten my location out of him pretty quick. Minty was a stand-up guy, but he wasn't tough.'

Shelby looks up at Tannahill, all the broken-toothed cockiness now gone and an expression of genuine concern on his face.

'Minty didn't know anything else, so after Billy had beaten all the information he could out of him he would have switched his attention to the next person on his list. I thought about who that might be, and what I'd do if I was Billy Carver, knowing what I know, knowing what he knows. He would have come to the address Minty gave him but found no sign I'd been there, because I made damn sure I didn't leave anything behind.'

'What's the address?' Shelby's eyes flick up at Tannahill but he doesn't answer. 'If your friend has given the address to Carver he might still be there, waiting for you to come home.'

Shelby thinks for a moment then comes to a decision. 'It's 9 Zoffany Street, Archway, N19.' He smiles. 'Last house on the last street in London, alphabetically speaking. Easy to remember but also not obvious.'

Tannahill checks the time on his phone and reaches for the record button. 'Terminating interview at twelve twenty-seven p.m.' He presses the button to stop the recording then rises from his chair. 'I'm going to have this address checked out. Maybe your friend just lost his phone or met someone in the pub and lost track of time.'

Shelby shakes his head. 'You're not listening to me. Minty was fastidious, he was practically OCD. If he said he was going to call at a certain time he would call. If you do find anyone at that address it won't be Minty it'll be Carver, waiting for me to come home. So whoever you're sending round there you should make sure they're armed and prepared for a fight, because if Carver's there, they'll get one.'

'Noted.' Tannahill rises from his chair and heads for the door.

'Wait,' Shelby calls after him. 'If Carver isn't there, he might be at Laughton's place.'

Tannahill stops by the door and turns back round. 'Why would he go there? Laughton had nothing to do with Operation Henry 8.'

'No, but her old man did and she now lives in his old flat. That whole murder mansion thing she and her old man were tied up in made it on to the news over in America. I followed it so I imagine Carver must have done too – not much else to do in prison but avoid getting stabbed and dream of the world outside. That means he'll know John Rees died and left everything to his only daughter. Carver hated John Rees. His name came up at trial as the copper in charge of the operation that nicked us, so he was on Carver's shit list too. I told all this to Laughton. Told her she needed to be careful, but you know how she is – never likes being told what to do. You should put some men on that address until you find Carver.'

'Already did,' Tannahill says, opening the door to the interview room. 'There's an unmarked car parked outside with two officers in it right now.'

Shelby nods. 'Good. That's good.'

Tannahill exits the interview room and locks the door behind him. He checks the time and calls the night despatcher with the address Shelby gave him, tells them to send a squad car round immediately and report back directly to him whatever and whoever they find there. He hangs up and stands for a still moment in the dead silence of the corridor, waiting for someone to call him back and enjoying the calm and quiet after the manic evening he's had.

The strip lighting flickers slightly against the corridor walls lined with the same ceramic tile they used in the tube stations and public toilets. He checks his phone and moves back towards the closed door of interview room 7 and peers through the observation window.

Shelby Facer is sitting in his chair, legs stretched out under

the table, hands folded behind his head, face tilted up to the ceiling. His eyes are closed and he looks relaxed, unbothered, more like a man stretching out in a hammock than one in the middle of a police interrogation. Tannahill thinks about their conversation and how Shelby had been trying to press his buttons about Laughton.

Why would he do that? Why risk pissing off a police officer and getting thrown in the cells a few short days after being released from a sixteen-year prison stretch?

Inside the interview room Shelby's head starts bopping slightly, like a catchy tune has started playing in his mind. The phone buzzes in Tannahill's hand and he moves away from the door before answering.

'DCI Khan.'

'Hi, this is Sergeant Derek Miller, I was given this number to call after we checked out an address at number 9 Zoffany Street, N19.'

'Yes, hi. Did you find anything?'

'No, sir. No lights on, no one answering the door. Curtains are still open so I had a quick look inside and it didn't look like anyone had broken in or anything like that.'

'OK, thanks.'

'Do you want us to hang around for a bit to see if anyone shows up?'

'No, don't worry. I'm sure you've got better things to do. Thanks for checking it out.'

'No problem, sir.'

The line goes dead and Tannahill moves back down the corridor to the door of interview room 7. Inside, Shelby is still bopping along to whatever music is playing in his head, the hint of a smile on his face making him look like a man with not a care in the world. Tannahill watches him for a minute, thinking how odd it is that he hadn't asked the usual questions – was he being charged? Was he under arrest? When would he be released?

Then it struck him.

He didn't want to be released. That explained why he'd been needling him about Laughton earlier. He'd been actively *trying* to piss him off because he *wanted* to be locked up. Clearly, as far as Shelby Facer was concerned, while Billy Carver remained on the streets and unaccounted for, he was much, much safer in here.

16

Mist smudges the surface of the Thames as morning breaks. The heavy black water moves slowly beneath like something stealthy and alive as the river, full and engorged, starts to empty again. In contrast, the city begins to fill with bleary-eyed people in suits who shuffle from trains and out of tube stations, clutching their coffee and listening to audiobooks and podcasts about true crime, and self-help, and how to earn passive incomes. Some listen to the news where the story of a headless body found on the banks of the Thames has been pushed down the agenda by the latest political scandal involving a friend of the Home Secretary and the awarding of a large government contract.

The story of the headless body has also made it into some of the morning tabloids – the *Mirror*, *Sun*, *Express*, *Daily Mail* – though none of the broadsheets have run with it. The same photo that accompanied the first reports online has helped bump the story above the fold on whatever inner page it appears. All these articles are low on facts and high on drama, rehashing the eyewitness reportage of the initial posts embroidered with details from Tannahill's press release. What these articles lack in substance, however, they more than make up for in sensationalist speculation, leaning heavily into the various

conspiracy theories that have sprung up online. There is a link to a Crimestoppers page in the online editions and a number to call in an attempt to give the article the veneer of being civic-minded rather than ghoulish.

In Westminster, in a busy, windowless post room in the basement of No. 2 Marsham Street – better known as the Home Office – Nadine Smith, a young woman who grew up in a Tower Hamlets tower block, with a first-class degree in economics but no family connections, stands at a table organizing the morning press drop. In front of her are neat piles of all the second edition newspapers, the edition most of the commuters/voters will be reading. She takes a copy from the top of each pile to make twelve new piles, two for each floor of the building. The front page of every newspaper carries the same story of the Tory party donor receiving a large government contract to supply new police uniforms without any previous track record, and without having to go through the correct bidding procedure. The story has been rumbling on for almost a week now, a trickle of new daily details keeping it current and moving it steadily up the news agenda. The latest revelation, after days of speculation and denials, is that the minister at the centre of it all, only referred to previously as 'an unnamed Tory MP', is actually the Right Hon. Charles Nixon MP, Home Secretary, the person in charge of the whole police force and also the building Nadine works in.

Nadine doesn't really like Charlie Nixon. On the few occasions their paths have crossed and he's deigned to speak to someone as low down the totem pole as her, she could tell he was dismissing her even as he pretended to engage. She knows why, of course; she's the exact opposite of him – female, black, young, poor – and though he knows he has to be professionally inclusive these days, he's still much happier dealing with people who look and sound like him. Like the white, male, Eton and Oxbridge educated Tory party donor he gave the police uniform contract to, for example.

Nadine pauses for a moment and arches her back to stretch some of the tension out. She's already been at work for over three hours doing a job she could have done several years and tens of thousands of pounds of student debt ago. It's a foot in the door, she reminds herself daily, a stepping-stone towards a proper job in this building, a job that could make a difference.

She opens one of the tabloids, flicking past the headlines to the inner pages, her eyes pausing briefly on the blurred-out picture of a body lying on the banks of the Thames next to the headline: HEADLESS BODY WASHES UP BY TOWER BRIDGE.

She is tempted to read it but hasn't got time, so she closes the paper and adds it to the last pile, the one destined for the sixth floor where the Home Secretary and his team are based. And even though Nadine feels patronized and ignored by Charlie Nixon, he is also her boss, so in the tribal world of politics where an attack on one of your team is an attack on everyone, the urge to defend is instinctive. So she grimly loads the day's newspapers on to her post trolley, knowing that it's going to eat up most of the office's attention today, and wondering if there's anything at all she might do to help.

17

The morning sun slants in through the floor-to-ceiling windows of Laughton's kitchen throwing slashes of light across the floor. Laughton stands by the kettle, her fingers tapping out sequences of threes as she waits for it to boil, half listening to the *Today* programme on Radio 4 as it runs through the morning news. Gracie has yet to put in an appearance, which is not entirely unusual, but after the events of last night her absence feels like it has extra weight today.

Laughton glances at the clock on the oven: 7:49

Gracie will have ten minutes to get dressed, eat breakfast, and leave the house if she wants to stand any chance of not being late for school – again, not entirely unusual. Gracie has a very casual relationship with time and always cuts things incredibly fine. This drives Laughton nuts, though she does her best not to show it. Laughton is never late for anything. She'd rather be an hour early than one minute late. Maybe that's why Gracie is how she is, an act of subconscious teenage rebellion. Or maybe not so subconscious. A new and unpleasant thought occurs to her, an unwanted collision between her early morning preoccupations and her daughter's continued and chronic lateness. Shelby had never been on time for anything either. Maybe Gracie's behavior wasn't

107

rebellious or deliberately adopted simply to annoy her, maybe it was genetic.

The kettle clicks off and she pours hot water into the teapot, her second pot of the day. She's been up since five thirty, trying and failing to distract herself from the events of last night through work. In the end she cracked and messaged Tannahill for an update on the case and to ask him why he had stuck a squad car outside her building when she had specifically told him not to. She had spotted it that morning shortly after getting up and had been both annoyed and touched that Tannahill had bothered. She was actually glad it was there now. Shelby's warning had been playing on her mind ever since she woke up and she has now started worrying about Gracie leaving the house to go to school, though maybe that wasn't so much of a worry, given how things currently stood.

She checks the time again: 7:51

She has a new message, Tannahill finally responding to her earlier text, the bullet points of information that suggesting he's busy:

Shelby in cells at Whitechapel, still being questioned but not yet charged.

No new info on the dead body. Nothing new to report.

He didn't mention the squad car. Laughton checks the time again: 7:52 now.

Unless Gracie appears fully dressed, like, right now, she is *definitely* going to be late for school. Laughton opens her mouth to call out but hesitates and listens instead through the low burble of the radio. She can hear movement, muffled banging behind the still closed door of Gracie's bedroom. Her daughter is awake at least.

Laughton picks up the teapot and swirls it around nervously. It's a source of both annoyance and curiosity to her that she can happily and fearlessly face off against the most

aggressive barristers, the most patronizing and dismissive police officers, the most infamous and dangerous criminals and yet her fifteen-year-old daughter has her fumbling and stuttering like Hugh Grant in an old romcom. Maybe it's because she had almost lost her a year earlier. Or maybe it's because she is a single parent. Perhaps traditional parents, with someone else to share the burden of responsibility, develop a kind of shared domestic courage that single parents never quite manage. When you're flying solo everything is down to you, every decision yours alone, and if you crash it's all your fault. The unfairness of it is that if, by some miracle, you manage to stay aloft and not come tumbling out of the sky, no one says a damn thing.

A loud bang sets her nerves jangling and she turns in time to see Gracie stomp into the kitchen fully, if messily, dressed in the bottle green of her school uniform.

Laughton smiles a greeting that is not returned. 'I think you might be pushing it if you wanted breakfast,' she says, nodding at the clock on the cooker.

'I don't want any,' Gracie stalks over to the island and grabs a banana then stares down at the island and the neat pile of her homework from the night before. 'Is he still in prison?' she asks flatly, no names mentioned.

'No,' Laughton replies. 'He's not in prison.'

'Jail then or whatever.'

'He's still being held for questioning if that's what you mean.'

Gracie looks up at Laughton with thunder behind her eyes. 'Why didn't you tell them you didn't want to press charges?'

'They haven't charged him with anything so nothing I said would have made any difference.'

'Where is he?'

Laughton pauses before reluctantly answering. 'Whitechapel police station.'

Gracie nods and breaks open the banana, digging her finger into the bottom rather than the stalk, something she has done

ever since they watched a nature documentary and learned this was the way chimpanzees in the wild did it.

Laughton glances at the clock again: 7:57

Her natural anxiety about lateness is peaking now.

'If you don't leave for school right now, you're going to be late. I promise I'll call Tann later for a further update and try and get some kind of timeframe on when Shelby will be released. Legally they can hold him for up to thirty-six hours without charge, but I'll repeat that we don't want to press any charges, OK?'

Gracie takes an angry bite of her banana. Says nothing.

'Also, there's a police car outside with two uniformed officers in it. I imagine one of them will get out and follow you to school. Just ignore him. Until we know more about what's going on we should be careful. I'll come and pick you up from school later. I should know more by then and I'll fill you in on everything on the way home. OK?'

Gracie takes another angry bite of banana.

'Don't be angry at me for this,' Laughton says. 'I didn't know your father was going to turn up out of the blue and bring all this with him and I'm trying to deal with this too, so help me out a bit here.'

Gracie seems to soften a little. 'If he's still in custody can I go and see him?'

Laughton closes her eyes in frustration. 'Maybe. To be honest I doubt they'll keep him in much longer because he hasn't really done anything.'

'Can I see him when he's released?'

'Let me find out more about what's going on, then we can talk about it.'

'That's a "No" then.' Gracie stuffs the rest of the banana in her mouth, sweeps up her homework and stomps out of the kitchen.

'We need to take a moment before rushing into anything is all I'm saying.' Laughton follows her out into the hallway in

time to see Gracie heave open the front door. In a split second of panic Laughton imagines someone standing there, but the corridor is mercifully empty.

'Don't forget to take your Imuran,' Laughton says.

Gracie slams the door in reply.

Laughton stares at the closed door for a beat then hurries across to Gracie's bedroom as a fresh anxiety seizes her. She pushes open the door into an Olympic-standard mess of clothes, shoes, make-up and soft toys that mark the transition from child to young adult. She picks her way through the devastation and enters Gracie's en-suite bathroom, which if anything is even messier than the bedroom; towels, tissues, bath mats, empty toilet roll holders all mingled together in a chaotic mess. Laughton ignores it all and yanks open the mirrored door of the bathroom cabinet, her eyes scanning the shelves for the bottle of Imuran, the immunosuppressant Gracie has to take following her liver transplant the year before. She searches through the cotton buds and cotton wool balls choking the shelves to make sure it isn't hidden, then scans the sink and the top of the toilet. Gracie has to take her Imuran after she's eaten, so she must have taken it with her.

Laughton takes a deep breath and blows it out. This is a good sign. Even in her anger Gracie has remained clear-headed and sensible enough to take her medication with her, demonstrating that she's neither self-destructive nor reckless, two things she has definitely been in the past, and traits she has, unfortunately, inherited from her mother.

Laughton closes the bathroom cabinet and retraces her steps through the carnage of Gracie's bedroom, comforted by the knowledge that the mess will camouflage the fact that she dared set foot on this private and hallowed ground. She closes the door behind her and heads back into the kitchen, the pot of tea abandoned on the side, the *Today* programme still broadcasting the morning's news to an empty room. She finds Tannahill's number and dials, then unlocks the door to the

balcony, sucking a blast of chilled morning air into the kitchen as she opens it.

Laughton leans against the railing and peers over the edge at the street below as the phone starts ringing in her ear. The squad car is still there, a uniformed officer standing next to it, staring out at the river as he sips on a takeaway coffee and puffs on a cigarette, known in police circles as a 'stakeout special' or 'the breakfast of champions'.

The phone connects. 'Hey!' Tannahill says, the hum of office conversation audible behind him.

Down on the street the uniformed officer glances in the direction of the building, his eyeline at street level.

'You put a car outside my house,' Laughton says, leaning forward a little and peering down the front of the building to where Gracie has now emerged from the entrance.

'Yes.'

'I told you I didn't need one.'

'You did.'

Gracie looks over at the police car and marches off down the street, heading for school. The police officer flicks his cigarette away, leans down and says something to his unseen colleague in the car, then starts following Gracie.

'Thank you for taking no notice of me,' Laughton says.

There's a pause filled with more background office noise before Tannahill replies, 'You're welcome.'

'So, any news?'

'Not really. Shelby's still in the cells. He still hasn't asked to speak to a lawyer or asked whether he's going to be charged with anything.'

'Are you going to charge him with something?'

'No, but I'd like to hang on to him for as long as we can. If we can locate Billy Carver I'd like to interview him again and compare their stories.'

'Any luck finding Carver?'

'Not yet. We checked the address he listed on his extradition

forms but there was no one home and the phone number we have for him rings out. News of the body has made it on to the morning news too, so we've got to assume he'll see the story and be extra careful now, if he is behind all this.'

'What about that other person Shelby mentioned?'

'Malcolm Fowler, also known as "Minty". We're drawing a blank on him too. Ditto with getting any more leads from the old case files for Operation Henry 8. What there is on file is heavily redacted. I've asked for it to be declassified, but I can't imagine it's going to be high-priority, given how old it is and the fact that there are already two successful convictions attached to it. I'm about to do the morning briefing, but we've got a pretty full caseload, so I can't see a potential blood vendetta between some old cons with a score to settle inspiring much willingness to investigate it. Dr Prior is scheduled to do the autopsy this morning, so that might give us something new. Maybe we'll get a match for Malcolm Fowler, maybe we won't. Obviously, there's no fingerprints to go on. Er, that's about it. If we don't have anything new by this time tomorrow we'll have to either charge Shelby with something or turn him loose.' There's a pause and Laughton hears a man laughing in the background, the kind of bawdy, chummy, locker room laugh particular to male-dominated spaces. 'Do you want us to charge him with something?' Tannahill asks, his voice low.

Laughton thinks about it for a second. 'No.'

'You sure?'

'Yes. He hasn't really done anything.'

'Well, he gave a false address on his parole documents, broke into a private address and intimidated a resident.'

'He didn't intimidate me. And if you're spread as thinly as you say, why waste resources on prosecuting something as flimsy as this?'

'Well, we do have a body with its head and hands missing so it's not nothing.'

Down on the street, Gracie stomps out of view round the

corner of a building. The police officer crosses the street to follow her. Laughton's eyes drift over to the river and the spot beyond Tower Bridge where she knows the body washed up.

Dead Man's Hole.

'Last night Shelby asked me if my dad kept any old files,' Laughton says, replaying their conversation. 'Said Billy Carver might come looking for them to find the names of the others who'd been involved in Operation Henry 8.'

'And have you?'

'No. There was nothing here when we moved in.'

'Shame. Listen, I've got to go,' Tannahill says, 'the morning briefing is about to start. I'll call you later with any updates.'

The phone clicks and Laughton is left listening to the morning rumble of London winding itself up for another day. She turns and heads back through the glass door into the kitchen. Yesterday's ghost post still lies on the island, the acid yellow of the bill from the storage company almost radioactive in the morning light. She picks it up and reads the address on the headed paper. Not local but not far.

Not far at all.

18

Nadine Smith exits the lift on the sixth floor, pushing the heavy post trolley past the seal of Her Majesty's Government, the Lion and Unicorn rampant either side of the crown. She heads into the executive offices, dropping the mail in the main in-tray and the first stack of newspapers on a low coffee table in the middle of a nest of stylish but uncomfortable-looking chairs in the main reception area. Immediately a flock of people in suits appear, grabbing at the pile like hungry crows pecking flesh off a corpse.

Nadine moves down the main corridor and on to the executive suite, the heavy trolley feeling heavier as the wheels dig into the deeper carpet that lines these particular corridors of power. Ahead of her, the door to the minister's office is closed, which is unusual. Normally the Home Secretary has an open-door policy with an actual open door to match, though it's almost impossible to get past his aides. She stops by the desk of Tom Kenwright, the Home Secretary's chief adviser, and hands over the bundle of post for the minister. He ignores it, grabbing the stack of newspapers from her trolley and starts shuffling through them like an enormous deck of cards.

'Tough day,' Nadine says, nodding at the closed door.

'Heavy is the head that wears the crown,' Kenwright

murmurs, all his attention on the headlines. 'And no matter how bad it gets for the king, it always ends up being ten times shittier for the courtiers.'

Nadine opens her mouth ready to offer her help with whatever might need helping with, but Kenwright cuts her off. 'You should probably scurry along to distribute the bad news to the rest of the building. I'm sure there's plenty of eager eyes desperate to read all about it.' He starts re-ordering the pile of newspapers on his desk, putting the worst ones at the bottom.

'Yes, of course,' Nadine says, feeling herself flushing hot, 'Have a good day.'

Kenwright looks up at her like she just told him to go fuck himself then watches her wheel the heavy trolley down the corridor. Only when he's decided she is far enough away does Kenwright tap his mouse to banish the lion and unicorn screen saver and quickly scans his morning emails, seeing what other landmines he needs to deactivate before his morning briefing with the minister.

He scrolls through the hundred or so messages that have come in overnight, interdepartmental nonsense mostly that the minister has to be copied in on and Kenwright has to read. He spots the police request near the top of the unread messages, triggered by a flagged alert on an old case file. Some chief superintendent on the North London Murder Squad has forwarded a request from one of his DCIs investigating a recent murder that might be connected to a sensitive historical case. The DCI's name sounds familiar, Tannahill Khan.

Kenwright taps his teeth with a fingernail as he tries to place it then resorts to Google for speed. Most of the results are from online news articles which remind Kenwright exactly why he recognizes the name. DCI Tannahill had been involved in that whole mess with John Rees a year ago. He was one of his protégés and had somehow managed not to go down in flames when his boss fell so spectacularly to earth. Kenwright studies a photo of Tannahill, noting the dark skin and hair

that match the exotic character of his name. Kenwright imagines Tannahill's multiracial heritage didn't hurt. At a time when the Met was being lambasted almost daily for being institutionally sexist, chauvinist, and racist, having a senior officer with a name like Khan was undoubtedly worth its weight in PR gold. If he'd been a gay woman as well he would have hit the box-ticking jackpot.

Kenwright opens the emailed request and speed-reads it, not entirely sure what it's about. He didn't put the alert in place so doesn't know what's in the files or why their contents have been censored. Nevertheless, the fact that *someone* thought it worth putting a flag on the files means he needs to find out why and decide for himself whether it's still a problem or not.

He opens his secure browser, logs into the National Crime Database and copies the case number from the email into the directory. The file for 'Operation Henry 8' opens up on his screen, redactions and all. He opens a drop-down menu, selects a tab labelled 'Security', carefully enters his details then hits *Return* and the case file refreshes, this time with all the redacted information removed by an algorithm responding to his higher-level security access.

He reads through the file and stops when he reaches the now visible names of the six so-called 'wives', their codenames listed next to their real ones. Now he understands why the files had been so heavily redacted.

He glances back at the closed door, his boss moving behind the frosted glass panel, back and forth, pacing around his office like a caged animal.

This is bad timing, very bad. There is no way this can be allowed to leak. And the easiest way to stop a leak, like the fabled thumb in the dam, is to plug it early.

Kenwright clicks back to the email alert and scans back through the communication path, looking at everyone who was copied in. It had been sent late last night and, happily, hardly anyone had seen it as it had automatically been funnelled to

the relevant department with the necessary clearance to process the request. Fortunately, this particular case file required a very high clearance level so he was most probably the first one to actually read it. And that is the way it needed to stay.

Kenwright hits *Return* to send a reply rejecting the request then pauses. A reply would extend the email chain and add his name to it. At the moment the request is only addressed to this department. Kenwright looks back at the email, checks the name of the chief superintendent he hadn't recognized, then opens the Home Office directory and looks up his direct line. He calls it from his desk phone on a line that is automatically anonymous and encrypted.

Behind the frosted glass his boss continues to pace and gesture with his spare hand.

Maybe all this was pointless.

Maybe this was just like closing a window on the *Titanic*.

But some people survived even that, he reminds himself; not everyone went down with the ship. And until he knows whether they've dodged the iceberg or not, he'll carry on doing his job, hoping for the best, and plugging the leaks.

'Chief Superintendent Grieves,' a voice answers, sounding distracted and stressed.

'Hello, yes, this is Tom Kenwright. I'm calling from the Home Office about an email you sent requesting the declassification of a sixteen-year-old case called Operation Henry 8?'

'Oh yes, that was me.'

Kenwright automatically adjusts his face into a well-practised mask of empathy and regret, even though the person on the other end of the line can't see it. 'It's not good news, I'm afraid.'

19

Gracie turns the corner and joins the flow of office-suited commuters and green-uniformed girls heading to work and school.

The Towers School for Girls sits in the middle of the street as it has done for over two hundred years, an ecclesiastical-looking building in Portland stone, now entirely surrounded by modern buildings in steel and glass. Some of the newer structures also belong to the school and Gracie tracks along the side of the science building, using the angled smoked glass of the revolving door as a mirror to check behind her without having to turn her head. He's still there, the uniformed policeman who's followed her all the way to school, ambling along behind her, the reflective strips on his vest catching the sun. She slows a little, wanting to make sure that he doesn't lose her in among the other identical green uniforms squeezing through the entrance of what everyone somewhat unimaginatively calls 'the old building'.

A sudden scuffing, scurry of footsteps nudges her wide-eyed, high alert even higher and she whips her head round as her friends Sophie and Elodie charge out of the crowd and leap on her.

'Gracie!!!!'

Gracie surrenders to the hug and sneaks a look over Elodie's shoulder to where the police officer is trying and failing to look inconspicuous on the other side of the street. He glances over, long enough for her to be pretty sure he's spotted her, then looks away again.

Elodie releases Gracie from her embrace. 'How was last night?' she asks as the three girls carry on in their slow creep towards the old building. 'Did you ask your mum about your dad?'

'Yep.'

'Oh my God! Who is he? Are you going to contact him?'

'He, er . . . I saw him last night actually.'

'Nooo! What, like, he came to your house?' Elodie's large eyes grow even bigger. Did your mum call him or something?'

'No, it was weird, we'd just started talking about him, there was a knock on the door, and there he was.'

'Oh my God, that is so random. It's, like, fate or something!'

They reach the entrance to the old building and pass through the arch of the main door into the gloom of the entrance hall. Gracie stops in the shadow and glances back outside at the sunlit street. The police officer is on the opposite side of the road looking over at the entrance.

'So, what's he like?' Elodie asks.

'I didn't speak to him,' Gracie murmurs.

'What? No way! Why?'

Outside on the street the police officer turns around and starts heading back the way he came.

Gracie turns to Elodie. 'Listen, can you cover for me this morning? If anyone asks tell them I threw up on the way to school or something and went home.'

Elodie looks at her uncertainly. 'Okaaay. What are you really going to do?'

'I'm going to try and talk to my dad.'

The wide eyes of Elodie go incredibly wide again. 'Coool!'

Gracie takes a step towards the entrance and looks back out

along the street at the police officer. She watches him until he disappears around the corner, then looks back at her friends. 'I'll be back by first break,' she says. 'Hopefully no one will even notice I've gone.'

Then she steps back out into the sun and walks away down John Fisher Street, in the opposite direction to the policeman, heading into the stone cold heart of Whitechapel.

20

Tannahill stands in the incident room, trying to get his laptop to talk to the large display board when his phone buzzes in his pocket. He checks caller ID and stands a little straighter before answering.

'Dr Prior.'

'Evelyn, please. Congratulations, Inspector Khan, you are a winner. I got the DNA tests back on your DB after working late and pulling some favours down at the lab and we have a match. Our floater now has a name – Malcolm Fowler.'

Tannahill traps the phone under his chin and fiddles with the cables plugged into his laptop. Shelby's hunch had been right. Which meant he was probably right about Billy Carver too.

'Thank you, Dr, P . . . er, Evelyn.' He looks up at the board where his laptop display has now appeared in foot-high letters:

OPERATION HENRY 8

Catherine A	Billy Carver
Anne B	Malcolm Fowler
Jane	Shelby Facer
Anne C	???
Catherine H	???
Catherine P	???

'Don't mention it,' Evelyn Prior's low, husky voice purrs down the line. 'My evening had been ruined anyway, and a girl's got to get her fun somewhere. Some people go dancing, some go fishing, I cut up headless corpses while listening to Mozart.'

Tannahill stares up at the names, his mind processing this new information and where it might lead. 'I spent a large chunk of last night in an interview room that smelled of old cabbage,' he says, 'so I guess neither of our evenings turned out exactly as planned.'

'Maybe we need to balance things out,' Evelyn's low voice sounds conspiratorial. 'Do you know Happiness Forgets?'

'Does it?'

'Lighten up, Detective, it's a cocktail bar on Hoxton Square. They do the best Amaretto sours I've ever tasted. Why don't we go there after work – no headless corpses, no smell of old cabbage. We could erase the memory of our ruined evenings by collaborating on a better one.'

Tannahill opens his mouth to speak but isn't quite sure what to say. Did Evelyn Prior just ask him out? A tapping sound makes him spin around and the white-shirted figure of his boss, Chief Superintendent Derek Grieves, stands framed in the doorway. 'Got a minute?' he mouths.

'Yes, sir.'

'Sir!?' Evelyn's voice snaps. 'Not very observant for a detective are you?'

'Sorry,' he says into the phone. 'I wasn't talking to . . . Listen, I've got to go. Work thing. I'll call you back.'

He hangs up and Grieves steps into the incident room and closes the door behind him. He looks up at the display board. 'Operation Henry 8,' he says, as if the words taste sour. 'This is that old case you asked to be declassified.'

'Yes, actually I was going to ask you to chase that up because there's been a new development. That was Dr Prior on the phone. We got a DNA match on our headless corpse. The victim was Malcolm Fowler. He was one of six people directly

involved in that case, as was Shelby Facer, who gave us the tip that the victim might be Malcolm Fowler. The third person we know about is Billy Carver, who is now our chief suspect.'

'Carver! Used to run with the Gallaghers, didn't he? I thought he was dead.'

'Not dead, sir, just out of the picture for a while. He spent sixteen-years in an American prison for his part in all this and returned to the UK a couple of days ago, as did Shelby Facer. Facer believes Carver may be going around settling old scores with everyone he blames for putting him away. That's why I wanted to have a look at the old case file, to find out who else was involved. If Shelby Facer is right, and it looks now like he might be, anyone else named in that file is potentially a target.'

'Hmmm.' Chief Inspector Grieves chews the inside of his lower lip and continues to stare up at the board, fists on his hips. 'Do you have any other evidence to back up this . . . theory?'

'Not yet, sir. We're trying to locate Carver but so far he's proving elusive, which again makes sense if he is on the warpath. I was hoping the old case file might reveal some known associates as well as the other three people on that list.'

'Well, I'm afraid you're going to have to try and find those names another way. The Home Office already got back to me regarding your request to unlock those files and I'm afraid it's a "No".'

Tannahill stares at his boss, waiting for more but nothing comes. 'Could you go back to them, tell them about this latest development? This is a solid lead now, maybe they'll reconsider.'

'Is it a solid lead though? I'm not going to go back to them with nothing more persuasive than the conspiracy theory of some ex-con. You're still holding him I believe?'

'Yes, sir.'

'Have you charged him with anything?'

'No.'

'Well unless you've got good reason to keep hold of him,

you should let him go. Get his contact details and cut him loose – you can always get him back. In the meantime, forget about the old case files and focus on what you've already got to work with. Victim background, now you have a name. Last known movements, the usual. And if this one proves to be too tricky, move on to one of your other cases. How many murders are we up to this month?'

'Eight, sir.'

'Jesus, I thought it was seven.'

'The body we fished out of the Thames takes it to eight.'

'Of course it does. Well, let's start solving some of them, shall we? And maybe prioritize the ones that are less likely to piss off the Home Office.'

'Did they say why they were denying the request?'

'No, and they don't need to.'

Tannahill nods. 'It's unusual for them to get back so fast, though. You normally have to send at least three emails before they even acknowledge the request.'

Grieves stares at Tannahill with the weary expression of someone tired of explaining that fire burns to people he knows are going to stick their hands in the flames anyway. 'If I were you I would view the speed of their reply as a sign. You've had the door slammed in your face, son, don't keep knocking. Take it from me, if the Home Office turns round and tells you to back off, you don't ask them why, you just back off and hope they remember your compliance fondly the next time you put in for a promotion. Do your job, chase the leads you have, gather evidence, solve some murders.'

He turns to leave and almost makes it to the door before Tannahill stops him. 'Could you forward me the email, sir?'

Chief Inspector Grieves stops and turns round slowly, looking annoyed. 'What email?'

'The one from the Home Office denying access to the unredacted file. I should attach it to my case file to show that avenue is a dead end to anyone else who might look at it later.'

125

Grieves stares at him for a beat before answering. 'There was no email,' he says. 'Someone called from the Home Office. Just write in the file that the request to open the old case documents was denied. You don't need to go into details.'

He opens the door, letting the noise of the outer office back into the relative quiet of the incident room. A few people glance up from their work as he weaves his way through the desks, their eyes flicking between him and Tannahill as they try to gauge what happened and whether Tannahill got a bollocking for something. Other people's fuck-ups are always a source of great interest, especially in a department as inherently competitive as the Murder Squad. People start moving toward the incident room for the morning briefing. Tannahill turns back to the display, thinking about what the chief superintendent said.

There was no email from the Home Office.

Why would someone high enough up at the Home Office to make that kind of decision bother to put in a call about something as seemingly low level as this?

He closes his laptop and the names disappear from the display as it disconnects from the projector.

Because it left no paper trail, that's why. A phone call was deniable in a way an email was not. Someone really did not want him reading the uncensored case files relating to what happened sixteen years ago in Operation Henry 8.

And that only made him want to read them even more.

SIXTEEN YEARS EARLIER

John Rees sat in his office, listening to the burble of voice outside in the bullpen as he studied the surveillance photographs spread out on his otherwise empty desk. He had been back full-time for a few months now. More than full-time. Truth was, if he could sleep in his office he would. Anything was preferable to going home to the empty house.

All the extra hours and workload, and the arrests that had come with it, had put him in line for a fast-track promotion, which was something positive, he supposed. A promotion would not only give him more responsibility and more things to fill his waking mind, it would also mean a pay rise. He needed to get out of the house and move somewhere new, somewhere central and anonymous, a place where the neighbours wouldn't know him or his story, and wouldn't smile sadly at him every time he passed them on the street. Given the speed at which London property prices were climbing, he would need the bump in his wages to be able to afford anything at all.

Rees took his keys from his pocket, found the smallest one and used it to unlock the bottom drawer. Inside were all the

things that used to stand on the desk: a framed photo of his wife with Laughton on her knee, both of them smiling at him as he took their picture; a picture of a policeman drawn in crayon by Laughton when she was about five; a studio photo of all three of them, smiling and together, the white background freezing them in some non-specific, happy period that no longer existed and possibly never had. This was the photo he found hardest to look at, the one with him next to the two people he loved most in the world and had let down so badly. He picked up the photo revealing the plastic evidence bag beneath it.

Rees had continued to hold on to the uncut diamonds after the raid, waiting for the right opportunity to properly notify the top brass of their existence and finally enter them into evidence. He had hoped Thorpe might belatedly declare the cash he had taken, especially as he knew Rees had seen him pocket it, but in the end Thorpe did nothing, and was clearly not going to. There was no real need for evidence, there was never going to be a trial. All the terrorists had been shot and killed trying to escape, as had the two arms dealers. They had seized quite a sizeable number of weapons and, as far as the department and the higher-ups were concerned, it was a win. Thorpe had been recommended for promotion and become something of a poster boy, even being wheeled out by the Home Secretary for various press junkets as the heroic face of the modern police force. All of this meant that coming forward now and telling everyone he'd seen Thorpe swiping cash and stealing evidence was not going to be easy or welcome. Throwing the new golden boy under the bus was going to piss everyone off, even if it was the right thing to do. It was also going to be his word against Thorpe's, and, right now, with his own recent history and inevitable large question mark hanging over his state of mind, they would believe Thorpe.

He stared down at the bag of diamonds, surrounded by the smiling faces of his lost family, then looked back at the surveillance photos fanned out across his desk. They showed Laughton,

somewhere on the streets of south London, fifteen years old and somehow looking even younger. He studied the man pictured with her, his arm draped over Laughton's shoulder as she leaned into him – Shelby Facer, not the kind of boy any father wants their daughter bringing home. Not that he was a boy. Shelby Facer was barely much younger than he was, yet there he was with his snakish grin and his arm resting on his daughter like she was now his property. He wanted to jump into the photograph, pull him off his daughter and punch the smile off his face. But that sort of behaviour wouldn't close the gap between him and his daughter. That kind of thing would only make things worse. No, if Laughton was going to find her way back to him, it would have to be on her terms and in her own time. All he could do was watch from afar and do what he could to keep her safe from people like Shelby Facer.

Rees looked back down at the drawer to the photos of happier times and the bag of uncut diamonds that no one but him and a bunch of dead terrorists knew about. Maybe he should use them to tempt Shelby away from his daughter, give him a handful of rocks in exchange for a promise that he would vanish, kill two birds with one stone. He would do it if he thought it might work. But people like Shelby Facer would never be satisfied with one payday. Give him a sniff of money and he would keep coming back for more and never go away.

There had to be another way, a way he could use the diamonds for good instead of the evil they had been intended for. A way to buy his daughter's freedom permanently.

21

Shelby Facer steps out of the door of Whitechapel police station and squints against the sunlight. The day seems way too bright after so long in the subterranean gloom and it takes a few long seconds for his eyes to adjust. He scans the busy street through narrowed eyes. He is still not used to seeing so many people teeming everywhere. It's chaos out here, a world he doesn't understand and that makes him feel anxious. In prison you could tell who was who at a glance. Everyone wore the same clothes for a start, the cons in their pumpkin orange jumpsuits, the guards in black uniforms with white shirts. There were people to avoid on both sides, but you learned how to spot that too: the little signs that told you who to trust and who to steer clear of, your people, their people, no people at all. It was simple. Easy. Ordered. London is none of these things.

He moves down the steps to street level and away from the police station, head lowered, eyes peering from beneath the shadow of his brow at the river of people flowing past. A stressed-looking woman walks by, dragging a couple of grumpy children behind her, a boy and a girl who might be twins. Shelby stares at them as they pass. One stares back.

One of the things that has surprised him since getting out of prison is how freaky children are in real life. You kind of

forget about them inside, then you come out from behind those walls and there they are again, these weird miniature humans with unformed features and strange, toddling ways of walking, like aliens among us. It's things like this that make him realize how much he has lost by being away for so long.

He looks away from the twins, or whatever they are, and tries to think about something else. If he thinks too much about what he has lost, it makes him sad and angry. He looks further up the street, trying to refocus, trying to concentrate only on the way ahead and what he needs to do next. Then he sees the face in the crowd, a face from his past, staring straight at him.

He stands there for a moment, frozen in place, the crowd flowing around him like water round a rock. He feels like a rabbit must feel, shocked into stillness in the middle of a road when the headlights of a car catch him. People pass between them but he continues to stare at the face from his past, totally unchanged despite all the lost years. It starts to move, coming closer now, drifting through the crowd like a ghost. He watches it come, unable to move, unable to tear his eyes away. The face stops in front of him.

'Hello,' Gracie says, sounding less like her mother than she looks, which breaks the spell a little and allows Shelby to gather himself.

'You're here because of me,' he says, more a statement of realization than a question.

Gracie nods. 'My mum told me they were keeping you here.'

Shelby smiles and opens his hands like a magician after performing a successful trick. 'Not any more.' He looks down at her bottle-green uniform, her school bag dangling from her shoulder. 'Shouldn't you be in school?'

'Yeah.'

Shelby nods, the smile still in place. 'Your mum will blow a fuse if she finds out you ducked school to come see me.'

Gracie shrugs. 'I'm not going to tell her. And my friends are

covering for me, so as long as I'm back before lunchtime I should be fine.'

Shelby nods. The more she speaks, the more the ghost of her teenage mother melts away and she becomes her own person, someone who looks almost identical but sounds different enough to break the unnerving spell. He smiles down at his daughter.

'You wanna grab a coffee or something?' He gestures at the various cafés lining the street. 'They kicked me out of jail before the food trolley came round, so I could eat a horse. Come on.' He starts walking down the street. 'Let me buy my daughter breakfast. It's about time, don't you think?'

22

Number 9 Zoffany Street – the last house in London – lies at the end of a short road with Victorian terraced houses on one side and an ugly slab of red-bricked new builds on the other. Tannahill presses the doorbell and an electronic chime sounds inside the house. Behind him Bob Chamberlain locks his car and limps over to join him by the door. Chamberlain is registered as disabled so gets to drive his car into work, and his blue disability badge enables him to park anywhere in London, making him incredibly useful for impromptu lifts and things like popping over to inner London police stations to pick up sets of keys, for example.

He stops next to Tannahill and peers through the front window. 'Anyone home?'

Tannahill listens for a few seconds to the silence beyond the door then shakes his head.

'Right.' Chamberlain produces the set of keys they got from Shelby Facer at Whitechapel police station earlier and starts the complicated process of undoing the various locks.

'Blimey,' Chamberlain huffs. 'What's this guy hiding in here?'

Tannahill watches on. 'I guess we're about to find out.'

Chamberlain works his way through three separate locks before finally opening the door to reveal a dingy hallway with

a couple more doors leading off from it and a set of stairs rising up at the end. An alarm starts beeping and Chamberlain steps forward to tap a code written on his hand into the control panel on the wall. On a mat by the door is a small pile of mail and a copy of today's *Daily Express*. Tannahill cocks his head to one side so he can read the name on the envelopes. They are all addressed to M. Fowler. Chamberlain taps in the last digit, hits *Enter* and the alarm falls silent. They both stand for a second, listening for the sound of voices or movement in the house.

'Hello?' Tannahill calls out. 'Anyone home?'

More silence.

'I think we can safely take that as a "No".'

'What are we looking for here?' Chamberlain stoops down and picks up the newspaper.

Tannahill enters the house and walks up to the first door. He peers through into a neat and unexceptional–looking living room. 'Signs of a break-in, signs of a struggle, pools of blood, piles of money, piles of drugs – the usual.'

He steps into the centre of the room and does a slow three-sixty as Chamberlain limps in behind him, shaking the newspaper open.

Everything seems in order, no broken glass or overturned furniture. A large TV on the wall faces an oversized, and quite ugly, brown leather Chesterfield sofa. An equally ugly coffee table sits in front of it with drinks coasters on it but nothing else. A long sideboard fills most of another wall with an old-looking but good-quality hi-fi on it, complete with a turn-table, an amp, and decent-sized speakers either side. Tannahill opens the doors of the sideboard and finds it filled with vinyl records, at least three or four hundred. He pulls a couple out and studies the covers – The Cure, *Kiss Me, Kiss Me, Kiss Me*; *Surfer Rosa* by The Pixies. At least Malcolm Fowler had better taste in music than furniture.

'Looks like our friend here has made it into the papers,'

Chamberlain says, holding the newspaper up for Tannahill to see. He looks at the grainy photo of the body on the riverbank, more suggestive than illustrative, which is probably why they could run it, nothing too graphic that might put people off their morning Shreddies. He speed-reads the accompanying article, recognizing the details from his own press release, then checks what page the article is on: page five, not prime real estate but definitely not buried. 'So weird!' he says, shaking his head.

'What's weird?'

'This case.' Tannahill heads out of the living room and down the hallway towards the back of the house. Chamberlain limps after him. 'Normally if one of our cases makes the papers it automatically becomes priority, right? You always try and solve the ones most people are looking at first, or at the very least make sure you're seen to be doing whatever you can to swing the sword of justice.'

'Yeah, so?'

'So, Grieves effectively told me to stick this one on the bottom of the pile. In fact, I kind of got the impression that if I put it in a drawer and forgot all about it he'd be even happier. And yet here it is on page five of a national newspaper.'

'Have you annoyed someone?'

'Maybe. Though this case is barely twelve hours old, so there aren't that many people I've spoken to. I asked for an old file to be unredacted and got a swift and resounding "No" from the Home Office.'

Chamberlain's bushy eyebrows shoot up behind his glasses. 'Ahhhh.'

Tannahill looks up at him and waits for more but none comes. 'What do you mean, "Ahhh"?'

Chamberlain turns the newspaper to the front page and holds it up. A photograph of the Home Secretary Charles Nixon stares out from it. He looks stressed and cross as he hurries between a very nice-looking front door at the top of a flight

of stone steps and a waiting ministerial car. The headline above the photo reads: NIXON NAMED AS MINISTER AT CENTRE OF POLICE UNIFORM PROCUREMENT SCANDAL.

'I'm still not sure why that's worth an "Ahh",' Tannahill says. 'If anything I would have thought that, on a day when the Home Secretary is being crucified on the front pages of every newspaper, his staff would have slightly bigger fish to fry than to bother rapidly processing a routine information request about an old case file. Unless there's something in the file that's related to this somehow. Half the names of the people involved were redacted, so it's hard to tell. The only names you can read are Shelby Facer, who Grieves told me to let go; Malcolm Fowler, whose house we're currently standing in and whose body is lying headless and handless in the morgue; and Billy Carver, who is currently at large.'

Chamberlain nods solemnly. 'Let's just hope he's not hiding here somewhere.'

They search the rest of the house in silence, Tannahill taking the upstairs and Chamberlain the rest of the ground floor. The upstairs is much the same as the downstairs – large, ugly, masculine furniture in each bedroom. A few clothes in one bedroom, nothing in the others but empty drawers and wire hangers in the wardrobes. There's no sign that Shelby Facer ever stayed here and not much evidence anyone lived here at all. It feels more like a rental, and Tannahill wonders if maybe this wasn't Malcolm Fowler's real home after all. He heads down the stairs and finds Chamberlain waiting in the hallway, leaning against the wall and reading the newspaper. 'Anything?'.

'Nothing in the house,' Chamberlain replies, 'but by the look of things, the Home Secretary is going to be out of a job fairly soon, so maybe the new one might declassify your case files for you.'

Tannahill smiles and feels his phone vibrate in his pocket. He pulls it out and checks caller ID. The number on the screen is a landline, somewhere in inner London. He doesn't recognize

it and neither does his phone. He swipes to answer it, straightening slightly before he speaks, something his mother taught him to do when he was young enough for it to be hardwired into his DNA.

'DCI Khan.'

'Yeah, hi.' The voice belongs to a woman Tannahill doesn't recognize. 'Someone called me last night and left a message to call 'em back.' She sounds old and with the deep, dry rattle in her voice of a dedicated smoker. Her accent is old generation East London, more cockney than MLE, the Multicultural London English that has since taken over. She also sounds worried, though that's not unusual when people return calls to the police.

'And what was the message regarding?' Tannahill pulls a notepad and a pen from his pocket and scribbles on the corner of a page to get it working.

'It's about my son.'

Tannahill's instincts bristle. 'And who is your son, Mrs . . . ?'

'Carver. Lizzy Carver.' Tannahill clicks his fingers at Chamberlain to grab his attention and puts his phone on speaker.

'My son's William. Billy.' The woman's voice sounds ghostly in the gloomy hallway. 'Is 'e in some kind of trouble?'

'No,' Tannahill says. 'No, he's not in any trouble. I was just hoping I might talk to him.'

'Oh, right.' She sounds almost disappointed.

'Would that be possible, Mrs Carver?'

A deep, rattling sigh whispers down the line. 'Nah,' she says. 'I don't know where 'e is.'

There's a click and it takes Tannahill a second to realize she's hung up. He stares at the phone for a moment, wondering if he should call her back. She had sounded worried at the start, then shut things down when she found out her son wasn't in trouble. Actually, she had hung up the moment Tannahill had asked to speak to him.

137

He looks up at Chamberlain.

'Come on,' he says, searching for a new number as he heads for the door.

'Where to now?' Chamberlain limps after him, dropping the newspaper back on the mat where he'd found it before resetting the alarm and closing the door behind them.

'Jamaica Street in the East End,' Tannahill replies, finding DS Baker's number and calling it as Chamberlain begins the lengthy process of locking up the house. 'I'll get Baker to meet us there. I think we may have found Billy Carver.'

23

Laughton enters the wood-panelled gloom of lecture theatre No. 2 at London Metropolitan University and dumps her bag on the chair by the lectern. Despite her restless night and early start she has ended up running late, which for her means being only ten minutes early instead of at least twenty. She pulls her laptop from her bag, places it on the lectern then clicks open a file.

The large screen blinks into life behind her, displaying the subject of her morning lecture in large, bold letters:

DEAD ENDS OR LOCKED DOORS?
LEARNING TO ASSESS OBSTACLES IN
POLICE INVESTIGATIONS

She looks out at the empty lecture theatre, the morning sun throwing dust-filled rays of light down into the sombre room from high windows. In ten minutes, the seats will all be filled and eager faces will stare at her, ready to learn whatever wisdom she has to share.

She doesn't feel very wise today.

She feels tired, and distracted, and, as she often does, like an imposter waiting for a whisper in her ear from a well-spoken

139

voice saying, 'I'm sorry, we seem to have made a terrible mistake, if you wouldn't mind leaving the premises'.

She feels it more keenly today, maybe because of the lack of sleep, or because she's worried about Gracie, or because Shelby Facer turned up out of the blue, a physical reminder of how low she had once been.

She pulls out her phone so she can set the countdown timer running at the start of her lecture and sees a missed message from Tannahill:

Just FYI – Shelby was released at 9:06 this morning. Expecting the post-mortem results later today. Gracie made it to school OK (you still OK to pick her up after school? I doubt I'll be able to keep the squad car in place much longer). Also, request to release unredacted Operation Henry 8 case files rejected!! Back to square one . . . T x

Laughton takes a deep breath that tastes of dust and wood polish.

Shelby is at large.

She opens her notebook to go through her notes before the keener students start arriving and sees the bill for the storage unit, trapped between the pages, the acid yellow letterhead almost glowing amid the gloom of the lecture theatre.

. . . *request to release unredacted Operation Henry 8 case files rejected*, Tannahill had said.

Back to square one, he had said.

She looks back up at the display board where the title of her lecture is displayed:

DEAD ENDS OR LOCKED DOORS?

There was really only one way to find out.

24

Shelby sits in the corner booth of a greasy spoon that has somehow managed to hold out against the relentless march of the coffee chains. Gracie sits opposite, her school bag wedged in the seat next to her, her eyes studying the gallery of signed, framed pictures of forgotten celebrities that cover the walls.

To my friend Vic, best fry up in the City, best wishes, Des O'Connor

To Vic, knockout food, Frank Bruno

Vic, king of the full English, all the best, Bobby Davro

The same man who took their order is in each photo, looking much younger and happier. His drooping moustache is now completely white, his hair thin, his waistline significantly expanded, and there don't appear to be any smiles left in him. Gracie studies the photos, her slight frown showing she has no idea who any of these people are. Gracie looks away from the photos and catches Shelby staring.

'Sorry,' he smiles. 'Whenever I look at you I see your mother.'

Gracie screws her mouth over to one side, another inherited gesture. 'Yeah, I get that a lot.'

Shelby continues to study her, shakes his head. 'I can't see any of me in you at all.'

Gracie shrugs. 'Most of my friends look more like their mums than their dads, so I guess it's normal. Except for this one girl called Belle who looks exactly like her dad, which is pretty unfortunate, given her name. Some of the mean girls at school call her the Beast, you know like in Beauty and the Beast?'

'Kids can be such assholes.'

'Yeah, though Belle is also a bit of a bitch, so it's kind of hard to feel sorry for her. Her dad is an investment banker and Belle never, ever shuts up about how much money they've got.'

Shelby smiles. 'You look pretty well set up yourself.'

Gracie shrugs. 'I guess.' She looks over at the mirthless owner frying the eggs for their order and the frown returns. 'You don't have to buy me breakfast. I have money, if you're . . . if you don't have . . .' She lets the sentence trail off, unsure how to finish it.

'Don't worry,' Shelby says. 'I can buy you breakfast. Still got some gate money burning a hole in my pocket. That's what they give you in America when you leave prison. It's supposed to help you in your first few days of freedom, only I don't think they've changed the amount they give you since the seventies, so it doesn't go very far.'

'How much do you get?'

'A hundred dollars, which is about eighty quid! I figured out on the plane ride home I'd been inside for fifteen years and seven months, which is a hundred and eighty-seven months, so a hundred dollars divided by a hundred and eighty-seven works out at around fifty cents a month, or six dollars a year.' He looks across at the menu board hanging by the till. 'That would make a cup of coffee here worth around nine months of my life.'

Gracie's eyes go wide in surprise. 'Let me buy breakfast. I want to get it.'

'No, it's OK,' Shelby smiles, 'I can afford to buy my daughter breakfast. I'd like to do it. Make up for all those times I haven't been around. Besides, I got more than just gate money.'

The café owner appears at their table, places a bacon and egg sandwich and a mug of black coffee in front of Shelby and a glass of weak-looking orange juice in front of Gracie, then puts the bill between them and shuffles off again.

Shelby picks up a bottle of HP sauce. 'I missed this,' he says, squirting a large, brown dollop into his sandwich. 'They don't do brown sauce in the States.'

He takes a huge bite then closes his eyes as he chews. 'Man, that's good. You never know how precious the simple things are until they're taken away from you.'

Gracie looks down at her hands and twists them together. 'What was prison like?'

Shelby jabs his thumb at his Miami Dolphins sweatshirt. 'You mean my extended holiday in the sunshine state?'

He puts the sandwich down and wipes his hands on a paper napkin. 'Prison is exactly how you imagine. Scary at first, but you get used to it. You decide who your friends are, and stick to them like glue. That was the biggest lesson I learned, you can't survive on your own. It's the same out here, really. People are always stronger together.' He smiles. 'And there's nothing stronger than family, right? You and your mom seem pretty tight.' He takes a sip of coffee.

Gracie shrugs. 'We're OK. She can be a bit controlling sometimes. I had . . . some health issues and that made her extra protective.'

'What kind of health issues?'

Gracie looks down at her hands, wondering how much to reveal about her suicide attempt.

'I had some issues with my liver,' she says, keeping it simple, 'I'm fine now, but Mum's extra protective of me because of it, which can get a bit much sometimes.'

'Mothers can be fierce when it comes to their young,' Shelby says. 'You never want to get between a mommy bear and her cub.'

Gracie takes a sip of juice. 'What was your family like?'

'Boring. My whole childhood was boring. I lived in a place called Ravenfleet, which might sound like some kind of smuggler's cove but is about as far from that as you can get. It's miles from the sea in a place called the Fens which is the flattest place you can imagine, drained marshland as far as the eye can see, no hills, no trees, nothing.

'My dad was like a ghost, worked his whole life in the local tax department while my mom stayed at home and cleaned obsessively. Maybe that's why I ended up doing everything I did, not because I wanted to turn to a life of crime especially, I was just desperate not to turn into them.'

'Are they still alive?'

'Dad died of a heart attack about five years into my little stay in Florida. My mother blamed me for that, said it was caused by stress brought on by the disappointment and shame I'd brought to the family, but I think it was more to do with the fact that they changed the tax rules and put him out of the job he'd been doing for over thirty years. He would probably still be alive and doing it now if he hadn't been given the boot.'

'What about your mum?'

Shelby shakes his head. 'I honestly don't know. I haven't spoken to her in ten years, not since she called me up to tell me Dad had died. I imagine she's probably still in Ravenfleet cleaning the house. I think she was worse than my dad, actually. He was just boring. She was . . . I don't know what she was. There was something missing in her is the best way I can describe it. Warmth, maybe, I don't know. She was a bitter woman, very judgemental, everything had to be perfect. Criticized everything, especially me. Whatever I did or didn't do, she would always find something wrong with it. She was the main reason I left home.'

'How old were you when you left home?'

'Sixteen, about the same age as you are now, right?' Gracie nods. 'I didn't really have a plan, just left for school one

morning, went to the station instead, hopped on the first train to London, jumped the barriers when I got to King's Cross, and so began my life of crime. I didn't plan on staying, I think I just wanted to stir things up, get some kind of reaction from my dad, give my mum something real to get angry about for once. But after a night away I felt like some great weight had lifted and decided I was never going back.' He pops the last bite of sandwich into his mouth and chews contentedly, licking spilled egg yolk and brown sauce off his fingers.

'What are their names?' Gracie asks.

Shelby shrugs. 'Does it matter?'

Gracie reaches into her bag, pulling a stack of papers from inside. 'I'm doing this project for school.' She finds the page with the outline of the family tree on it and slides it across the table. 'It's more than that though. I guess I'm also trying to figure out where I fit into all this.'

Shelby stares down at his name written in the box for 'Father' and his eyes gloss with tears.

'Sorry,' he rubs his eyes with the palm of his hand. 'Christ, sorry, that took me by surprise. It's just, seeing my name there next to your mother's, and with your name underneath. It's like . . .' He frowns as he searches for the right words. 'It's like glimpsing a life I might have had.'

'This is still part of your life,' Gracie says, unzipping her pencil case. 'Family is family.' She hands him a pen.

Shelby looks down at the outline of the tree for a long beat then writes 'Graham Facer' in the space for his own father and 'Iris Ashcroft' in the space for his mother.

'Graham and Iris,' Gracie murmurs.

'Your granny and grandad,' Shelby says, raising an eyebrow. 'God help you.'

He takes another swig of coffee and waves at the miserable owner for a refill.

'OK,' he says, sliding the family tree back across the table. 'Enough about me and my boring past.' He points at Gracie's

145

name, written at the bottom of the page. 'I want to hear all about this person.'

Gracie shrugs. 'What do you want to know?'

'Everything.' Shelby smiles, revealing his broken front tooth. 'I want to know absolutely everything.'

25

Jamaica Street.

An out-of-the-way, run-down part of the East End of London. Extensively bombed in the Second World War and cheaply rebuilt in the sixties using poor-quality materials that were only supposed to last until the economy recovered. But the economy never did recover, not in a way that reached places like Jamaica Street, and so the temporary fix became a permanent solution.

Chamberlain pulls to a halt in the fractured shade of a skinny tree that looks like it died and no one noticed. He and Tannahill peer up through the bare branches at the faded and flaking slab of Albion House, all brick and crumbling concrete with open walkways on the front linking the apartments together. The building wouldn't look out of place in Soviet Russia, the ugly white, plastic-framed double glazing the only vaguely modern thing about them.

'If Carver is in there,' Chamberlain murmurs, 'we're definitely going to need more backup.'

'We could ask, but I doubt we'd get it,' Tannahill replies. 'Besides,' he nods at a figure walking up the street towards them. 'Backup is already here.'

DS Baker spots them and heads over to the car, looking exactly like a copper trying not to look like a copper. Tannahill

winds his window down and scans the second-floor balcony of the crumbling building until he spots the number of Lizzy Carver's flat in grey plastic letters. The fact that it's on an upper floor is good, it reduces the number of entrances and exits. There's probably only one way in and one way out and he's looking at both of them.

'Morning, gents,' Baker says, leaning down so his head is level with Tannahill's. 'Fancy meeting you here.'

Chamberlain grunts, clearly unimpressed by Tannahill's idea of backup.

'OK,' Tannahill says. 'There's a strong chance that my main and only suspect in the headless floater investigation is in a flat up there. I want you to cover the front and back for me. I'll go knock on the front door, and if some guy in his early sixties who looks like he might have spent the last sixteen years in an American prison comes hurtling out of the building, I want you to arrest him, or at least call it in and keep your eye on him so someone else can arrest him. I'm not asking you to do anything risky.'

Baker nods. 'So you want us to watch your back while *you* do something risky?'

'I don't think it's that risky. If my suspect is in there, he'll probably run and then we can catch him. If he's not there, I'll have a little chat with his mum and see what she knows.'

Baker looks over at the main entrance to the apartment block where two women are standing and chatting next to a large metal door that is scarred and gouged, as if someone forgot their key and tried to break in using a crowbar. 'How you going to get in through that without a key?'

'Let me worry about that. All I want you to do is go round the back and watch the fire escape while Chamberlain covers the front. If anything goes wrong, call for help.'

'And how will we know if something's gone wrong if you're in the flat, I'm in the car and Baker is standing round the back with his thumb up his arse?'

'Oi,' Baker says. 'There's going to be no thumbs up no arses on this job.' He turns to Tannahill. 'He does have a point though. What happens if, for example, no one comes running down the fire escape because they're too busy hacking you to death with an axe?'

'Well, that would be unfortunate and I will try my hardest not to let it happen. Tell you what I'll do . . .' He pulls his phone from his pocket, opens a blank text message and types something into it. 'I'll go up there and knock on the front door, and if everything's cool I'll text you this.' He shows them his phone.

Baker squints at the thumbs-up emoji and snorts. 'If my kids were here, they'd say that was the most boomer thing they'd ever seen.'

'Yeah, well they're not here, so are we good? If you don't get the thumbs-up, call for backup and blame me for dragging you both into this, OK?'

Baker squints up at the building. 'I'm not sure we're "good" exactly, but since you're really dead set on knocking on that door, I'll happily call an ambulance for you if it all goes south.'

Tannahill smiles and gets out of the car. 'That's what I like about you, John, your boundless optimism.' He checks the time on his phone. 'I'll give you five minutes to get in place round the back then I'll text you both to let you know I'm going in. If you don't get my thumbs-up emoji within a minute of that, you can call for support.'

Baker shakes his head. 'It's your funeral.' He heads away, back down the street, the two women by the entrance watching him as he walks past before disappearing round the corner of the building.

Tannahill nods at Chamberlain. 'All set?'

'I hope for your sake Carver's not there,' Chamberlain replies grimly. 'You should never corner a rat.'

'I'll be fine,' Tannahill says, more cheerfully than he actually feels. 'Just keep an eye on that front door.'

He straightens up, buttons his jacket and emerges from the thin shade of the tree then heads over to the two women standing by the scarred front door. One is vaping, the other is bouncing a pushchair up and down so violently Tannahill half expects a baby to come flying out of it any second. They side-eye him as he draws closer but carry on their conversation, lowering their voices the nearer he gets.

'Morning,' Tannahill says, treating them to his warmest smile and nodding at the ugly pile of bricks behind them. 'Do either of you live here?'

The two women regard him suspiciously, like he's asked them a trick question.

'Only we got a report of a smell of smoke on the second floor,' Tannahill squints up at the block of flats. 'I'm from the management company,' he explains, his smile still firmly in place. 'I'm supposed to be meeting a key-holder here but they're snagged up in traffic. I don't suppose one of you could let me in so I can have a quick look before he gets here? It's probably nothing, but in these old buildings you can never be too careful.'

26

Gracie looks up at Shelby, feeling suddenly self-conscious that she's been babbling for twenty minutes in an almost constant stream of consciousness about school, friends, how miserable she had once been, how much happier she is now. She even found herself telling him about her overdose, about her partial liver transplant, about her recovery – things she hasn't even told her best friends at school.

'Sorry,' she says, 'I must be boring you.'

'God no.' Shelby flashes his broken-toothed smile. 'You've packed a lot more into your life than I've done in mine.' He stares down at the egg and brown sauce smears on his plate. 'I'm just sorry I wasn't around for any of it. Not that I would have been much use.' He looks back up and brightens. 'Still, looks like you and your mum are doing OK now. Nice apartment, private school, a bit of money in the bank. I guess you inherited something from your grandad?'

'Yeah, I suppose, but Mum's pretty successful too. She works really hard. She's always working. I think we were OK before we moved to where we are now, but, yeah, I suppose it is much nicer than before.'

'Where were you before?'

'We lived in a flat off the Holloway Road.'

151

Shelby smiles. 'Yep – unless things have changed drastically while I've been away, the place you're in now is *much* nicer than anywhere off the Holloway Road. So, what does she do, your mum; is she like a police officer or a lawyer something?'

'She does all sorts of things to do with crimes and things. She works for London Metropolitan University, mainly, as a lecturer in police stuff. She's written a couple of books too, and she helps out on actual cases sometimes.'

Shelby nods. 'I read about one of those, big case last year, involving some crazy guy and your grandad, is that what you call him – grandad?'

'Grandpa. He's grandpa. Was.'

'Yes, I read that he'd passed. I'm sorry for your loss.'

'That's OK. I didn't really know him. Only at the end . . . a little.'

Shelby smiles as something occurs to him. 'Did you know your grandpa was the guy in charge of the operation that put me in prison?'

Gracie nods.

'That's some messed-up family stuff, right?' He shakes his head. 'I used to hate him for that but now I see that he was only doing what any father would do, protecting his daughter from a bad situation, and believe me, back when I first met your mother, I was one bad situation.' He frowns as he remembers who he used to be, then looks up at Gracie. 'I guess if you got involved with someone like me, like who I used to be, then I'd do anything I could to get you away from them too.' He smiles and shows the broken front tooth again. 'So, what do you want to be when you grow up – a lawyer? a politician? Be great if you ended up as a lawyer.' He winks at her. 'Could always use a good lawyer in the family.'

Gracie smiles and looks away. 'I don't know what I want to do. Go to uni, for sure, but I've got to get good A-levels first.'

'Well, you should be studying then, not ducking out of school to have breakfast with an old con like me.' He smiles at her.

'I'm glad you did, though. It's nice to catch up, find out a little bit about you. When I flew to the States to try and pull off this deal I didn't know your mother was . . . well, I didn't know about you. I'd like to tell you that if I had known I would have done things differently, stayed here and tried to turn my life around, support your mother, be around for you. I'd like to tell you that, but that wouldn't be the truth. The person I was back then, I would most likely still have gone, probably run away even faster, truth be told.'

He looks up at her, his eyes clouded by pain and regret. 'I'm sorry to tell you that, but I'm trying to be honest. After everything that's happened to me and all the things I've seen, all the things I've lost, I'm trying not to waste any more time. I'm trying to do the right thing. I would never walk away from you or your mother now because I'm a different person. That's why I came round last night, to warn you about this guy who might come looking for information. This guy, Billy Carver, he's bad news. I think people like him are broken from the get-go. I'm not sure your mum was listening to me, though. She doesn't trust me. I mean, why should she?' He stares down into his coffee, his shoulders slumping as if all the energy has suddenly drained from him.

Gracie feels awkward, like she should be doing something to comfort or reassure him, but she doesn't know what to say or do. She's not used to having a dad in her life, let alone a sad one. 'Do you really think he's dangerous, this Billy . . .'

'Carver? Oh yeah. He's like the Terminator; you ever see that film?'

Gracie nods.

'That's what we're dealing with. Billy Carver will not stop, ever, until all scores are settled and everyone on his shit list is dead. Pardon my French.'

'I've heard worse.'

'Does your mum curse?'

Gracie smiles. 'All the time.'

Shelby nods. 'Good for her.'

He looks up as Vic shuffles back to their table and picks up Shelby's empty plate.

'Need anything else?' he says, in the toneless voice of the clinically depressed.

Shelby looks at Gracie but she shakes her head. 'I should be getting back.' She reaches for the bill but Shelby snatches it up.

'My treat, remember. Got to spend all that gate money on something.' He hands over a twenty and waits for Vic to shuffle off and get change before he speaks again.

'Have you got a number I can call you on, or text you or something? I'd like to be able to talk to you again.'

Gracie nods and pulls out her phone. She opens her contacts, pauses for a second then types DAD into a new contact and hands it to him.

Shelby smiles when he sees what she's written. 'Maybe don't put me down as that,' he says as he taps in his number. 'Just in case your mother spots it. Probably don't tell her about this little chat either, I doubt she'll be too happy that you cut school in order to come visit me. We should keep all this as our secret, until things settle down a little.'

He hands the phone back and Gracie deletes the word DAD and puts him in as D instead. Half her friends at school are listed by initials or nicknames, so for now he can be just another new friend her mother doesn't need to know about.

Vic shuffles back and places a saucer on the table with the change all in coins to encourage them to leave a tip.

'I'll get the next one,' Gracie says, sliding out from her seat.

'OK,' Shelby replies. 'I'll book a table at the Ritz and order everything on the menu.'

Gracie smiles. 'You can if you like. I'll see you.'

'You can count on it.' Shelby watches his daughter walk away, thinking again how she looks exactly like her mother did sixteen years and a whole lifetime ago.

SIXTEEN YEARS
EARLIER

SHELBY FACER

Shelby placed his suitcase on the ground, looked up at the house and checked the address: 9 Zoffany Street, N19. The last house in London Minty had called it, like it was something special. It didn't look that special. It looked exactly the same as a million other houses built at the height of the Empire in the scruffier parts of an expanding London.

Chance to get in on a major deal – the message had said.
A simple courier job. Bring your passport and an overnight bag.

If the message hadn't come from Minty Fowler, Shelby would have thought it was a wind up, but Minty was serious and well connected. He figured it wouldn't hurt to come along and hear him out at least. So here he was. He picked up his suitcase and headed to the house.

'There he is,' Minty said, all smiles as he undid the last of many locks and opened the front door to let him in. 'Go on through, someone's here already.'

Shelby headed down the short hallway and stepped into a sparsely furnished living room with a large TV in one corner, a coffee table in the centre of the room with a mobile phone, and what looked like a travel wash bag on it. Facing the table was a large brown Chesterfield sofa with a solid looking man sitting on it.

'Hi,' Shelby held out his hand and turned on his warmest smile. 'Shelby Facer.'

The man looked up at him like he wanted to take his hand and rip it off.

'No names,' Minty said, stepping into the room. 'I should have said that in my message. Sorry.'

Shelby kept his smile in place but lowered his hand. 'Then I guess you have the advantage.' He held the man's gaze for a moment, trying his best to show that he wasn't intimidated by his silence, even though he was, then turned back to Minty. 'So, what's the deal?'

'We need someone to deliver a package.'

'Who's "we"?'

Minty pursed his mouth like he'd sucked on a lemon. 'I'm not going to give you any names. I can tell you that I've done business with these people before and they're proper, I can vouch for them, like I vouched for you to them.' He picked up the phone from the coffee table and checked the time. 'Someone is going to call you on this in exactly . . . four minutes.' He handed the phone to Shelby. 'We're also going to be joined, by two more people, though they seem to be running a little late.'

Shelby looked at the phone in his hand like it was a grenade with the pin removed and tried to act as if it was no big deal.

'All sounds very cloak and dagger,' he said, shooting a wink at the guy on the sofa. The man stared back, his face

156

hard and unreadable. There was something dark and unsettling about him, and it wasn't just because of his unfriendly manner and brooding presence. He made Shelby's lizard brain scream in warning, as if he had happened upon a hungry bear in the forest, or come face to face with a shark in the ocean. It was a presence he had, a dark energy that felt violent and frightening.

A sudden knock on the door made both Shelby and Minty jump. The guy on the couch didn't flinch, didn't show any indication he'd even heard the knock. It was as if he was carved out of stone. Minty scurried out into the hallway to answer the door and Shelby glanced at the wash bag on the table, wondering what it contained.

'Gentlemen,' Minty said, stepping back in the room. 'Please excuse the lack of introductions but I have been instructed to keep this businesslike and anonymous.' He moved aside and two men stepped into the room, making it feel instantly cramped and uncomfortable. One of the men looked Italian – dark hair, dark skin, and a suit that looked like it cost more than a family car. The other man also had a suit on, but his didn't really fit and the elbows were shiny, like he spent most of his waking hours leaning on them. Shelby smiled at them both and nodded a greeting.

The man in the expensive suit looked at the others like he was sizing them up. 'Which of you has the diamonds?' he asked, his voice sounding more Spanish than Italian.

'We should wait for the call,' Minty replied, sounding a little flustered. 'Why don't you take a seat?'

The guy in the expensive suit looked at the man already sitting on the sofa then turned to the other man who seemed as jittery as Minty. 'You sit,' he said, more a command than a request.

The nervy man sat, leaving Shelby, Minty and the Spanish guy standing. No one said anything and an uneasy silence settled, but not for long.

157

The ringtone seemed extra loud in the heavy silence of the room, something classical that Shelby recognized. He answered and raised the phone to his ear. 'Hello?'

'Could you put the phone on speaker, please,' a man's voice said, sounding a little muffled, as if he was making some vague attempt to disguise his voice.

Shelby put the phone on speaker and held it up.

'Good evening, gentlemen,' the voice said, 'and thank you for coming at such short notice. On the table in the room there should be a small bag; can someone please confirm.'

'Yes,' Minty said, stepping forward. 'It's here.'

'Good,' the voice on the phone replied. 'If the seller wants to open it and select a sample.'

The nervy man on the sofa looked at the Spanish-looking guy, who nodded once, then leaned forward and unzipped the wash bag to reveal a small plastic bag, the kind you might put a sandwich in. Inside was what looked like a fistful of dull, white gravel. The nervy guy placed it on the table, took a scroll of black material out of his pocket and unrolled it to reveal a flat grey stone and an oblong black box with lights on the side and a sharp, metal point on one end. It looked like a digital thermometer or a probe an electrician might use. He shook a few stones on to the material, flicked a switch to turn on the electronic probe and touched the tip of it to the first stone. All the lights lit up immediately.

'What is that?' the man in the expensive suit asked.

'It's a tester pen,' the nervy guy explained. 'It checks a stone's thermal conductivity. Diamonds conduct heat better than any of the cheaper alternatives, so if all the lights come on like this, the rocks are genuine.'

He proceeded to touch the probe to each stone in turn, getting the same result each time. Next, he took the largest of the rocks and scratched it along the surface of the grey stone, leaving a clear line.

'This is carborundum,' he explained, 'only slightly less hard

158

than diamonds, so if these are glass, or moissanite, or cubic zirconia they will leave no mark.' He took each stone and scratched it on the surface, leaving marks behind each time, then looked back up at the man in the expensive suit and nodded.

'OK,' the man in the suit said. 'Looks like we're in business. So, what now?'

'Now, you return to Miami,' the voice on the phone replied. 'We have shown you we are serious and properly funded, now it's over to you. Our courier and security guy will meet you there in twenty-four with the stones.'

The man in the nice suit surveyed the room and nodded. 'OK,' he said. He looked at Shelby. 'See you in Miami.' He turned and walked out of the room.

Bring your passport and an overnight bag, Minty's message had said.

Shelby glanced down at the diamonds. Looked like he was going to Florida. He regarded the scary guy on the sofa. The only downside was he was not going alone.

27

Tannahill steps on to the cracked concrete walkway of the second floor of Albion House and checks his phone. He'll give Baker another minute to get in place.

He looks out at Jamaica Street, the buildings opposite identical in design and decay like a kind of depressing reflection. He leans over and looks down the front of the building, wondering how many people have jumped. Not enough to warrant the installation of safety barriers obviously, unless the cost of the lives lost was deemed to be less than the expense of trying to save them. The two women are still deep in conversation by the front door, the baby in the pushchair still being bounced so violently it might almost qualify as child abuse. One of the women looks up and catches his eye. He smiles down reassuringly then looks back at his phone, as if expecting the fictional key-holder to call, and checks the time again. Baker should be in place round the back now. He sends him and Chamberlain a quick text:

All good?

Three dots pop up showing someone's typing a reply then the thumbs-up emoji pops up from Baker.

Tannahill hits *Reply* and puts his own thumbs up in a message but doesn't send it. He keeps the phone in his hand and heads along the crumbling walkway, counting down the numbers until he reaches number 27, the address Billy Carver had written on his extradition papers. He stops by the door and holds the phone in his left hand, his thumb poised over the *Send* button in case anything goes wrong. He takes a breath and presses the doorbell.

An electronic *Ding Dong* sounds inside the flat then fades away to nothing.

Tannahill leans in and listens through the background noise of distant traffic and sirens for any sound inside the flat. He is about to press the bell again when he hears a shuffling sound, soft but getting louder. He straightens up and smiles at the lens of the peephole drilled into the door at eye-level.

"Oo is it?' a voice demands, the same smoke-soaked voice he had heard on the phone earlier.

'My name is DCI Khan, Mrs Carver. I'm with the Metropolitan Police. We spoke on the phone about twenty minutes ago.'

There is a pause followed by the rattle of a chain and the muffled *thunk* of a deadbolt being unlocked. The door opens a little, banging to a halt as the security chain engages. A deeply lined, almost grey face peers out at him, a half-smoked cigarette dangling from thin lips lined with the deep creases of a lifelong smoker.

'Got any ID?' she asks, the cigarette moving up and down as she speaks and dripping ash down an old-fashioned-looking, pale blue housecoat, peppered with tiny holes from previous burns. Tannahill pulls his warrant card from his jacket and holds it up for her to see.

She peers at it, sucking on her cigarette and making the end glow red. Finally she looks back at him, breathing the smoke out as she speaks. "Ave you found 'im then?'

'No, Mrs Carver. We haven't, and like I said on the phone earlier, he's not in any trouble. I'd just like to talk to him if I

could.' He looks past her into the smoky gloom of the flat. 'So, if he is here, you can tell him I'm not here to arrest him or anything. I only want a quick chat.'

Mrs Carver takes another deep pull on her cigarette and peers at Tannahill like he's stupid. 'I told you, 'e's not here any more so you've wasted your time.' She moves to close the door but Tannahill sticks his foot into the gap, keeping it jammed open.

'Sorry,' he says, 'did you say he's not here "any more"? So, he has been here?'

Mrs Carver looks up at him and he can almost see her mind whirring behind her black, suspicious eyes. 'Yeah,' she says finally.

'When was your son here, Mrs Carver?'

Again she pauses, weighing up whether she should tell him or not. The phone buzzes in Tannahill's hand and he glances down to find a message from Baker saying – *All good?*

Tannahill sends the thumbs-up emoji in reply.

'Friday,' Mrs Carver says. ''E stayed here Thursday and Friday night. Saturday 'e went off somewhere and said e'd be back late. Ain't seen 'im since.'

'Did he say where he was going or who he was seeing?'

She lets out a snort and more ash spills from the end of her dying cigarette. 'Billy never told me nuffin'. I thought being away for so long might of changed 'im for the better, calmed 'im dahn a bit, but 'e was still the same. Still angry at everyfing. All 'e said was 'e needed to see a man about a dog and sort some fings aht, but 'e didn't say what and 'e didn't say where.'

'May I see the room where he stayed?' Tannahill asks, pushing his luck.

Mrs Carver regards him coldly again through the gap and the veil of smoke. 'Got a warrant?'

'No,' Tannahill admits with what he hopes is a winning smile. 'But I don't need one if you let me in voluntarily.'

'And why would I want to go and do that?'

'Because I'm trying to find your son, Mrs Carver. I'm not looking to arrest him or cause any trouble, I only want to find him and talk to him, and having a quick look at the last place he stayed might help me find him a bit quicker.'

Mrs Carver takes another deep drag on her cigarette, a reflex which seems to accompany her thought processes. Her face screws up as she tastes the bitter smoke from burning filter and she plucks the dead cigarette from her thin, puckered mouth and crushes it out in a half-full ashtray on a shelf by the door. She pats the pocket of her housecoat and looks genuinely panicked when she finds it empty. She looks back at Tannahill, chewing her lower lip in thought.

'Go on then,' she says, closing the door a little in order to unhook the chain. She lets the door swing wide and heads back into the flat in search of cigarettes. Tannahill waits for a moment for some kind of invitation before stepping through the door and following her down the short hallway. Everything in the flat has been tinted a kind of browny-grey: the paintwork, the carpet, even the air.

'In there,' Mrs Carver says, nodding at a door off the hallway. 'I ain't tidied cos I weren't expecting no visitors. Billy never likes me touching 'is stuff anyway.' She shuffles on into a tiny kitchen as grey as the rest of the flat, where a packet of cigarettes is visible on a small table next to a half-drunk cup of tea. The cigarette packet has a picture of a diseased lung on it beneath the words 'SMOKING CAUSES EMPHYSEMA'. Mrs Carver ignores it and pulls one out, sparking it up with a disposable lighter from the pocket of her housecoat. Tannahill twists the handle and pushes the door open to reveal the room beyond.

The bedroom is like a time capsule: a single bed pushed up against one wall, an old wooden wardrobe in the opposite corner and slightly crooked shelves screwed to the walls. The shelves are filled with trophies and a few framed photographs. The bed is still unmade, creating the feeling that someone has

just got out of it and might return at any moment. There are clothes on the floor, a grease-stained Domino's Pizza box and some empty cans of Stella that have been crushed and thrown at a waste bin in the corner by someone with terrible aim.

Tannahill steps inside and looks around, trying to get a feel for the room and the person who stayed here. It feels more like a teenager's bedroom than an adult's. He walks over to the shelf and picks up one of the trophies, a boxer with gloves raised, silver-plated plastic on a black plastic base. An engraved metal plaque on the front reads *U14 division – Runner up*. The trophy is thick with dust and there's a square mark on the dusty shelf showing where it has stood for God knows how long. It looks like Mrs Carver hasn't been expecting any visitors here for quite some time.

Tannahill places the trophy back on the shelf and picks up one of the framed photos. It shows a group of boys standing in front of a boxing ring, their meaty arms draped over each other's shoulders, their hair cut short and wet with sweat. He recognizes the one in the middle from the mug shot in the case file – younger, slimmer, but even at that age with the same dark air of someone you did not want to tangle with.

'That's Billy wiv 'is mates dahn the club,' the dry smoker's voice rasps behind him. 'It was me what signed 'im up for it. Thought it might channel 'is aggression. It worked for a bit, that's 'ow he won all them trophies. Then 'e nearly killed some poor lad in the ring. They 'ad to pull Billy off of 'im after the bell went, he just kept 'itting him, even though the other lad was on the floor and weren't moving no more. They banned 'im after that. Kicked 'im out the gym. That's when it all went wrong really. Fell in wiv some bad people who could see a use for someone like Billy, someone wiv a temper who was quick wiv his fists and not afraid of nuffing. 'E got that from 'is old man 'n'all. Maybe if he'd been able to stick to the boxing . . .' Her voice trails off in a cloud of fresh smoke and old memories.

Tannahill turns to her. 'Do you have any more recent photos of your son, Mrs Carver?'

She takes another deep drag on her cigarette, pulling on it like she's breathing in pure oxygen rather than smoke. She shakes her head and blows the smoke into the room. 'Only ones of him in prison, but I don't like looking at those.'

Tannahill turns to her and points at the wardrobe. 'May I?'

Mrs Carver shrugs, which he takes to be a 'yes' so he opens the door.

Inside is an odd mix of clothes, Hawaiian-style shirts next to newer, larger, more formal shirts that have clearly been ironed.

'I bought them shirts,' Mrs Carver says bitterly. 'Told Billy 'e needed to smarten 'isself up and go out and get a proper job if 'e wanted to stay here wi' me. Told 'im there was plenty of temp jobs in the city, but you know what 'e said? 'E said I ain't never working in no office.' She shakes her head. ''E's still the same as always. Big chip on 'is shoulder and angry at the world.'

Tannahill closes the door and looks down at the wastebasket in the corner. A few of the crushed beer cans made it inside, and there's something else in there too. Tannahill bends down to take a look.

'I told 'im he needed to do somefing, his bleedin' pride weren't gonna pay no bills or put no food on the table.'

The object in the wastebasket is a wrapper, clear plastic with a ripped, red cardboard label on the top.

'I said I was too old to still be lookin' after 'im, and that 'e should be lookin' after me by now.'

Tannahill tilts the wastebasket over a little and frowns when he sees what it says on the label – *Learner Driver Plates.*

''E told me to stop my noise,' Mrs Carver says. 'After all 'e's put me through. "Stop your noise," 'e says! I'll get a job, but not in no office wearing no monkey suit.'

Tannahill snags the clear plastic wrapper by a corner and

holds it up, wondering why Billy Carver would need L-plates. Learning to drive a car seems like a strange thing to do immediately after getting out of prison. Then it struck him. There were other things you needed L-plates for.

He turns to Mrs Carver, leaning on the door frame in the centre of a cloud of cigarette smoke. 'Did he get a job in the end, Mrs Carver?'

She rolls her eyes and takes another industrial-sized drag on her cigarette. 'Delivery boy,' she says, blowing a fresh cloud of smoke into the bedroom. 'Can you believe that, fifty-six years old and 'e wants to work as a bleedin' delivery boy. 'As the cheek to ask *me* to take out a lease on a scooter for 'im, you know, like, a moped. 'E can't rent one hisself, see, cos of 'is record. So now I'm on the 'ook for a few grands' worth of bike. I told 'im, if 'e put so much as a scratch on it 'e'd be out on his ear.'

'Do you still have the paperwork, Mrs Carver?'

She looks at him like he's an idiot. 'Yeah, course. It was me what 'ad to sign it all.'

'May I see it?'

She shrugs and shuffles back into the kitchen, trailing a cloud of smoke behind her. Tannahill pulls his phone from his pocket and quickly takes photos of the inside of the wardrobe, the wastebasket with the empty L-plate packaging inside, and a wide view of Billy Carver's boyhood bedroom, then heads into the kitchen to find Mrs Carver rummaging around in a drawer filled with envelopes, bills, and takeaway menus.

''Ere you go.' She pulls out the yellow copy of a lease agreement with a drawing of a motor scooter on the letterhead and BIKE-U-LIKE written across it in leaning lettering probably intended to suggest speed. 'They swiped my credit card for a seven 'undred quid excess before they'd 'and me the keys, and I won't be seeing that again if anyfing's 'appened to that bike.'

Tannahill scans the document and spots the registration number at the bottom.

'Thank you, Mrs Carver.' He pulls a business card from his pocket and hands it to her. 'This will help us find him and make sure he's OK.' He finds Chamberlain's number on his phone and dials it. 'And if Billy does call in the meantime, please let me know. You can get me on any of those numbers at any time.'

The phone connects and a concerned-sounding Chamberlain answers. 'Everything OK?'

'Yeah, all good. Listen, I need you to run a number through ANPR for me.' Tannahill reads out the registration number from the hire document then catches the worried look on Mrs Carver's face. 'ANPR is Automatic Number Plate Recognition,' he explains. 'It will tell us where the bike has been and hopefully where Billy is now.'

She nods and inhales another soothing lungful of carcinogenic smoke. 'So long as that moped comes back in one piece,' she says. 'That's all I really care about.'

28

Traffic flows, a river of metal and glass down the straight, wide course of the Holloway Road.

He sits on the western shore of it in the shade of the lone tree by the bike stands outside London Metropolitan University. The moped engine ticks as it cools down. His eyes – hidden behind the darkened plastic of his visor – are fixed on the strange, twisted-metal building opposite and the traditionally built clock tower beyond.

She works here.

He had gleaned that little fact in the newspaper coverage of her involvement in the murder mansion case the previous year. More detail had been available online – her name on the London Metro website listing her as one of the lecturers, another list of the university's buildings revealing where all the different faculties were housed, even her schedule of lectures was online, which is why he knows she is here right now.

He stretches, squeezing some tension out of his back, then goes back to pretending to look at his phone while his eyes remain fixed on the two buildings opposite. Her scheduled lecture is due to end soon and he wants to be sure he catches her as she leaves. She might remain inside, of course, go to the library in the graduate building, the strange, crumpled structure

opposite that looks like a giant crushed can, or she might go and work in her office. He presumes she has an office, though he was unable to find any details online. She will come out eventually though – for lunch, at the end of the day, sometime – and he is happy to wait. Killing time is something he learned in a Florida prison, a lesson that took a decade and a half to be taught. His education was forced upon him, unlike the one the pampered, entitled idiots were getting in these bullshit buildings surrounding him.

A bunch of students pass him now, laughing and talking animatedly about some bollocks they'd just read, someone else's opinion they will now steal and pass off as their own until something shinier comes along.

'I think Kafka is hilarious,' one of them says, 'I reckon he'd probably be doing some kind of deadpan stand-up if he was alive today.'

Everyone laughs like it's the funniest thing they've ever heard and they head off down the Holloway Road, looking for a café where they can continue their loud, self-satisfied conversations.

These kids – and they are still kids despite their fluffy beards and piercings – strut around like they have it all figured out. They don't know anything, not about the real world at least. He'd like to see how many jokes they'll be cracking after they graduate with a ton of student debt and a degree in something useless that won't even begin to help pay it off. He'd read Kafka in prison and it hadn't cost him a dime – only time – and he bet he understood it way more than any of these idiots because he'd lived it; *The Trial* was more like a memoir to him.

He'd pieced his own story together in jail too, going through all the documents from his case again and again, until he saw the pattern they made. It was a strange experience, collecting and assembling fragments of the blueprints for the trap that had imprisoned you.

Operation Henry 8.

Such a *Boy's Own* name for something that had taken away his entire life.

He had lain, night after night in his prison cot, turning it all over in his mind as he stared up at the stained concrete ceiling of his cell, sweat beading on his skin from the solid heat pressing down on him, looking for some meaning in it all as the grunts and whimpers, deep snores and high-pitched whine of mosquito wings pierced the darkness all around. He had lain there, wondering if there had ever been a way he might have escaped the trap, or if his destiny had already been set, just as Henry's wives had been doomed the moment they fell into his orbit – divorced, beheaded, died, divorced, beheaded, survived, their fates repeating in his head like a mantra – a rosary of the doomed.

Was he the same – he had wondered – had he too been condemned by fate?

And then he had realized something profound. To think like that was just another trap. If you acted and thought like a victim, you became a victim and you remained one. The trick was to learn how to think like a victor.

So, he decided to change his story by embracing his existing one.

There were no details of the executioners used to rid Henry of his unwanted wives, their names lost to history. The only record he could find was of a man known as the Sword of Calais, a Frenchman imported specifically for the execution of Anne Boleyn, and at her request. She wanted her death to be quick and painless so she called for the best.

The Sword of Calais. The best. He repeated this name in the long, hot nights, imagining what sort of man he had been, what sort of life he had lived until he had started to imagine himself as this person, someone whose identity was tied to his purpose, and – like a god – had the power to end or spare a life. He tried to forget everything he had been – his past, his name –

170

untethering himself from the details of his former failure in order to become this new, victorious entity.

Then one day he had come to his cell and found a new cellmate unfolding his bedroll and acting in that jumpy way all new inmates did.

'Hey man,' the newbie had said, flashing him a hopeful but guarded smile. 'I'm Gene.'

'Calais,' he had replied without thinking. 'My name is Calais.'

And that was it, his transformation completed in that simple statement. Everything he had been was now gone – his past, his failures, even his name.

Calais takes a deep breath now, in through his nose and out through his mouth, something else he'd learned in prison on one of the many anger-management courses he'd been forced to take in the early days. The crowds of smug students had managed to wind him up and he needed to calm down and stay focused – head in the game, eye on the prize.

And there she was.

He follows Laughton with his eyes as she exits the crushed-can building, a large bag slung over her shoulder, her attention fixed on the solid line of traffic flowing down the Holloway Road.

He'd read somewhere that the Holloway Road got its name from the hollow carved into it by the hooves of all the livestock that used to be driven along it on their way to the city markets. Nowadays it was trucks and vans, but the principle remained the same: goods heading into the city to be turned into money.

Laughton holds her hand up and a black cab peels away from the river of cars and vans and pulls to a halt beside her.

He puts his phone away and starts his engine, flipping the kickstand up with his foot, ready to roll as soon as she does.

Another crowd of pimples and opinions walks past him, laughing and talking and knowing nothing. He could tell them everything they needed to know in five seconds flat, all the wisdom he had accumulated distilled into a simple mantra.

Time and money are the only two things worth a damn, the only two things you can never have enough of. And though he can never get the time he lost back, the money is a different story. *That* he can do something about.

Laughton disappears into the back of the cab and it moves off, re-joining the flow of metal, glass, and rubber. Calais waits for a few seconds then eases forward, steering the bike into the traffic and following the cab at an anonymous distance, down the Holloway Road towards the distant shining towers of the city along with the ghosts of all the slaughtered livestock that passed this way before.

29

Tannahill smiles at the two women still hanging around the front door as he exits Albion House.

'False alarm,' he says, glancing down at the toddler in the pushchair who is now finally asleep, or possibly concussed. 'Someone's toaster went a bit haywire.'

The women raise their eyebrows and nod, as if this is what they suspected all along, then go back to their conversation as Tannahill heads down the street to the parked car. Chamberlain is on his phone as he approaches, nodding and scribbling in a notepad.

'We got a hit on that registration plate,' he says, still writing frantically. 'Several hits actually. He's mobile right now.'

'Where?' Tannahill opens the door and jumps into the passenger seat.

'Heading east on the Mile End Road. Last hit we got was six minutes ago. There was another eight minutes earlier, and another fifteen minutes before that. He's travelling out of central London along a bus lane and getting picked up by all the traffic cameras.'

'Anything near Tower Bridge?'

'Yes.' Chamberlain checks back through his notes. 'The last hit from yesterday evening was eight-oh-nine on Lower Thames

Street, that's a stone's throw away. Then nothing new until about half an hour ago. Looks like maybe he parked up for the night and is now on the move again.'

Tannahill's jaw clenches. The thought that Billy Carver had been near Laughton's flat, possibly watching it all night long, makes him feel sick. He must have spotted the squad car parked outside and that had been enough of a deterrent to keep him away. But there was no way he would be able to keep the car there for another night, not now Grieves had told him to drop it altogether. He had to catch Carver quickly, and this was his best chance.

'Swing round the back to pick up Baker,' Tannahill yanks the seat belt across his chest. 'Then head to Carver's last reported location.'

Chamberlain looks across at him. 'You're going to try and chase down a moped using ANPR?'

'He's travelling down a bus lane,' Tannahill replies, 'and the Mile End Road is only five minutes from here. If we're quick then maybe we can get ahead of him.'

30

The Big Yellow Storage Company in East London occupies an old stationery factory and looks like something a child built from over-sized plastic bricks. The cab pulls up in front and Laughton steps out. She looks up at the building, taking in the sheer vast, yellow-ness of it, three storeys high and big enough to house several jumbo jets.

The cab pulls away as Laughton heads to the entrance, pushing through the main door into a bright reception area lined with shelves containing flat-packed boxes, packs of permanent markers, padlocks, rolls of bubble wrap and other packing paraphernalia. A man of around sixty looks up from his book and discreetly stashes it under the counter as he fits a smile on his face. The badge on his yellow T-shirt identifies him as 'Dave'.

'Can I help?' Dave asks.

'I hope so yes,' Laughton pulls the invoice from her bag and slides it through a slot in the Perspex screen running the full length of the counter. 'I wondered if you could tell me how I go about gaining access to my father's storage unit.'

'Do you have his permission?'

'No, I . . . he died . . . so . . .'

'Oh, I'm sorry. Yes, of course I can help, let me take a look at this.' Dave picks up the invoice and peers at it through the

pair of half-moon reading glasses perched delicately at the end of his nose.

'Right. Well, first I'll still need to see some ID.'

Laughton pulls her driver's licence and Metropolitan Police ID card from her bag, then slides them through the slot in the Perspex screen. The man takes them and turns to a scanner on the desk behind him. 'Just need to make copies of these, if that's OK, then we can fill out the transfer forms and assign the contract to you. Will you be wanting to keep the storage unit open, or are you here to make arrangements to empty it?'

Laughton considers the question. 'I'm not sure. I don't really know what's in it so it's hard for me to say. I don't even know how big it is.'

'Oh, it's one of our largest units.' The man slides her ID cards back across the counter and staples the photocopy to a form. 'Four hundred square feet, so about the size of two double garages. You could easily fit the contents of a six-bedroom house in one of those.'

Laughton feels suddenly light-headed at the prospect of such a potentially huge cache of things from her father's life.

'If you could fill in your details on this form . . .' Dave slides another document across the counter. 'I'm afraid there is also the matter of the outstanding balance.'

Laughton takes a credit card from her bag as he taps an amount into his terminal.

'Shall I charge another month on top of the outstanding balance for now?' he suggests. 'Until you've had a chance to take a look inside and think about what you want to do going forward?'

Laughton nods. 'Yes, let's do that.'

He adds a few more figures to her bill and holds the card machine out for her.

'How long has my father had this unit?' Laughton asks, sliding the card into the machine and tapping in her PIN.

'Let me have a look.' He taps something into the computer

and starts scrolling. 'He's definitely had it as long as I've been working here, so at least ten years.' He scrolls onward then leans in and peers at the screen 'The account was opened almost sixteen years ago, so your father must have been one of the very first customers after they converted the old factory.'

Sixteen years!

Her father had first rented the unit at around the same time her mother was killed. The timing seems ominous and makes Laughton wonder again what exactly might be stored here. If it turns out to be full of her mother's old things, she's not sure she'll be able to deal with that.

She looks up at Dave 'You don't happen to know what's inside the unit do you?'

'Oh no, that's all up to the customer. There's a list of banned items – guns, fireworks, flammable things like fuel and paint – but other than that we have nothing to do with what's kept here and don't keep any inventories. We don't even have master keys for the units once they're rented; that's down to the customer too.'

Laughton nods. She hadn't thought that she might need a key. The only experience she's had of places like these is through the pages and photographs of certain cold cases that have taught her that people keep all kinds of things in facilities like this: souvenirs from murders and serial rapes, weapons, stolen goods. They had even found a corpse once in a storage unit in Bradford. The killer had kept it in an old cast-iron bath filled with sacks of kitty litter to mask the smell. Self-storage units were perfect for people with double identities who needed to keep their shadow selves hidden from their regular lives. People like her father, apparently.

'OK,' Dave says breezily, 'your payment has gone through.' He produces a leaflet from beneath the counter and slides it across the counter. 'This is a map of the facility. Your father's unit is here on the second floor.' He circles a large rectangle at the end of what looks like a very long corridor. 'There's a

goods lift over there, or there are stairs through those doors if you're feeling energetic. Any problems, let me know. There are cameras on all floors that connect directly to me here, so you don't need to come all the way down if you have trouble getting into your unit; wave at a camera and I'll pop along and see what I can do to help.' He bends down below the counter and reappears holding an industrial pair of bolt-cutters. 'We may not keep keys, but this tends to unlock most things.'

Laughton smiles and picks up the map. 'Thank you,' she says, 'I'll wave if I need anything.'

Then she turns and heads away into the bright yellow guts of the building to find out exactly what her father has kept hidden here since before her daughter was born.

31

Calais sits across the road from the Big Yellow Storage, the engine of his moped idling, phone in hand as if consulting a map, his face hidden by the dark visor of his crash helmet. Following the cab had been easy on the bike, weaving between the traffic to keep it in sight as it eased past the jams in the bus lanes. London was lousy with delivery bikes these days so it was the perfect disguise, and the crash helmet kept everything nice and anonymous.

He keeps his head angled down towards his phone but his eyes on her, as she talks and talks to the man at the reception desk, filling in forms and talking shit. He wonders what on earth they can be banging on about for so long. Finally, she steps away from the reception desk, passes through a set of yellow doors and disappears into the bowels of the building.

Calais slips the bike into gear and eases forward, riding slowly along the front of the vast yellow frontage of the building. He reaches the end of the building and spots a parking area with a line of mopeds and delivery bikes clustered in the shadow of the wall of another, smaller warehouse next door. Opposite the line of bikes a delivery van is parked at a slight angle, its rear backed up to the side entrance of the Big Yellow. A young couple stand next to it, struggling to offload a large sofa on

to a large trolley that keeps rolling away down the delivery ramp. He turns the bike in a complete circle, shimmies past a parking barrier and pulls to a halt near the van, lifting his visor but keeping his helmet on.

'Need a hand?' he calls out.

The guy looks flustered, his alpha male mind struggling to accept help from another man.

'Yes,' his girlfriend answers, making his mind up for him. 'That would be amazing, thank you.'

Calais turns off the engine, rests the bike on its kickstand and walks over, side-eyeing the open door of the delivery bay.

'You hold the trolley,' he says to the woman, 'stop it from rolling away while me and your boyfriend do the heavy stuff.'

He nods at the open delivery door in the side of the building and the yellow corridors beyond.

'Then I'll help you carry it inside.'

32

Tannahill stares ahead. Chamberlain drives. They move swiftly down the bus lane of the Mile End Road. Tannahill had never realized there were so many delivery scooters in London until he started looking for one. He listens to background office noise and tapping of keyboards through his phone which is connected directly to a sergeant at the ANPR control centre.

'Got another hit,' the sergeant says, 'three minutes ago.' There's a pause. More keyboard tapping. 'Looks like the suspect has stopped right next to a traffic barrier. I'm looking at the live feed now.'

'Can you see anyone?'

'No, sir, it's parked. I can see the bike but not the rider.'

'What's the address?'

'I'll send it through to your phone, it's on an industrial estate in Bow, close to the London Stadium.'

Tannahill covers the phone with his hand. 'How far to the London Stadium?' he asks Chamberlain.

'Ten minutes, maybe five if I stick the lights on.'

'No lights, no sirens,' Tannahill says. 'I don't want anyone to know we're coming.'

His phone buzzes as the address comes through. Tannahill checks it. 'Keep your eye on the feed,' he tells the sergeant. 'I'll

181

put you on speaker and stay on the line. Let us know if you see anyone. We should be at location in seven or eight minutes.'

'Got it.'

'I know I'm beginning to sound like a broken record,' Baker murmurs in the back seat, 'but shouldn't we hold back and call in some backup?'

'No time,' Tannahill says. 'And there's three of us anyway, who needs backup?'

33

Laughton reaches the second floor and pushes through a set of big double doors that make an unpleasant sucking sound as they open. She stops for a second, checking the map against the floor layout and listening out for signs of anyone else who might be around.

The building is eerily silent. Bright strip lights reflect off the shiny floor and illuminate the numbered doors of identical units stretching away almost to infinity. It's so quiet it feels like even sound has been squirrelled away here, carried off and locked away behind one of these numbered doors.

She heads down the longest corridor, away from the stairs, her footsteps squeaking on the shiny floor as she counts down the numbers to 301, her father's storage unit. She imagines him walking down this same corridor, carrying his boxes, or bags, or wheeling a trolley filled with whatever it was he brought here to keep safely hidden away from his regular life. Most of the units are padlocked with the branded Big Yellow locks they sold in reception. Laughton hopes her father's unit is no exception as the locks, though solid, look pretty basic and she feels pretty confident she can pick one without needing to call on Dave the friendly receptionist and his industrial strength bolt-cutters.

The door to one of the units stands slightly ajar and Laughton slows as she draws near, the unsettling silence of the building coupled with having watched way too many B-movie horror movies, leading Laughton to expect something horrible to jump out at her the moment she reaches the door. She stops in front of it, her heart pounding a little harder in her chest as she studies the column of darkness between the edge of the open door and the frame.

Nothing jumps out. No glowing eyes stare back.

She reaches out, pulls the door open a little further and lights blink on in the unit in response to the opening door.

The room is about the size of a single bedroom with a grey, painted concrete floor and walls made from corrugated steel. It smells vaguely of paint and is almost clinically clean. Laughton imagines that with a rug, some nice lighting and some pieces of furniture it could be made quite cosy, and wonders how much one of these units goes for, if it's less than the average London rent, and how soon it will be before people start renting these units out to store themselves rather than their possessions.

She pushes the door closed and carries on down the corridor with only the sound of her squeaking shoes for company.

. . . 312 . . . 311 . . . 310.

She starts saying the numbers aloud to push away the silence, clicking her fingers at every third number, then realizes what she's doing and forces herself to stop. Counting in threes is one of her tics and, though she has been largely successful in conquering her compulsions over the last year or so, it still manifests itself in times of great stress. She takes deep breaths instead, in through the nose and out through the mouth, breathing through her desire to click, all the way to the end of the hallway. She turns the corner and is confronted with another, much shorter stretch of corridor with a large yellow door at the end and the number 301 stencilled on to it.

Her father's storage unit.

Laughton takes another deep breath and steps forward, her

attention fixed on the heavy-duty padlock threaded through the thick steel hasps on both door and frame. She stops in front of it and picks up the lock. It's a Titan, a high-end make she recognizes, though she has never seen this particular model before.

She turns it upside down and looks at the base, expecting a keyhole or a combination but finding neither. The bottom is blank, just a solid plate of brushed, tempered steel. She turns the lock over slowly in her hand, trying to figure out how to open it, and one side lights up revealing a display about half the size of a phone screen. There are five empty boxes and a keyboard displayed on it. There's a shift key too, which turns the keyboard lowercase when she taps it. The option of using both lower and uppercase letters means the possible combinations are instantly multiplied. Laughton does a quick calculation in her head to figure out the odds of cracking the code – twenty-six letters times two equals fifty-two, so each of the five blank spaces can be filled fifty-two different ways. Fifty-two to the power of five is . . . over three hundred and eighty million permutations!

Laughton yanks at the lock in frustration, as if that might make it miraculously spring open, but all it does is re-emphasize how heavy and solid it is. She doubts even helpful Dave in reception will have any joy opening it with his bolt-cutters.

She lets go of the lock and it clangs heavily against the door, the sound echoing away down the corridor until it's swallowed up and stored away wherever the building keeps all the other sounds.

Laughton stares at the screen on the side of the lock, the five empty boxes glowing in the gloom like a challenge.

She tries the most obvious ones, typing in first JOHNR and then JREES, with various combinations of upper and lowercase letters, but nothing works. She hadn't really expected them to. Why go to the trouble of installing an expensive lock like this then using your own name as the password?

She screws her mouth to one side, frustrated by the knowledge that the only thing standing between her and a large room filled with a decade and a half's worth of family secrets and memories is this lock.

She looks back over her shoulder and up at the security camera fitted high in the corner where the corridor turns. She takes a step toward it and is about to wave to alert helpful Dave in reception when a new thought strikes her.

She turns back to the door, pulls her phone from her pocket and googles 'TITAN COMBINATION PADLOCKS'.

The company website comes back as the top result. She opens it and finds a page listing all the company's products. She checks the model number on the lock against the inventory. The lock she is holding is the Titan CB48X, one of the newest models, launched less than two years earlier. That means her father must have upgraded the lock only a few months before he died.

Laughton thinks back to that time, before the two of them were reconciled, and tries to imagine all the things he would have been thinking about. A five-letter name surfaces in her mind and she types it reluctantly into the lock – MCVEY – the name of her mother's killer. She types it again in lower case, then with a mix of caps and lower case, but the padlock remains sealed.

Not McVey then.

Next she types in variations of E-V-A-N-S – the other five-lettered monster from that period – but that doesn't work either.

She takes a deep breath and blows it out in frustration. Maybe she will need the services of friendly Dave after all, if only to call a proper locksmith to come and solve her problem. Or . . . maybe she should call one herself.

A few months earlier she had worked with a guy on a cold case involving an Edwardian trunk filled with human remains that had been secured by a strange, clockwork lock. The lock, ironically, turned out to be the key to the whole mystery, as

186

only one man, a clockmaker and the inventor of the lock, had access to this type of locking mechanism at the time the trunk had been shipped to the Edwardian equivalent of the place Laughton was standing in now. The man who had figured all this out, the gloriously named Percy Perryman, was a clockmaker who worked for the National Trust keeping all its hundreds of antique clocks in working order. He was also a lock enthusiast with an encyclopaedic knowledge of the subject, so if anyone knew a workaround for a Titan CB48X – or at least the best tools to crack one open – it would be him.

Laughton pulls her phone from her pocket ready to dig out his number but stops. She stares at her lockscreen, the photo of Gracie smiling out at her. She tentatively types G-R-A-C-E into the five blank boxes.

A faint noise sounds inside the lock and the main body drops slightly as it releases.

Laughton stares at it, her vision swimming slightly as tears appear. It was her daughter, or maybe her own mother who she'd been named after, or maybe both of them who had been uppermost in her father's mind when he'd last upgraded the security here. It was *their* name he had used to protect whatever was in this room.

Somewhere behind her a door bangs, shattering the moment.

Laughton turns and listens to the squeak of distant footsteps until they too are swallowed by the hungry building. She turns back to the unit, removes the padlock from the locking hasps, and pulls open the door.

34

'Pull over here and let me out.' Tannahill points at a bus stop and checks the address. He puts his phone back on speaker and holds it up so Chamberlain and Baker can both hear. 'Any developments?' he asks.

'No, sir,' the ANPR sergeant responds. 'The bike's still parked in the same place and, still no sign of the rider.'

'OK, thanks.' Tannahill hangs up as the car pulls in to the bus stop.

'Right, so I'll get out and approach on the street, you hang back and wait for my signal. As soon as the rider appears I'll give you a wave and approach on foot while you two swing round to intercept. If he rabbits, you pursue, don't wait for me, OK?'

Baker nods. 'Got it.'

Tannahill turns to Chamberlain. 'And if he looks like he's pulling a knife or trying to stab me, run him over, OK?'

Chamberlain nods. 'With pleasure.'

Tannahill gets out of the car and walks up to the corner, looking around to familiarize himself with the environment.

The whole area is covered with warehouses and industrial units, big grey rectangles built from breeze blocks and corrugated steel with little clue as to what each building contains.

He slows as he reaches the corner and moves closer to the wall, stopping short so he can peer round the edge.

'Shit!' he mutters under his breath.

Billy Carver's bike is parked about twenty feet away on the opposite side of the street. Unfortunately, what the ANPR camera had not shown was that there are around thirty other mopeds and motorbikes parked in the same location, along with a few vans and cars. They are lined up along the side of one of the non-descript grey buildings, this one with industrial ducting fixed to the side walls and a tall chimney rising above the roof level pumping out a steady cloud of steam.

Two picnic tables are set up out front and at least twenty motorcycle riders are sitting or standing around them, eating what look like burritos from silver foil wrappers. Some are wearing tabards with Deliveroo or Just Eats logos on them, and most of the bikes have large, thermal delivery boxes on the back, many with the same logos. A rider emerges from the building carrying a large paper bag with Taco Bell written on it. He carries it over to one of the bikes, places it in the box on the back then starts up his moped and buzzes away, heading west towards the city.

The warehouse must be a dark kitchen, one of the hundreds of delivery-only outfits that had been set up by the big chains to service the booming takeaway market. It looks like Billy Carver is doing exactly what he had told his mother he was going to do, working as a delivery driver.

Tannahill scans the faces of the riders, looking for Billy Carver, but can't see him in the crowd. He studies the ones with their backs to him, and the few who have chosen to keep their helmets on, dismissing the ones that are too tall, too skinny, or look too young. There are only two likely candidates out of all the riders – one seated, one standing. The seated one appears to be joining in the conversation at the table, laughing at the jokes, slapping one of the other drivers on the back.

The other guy, the one standing and leaning against the wall

of the dark kitchen, is an altogether different story. He seems as removed from the group as the other guy seems part of it, saying nothing, reacting to nothing, preferring instead to stare down at his phone, his attention entirely focused on whatever he's scrolling through. He could be waiting for his order to be ready, of course, which would explain why he hadn't taken his helmet off, but he definitely seemed like more of an outsider, like the new guy, perhaps, someone who doesn't yet feel comfortable enough to join in, or even park his bike with the others.

Tannahill looks back at the moped, tilted over on its stand by the traffic barrier. It's definitely the right number plate. He checks the rest of the area – a loading bay, a fire escape, another couple of emergency exit doors. Maybe Carver is in one of these other buildings. If Tannahill breaks cover now only to find that the rider leaning against the wall isn't Carver, he might spoil his chances of an arrest.

He stays where he is for the moment and looks back at the lone rider, willing him to take off his helmet so he can see his face.

35

The sofa lands on the concrete floor of the storage unit with a solid *thunk* and the boyfriend immediately tries to reclaim some kind of macho authority by sliding it snugly into the corner all on his own.

'Thank you so much,' the girlfriend says. 'Can we give you some money to buy yourself a drink or something?'

'Not necessary,' Calais says, holding his hand up. 'Just point me in the direction of a toilet and we'll call it even.'

'OK, great – thanks. I think there's probably one through there by reception.'

'Thanks.' He smiles at her and also her boyfriend, who nods but does not smile back.

By the time Calais is through the double doors and looking back, they are already having a heated argument.

Calais smiles and turns away, grabs a map from a display on the wall and starts walking down the shiny yellow corridor, listening out for sounds and looking for any door that is unlocked and open. Any unit that might have her inside it.

36

Lights flicker on as the door slowly opens. Laughton stands for a moment like a vampire on a threshold, waiting to be invited in.

The storage unit is even larger than she had imagined it would be, with high shelves lining the walls that stick out into the room at regular intervals, making it feel like a small library or some long-forgotten filing room. The shelves are crammed with paperwork, boxes, lever arch files, overstuffed envelopes – and there is an old card table in the centre of the room covered in green baize, with a black and chrome Herman Miller chair pushed under it, the exact same design and colour as the one in his old study at home. A pad of paper and a couple of pencils lie on the table in front of it and a whiteboard hangs on the wall opposite, the kind they have in incident rooms, with different-coloured magnetic fixings to pin documents and photographs to it, and dry marker pens to add notes. It all seems very ordered, the methodical neatness emblematic of the man who created it. Laughton almost feels like the ghost of her father is still here and she shivers despite the stuffy warmth of the place.

She steps into the room and pulls the door closed behind her, instinctively wanting to lock it but discovering that she can't. She unhooks the padlock from the hasps outside and

carries it in with her, having a sudden fearful notion that someone will creep up the corridor and lock her inside. She places the padlock on the nearest shelf, which has a label on the front with an 'A' written on it. The next shelf also has an 'A' and the one after is labelled 'B'.

She lifts the lid on the first box and peers inside. A single sheet of paper sits on top of a deep stack of documents with her father's neat, precise handwriting listing what must be the case contents of the box:

ALISON MAINWARING
ANNIE SEWARD
AYLESBURY ABBATOIR – THREE BODIES

She takes out the list to reveal a photocopied sheet of paper with a picture of a young woman, a brief description, and a single word: MISSING. In the photo she is smiling, as if she's delighted to have been discovered after lying so long alone in the dark.

Only she isn't alone.

Laughton looks around the room, estimating how many boxes are stored here, each containing cold cases exactly like this one, unsolved mysteries with victims like Alison Mainwaring, forgotten by almost everyone, but apparently not by her father.

It was a tradition in every police force that whenever a new chief inspector took office they were given all the cold cases to review. The idea was that fresh eyes, coupled with advances in investigation techniques, might crack open cases that had previously remained a mystery. In reality, the old cases quickly got pushed further and further down the priority list as new cases popped up, and so there was rarely time for any new chief inspector, no matter how keen and well intentioned, to properly reinvestigate them. Some cold cases did get solved from time to time, but mostly this was through deathbed confessions, or because the perpetrators, imprisoned for something else, would

offer new information on an old case, figuring they would garner a few new headlines to further burnish their notoriety and maybe earn them a trip or two out of the prison they were going to die in anyway, in order to point out the burial grounds of their missing victims.

Laughton puts the handwritten list back in the box and replaces the lid, feeling a slight pang of guilt as she covers up Alison Mainwaring's hopeful smile. She moves further into the room, passing the first line of shelves that jut out, following the alphabetized labels until she finds the shelf labelled 'H'. There is only one box and she pulls it out slightly and removes the lid. Inside is another neat stack of documents with another of her dad's handwritten notes on top listing the box's contents:

OPERATION HENRY 8

Beneath the title are the names of Henry's wives with six other names written beside them.

Catherine A	Billy Carver
Anne B	Malcolm 'Minty' Fowler
Jane	Shelby Facer
Anne C	Jimmy 'Mia' Farrow
Catherine H	Adrian Shanklin
Catherine P	Brendan Webber

Laughton moves to lift the box off the shelf then stops as she notices something else in the furthest corner of the room. A stack of plastic crates has been pushed against the far wall next to a large object with a dust sheet draped over it. She stares at the shrouded object for a moment, wondering what lies beneath the sheet, then looks away, forcing herself to focus on the task in hand.

She picks up the box, carries it to the table, then removes the lid and takes out two large bundles of documents, laying them on the table in neat piles next to the note pad. Both bundles have OPERATION HENRY 8 written on them in large letters.

She sits down and looks at the whiteboard opposite, blank now but still carrying faint marks where her father had written things on it. During his time in office as commissioner, the Met had recorded a significant increase in the number of cold cases being solved, something that had largely been attributed to advances in forensic science and a more efficient review system. Laughton wonders now if it had been more down to her father's solitary work in this quiet room, working through these boxes and the files they contained. She pictures him sitting at this desk, documents spread out in front of him and pinned to the board opposite, thinking his way through old cases, surrounded by the ghosts of all these restless, forgotten victims.

The thought of ghosts prompts Laughton to look back at the far wall of the room where the large, shrouded object is still visible through a gap in the shelves, looking like a huge cartoon spook. Her curiosity has always been one of her greatest assets and, sometimes, also something of a liability. Right now she knows the files should be occupying her full attention, but the mystery object at the back of the room is tugging at her focus and she knows herself well enough to realize that it's better to give in to her curiosity than waste time and energy fighting it.

She rises from the chair, the wheels rolling smoothly across the concrete floor, and heads back towards the back of the unit, peering at the semi-transparent plastic boxes stacked next to the shrouded object and trying to see what they contain. Whatever it is, they don't look like files.

She stops in front of them, pulls the lid off the first box and catches her breath when she sees her mother's face smiling back at her. She reaches out to steady herself, her hand finding the solid object hidden beneath the dust sheet shroud. The box is filled with framed photographs. She picks up the top one and

finds another photo of her mother beneath. She remembers it hanging in the hallway of her childhood home. Her mother had filled the entire hallway with photographs. They had mostly been of Laughton throughout various stages of her childhood, which embarrassed her whenever her friends came round on playdates. She had forgotten all about them but here they were in this box full of memories.

She rummages through the plastic crate, her eyes misting slightly at the sight of her mother and her girlish self, innocently smiling in that time before the tragedy. She thinks of her father, all alone after her mother died and after she ran away, taking these photos down from the wall, stacking them carefully in this box, then bringing them here so he didn't have to look at them any more.

She spots a larger frame tucked behind the stack of crates and another forgotten memory comes flooding back. Inside the frame is an old movie poster showing a hard-faced, handsome man holding a blonde woman in his arms, the words 'Love' and Hate' tattooed across his knuckles. The hand labelled 'Hate' is also holding a knife. It's an original poster for *The Night of the Hunter*, her father's favourite film and also the origin of Laughton's name. She traces her fingers over the printed name of the director – Charles Laughton – wondering if seeing her name every day on this poster had been as painful as seeing his dead wife's face smiling out from all these photographs. Now she understood why her father had rented this place the year her mother died. He had needed somewhere to keep the things he couldn't bear to look at any more, but could never throw away either.

She puts the film poster to one side so she can take it back to the flat later, along with the crate of photographs, then looks back up at the large, shrouded object. She grabs the edge of the dust sheet and pulls it away in one, quick motion, to reveal the object beneath.

A cascade of memories rushes through her mind the moment she sees her mother's wardrobe. It had stood in the corner of her parents' bedroom in their home in Acton, the doors always

196

open as if it could not contain the riot of colour inside – dresses hooked over the doors, shoes scattered in front like offerings at a messy shrine. She remembers playing hide-and-seek, and climbing inside it, and the comforting smell of her mother enveloping her as she hid in the dark, staying very still, listening out for the countdown, and the 'here I come', and the exhilarating terror of the thump of footsteps getting louder as they mounted the stairs. Then the memory shifts, and she's hiding in a different cupboard, her mother next to her this time because someone else was coming, a real-life monster, and there was no exhilaration this time, only terror.

Count to three – her mother had whispered.

On three we run. We run and we keep on running. OK?

But Laughton had run on two and her mother had died because of it.

Again, she imagines her father, standing in the bedroom alone, staring into this wardrobe, his wife's blood still staining the hallway carpet outside as he stared at the dresses she would never wear again. Laughton imagines these must have been the very first things he had stored here, which was why they were at the back of the unit.

Laughton grips the handle of the wardrobe door and twists it open, releasing a breath of perfume so faint it could almost be a memory. The wardrobe is still crammed with colour, a rainbow of half-remembered dresses, her mother's shoes now stacked neatly beneath them.

Laughton closes her eyes and leans forward, pushing her face into the soft material, breathing in what she can of her mother's scent beneath the fragrance of old clothes and moth repellent. She's still there, just about, and Laughton reaches in, her hands pushing through the soft material until they touch the back of the wardrobe, then she gathers the dresses in her arms, holding them tight as tears sting her eyes, breathing her in, remembering and mourning as she gets lost in the soft memory of her mother.

37

Calais opens the door to the third floor and listens for a moment, looking both ways for any sign of activity. He sees nothing, hears only silence. He steps out of the stairwell and starts heading down the long corridor.

It is hot inside the bike helmet, but he keeps it on, mindful of the security cameras fixed above the doors and high in the corners of the corridor. If he has to do something here and the place becomes a crime scene he does not want his face recorded on CCTV.

The warehouse is quiet, lunchtime on a weekday clearly not prime time for hoarders and whoever else uses places like these, so he has been able to work quickly through the lower floors, checking only the open units, of which there have not been many. Fewer witnesses, less risk – perfect for him. All he needs to do now is find her.

He works his way down the corridor, scanning the doors ahead, looking for the ones without locks that suggest someone might be inside. He spots one ahead and slows his place as he draws nearer, carefully placing his footfalls on the painted concrete to silence the squeak of his shoes.

He stops by the door, listens for sounds of movement, then pulls it open slightly. Lights flicker on showing the room is

empty. He closes the door quietly and continues on his way, keeping his footfalls light, slowing again as he draws closer to the corner, stopping just before it.

He peers around the edge.

There is a short corridor with a door at the end, no lock on it and light spilling out from the narrow gap where the door doesn't quite meet the frame. He listens for movement beyond but hears nothing. This is the last room on the last floor so, unless she has somehow managed to sneak her way past him, she *has* to be in here.

Calais moves around the corner and walks carefully towards the door, his footfalls totally silent now and the lyrics from an old Motown song playing in his head about having no place left to run. He reaches the door. Listens again.

Still nothing but he can *feel* her in there.

He reaches out, hooks his fingers round the edge of the door then slowly, very slowly, pulls it open.

The room beyond is bigger than he had expected and filled with shelves and file boxes, but there is no sign of her. He takes a single step into the room and spots a heavy-looking padlock on the shelf by the door. He picks it up, feeling the solid weight of it, then spots something else, two files on a green baize table with OPERATION HENRY 8 written on them.

Calais moves over to the table, eyes scanning the room, watching and listening for any sound. And there she is.

He spots her through a gap in the shelves, standing at the back of the room, facing an open wardrobe, rocking from side to side slightly with her face buried in an armful of old dresses.

He glances down at the table, places one of the files on top of the other then looks back up at her, checking she doesn't turn around as he slides the files across the table towards him.

He doesn't see the pencil, rolling across the baize, pushed by the files. Doesn't see it fall off the edge of the table and tumble down to the painted concrete floor. He doesn't see it, but he hears it.

And so does she.

38

The noise is sudden and sharp and snaps Laughton out of her reverie. Her head whips around, looking for the source, and a silent scream sounds in her head when she sees the dark figure standing by the table, his black, featureless face looking straight at her. For a second she imagines he is the monster from her past, her mother's killer summoned by the spell of her memories. But then she sees what the figure has in his hands and is moving before she's even aware of it, her fear transformed instantly to anger and righteous rage.

Those files belonged to her father. And this thief is not going to have them.

She is round the edge of the shelves before the figure reacts, stepping back in surprise at her aggression and lack of fear. He reaches out with his free hand, grabs the back of the chair and launches it at her, wheels rattling as it spins across the concrete floor. Laughton jumps to the side but a wheel catches her on the ankle, sending pain shooting up her leg and knocking her off balance. The chair smashes into something behind her and she stumbles for a second then scrambles forward. But he is already moving, seizing the opportunity her stumble gave him, and is through the door and slamming it shut behind him before she even reaches the table.

Laughton snatches up the other pencil from the baize, figuring the point will do for a weapon, then slams into the door, expecting it to fly open, but instead she bounces off it and more pain blooms in her shoulder.

She staggers backwards, grabbing at the shelf nearest the door to stop herself from falling, regains her balance and tries the door again, kicking it this time with the flat sole of her shoe. A deep boom echoes in the room and away down the corridor beyond, but the door stays shut. She glances over at the shelf where she'd left the padlock.

It's not there.

He must have grabbed it on his way out and locked her in.

Laughton listens helplessly to the rapid squeak of shoes on the painted concrete getting fainter outside and feels frustration expand inside her. He's getting away, and there's nothing she can do about it. She turns and lets out a primal roar of rage when she sees what the chair had smashed into. The film poster lies on its side, the frame crooked and bent, tiny pebbles of broken glass littering the concrete floor in front of it. One of the chair wheels has gone straight through the poster leaving a large rip.

'FUUUCK!!' Laughton howls.

She yanks her phone from her pocket, stabs the screen, her adrenaline-fried fingers trembling as they navigate to her *Recents*.

She finds a number and calls it.

39

Tannahill feels the phone buzz in his pocket at the same time as the rider emerges from the building and starts heading directly towards the parked bike. He has his helmet on so his face is hidden but he looks right – big and wide in the shoulders. He is holding something in his hand, packages of some sort, thick envelopes or folders. He also looks like he's in a hurry.

Tannahill pulls the phone from his pocket and checks the caller ID. Laughton. He's been wanting to talk to her all morning but now is absolutely the worst time, so he rejects the call and looks back at the man.

He is almost at the bike now, nowhere else he could possibly be going. Tannahill looks over his shoulder to where Chamberlain is parked and raises his hand. Baker in the passenger seat acknowledges with a wave.

Tannahill turns back to the rider, standing by the bike now and lifting the lid of the box strapped to the back. Has to be him. He drops the packages inside then closes it. The visor on his helmet is open slightly and Tannahill tries to catch a glimpse of his face but he's too far away and the gap too narrow.

His phone buzzes.

Laughton again.

He answers it to tell her he can't talk but doesn't get the chance.

'CARVER!!' Laughton shouts before he can say anything. 'I've just seen Carver. I'm in my dad's old storage unit, he kept copies of everything. I found the old Operation Henry 8 case files but Carver showed up out of nowhere and took them. I'm locked inside but if you've got any units in the area you could still catch him, I'll give you the address.'

'No need,' Tannahill replies, breaking cover and heading quickly towards the rider. 'I'm looking at Carver right now.'

He lowers the phone but doesn't disconnect. Keeps moving, eyes on the rider's back as he closes the distance. Behind him he can hear Chamberlain's car racing towards him.

He reaches the barrier and calls out. 'Hey!'

The rider looks up, struggling at first to locate the source of the voice, his head turning left and right until he finally locks eyes with Tannahill.

Tannahill tenses, fully prepared to leap forward and knock him off his bike if he attempts to run. But he doesn't, he just stares.

Chamberlain's car peels around the corner and screeches to a halt in front of the barrier, blocking the gap and making sure the rider has nowhere to go.

Baker leaps out of the car and the rider automatically raises his hands, his head swivelling between Baker and Tannahill.

'Step away from the bike and remove your helmet, please,' Tannahill instructs.

He obeys, tilting his head back so he can unsnap the chin fastening. He pulls the helmet off, giving Tannahill his first proper look at the rider's face.

It's not Carver.

Not even close. The man is at least twenty years too young and his hair is dirty blond, not thinning and black like in the most recent pictures of Billy Carver.

'What's your name, sir?'

The rider frowns. 'Raul,' he says in a heavily accented voice. 'Raul Braga. Is problem?'

'What's in the box?' Tannahill points at the back of the bike.

Raul looks confused. 'Is package.'

'Can I see?'

Raul nods and flips the lid open.

Inside is a large envelope with a DHL label on it with a name Tannahill does not recognize and an address in the city. He raises his phone to his ear, remembering that Laughton is still there.

'The case files,' he says to her, 'what did they look like?'

'They're in pale blue folders and have Operation Henry 8 written on them in big letters.'

Tannahill's jaw clenches. Wrong man. Wrong package. But it's the right bike.

Tannahill crouches down and studies the screws holding the plate to the back of the bike, sees faint scratch marks on them.

'That not mine,' Raul says, pointing at the number plate. 'That not my number.'

Tannahill nods, realizing now what happened. 'They've been switched.' He looks up at Raul. 'Do you know your registration?' Raul nods. 'Give it to him.' Tannahill turns to Baker. 'Run it through ANPR, see if you can find out where that plate is now. Hopefully Carver hasn't swapped it again and we can track his new number.'

He stands and moves away, raising the phone to his ear to talk to Laughton again.

'It wasn't Carver. He must have swapped plates earlier today or sometime last night, so we've been chasing the wrong bike. Let me know where you are and I'll see if we have anyone in your area, hopefully we can intercept him.'

'I'm in the Big Yellow storage facility on Wick Lane in Bow.'

'Bow? That's pretty close to where I am now.' He covers the phone with his hand and turns to Chamberlain leaning out of the driver's window. 'How far are we from Wick Lane?'

'Couple of minutes.'

'I'm coming,' Tannahill tells Laughton. 'Hold tight and I'll come and get you.'

'Don't worry about me,' Laughton says. 'Just get Carver.'

40

Laughton paces the concrete floor of the storage unit. This room had seemed large when she'd first opened the door; now it feels like the walls are closing in around her. She doesn't like being locked up. Doesn't like feeling helpless either. She tries to focus but keeps running through what had happened. She shouldn't have left the padlock by the door, shouldn't have left the files on the table, should have reacted faster, moved quicker, jumped out of the way of that damn chair. Her ankle still hurt where it struck her, but her pride hurt more.

She hears the squeak of approaching footsteps.

And now she was having to be rescued and she hated that even more.

There is a loud clatter of metal as the padlock is removed, then the door swings open and a wave of relief floods through her when she sees Tannahill standing there.

Laughton practically falls into him, wrapping her arms around his back and holding him as tightly as she had hugged her mother's dresses. 'How did you unlock the padlock?'

'It wasn't locked, it was just threaded through the door.' Tannahill looks around. 'Wow, look at this place, it's like a serial killer's lair.'

'This was my dad's, so be careful what you say. It's also the

reason your case isn't dead in the water.'

'Poor choice of words, given the reason we're here.'

'What? Oh, shit, yes, sorry. Didn't literally mean dead in the water. How about, this place is the reason your case isn't . . . I was going to say "belly up", but that's almost as bad.'

'"Up shit creek without a paddle"?' Tannahill suggests. 'This is actually quite hard, isn't it?'

'That'll do. Anyway, the point is you shouldn't diss this place, you should be thankful for it.' She nods over at the whiteboard. 'Look at this.'

Tannahill reads the names Laughton has written there:

OPERATION HENRY 8

Catherine A	Billy Carver
Anne B	Malcolm 'Minty' Fowler
Jane	Shelby Facer
Anne C	Jimmy 'Mia' Farrow
Catherine H	Adrian Shanklin
Catherine P	Brendan Webber

'These were the names on the index sheet for the files Carver took. It was the only thing I managed to read before he took everything. Any of them ring any bells?'

Tannahill shakes his head, pulls out his phone and snaps a picture. 'I'll run the names, see if I can track any of them down, not least to warn them that a vengeful psycho from their past is now on the large and looking for them.'

'You didn't catch him?'

Tannahill shakes his head. 'He was gone by the time we got here and he's switched plates again. The original ones from the bike we'd been following showed up on a different bike at Heathrow, Terminal 5. Carver must have swapped a whole bunch of number plates to throw us off the trail, and it worked, we've lost him.'

Laughton nods. 'You should contact Shelby. Tell him what happened here, tell him to be careful and maybe give him these names. Maybe he'll know who they are and can help us find them.'

'Or . . . you could tell him?' Tannahill suggests.

Laughton thinks about this for a second then shakes her head and stares back at the name. 'No, you tell him.'

Unseen by Laughton, Tannahill smiles. 'OK.'

His phone buzzes, sounding like a trapped insect. Tannahill checks who's calling then puts it on speaker and answers.

'We've got another body,' Baker says the moment the call connects.

Tannahill looks across at Laughton. 'Where?'

'Kew Gardens,' Baker replies. 'Same deal as before: middle-aged male found washed up on the banks of the Thames with no head, and no hands.'

41

Calais parks the moped in a line with several others outside a Domino's Pizza and checks the streets for cameras from behind the safety of his dark visor. He spots one above a bank and another by a set of traffic lights. He also sees a café opposite with photos of burgers and English breakfasts in the window instead of a menu. He leans the bike against its kickstand, lifts the files out of the delivery box and heads across the road to the café, figuring they're unlikely to have cameras in there.

The café smells of oil and burnt toast and feels as if a fine layer of grease has been sprayed over everything. It's also not busy, despite it being lunchtime, with several tables standing empty. He checks the room for cameras and only takes off his helmet when he's satisfied there are none.

He orders a mug of tea, pays in cash, and carries it over to an empty table in the furthest corner of the room. He places the files and his helmet on the table, then sits facing the door with his back to the wall, something he learned in prison. You never want your back to the room, not when you're the only English guy in a warehouse full of bored American psychos with time to kill and nothing to lose.

He takes a sip of tea. It tastes of tannin and the stainless steel of the tea urn it had been poured out of. He stares out

209

through the grimy window and the passing traffic to his moped across the road, blending in with the other delivery bikes. He feels safe here. Anonymous.

He opens the first file and starts reading: OPERATION HENRY 8 – Co-agency, covert operation between The London Metropolitan Police Force and the US Drug Enforcement Agency, operating out of MIAMI, FL, USA.

SIXTEEN YEARS
EARLIER

SHELBY FACER – MIAMI

Miami was too bright and way too hot for Shelby.

He felt fuzzy from the jet lag and the after-effects of all the free booze on the business class flights. He had never flown business before and could see no way back to coach now – more leg room, unlimited free drinks, nicer seats that went almost horizontal. The only thing that had spoiled it had been his travelling companion.

The unsettling guy from the sofa had seemed to hate all of it. His name was Carver. Shelby had spotted it on his boarding pass and tried his best to loosen him up in the business lounge at Heathrow by engaging him in conversation, but the guy clearly wasn't the chatty type so he'd given up and done his best to ignore him for the rest of the trip. Carver was sitting silently next to him now in the passenger seat of their hired car, giving off his usual air of menace.

'There it is,' Shelby said, nodding ahead at a big square building on the side of the road with STORAGE written on the front in faded letters, part of a row of warehouses close to the harbour. They had come here straight from the flight, which suited Shelby just fine. He wanted to get rid of the diamonds and away from Carver as fast as possible, so he could check out the beach and the nightlife for a few hours before flying back.

Getting the diamonds through customs had been easier than he thought. He had bought a fancy, overpriced jar of Dead Sea bath salts, emptied most of them into the toilet and replaced them with the rocks. Mixed in with what was left of the salt they had become practically invisible. Customs had waved him through anyway, easy peasy. Now all he needed to do was secure the deal and get the fuck away from the human storm cloud next to him.

He pulled off the road and brought the car to a standstill in front of the warehouse. Several other cars and vans were parked nearby but there was no sign of any people. He turned to Carver. 'You ready?'

Instead of answering, Carver got out of the car and slammed the door behind him. Shelby shook his head. 'What an arse,' he murmured, then reached into the back for the jar of bath salts and stepped out into the full blast of the Florida sun.

The heat felt like someone had wrapped a hot, wet blanket round him. He was dressed for London weather and could feel his shirt already starting to stick to his skin beneath his jacket. The only silver lining was that Carver was similarly dressed, and all in black so undoubtedly felt even hotter.

The message had popped up the moment he'd turned the phone on in the terminal building of Miami International. It gave him an address and instructions to hire a car and head straight here. Someone would meet them at the side door. Shelby spotted a door at the side of the building and headed towards it. Carver walked beside him, turning his head slowly, checking

212

the parked cars and surrounding buildings like he was in the secret service or something. For all his attitude and air of menace, Shelby wondered how much use he would be if things went south. Carver didn't have a gun or any weapon at all so far as he knew. All he had was his threatening demeanour, which was not going to be much use if the other side had Uzis and superior numbers, which they probably would. This was America after all, home of the free and the concealed carry. He reached the door then paused as a sudden, unhelpful flash memory of a scene from *Scarface* popped into his head, the one where Tony Montana is chained to a bathtub while his friend gets chainsawed to death next to him. That had been in Miami too, hadn't it?

He took a deep breath and waited for Carver to finish his bullshit secret service routine then knocked on the door. He stood back, trying his best to look cool and calm, despite the heat and unhelpful memories of Al Pacino.

He heard footsteps inside the building and turned to Carver as something new occurred to him. 'Are you here to protect me or the diamonds?'

Carver looked at him like he was something he'd stepped in but said nothing.

Shelby nodded and turned back to the door. 'That's what I figured.' He forced a smile as the noise of a deadbolt banged inside the door, sounding like a gunshot, then the door opened a crack. The sun was so bright that Shelby couldn't make anything out in the dark interior. He squinted at the column of black, smiling at the spot where he imagined someone's face might be.

'Greetings from England,' he said. 'I believe you're expecting us?'

There was a pause then the door opened wider, letting enough light in to reveal a short, stocky man whose head was at least a foot lower than Shelby had guessed. He was Latino and dressed in loose-fitting clothes that had a shabby, military air

about them. He also gave off the same menacing vibe as Carver and seemed to recognize a kindred spirit when they locked eyes.

'Can we come in?' Shelby said. 'We're British, so we start shrivelling up if we stand in the sun for more than two minutes.'

The man looked back at him for a beat then stepped aside and let them in, checking the street behind them before closing the door.

'Through there,' he said, pointing down the hallway to a partially open door.

Shelby strode towards it, trying to project calm confidence. In truth he felt like a dead man walking but couldn't let anyone see that. One thing he had learned since leaving home and striking out on his own was that it was all about confidence. If you had confidence in yourself then other people would have confidence in you too. Fortune favours the brave, wasn't that what they said? And a fortune was exactly what was at stake here.

He stepped into the room and looked around as if he was planning to buy it. It was lined with shelving units crammed with luggage of all shapes and sizes, suitcases mostly, but some backpacks and smaller bags. Airport lost-luggage storage, most likely, a smart place for a meeting like this. People must come and go from here all the time, arriving with nothing but leaving carrying suitcases containing who knew what?

In the middle of the room, lit from above by a skylight, was a high table with three men standing around it. The man in the expensive suit from London was in the centre of the group. The other two were wearing the same vaguely military clothing as the guy who had answered the door.

'Hello again,' Shelby said, smiling at the man like he was an old friend.

The man regarded him for a second. 'You have the stones?'

Shelby held up the jar and shook it, making the contents rattle softly. 'Do you have something for me?'

214

The man's eyes shifted briefly over to Carver, then he nodded and the guy on his left peeled away and walked over to the wall of suitcases. He pulled one out of the stack and returned to the table, placed it in front of Shelby, flipped the catches and opened the case. Inside was a neat assortment of holiday clothes – T-shirts, shorts, sandals – surrounding a large white object wrapped in plastic. It was about the same size and shape as a house brick. Shelby looked at it, forcing himself to have no reaction.

He had made buys before, but never anything remotely on this scale. The brick of cocaine had to weigh at least a kilo, maybe a kilo and a half, and would be worth around fifty or sixty grand in London, probably double or treble that once it had been stepped on a few times. And this was only the sample.

He took the brick out of the suitcase and felt the weight of it in his hand, maybe even two kilos. He placed it on the table, took a key from his pocket and a small bottle of clear liquid. He unscrewed the cap, dug the key into the plastic and pulled out a small sample of the white powder which he tipped into the bottle. He put his finger over the neck of the bottle and shook it to mix the drug into the liquid, then held it up to the light. The liquid was a reagent that reacted to cocaine to tell you how pure it was. Clear meant there was no cocaine present at all, yellow showed low content, orange slightly more, all the way through to red for very high content. The liquid in the bottle was almost purple. Shelby had never seen a reaction like this before. The cocaine was close to 100 per cent pure. You could cut this four or five times and it would still be better than most of the street drugs currently in London. That meant this one brick in front of him was worth about a quarter of a million quid.

The words of Minty's original message resurfaced in his mind:

Chance to get in on a major deal . . .

No shit! When he got back to London he needed to take

215

Minty out for one eye-wateringly expensive 'thank you' meal.

He looked across at the man in the nice suit and nodded, trying hard to act cool and not show how fast his heart was beating.

'Looks like we're in business.' He placed the bottle down on the table and pushed the jar of bath salts across the table towards him.

The man made no move to pick it up. He just stared at Shelby for a moment, his face unreadable, and again Shelby thought of *Scarface*. Then the man nodded and held out his hand for Shelby to shake. Shelby smiled. All he had to do now was kill time until the flight back home. He reached out to shake the man's hand and that's when it all turned to shit. Sunlight seemed to explode all around him, followed by a bang so loud he only heard the start of it before his ears stopped hearing much of anything at all.

The force of the explosion knocked him backwards, his hands covering his ears, eyes screwed tight against the blinding light. He rolled to his side and tucked himself into a tight ball as all around he heard muffled shouts, as if he had been plunged underwater. He tried opening his eyes but could see almost nothing beyond the residual flash damage burned into his retina. Someone grabbed him, spun him on to his front and knelt on the small of his back as they cuffed his hands behind him.

It had all happened so fast.

One moment he was about to step through a door into the life he'd always wanted for himself, the one he felt he deserved. The next he was deaf, blind, and face down on a dusty warehouse floor.

Rough hands grabbed him from behind and dragged him to his feet. He could still hardly hear anything through the high-pitched whine of noise damage and tried to blink away the bright patches burned into the centre of his vision. Three men dressed like soldiers were standing in front of him. The middle one was talking to him but he couldn't make out the words.

They each had DEA stencilled on their bulletproof vests and were pointing machine guns at him. Shelby instinctively tried to raise his hands, forgetting they were already cuffed, and stumbled forward. One of the men jabbed him backwards with the barrel of his gun. To his right the man in the nice suit had also been cuffed and had blood running down the side of his face from one ear. He was staring in front of him, his expression impassive, saying nothing.

A shout pierced the muffled rumble of Shelby's hearing and he turned to see Carver thrashing around on the ground with five men on top of him, struggling to hold him down. Carver was screaming and fighting. He looked over at Shelby and they locked eyes for a moment. Then Carver spat at him and surged forward, dragging three of the men along and gaining some ground before they managed to pin him down again.

Shelby turned away and thought about the vans parked outside. They must have been filled with men, waiting for the deal to go down before they moved. They'd been tipped off and Carver clearly thought he had done it. Shelby looked back at the table with the open suitcase, the brick of cocaine, and the small bottle of purple liquid.

100 per cent pure.

A quarter of a million per brick.

All gone now.

Someone grabbed him by the shoulder, spun him round toward the door, but then he realized something and craned his neck back round to check. A blow to the side of the head forced him to face forward again.

'Move!' a voice shouted at him, and he began to walk towards the door, thinking about the table behind him and what was no longer on it.

The diamonds had gone.

Someone had taken them.

42

Tom Kenwright raps once on the door of the Home Secretary's office while clutching a thick bundle of the day's business and a selection of the morning papers under one arm.

'Yes,' Charles Nixon calls from inside, sounding tetchy.

Kenwright pushes into the office and sees his boss standing fists on hips by the window, silhouetted against the Lambeth skyline beyond.

'Don't do it,' Kenwright jokes in an attempt to lighten the mood.

Nixon grunts. 'I wouldn't give them the satisfaction.' He turns and heads over to his desk where a red ministerial box is serving as a stand for his laptop, suggesting he has been on Zoom calls most of the morning. He slumps in his chair and leans forward, shirtsleeves rolled up and tie worked loose in his trademark 'Ready for Business' pose. 'What you got for me?'

Kenwright places the stack of documents down on the desk and starts sorting through them. 'Policy review mainly.'

'Great. If ever there was a day I could have done without the mind turd that is policy review, it's today.'

'There's the immigration white paper, which I've proof-read and marked with some concerns for your attention. There's

also a long list of media requests for comments about today's headlines. I've said you're unavailable but there's the list anyway in case you do want to go on the record with a friendly.'

'Fuck that,' Nixon, grabs the list of requests, screws it up into a tight ball and flings it at a wastebasket he deliberately keeps on the far side of the room so he can launch things at it. 'You would have thought I'd passed a law to make the police wear Nazi uniforms or something the way everyone's jumping on this fucking non-story. Everyone does business with people they know, that's all this is.'

Kenwright smiles indulgently. Effectively handing an old friend tens of millions of pounds of taxpayers' money by giving them a plum government contract without proper tender isn't exactly the same as just doing business with friends, but he's not going to say that. 'Yes, sir,' he says instead. 'I'm sure it will all blow over.'

'Yes, but when, Tom? This bloody thing has been rumbling on for days and it's now on every sodding front page. I've had Nigel on the phone this morning for an hour with his knickers in a twist.'

Nigel was Nigel Clarke, the prime minister, a friend of Charlie's from way back, something he reminded everyone about whenever possible by namedropping him and eschewing his official title.

'Apropos of this,' Kenwright takes one of the tabloids, turns to page five and slides it across the desk. 'There is something else you should probably be aware of.'

Nixon leans back and scowls at the article, his vanity leading him to generally try and read things at arm's length rather than reach for his glasses. He squints at the headline, HEADLESS BODY WASHES UP BY TOWER BRIDGE, above the grainy photo of the body. 'What's this?'

'Hopefully nothing, but I intercepted a request from the Met this morning to open up a redacted file in relation to their investigation into this murder. The file in itself was nothing to

worry about, an old drug bust involving the Met and the DEA, but one of the people involved was someone connected to you.'

'Who?'

'Brendan Webber.'

'Brendan?' Nixon stares down at the newspaper. Brendan had been one of the biggest donors to his re-election campaign. 'What's Brendan got to do with this?'

'Before he went into property, Brendan had an import/export business that got into difficulties. In order to try and dig himself out he made some unwise choices. "Desperate times" and all that. Anyway, according to the file, the police were watching him, made an approach and he became instrumental in helping them set up the sting that resulted in two arrests.'

Nixon opens his arms and smiles. 'Well, where's the problem then? Brendan was helping the police, not breaking the law.'

Kenwright's thin lips disappear as he presses them together and Nixon's smile fades as he recognizes what this means. 'Technically, yes,' Kenwright admits, 'but the only reason he was helping the police was because, if he hadn't, he would have gone to jail for a long time. He may not have been charged with anything, but that's only because he cooperated. This is all sealed in the file, of course, and I denied the request to declassify it, hoping that might shut down this line of enquiry and keep Brendan's name out of the investigation.'

Nixon looks at him, his eyebrows shooting up in a question. 'But? I'm sensing a "but".'

Kenwright nods. 'But, I just heard from one of my newspaper sources, who heard it from their source inside the Met, that another body has been found. As a result this story is going to be promoted to page two in the evening editions.'

'Shame it won't be promoted to page one,' Nixon mutters.

'Page one would actually be worse, sir.'

'How so? Anything that knocks me off the front page has got to be a good thing, no?'

'Not necessarily. The problem is, the higher profile this story

gets, the more reporters will be looking into it, and the greater the chance they'll discover that Brendan Webber was involved in the case at the heart of it, and, obviously, your friendship with him is public record. In normal circumstances that wouldn't be a problem. It's an old case, water under the bridge and all that, but given where we currently are in terms of news coverage, any associate of yours involved in anything criminal, no matter how ancient or tangential, will be a big story and you could end up fighting a reputational war on two fronts instead of one. I'm sure the very last thing you want is to have to have another long conversation with the PM explaining all this.'

Nixon nods gravely and stares back down at the newspaper, his finely honed, politician's survival instinct kicking into gear as he processes everything Kenwright has told him. Brendan Webber had donated significant sums to the Tory party as well as campaign funds to him specifically. He was a friend and a colleague, but none of that counted for anything if he became a political liability.

'So how do we distance ourselves from all this?'

'Well,' Kenwright says, trying to inject some cheerfulness into his voice, 'I'm hoping we won't need to. I've denied access to the declassified file so Brendan's name will not come out that way. Hopefully the police will simply do their job and catch whoever's running around killing everyone, case closed.'

'And no one needs to know.'

'No one needs to know.'

Nixon nods. 'We should probably tell Brendan though.'

Kenwright raises an eyebrow. 'Should we?'

'Of course we should. If there's a nutter on the loose from his past and he's in potential danger, we should at least give him the heads-up. He's been a good friend to us. He's got a wife and two kids. I'll call him.'

'No,' Kenwright says, 'I'll do it. If this thing blows up I don't want any recent communications between the two of you.

Imagine if the press caught wind of that. Leave it to me. You don't know any of this.'

Nixon nods. 'Understood. Thanks, Tom.'

Kenwright smiles and turns to leave.

'And Tom,' Nixon calls after him.

Kenwright turns back and sees his normally iron-faced, unflappable boss looking uncharacteristically worried as he stares down at the article and the photo of the headless body. 'Make sure you call him soon, eh?'

43

Kew Gardens in south-west London occupies three hundred acres of lush, green land that stretches along a bend on the south bank of the River Thames. Founded in 1840 it contains, according to the leaflets at least, 'the largest and most diverse botanical and mycological collections in the world'. Laughton had looked up 'mycological' the first time she had come here and found out it was just a fancy word for 'fungus'. She had been here several times before doing background research on cases involving bodies that had been found in forests, but she's never been in this part of the gardens before.

They crunch their way down a narrow gravel path through thick trees, she and Tannahill following a brisk, military-type who had crushed her hand in greeting and introduced himself as Tim. Tim is wearing the dark blue jumper of the Kew Constabulary and what looks like a cowboy hat. Laughton knew the botanical gardens had their own police force but has never met one before, her work here usually requiring the skills of the scientists and seed experts.

Tim met them at the gate to lead them through this shadowy, wooded part of the gardens no tourists ever see. It reminds Laughton of the ancient Forest of Dean and she shudders at the still-fresh memory of that place. She forces herself to focus

ahead where the trees part and the river is visible, reminding her that she is still in London.

They emerge into bright sunlight and a broad grassy beach with thick reeds lining the water's edge. It's so pretty that on any other day it would be the perfect spot for a picnic, but today a sombre air hangs over the place, radiating out from a group of serious-faced people clumped together at one edge of the embankment. Gardeners wearing green look on as crime scene investigators wearing paper suits unpack evidence boxes. Two more paper-suited figures are visible standing at the end of a thin, wooden jetty that juts out into the reeds. They squat on one side, peering down at what must be the body, though the vegetation is too thick to see properly. One of the figures stands and turns enough for Laughton to recognize Dr Evelyn Prior. Tannahill notices her too and clears his throat as if he's about to speak, but ends up saying nothing.

'That's Clive,' Tim, the Kew Gardens constable murmurs, pointing at a man in his fifties sitting alone on the grass. 'He's the gardener who found the body.'

Laughton studies him, his arms wrapped around his knees, his attention fixed on a spot on the ground a few feet in front of him, and imagines him out here alone, minding his own business and getting on with his normally peaceful job until he stumbled on to the horror-show of a body with no head.

'I'd better go and get suited up,' Tannahill says, heading off towards the crowd of people by the evidence boxes.

'So, what are you, a WPC or something?' Tim asks.

Laughton looks up at him, tall and content in his uniform. He seems like he's ex-military, ex-public school certainly, and has probably spent most of his life in male-dominated environments where women were largely subservient, junior and decorative. She could respond by listing all her academic qualifications and insist he refer to her as 'Dr Rees' but she's not sure he's worth the effort.

'Something like that,' she says, before walking away without

another word, dismissing him with her silence and imagining him thinking that she's rude without ever realizing that he started it.

The gardener looks up as she draws closer and she smiles reassuringly at him. 'Hi,' she says, 'I'm Dr Laughton Rees. I'm with the investigation.'

He nods. 'Clive Emerson,' he frowns. 'Laughton? That's an unusual name, what is it, Welsh?'

'It's . . . nothing,' Laughton replies. 'My dad chose it because of an old film.'

The gardener nods as if this makes sense. 'My dad picked Clive too, named me after his grandad. When I was younger I always wished his grandad had been called Jack or Clint or something a bit more exciting than "Clive" but you get used to anything in time.'

Laughton smiles. 'I don't know, there's some pretty groovy Clives in history. There's Clive of India, although he was a bit of a colonial bastard by all accounts. C. S. Lewis, he was a Clive, I think.'

The gardener shakes his head. 'Who's that?'

'He wrote the Narnia books, you know – *The Lion, the Witch and the Wardrobe*.'

The image of her mother's wardrobe flashes into her head and the sadness she felt earlier blooms inside her again.

'Oh, yeah.' Clive nods. 'I saw the film with my kids I think. Not as good as Harry Potter, but it was alright.'

Laughton takes deep breaths, pushing down on the emotions threatening to overwhelm her. She forces herself to focus on something else, something she has more control over.

'What time did you discover the body?' she asks.

''Bout an hour ago, maybe a bit less. I was cleaning out the reedbed, which I do every two or three weeks. The reeds act like a kind of filter, you see, pull all sorts of stuff out of the water, especially on the spring tides. Plastic mainly, stuff that doesn't break down, so if you let it build up it starts to choke

the plants. That's why you don't see many reedbeds along the river any more, too much crap in the water. These beds here are only healthy because I keep 'em that way. You got common reed here mostly, but there's some bur-reed in there too.'

He looks up at the two paper-suited figures at the end of the wooden jetty.

'Anyway, this morning I found a bit more than plastic bags and empty bottles. I used to work in a hospital, so I seen bodies before.' He shakes his head. 'Never seen anything like that though.' He looks up at Laughton, his eyes screwed up against the brightness of the sky. 'Do you ever get used to it, seeing stuff like that?'

Laughton nods. 'Kind of. You start to treat it as part of the job rather than dwelling on any of the more tragic or gruesome aspects of what you're dealing with. But every once in a while, something comes along that still gets you.'

Over on the jetty, Evelyn Prior rises up and starts making her way back to shore, where Tannahill is now shrugging his way into a paper suit.

'I'm sorry you've had such a crappy morning, Clive,' Laughton says.

Clive gives her a thin smile. 'Ah that's OK. My morning hasn't been nearly as crappy as whoever that is lying in the reeds.'

Evelyn Prior steps back on to the grassy shore and slips the hood off her paper suit, shaking her hair loose and somehow managing to look instantly perfect.

'Who's *that*?' Clive asks.

'That's the forensic pathologist,' Laughton replies. 'She's seen more dead bodies than anyone. You should ask her if she ever gets used to it.'

Clive nods. 'I'd rather ask her out on a date.'

Laughton smiles. 'Join the queue. I better go do some work. You OK?"

'Yeah, I'm fine.'

Laughton smiles then heads over to the jetty, where Tannahill is talking to Evelyn Prior. He sees Laughton approaching, nods at her, then heads over to the reeds, looking like he's in a hurry. Dr Prior regards Laughton from beneath a perfectly arched eyebrow.

'We must stop meeting like this,' she says, her low voice sounding amused. 'DCI Khan says I should give you a rundown of the results on last night's DB.'

'You've done the post-mortem already?'

'Well, my evening was ruined anyway so I thought I might as well do something useful with it. Good job I did.' She turns and looks back at the reedbed where Tannahill is now picking his way through the tall grasses, video camera in hand, recording his approach to the crime scene. 'I had planned to spend today catching up on paperwork.'

She unzips her paper suit. Laughton half expects her to be wearing another cocktail dress or evening gown, and is almost disappointed at the fairly regular, black office suit revealed beneath.

'Headlines about last night's floater are that the single stab wound to the chest was indeed the cause of death. The wound, to the left of the sternum between the fourth and fifth ribs, was a little under nine centimetres deep and had pierced the inferior tip of the heart causing fatal haemorrhage. There was still a large amount of blood inside the thoracic cavity, despite it being in the water.

'However, my other discovery, which needs to be confirmed through the tox report, is that the subject was almost certainly drugged prior to death. I collected stomach samples, which I've sent to the lab and will stick a red flag on now we have a second victim, but there were also physical signs of a possible overdose. The main one being evidence of urinary bladder distension.'

'Opioids,' Laughton murmurs.

Evelyn Prior regards her again from beneath the arch of her eyebrow. 'Yes. The opioids inhibit the parasympathetic nerves causing the subject to lose the urge to go to the toilet resulting in the bladder becoming unusually distended.'

Laughton frowns. 'So, the victim was unconscious when the fatal blow was delivered?'

'Most likely. That would also explain the absence of defence wounds. I should get the tox report back later today, but my money's on a synthetic opioid, one of the Nitazenes or fentanyl.'

Laughton nods. 'Easy to source. Can be crushed up and dissolved in a drink or mixed with food.'

Evelyn Prior looks back at Tannahill, his camera angled down at the body. 'I imagine we'll find the exact same with this new DB. All the other factors match: no head, no hands, single stab wound to the heart, no sign of defence wounds.' She turns to Laughton. 'One more body and a few more weeks and we'll have a serial killer on our hands.'

Laughton nods. 'Serial killer' was a term that was regularly thrown about and often mis-used on true-crime TV shows and podcasts, but the actual definition was very specific – someone who killed three or more people over a period of a month. Any shorter time and they were a spree-killer or mass-murderer. The thing that distinguished serial killers from the other classifications of murderer was that they killed again, at least twice, *after* they'd had time to reflect on their first murder. Their victims therefore did not fall into the usual categories of crimes of passion or moments of madness; they were deliberate acts, with each murder often displaying specific hallmarks of the killer as distinct as fingerprints. And there was nothing more deliberate than drugging someone in order to stab them through the heart then cutting off their head and hands.

'You're being summoned,' Evelyn Prior murmurs, her low voice making it sound vaguely ominous.

Laughton looks up and sees that Tannahill is looking at her, his hand raised and beckoning her over.

'I wonder . . . ?' Evelyn Prior says mysteriously, pulling a lipstick from her pocket and twisting it open. 'Is it just business with you two, or is there also pleasure?'

Laughton looks at her and catches a twinkle of mischief in her eyes.

'Please feel free to tell me to fuck off if it's none of my business,' Evelyn adds, shocking Laughton slightly with the unexpected F-bomb, 'only I invited him for cocktails earlier and he behaved like I'd dropped a spider down his shirt, which is not the response I'm used to. Then I remembered your little spat last night.' She carefully redoes lips that don't look like they need redoing. 'You got very cross with each other very quickly, and that doesn't generally happen unless there's something else going on. So . . .' She snaps the lid back on her lipstick and drops it back in her pocket. 'Is there?'

'Maybe . . .' Laughton has a weird out-of-body moment as she realizes she's discussing her love life with Dr Evelyn Prior. 'We're trying to figure it out.'

Evelyn nods knowingly, as if this was the answer she had expected. 'So, which one of you is holding back?'

'What makes you think—'

'*Trying to figure it out* generally means one person wants to commit and the other is hesitant, so – which one of you has the cold feet?'

Again, Laughton finds herself in the strange spotlight of Evelyn's attention. 'Well,' she says, *really* wanting to change the subject but unable to figure out how. 'I suppose I'm the one wanting to take things more slowly. I have a teenage daughter, which makes things . . . complicated.'

'Ahhh,' Evelyn says, as if this explains everything. 'A word of advice from someone whose instinct for all things vital has been sharpened by a life spent among the dead. Don't wait too

long.' She looks back over at Tannahill, still beckoning Laughton to join him. 'If you don't grab him, he *will* slip through your fingers. There aren't many men who manage to look that good in a paper suit.'

Laughton feels a weird protective rush and before she even knows she's doing it, she turns to Evelyn Prior and says, 'He looks even better out of it.'

She walks away quickly, breathing heavily and flushing slightly. She can't work out whether she's been given some friendly advice or a very unfriendly warning. Either way it's made her feel protective towards Tannahill and the strength of her feelings surprises her.

She steps on to the jetty, her footsteps sounding loud on the wooden boards as she heads towards Tannahill, who she has to admit, does look pretty fine in his shapeless CSI suit. She stops in front of him. 'I just had a really weird conversation with Evelyn Prior. Did she ask you out on a date?'

Tannahill blinks, his blue eyes looking almost the same colour as the sky. 'Er, sort of,' he says, seeming distracted. 'Listen, I need you to—'

'Do you *want* to go on a date with her?'

'What? No!'

'Why not? She's gorgeous.'

Tannahill shakes his head in exasperation. 'I don't want to go on a date with Evelyn Prior. Listen, can we talk about this some other time?'

'Yes, sorry. What is it?' She tries to look past him to where the body is lying in the reeds, but he steps in front of her and lays his hand on her shoulder in a way that is almost tender and also quite worrying.

'I want you to tell me exactly what your first impression is,' he says, the edge of seriousness in his voice making Laughton snap back into work mode. 'You ready?'

She nods. Tannahill steps aside.

Laughton looks down at the body in the reeds, ready to

engage her usual professional objectivity. But she can't. Not this time. The moment she sees the single puncture mark in the middle of the Miami Dolphins sweatshirt, all that goes flying out the window.

'Shelby,' she says, staring at the body lying on its back with no head and no hands. 'Oh my God, it's Shelby.'

44

By the time Calais has read through both files, his tea has gone cold but he drinks it anyway. Never waste food, something else he had learned in prison.

He slides the single page of handwritten paper in front of him and reads the names on it:

Catherine A	Billy Carver
Anne B	Malcolm 'Minty' Fowler
Jane	Shelby Facer
Anne C	Jimmy 'Mia' Farrow
Catherine H	Adrian Shanklin
Catherine P	Brendan Webber

Six wives. Two dead.

He takes a Sharpie from his pocket, the same one he had used to write on what was left of Minty Fowler's arm, and underlines the three that are left.

Anne C	<u>Jimmy 'Mia' Farrow</u>
Catherine H	<u>Adrian Shanklin</u>
Catherine P	<u>Brendan Webber</u>

There are photos in the file of all the 'wives' and he finds the ones for these three. He pulls out Minty Fowler's smartphone and googles 'Jimmy Farrow', then clicks on *Images* and scrolls through pages of idiots posing for Instagram or Twitter, teenagers and twenty-somethings who are all too young and look nothing like the mugshot in the file. He scrolls on, past the more sober photos of people on LinkedIn and a few photos of both Mia and Ronan Farrow, until he reaches the older people who seem to inhabit the lower levels of the page, like strange-shaped fish at the bottom of the ocean. And there he is, Jimmy Farrow, looking older than his mugshot, but most definitely him.

He clicks on the image and a website for a funeral home in East London opens, the photo of Jimmy part of an obituary that reads:

> *James Farrow, husband of Dawn Mary Farrow for 38 years, went to be with the Lord on Wednesday, 11 March after a long and courageous battle with cancer.*

He scans the rest, a strangely emotionless list of hobbies, various sports affiliations, and his surviving children and grandchildren. At the end is an invitation for friends and mourners to join the family at a memorial buffet to be held in Jimmy's honour at the family home. He copies the address into Google Maps and looks it up on Street View.

The house is a shithole; some prefab, 1950s bungalow in a part of London that's not really London at all. If this was where Jimmy 'Mia' Farrow had spent his twilight years, then he definitely wasn't the one who had waltzed off with the diamonds. He crosses Jimmy Farrow's name off the handwritten list and looks at the two remaining.

Catherine H   Adrian Shanklin
Catherine P   Brendan Webber

He types Adrian Shanklin into Google and this time the page of images that comes back contains several instant matches.

He clicks on the first one and a news site opens. The photo of Adrian Shanklin is part of a lengthy article detailing his arrest and conviction for a series of armed robberies on betting shops in south-east London. The article describes how he had stolen over eighty thousand pounds over a two-year period and been sentenced to twenty years in prison due to previous convictions and the violent nature of his offences.

Eighty grand over two years!

He could have earned more than that driving a cab. There's no way this guy stole the diamonds, unless he buried them somewhere and forgot where they were.

He crosses him off the list and googles the last name – Brendan Webber.

Again he gets a bunch of instant matches, but this time the photos and the websites they are on make him sit up.

He clicks on the first photo, a professional portrait showing a trim-looking man in his fifties with a deep tan and expensive teeth standing in front of the London skyline. His arms are folded across his chest and he's holding a roll of paper that looks like it might be blueprints. The photo is part of the 'People' section of a property development and management company website called WN Property. Brendan Webber is listed as one of the founding partners.

He clicks through the website, page after page of photographs showing shiny modern apartment complexes built, owned and/or managed by WN Property. He stops at one in particular, an apartment building with wide, glass-fronted balconies and Tower Bridge in the background. It's the Brannigan building, current home of Laughton Rees, former home of John Rees, the man who had been in charge of 'Operation Henry 8'.

Calais taps the Sharpie against his teeth.

In the case files Webber had been described as the owner of an import/export company that had gone belly up owing thousands in bad debts. He was the one who had the connections to bring the shipment into the UK. So how come a failed importer and exporter suddenly turned himself into a successful property developer? Where did he get the money to set up a company like that if he was broke?

He clicks on the 'About Us' section of the menu and speed-reads all the self-congratulatory guff about how Webber started the company by leasing an empty building, renting it out at a discount to blue-chip companies, then borrowing against the income to lease more buildings. After a few years he started buying buildings, then moved into construction, working with an award-winning team of architects called Stanford and Fuller, who sounded as wanky as him. Webber had even written a book about it all called *Borrow Money to Make Money* and ran property investment seminars and workshops.

Calais checks the date when the company was founded: 2008. The same year he went to prison. He sits back and stares at the glossy website. This was like looking through a window into the life he could have led if things had gone differently. But he had gone to prison and this guy had ended up with millions.

He clicks back to the main page where the photo of Brendan Webber beams out at him with his white teeth and tanned skin, eyes shining with energy, an entirely different person from the shabby, defeated-looking photo in the file. In sixteen years Brendan Webber had managed to completely transform himself, whereas Calais had remained the same, become a lesser version of himself even.

It isn't right; it isn't fair. Everything Brendan Webber has should be his. It *will* be his. Because the only problem with

having nice things is that there's always someone out there prepared to take them away from you.

He clicks back to the image results and looks through the thumbnail snapshots of Brendan Webber's life – him pictured in front of a shiny new building, him wearing a dinner jacket and smiling as he receives some award, him standing next to the prime minister and some other well-stuffed politician outside the door of Number 10, the caption beneath it reads – 'Tory donor and property entrepreneur Brendan Webber joins the government's Housing Task Force.'

While Calais had been watching his back in the shower-blocks, this smug arsehole had been having tea and cakes at Downing Street.

He opens another photo, Brendan Webber smiling for the cameras at what looked like a film premiere, his arm around the bony shoulders of a flinty blonde woman with a deep tan and a tight dress that showed off her yoga-toned body. In front of them stood two mini-me versions – one girl, one boy – grinning away like they'd won the lottery, which, in many ways, they had.

Perfect family. Perfect life. But not for long.

He navigates back to the company website and scans the 'About Us' section again, looking for the name of the architect firm Webber works with. He clicks on the 'Contact Us' section, finds a number for the main reception and taps to call it.

Outside, the traffic slides by as if greased by the same stuff covering the windows.

'WN Property,' a girl answers, sounding chirpy and posh, like someone who never had to worry about money or anything at all in her entire life.

'Yeah, hi, I've got some documents from Stanford and Fuller for Brendan Webber.'

'Brendan is actually on site this afternoon.'

Brendan! First-name terms with the boss, because that's the kind of guy he is.

'Oh, I think he's expecting these documents urgently, so if you could . . .'

'Sure, no problem, he's at Millennium Mills in Silvertown. Do you have the address?'

'Remind me,' Calais says, uncapping the Sharpie. 'Save me looking it up.'

45

Brendan Webber is in his element and doing what he does best, namely talking to people who are paid to listen.

'And that's going to be the show flat.' He points at a corner of the blue scroll of architects' plans rolled out on the large table in front of him. Eight men and one woman lean in to look at the plans. Webber stands back and allows a moment for what he's said to sink in. He is trim and athletic with silver hair worn in an old-fashioned, short back and sides cut with the top left long, a style that has become trendy again. His tracksuit and work boots make him look like a fitness instructor who headed out on a run, took a wrong turn and ended up on a building site. He also can't stand still and is as energetic as the rest of the group is subdued.

'Now I know it's going to be a massive pain in the arse, Mike,' he turns to the bear of a man standing next to him. 'But I'm going to need that unit up and running within six weeks – four would be better.'

Mike frowns down at the plans and shakes his head. 'In four weeks we'll barely be done with first-fixings.'

'For the whole project, yes, but we need to treat this unit separately and it needs to be priority. We can organize separate services for it so you can carry on fiddling with the electrics

238

and everything in the rest of the building, but this unit needs to be fully functioning ASAP. I want to use it as the sales office and show flat combined, so we can start selling off-plan.'

'Can't you do a brochure or something?'

Webber shakes his head. 'We've tried using CAD for sales in the past but it's *way* harder to get people to put down a large deposit on a bunch of glossy photos and a 3D model than it is on actual bricks and mortar. Give me my show flat, make it happen in a month and there's a ten-grand bonus in it for you, and five for everyone else.' He looks around the table, watching any resistance there may have been in the group melt away in the face of cold, hard cash.

Mike continues shaking his head. 'I don't know, Brendan.'

Webber slaps him on the back. 'Tell you what I'll do, Mike: I'll make it fifteen for you, seeing as you're the one who'll get the earache from everyone pulling double shifts in order to get this done.'

Mike stares down at the plans. 'You're going to rack up a shitload of overtime over this.'

'Not an issue, my friend,' Webber says, holding up his hands as if in surrender and shifting his weight from foot to foot like the floor is hot. 'Get me my show flat in a month and then we can all slap each other on the back and focus on the other two hundred and seventy-nine units.'

His phone buzzes in his pocket and he pulls it out and sees the number is withheld.

'I better take this,' he says, moving away from the table and towards a large window with most of the glass missing. He waits until he's out of earshot then answers the call, still fidgety from all his nervous energy.

'Hey?' he says, expecting to hear his girlfriend's voice as her number is usually the one that comes up unrecognized, a precaution in case his wife happens to be looking at his phone when it rings.

'Brendan, it's Tom Kenwright from the Home Office.'

Webber frowns as he tries to picture the face belonging to this smooth, posh voice. 'Hello,' he says, wondering why Charlie isn't calling himself.

'Have you seen the papers today?'

The frown deepens. He knows Charlie Nixon has been standing in the middle of a shower of shit for the last few days over this police uniform business, but is not entirely sure what that's got to do with him. 'Yeah, I've seen them.'

'There's a story on the inner pages. A body was found last night on the banks of the Thames. Another was found this morning. Both individuals are believed to have been involved in an enterprise sixteen years ago. The first body has been identified as Malcolm Fowler. Is that name familiar to you?'

Webber stops moving and stares out at the black waters of Royal Victoria Dock through the sharp, broken edges of a shattered pane of glass. 'Yes.'

'What about the name Billy Carver?'

Webber closes his eyes and nods. 'I know who he is.'

'So you know what I'm talking about.'

'Yes.'

'This is a friendly call to let you know that Billy Carver was released from prison a few days ago and is back on UK soil,' the smooth voice says, as if he's simply informing him that his dry-cleaning is ready for collection. 'Our mutual friend has also asked me to pass this message on to you,' the velvet voice continues. 'Be careful.'

The line clicks as it disconnects.

Webber keeps the phone pressed to his ear and stares out through the broken glass at a huge black bird moving slowly across the flat surface of the water, its dagger beak twitching back and forth as it searches for movement below. He had known Billy Carver was due to be released thanks to a news alert he'd set up to keep tabs on him, but hadn't realized it had happened already. He'd never forgotten what Carver had said after he'd been sentenced sixteen years earlier, about how

he would get even with every single person who had crossed him. He always figured he'd be back one day, asking for money, looking to settle old scores. And now he *was* back, and two people were dead.

He wonders who else Carver has caught up with, apart from Malcolm Fowler. He only personally knew two of the others. One of them had died and the other was in prison for armed robbery. The other three, the ones who had been on the front end of the deal, had only ever been names to him – all except Billy Carver. Billy Carver he had met once, in the cells of Lime Street police station when their paths had crossed at the lowest time of his life. Webber didn't believe in God and so didn't believe in the devil either but, if he did exist, he imagined him to be something like Billy Carver, a black void in the shape of a man.

Down on the water the bird arches its snakelike neck then disappears into the black water, leaving nothing behind but ripples. Webber shudders and takes a deep breath, fits a smile on his face and turns back to the group.

'Right, I think we're all done here, unless anyone has any questions?'

'Yes, I have one,' Webber looks at the speaker, a rat-faced man who represents the development office of the City of London and whose sole purpose in life seems was apparently being a constant pain in the arse.

'Declan,' Webber says, forcing a smile, 'of course you have a question, I'd be disappointed if you didn't.'

'These bonuses,' Declan says, squinting down at the printed sheets fixed to his clipboard. 'Which schedule will they be coming out of? Because they're not in the budget as it currently stands.'

Webber glances over at the plastic sheet hanging over the exit, feeling a strong urge to head home, lock the door and deal with all this later. But this project is too big and way too important so he forces his smile wider instead.

'This is exactly why our partnership works so well,' he says, putting his arm round Declan's bony shoulders and steering him away from the group. 'You focus on the detail while I keep my eye on the bigger picture. Let's have a look at these figures, shall we, see if we can't shake loose a bit of contingency.'

46

Laughton sees Gracie before Gracie sees her.

She is on the other side of the road, talking with a group of friends, part of the tide of green uniforms spilling out of the doors of the Towers School for Girls into the afternoon sunlight. She laughs at something one of her friends has said and Laughton feels the heavy weight of guilt settle upon her. As soon as Grace sees her she'll know something is wrong. Then Laughton will have to tell her that her father, a man whose name she learned less than twenty-four hours earlier, is dead and she will never see him again.

She stands still amid the afternoon crowd, watching her happy, oblivious daughter laughing in the afternoon, almost wishing that she won't notice her, that instead she might walk on down the road, still laughing, still happy, and avoid the conversation that will change all that.

But Gracie does notice her. She looks up, as if tugged by instinct, and her laugh melts away the moment she sees the sombre figure of her mother looking at her from across the street.

Gracie says something to her friends and they hug each other and head away, leaving Gracie alone. She looks at her mother but doesn't move, like she knows something bad is coming and

243

is keen to put it off for as long as she can. It is Laughton who eventually makes the first move. She nods in the direction of home and starts walking. Gracie pauses for a moment before following suit. Neither of them crosses the road to join the other, they walk in parallel, together but not together, putting off the difficult moment that both of them know is coming.

Gracie breaks first, her curiosity overcoming her reluctance to know what has brought her mother here. She weaves through the slow-moving traffic and stops directly in front of her mother.

'Hi,' she says.

'Hey.'

'What's up?'

Laughton opens her mouth to speak but the words get caught in her throat. She shakes her head, fighting back a sudden and unexpected flood of emotion. She remembers when she was told her father had died and how hollow and empty it had made her feel. And now she is about to make her daughter feel the same way.

'It's dad, isn't it?' Gracie says, guessing the thing her mother is struggling to say.

Laughton nods.

'What happened?'

Laughton steps forward, places her hands on her daughter's shoulders and looks her directly in the eye. 'We found his body in the river about an hour ago.' Gracie shakes her head and takes a step back. 'They still need to formally identify him, but he's not answering his phone and he was wearing the same clothes as . . .'

'What do you mean, formally identify him?' Gracie's eyes open wide and her hands cover her mouth as she figures it out for herself. 'Oh my God, he's like the one last night, isn't he?' Tears spring to her eyes at the horror of her realization.

Laughton tries to take her hand but Gracie snatches it away. 'This is your fault,' she says, backing away.

'Gracie, hun . . .'

244

'He came to you looking for help and you turned him away. And now he's dead and it's your fault.'

Again, Laughton opens her mouth to speak but no words come, because she knows Gracie is right. She could have done more, could have let him in at least. She could have stepped in when the police put him in cuffs and dragged him away. But now it's too late.

'I'm sorry,' she manages, but Gracie screws her face up in something like disgust then turns and half runs, half staggers away, heading towards the river and home.

Laughton watches her go, feeling wretched in the realization that things have somehow come full circle. She had once blamed her father for the death of her mother and now her daughter is doing something horribly similar. Only she had been wrong, her father had been innocent, and Gracie is right, she is partly responsible. But the person most responsible is Billy Carver, and she is going to find him and nail him to the wall for what he's done.

47

The moped slips along the straight roads, past shiny new-built blocks and construction sites. When Calais was last here the docks had been a post-apocalyptic wasteland, crumbling warehouses and rusting cranes standing beside the cold, empty troughs of the man-made, deep-water harbours.

He turns a corner and eases past a Starbucks, looking for the address the helpful receptionist had given him. A cold breeze blows off the water, the same breeze he remembers from before. It was always windswept and bleak here. Still is, despite the overpriced boxes stacked on top of one another. No amount of gentrification can change the weather.

He nears the end of the street, where the new builds end abruptly and give way to a chain-link fence. An expanse of cracked concrete and scrubby wasteland lies beyond with a huge monolithic building rising up by the water's edge. It's almost Soviet in its scale and brutality, with large, Crittall upper windows adding a vaguely art deco feel, and flaking red letters on the upper floor spelling out the word 'SPILLERS'. The windows are mostly broken and the cream paint is peeling badly. This is what he remembers, decay and abandonment – desolation. It's like someone has drawn an invisible line across the road with the present on one side and the past on the other.

He slows the moped as he approaches a gate in the chain-link fence with a large hoarding next to it announcing:

MILLENNIUM MILL REDEVELOPMENT
A PARTNERSHIP BETWEEN
THE CITY OF LONDON and WN PROPERTY

He pulls to a stop and looks through the gate at an access road with a couple of shipping containers at the end of it with windows set into their steel walls. Several cars are parked next to it, mostly compact, city models, but there is also a large olive-green Land Rover Defender with blacked out windows and alloy wheels that looks very much like a boss's car.

Calais eases the moped in a wide circle and heads back up the road, crossing over the invisible line between past and present before coming to a stop in the shadow of the apartment block. He kills the engine, flips out the kickstand then peers round the edge of the building, listening to the tick of cooling metal and the low moan of the cold wind. From his new position he can see the derelict warehouse, the car park, the Land Rover – everything. He spots a couple of security cameras by the shipping containers and one by the gate, but the car park is clear. Total blind spot.

He settles back on the moped seat.

He waits.

48

Tannahill enters the fourth-floor office of NoLMS HQ and heads straight across to the open door of the chief inspector's office. He knocks on the doorframe and Grieves glances over his reading glasses as he steps into his office, then returns his attention to the paperwork on his desk.

'Sir, I need you to resubmit the request to declassify the Operation Henry 8 files,' Tannahill says.

Grieves takes a deep breath and shuffles some of the papers into a neat pile in front of him. 'Are you sure, DCI Khan? Are you sure you *need* to do this?'

'Absolutely, sir. Another body washed up in the Thames this morning, same as the one before – no head, no hands. That's two victims in two days and both have been identified as being involved in Operation Henry 8, which means anyone else named in that file is also likely to be at risk, so it would be of huge benefit if I could read through the unredacted files and see exactly how everyone was connected and who we should warn.'

Grieves takes off his glasses. 'You see this paperwork on my desk?' He opens his hands and gestures at the documents in front of him. 'This is everything I need to square away before I head off on a holiday I've been promising my wife and kids for the last three years. I've got about two days' work here

that I'm trying to get done in' – he checks his watch – 'a little over three hours. What I really don't need is more work right now, especially work that might piss off anyone important. Now you already asked for this file to be declassified; they already said "No". I told you not to keep knocking at a door that's been slammed in your face.'

'Yes but, respectfully, sir, when I first put in the request it was one possible lead, now it's my main lead in a double murder investigation and the request is not some fishing expedition, it's a time-sensitive hunt for a killer who I believe will kill again if we don't catch him.'

Grieves looks up at him, his eyes weary and resigned. He shakes his head and stares back down at the paperwork standing between him and his holiday. 'I'll tell you what I'll do,' he says fitting his reading glasses back over his ears. 'I will submit a new request to declassify the files. But, as I'm going to be on a beach for the next fourteen days, drinking cocktails and reading crime novels where the bad guys *always* get caught, I'm going to copy you in, make it very clear the request comes from you, and request that all replies and correspondence going forward should be addressed to you. I'm also not going to press *send* on this email until I'm literally about to step foot out of the door.'

Tannahill nods. 'Thank you, sir.'

'You're welcome.' He looks back down at the documents and reads the top one for about ten seconds before looking up again. 'You appear to still be here, DCI Khan.'

'Sir. There's something else I'd like to request.'

'Really?' he deadpans.

'I've had a squad car acting as an obs and security unit in relation to this case. It's been parked outside the former home of Commissioner John Rees, the officer in charge of Operation Henry 8. I had reason to believe the killer might call round there as part of his . . . vendetta.'

'Why would your killer do that? John Rees is dead.'

249

'Yes, sir, but his daughter is not and she now resides at that address.'

'Is *she* mentioned in this file you're so desperate to wreck your career on?'

'No, sir.'

'Well then, no, you may not keep this unit in place if that's what you're getting at. In fact, I'm a bit pissed off it was there in the first place, seeing as this is the first I've heard about it. I'll put in your request for the file but your request to extend this unauthorized surveillance unit is denied. And if I were you I would get out of this office before I change my mind about the file request too.'

49

Laughton opens the front door of her apartment and listens.

She can hear music coming from Gracie's bedroom, something particularly dark and depressing, though not really anything out of the ordinary.

She closes the door, touches her father's photo, kicks off her shoes and pads softly across the marble, feeling the cool stone under her feet. She stops outside Gracie's bedroom and the music gets louder as she presses her ear to the door. She tries listening through it for any other sounds – crying, pacing, the sound of things being broken – but all she can hear is the relentless dirge of mournful music.

She steps back and reaches out, laying her hand flat on the wooden surface of the door, wondering whether to knock and try and talk about everything, painful though that might be.

The music fades between tracks and she listens again, and can hear the hiss of the shower.

She takes a breath, grateful for the brief respite, and heads into the kitchen, filling a glass of water from the cold-water dispenser on the fridge before sliding the door open and stepping out on to the balcony. She closes the door behind her, cutting out the distant resurgent sound of Grace's music, then

stares out at the river, sipping her cold water and enjoying this brief moment of calm in her rollercoaster of a day.

She looks down at the spot where the squad car was parked earlier and feels slightly uneasy when she sees that it is no longer there. She thinks of Carver, still out there somewhere, only now with her father's files and all the information they contained. She wonders where they will lead him, who it will lead him to, and when he might get there. Theoretically, she and Gracie should be safe. He had been looking for the files and now he has them, and if he'd wanted more, revenge on her family or whatever, then he could have attacked her in the storage unit. She pulls her phone from her pocket, finds Tannahill's number and listens to it ring as she takes another sip of cold water.

'Hey,' he says, the hubbub of the office noisy in the background. 'You OK?'

'Yeah, I'm fine. Gracie . . . not so much.'

'How did she take it?'

'Well . . . she kind of blamed me for his death. Said I should have done more to help him.'

'It's not your fault, you know that, right?'

'I don't know. I probably could have played it differently.'

'You didn't kill Shelby. Carver killed Shelby.'

Laughton nods. She had used exactly the same argument on Gracie, but hearing it now makes her realize how unconvincing it sounds. She stares down at the grey waters of the Thames, wondering if there was already another headless body in it, somewhere along its serpentine length.

'How's the manhunt going?' she asks, keen to change the subject. 'Give me some good news.'

'OK, so Grieves agreed to send a new request to declassify the file. By "agreed" I mean he made it out like I was putting a gun to his head and is only going to send it at the end of today as he heads off on holiday, so we won't hear anything back on that until tomorrow at the very earliest. The good thing

about that is that he's copying me in on the email so I'll be able to hassle the Home Office about it directly now. Er, what else?' Laughton hears papers being shuffled and can picture his messy desk. 'Oh yeah, we got the tox result back on the first body.'

'That was fast.'

'Yeah, I think Evelyn pulled some favours at the lab to get it bumped up. Our man was dosed with fentanyl before he was fatally stabbed, so I guess at least he didn't feel anything.'

Laughton frowns at this new information, mainly because Tannahill referred to Dr Prior as 'Evelyn'. 'That was nice of her,' Laughton says, trying to keep the snark from her voice and not altogether succeeding. 'She seems to be doing you a lot of favours lately.'

'You sound annoyed.'

'Why would I be? I can't tell you what you can and can't do. You're a grown-up. If you want to go out for cocktails with a beautiful, if slightly older, woman, then go for it.'

'*Slightly older!?* Oh my God, you're jealous. Listen, Laughton, I'm not interested, OK? I mean, I'm flattered, Evelyn Prior is an impressive woman.'

'And she looks like a nineteen fifties Italian film star.'

'She does, but the thing is, she's not you.'

Laughton feels a lump form in her throat and smiles despite it. 'Yeah, but I'm a pain in the arse. I'm grumpy, I'm always working, I can't cook, I have OCD, *major* unresolved daddy issues, and a teenage daughter who barely talks to me and now thinks I'm complicit in getting her father killed. I'd *SO* go for cocktails with Evelyn Prior if I were you.'

There's a pause on the other end of the line, filled with office noise and men's laughter.

'I'm not interested in Evelyn Prior,' Tannahill says. 'Since I met you, I'm not interested in anyone else. Partly because, as you just proved, you have no idea how amazing you actually are. Listen, I'm going to finish up here soon; why don't I come round?'

Laughton smiles again and is about to say how much she would actually love that, when a noise behind her makes her turn round. Gracie is standing in the kitchen, a bathrobe drowning her tiny frame and a towel piled up on her head. She grabs an Actimel from the fridge then looks over at Laughton with a blank, unreadable expression on her face. Her eyes are pink, like she's been crying. She shakes the Actimel and walks away, heading out of the kitchen and back to her bedroom.

'I'd love you to come round,' Laughton says. 'Honestly, I'd like nothing more, but I don't think it's a good idea right now. Gracie has just found, then lost her father, and she's furious at the world – me especially. If I invite what she might well see as a potential new father figure round, she'll probably never forgive me. It's all too soon and too raw.'

She hears a deep sigh on the other end of the line. 'Yeah, you're right – bad idea.'

'You see, I *am* a pain in the arse. Nothing is ever easy with me. I bet Evelyn Prior hasn't got a teenage daughter who hates her.'

'Your ongoing obsession with Evelyn Prior makes me think that maybe you should go for cocktails with her.'

Laughton smiles. 'No way. I'd be terrified. She's *way* too glamorous for me.'

'Yeah, me too. I prefer 'em bookish and weighed down with baggage. Listen, I should go, I've got a bunch of stuff I need to be getting on with.'

'Before you go, have you managed to get hold of any of the other "wives" on the list and warn them about Carver?'

'That's literally what I'm about to do. Hopefully we can identify the next likely target and stake him out. Carver only got these names a few hours ago, so we're not that far behind.'

'Good luck.'

'Thanks. I'll call you as soon as I have anything to report.'

The phone clicks, leaving Laughton feeling suddenly very, very alone on the balcony.

50

Tannahill sits back in his chair and looks up at the water stain above his desk. It seems to have grown bigger and definitely looks more like Africa now.

His phone buzzes in his hand and he sees that he has one new message and several missed calls, mostly from his mother. He thinks about calling her back, then decides against it. She'll only ask him about Laughton and how things are going and, right now, he has absolutely no idea.

He leans forward, taps his mouse to wake up his terminal and googles the names of the 'wives' one by one, following the same digital path the man he was hunting had gone down a few hours earlier. He finds the same information in the same places – one 'wife' dead, another in prison, and a third looking very much like the man who ended up with the diamonds all those years ago.

He logs on to the police database, finds contact details for Brendan Webber, and dials his number. He leans back in his chair and listens to it ringing.

51

Brendan Webber emerges from the gloom of Millennium Mill and squints against the light as he removes his hard hat and heads over to his car. He scans the dockside – car park, storage yard, site office, the derelict expanse of wasteland that surrounds it all.

He is still feeling a little edgy after the earlier phone call, a mood which has not been made any better by the last twenty minutes going through the budget with Martin. Martin might be an irritating jobsworth but his attention to detail was actually reassuring. This project was huge, the biggest he had ever taken on, and he needed to focus on it and not be distracted by the threat of some ghost from his past turning up and wanting revenge, or a handout, or whatever.

He pulls his key fob from his pocket and fires it at his car, making the hazards flash and the side mirrors fold out. He shrugs out of his hi-vis vest and it catches on his site visitor's lanyard. He lets out a groan as he realizes he hasn't signed out – another bullshit piece of bureaucracy Declan had insisted on for everyone, himself included.

He changes course and is about to open the door to the site office when his phone buzzes in his pocket. He fishes it out and checks the caller ID.

Number withheld.

He thinks about whether or not to answer. It could be Charlie Nixon, but he doubts it. Why get a minion to call him earlier then call himself half an hour later? The chances are it's someone else, someone his phone doesn't recognize, and he definitely isn't in the mood to talk to some rando right now. He rejects the call. They can leave a message if it's urgent.

He opens the site office door and holds his lanyard up to the reader until it beeps, turns around and heads back to his car, resuming his scanning of the larger bushes and areas of scrub around the edge of the car park. He makes a mental note that they need to clear this area as well; no good having a shiny new show flat if buyers have to walk through something that looks like the set of *The Walking Dead* to get to it. That was another thing Mike would grumble about, but he'd do it, Webber knew that. Mike would do any extra work that came his way because he had two kids at private school and Webber knew exactly how painful *that* was. The bonus would pay for a term at least, maybe even chuck in some flute lessons if there's change.

He opens the driver's side door, slips behind the wheel closing the door behind him with a deep and satisfying *thunk*. He presses the button to lock the doors and blows out a long breath, feeling a moment of peace and calm. He loves this car, it makes him feel important, which of course he is, but it also makes him feel safe. It's built like a tank and the riding height is higher than most cars, so even if something absolutely piled into him, the worst he would suffer was a broken ankle.

He slots his phone into the charging dock and puts on his seat belt, checking outside again through the tinted windows.

'Call Macy,' he says, then presses the button to start the car as he listens to it ringing.

'Hey, Dad!' He smiles at the sweet, light sound of his daughter's voice.

'Hi, hun. You home yet?'

'Yeah, just got in.'

'Is Danny with you?'

'Yes, he's gone upstairs, do you want to speak to him?'

'No, it's OK. Just checking you both got home OK.'

'Yeah, course. Why wouldn't we?'

'Oh, no reason. Is your mum there?'

'I think so, hang on.' He listens to the sound of footsteps and puts the car in gear, driving it in a wide circle around the car park until he's pointing back down the access road cut through the weeds.

'Hi!' His wife sounds distracted.

'You OK?'

'Yeah why?'

'You sound stressed.'

'I'm cooking.'

'Oh, right.' Beth's latest self-improvement project was cooking, which was better than life drawing, but not as good as yoga, which had made her sex drive go through the roof. Or it had until she'd given it up, like she did every other hobby she'd ever tried.

'What time you going to be home?' she asks.

Webber checks the time on the dashboard: 4:28. He could make it across town to Notting Hill in maybe forty minutes if the traffic isn't too horrible. Or he could take a detour, spend an hour in the flat with Carol and still be home for bedtime stories. Whatever his wife was cooking, he was pretty sure it would taste the same heated up in the microwave.

'Probably going to be another couple of hours,' he says, passing through the gate and checking both ways. He spots the motor scooter parked on the pavement by the corner of the next-door building.

'OK, hun,' Beth says, clearly distracted. 'I'll save you some dinner. Love you.'

'Love you too,' Webber murmurs, but the phone has already disconnected.

He eases out on to the road, looking over at the motor scooter, wondering where the rider is as he reaches for the phone to dial Carol's number from memory.

The voice behind him makes him freeze.

'Looking for me?'

Webber instinctively turns his head to look behind him but something hard hits him on the side of the temple.

'Don't turn around,' the voice says calmly. 'Don't say anything. Just drive.'

Webber drives, eyes wide and staring straight ahead at the road. A trickle of blood starts to run down his temple but he doesn't move to wipe it off. He concentrates on his breathing instead, keeping it deep and steady. He risks a glance in the rear-view mirror but whoever is in the back is sitting right behind him so he can't see his face. He doesn't really need to. He knows who's sitting behind him.

He focuses on the road and starts thinking about how he might get out of this situation. His normal instinct would be to talk, try and find common ground, start negotiating, but the rider had told him not to speak and he doesn't fancy getting hit again. He has to do something though, so he risks a question.

'What do you want?' he asks.

The man says nothing and Webber braces himself for another bang on the head.

'Everything,' comes the eventual answer.

'OK,' Webber says. 'I have money.'

'Money isn't everything,' the voice replies.

Webber drives. Thinks.

He could try slamming on the brakes and making a grab for him. He's in pretty good shape, goes to the gym five times a week, does a bit of boxing. But a memory surfaces about Billy Carver being an amateur boxer in his youth. He swallows drily. Sixteen years in prison might have weakened Carver, turned him soft. Then again, it might have done the opposite.

259

And he might have a gun. If he has a gun or a knife, that will be a different story.

Blood continues to drip slowly down the side of Webber's face and he thinks again about what he'd been hit with. It could have been a gun. Something hard and metallic for sure. He risks another quick glance in the rear-view mirror and his hopes sink when he catches a glimpse of the bike helmet. That means fighting is not going to work. If he punches Carver or batters him while he still has the helmet on, he'll only end up breaking his own hand.

He takes another breath to calm himself and keeps his speed steady and his eyes on the road.

He could run.

Maybe that's the thing to do.

Wait until they get somewhere with a few more people around and make a dash for it. They'll have to stop sometime – at traffic lights, or when they get snarled up in the evening traffic. He could do it then. Jam the brakes on hard to knock the guy off balance, jump out the door and make a break for it.

If Carver had a gun he could shoot him. But would he? Maybe not if there were people around. He'll be taking a risk but, on balance, running seems the best option. Maybe his only option. He looks ahead, thinking about where he might do it, somewhere with a crowd he can disappear into.

'Where are we heading?' he asks.

There's a pause before the muffled reply: 'West.'

Webber's hands grip the wheel a little tighter and he forces himself not to smile. West will take him right through the city at a time when everyone will be leaving their offices and heading for home. Lots of people, lots of opportunities for him to run.

He turns a corner into another street of anonymous apartment blocks and can see the gleaming towers in the distance. Once he reaches them, he'll have a chance. Only a mile or so more.

'Pull over,' the voice instructs him. 'Over there, at the bus stop.'

Webber's eyes grow wider as they stare at the distant city tower blocks, much too far away. As he slows the car, his mind races. His eyes dart around, looking for any kind of an opportunity but there's no one here; no cars, no pedestrians, not even a narrow alley he could dash into. He eases the Land Rover towards the empty bus stop and pulls to a halt.

'Turn off the engine.'

'Why have we stopped?' Webber asks, stalling for time as he tries to figure out what's going on.

Something cold, hard and round presses into the base of his neck. He *does* have a gun.

'Turn. Off. The engine,' the voice insists.

Webber presses his foot on the brake and slides the gearstick into park, causing the hybrid engine to automatically cut out. He can hear his heart beating in his ears in the muffled silence that follows.

He feels the barrel of the gun shift slightly against the skin of his neck then something passes over his right shoulder and falls heavily into his lap, making him flinch. He looks down and sees a clear plastic bottle of water lying in the gap between his legs.

'Drink it.'

'What?'

The gun presses harder into his neck.

'Drink.'

Webber looks at the bottle. Sees that the plastic seal is broken.

'What's in it?'

'Something to make you sleep.'

Webber stares down at the bottle but makes no move to pick it up. The gun barrel presses into his neck again, as if to remind him that it's still there.

'You have a choice,' the muffled voice says. 'Either drink the water and sleep for a bit. Or don't drink it and sleep forever.'

Webber swallows and runs his tongue across his lower lip, his mouth feeling rough and dry.

'We don't have to do this . . . whatever it is,' Webber says.
'Yes we do. Drink.'

Webber thinks about the conversation he had with his kids and his wife, everyone distracted, everyone doing their own thing, him worried about them when all the while the cause of his concern was crouched down behind him in the back of his car. He wonders how he managed to get in without the key and remembers that he had unlocked the car himself. He had unlocked the car then remembered he needed to sign out, so had gone to the site office instead. Carver must have slipped in then. It was that fucker Declan with his petty rules that had caused this. If he managed to get out of this, *when* he managed to get out of this, he was going to fire him.

'What's this about?' Webber says.

'You'll find out after,' the voice says. 'Drink.'

Webber takes a deep breath and lets it out wearily as he resigns himself to what is about to happen. He picks up the bottle, twists off the cap, and drinks.

The water is cool and actually feels refreshing in his bone-dry mouth. It also tastes fine, no bitterness, no chalky aftertaste. He wonders if maybe there is nothing in it at all and this was some kind of test to gauge his willingness to cooperate.

Then it hits him.

It starts as a kind of rising lightness, like the feeling you get in your stomach when you drive over the brow of a hill too fast. Only this sensation continues, building inside him and spreading, a sense of intense relaxation throughout his body.

He closes his eyes and tilts his head back slightly to let the water flow down his throat as he continues to drink. The water is the source of this bliss and he craves more of it and the calm it brings as it washes away the fear and anxiety that had gripped him only moments earlier.

He starts to feel lighter, like he is floating up out of his seat, but at the same time his arms feel heavy and the water bottle starts to droop. He feels something take hold of his hand and

opens his eyes to see that the man behind him has reached over his shoulder and is now holding the bottle for him, raising it up to keep the bliss flowing.

He lets go of the bottle, his arm too heavy to keep holding it anyway, and his hand drops into his lap.

He closes his eyes, his eyelids too heavy now too, and feels a burst of love for the man behind him, the one he had been afraid of only minutes before.

He can't be so bad if he is doing this kindness for me – he thinks as his mind expands into a joyful nothingness.

And nothing bad can happen in the midst of all this bliss.

DAY THREE

52

Brendan Webber comes to slowly.

It feels like he is rising up gently through thick water, only it doesn't *feel* like he is in water. He isn't wet and he seems to be breathing normally, though he can hear the sound of rushing water close by.

He tries to remember where he is but his mind is foggy and his memories vague and unfocused.

He opens his mouth, takes a deep breath and is surprised by how dry his mouth is.

He tries to open his eyes and finds that he can't. He *wants* to open his eyes. His brain is *telling* his eyelids to open but somehow the message isn't getting through.

He runs his sandpaper tongue around his cotton mouth and tries again to remember where he is.

A vague memory of driving surfaces. He was talking on the phone, first with his kids, then with Beth, and then . . .

Carol!

He must be at Carol's.

He must have come round here before going home and she must have been in a party mood, slipped him a pill or something that would be low-key entry level for her but has ended up knocking him for six. It's one of the hazards of having a

much younger girlfriend, she can out-party him on every level and wake up smiling the next morning.

He wonders what time it is, how long he's been comatose, and how much explaining he's going to need to do once he gets home. He'll blame it on the Millennium Mill project. As long as Beth thinks he's been working on that she'll cut him no end of slack because he's walked her through the figures and she knows how much he stands to make on the project. Hell, she's already started spending it.

He takes another breath and notices something new, a smell like damp bricks and . . . piss. He frowns, or attempts one at least, his forehead seeming as uncooperative as the rest of his face. It certainly doesn't smell like Carol's place, which is generally a mix of weed and scented candles.

He tries to open his eyes again and this time his left one opens a tiny bit, enough to see that his head is flopped forward and staring straight down into his own lap. There is a large damp patch radiating out from his crotch and he realizes with disgust that the smell of piss is coming from him.

He tries to raise his head but it feels too heavy so he lolls it over to the left and side-eyes the room instead.

It is gloomy, lit by a single weak overhead lamp – rough brick walls, some shelves with things on them that he can't make out. He tries to place the room but can't. A storeroom? Maybe a garage where he parked his car and fell asleep. Only he's not in his car. Where's his car?

His other eye flutters open as it all comes back to him in a rush.

Carver!

He remembers the voice from the back seat, the gun in his neck, the bottle of water, the spreading feeling of bliss. But he's not feeling bliss any more. Now he feels afraid.

He tries to lift his head but it's still way too heavy. Tries to lift his hands but they won't move either. He feels something tugging at his wrist and slides his eye over to his left hand

where a belt or a strap of some kind binds it flat to the broad, wooden arm of a heavy chair.

His breathing quickens, the taste of damp brick and urine coating the back of his throat. He tugs both hands but they are firmly strapped to the arms of the chair. He tries moving his feet but they are held fast too. He lolls his head over in the other direction and side-eyes the right-hand section of the room: same brick walls, same weak light, but there's also a wooden butcher's block with some tools laid out on it.

He licks his lips again, swallows against the dryness, tries calling out. In his head the word he is shouting is 'Hello', but the sound that comes out is a long and mournful moan. It fades away as he runs out of air and he takes another breath, ready to shout again.

'No one can hear you.' The voice is close and soft and comes from directly behind him. 'You can shout all you like, no one will come.'

'What do you want?' Webber tries to say, but again the words come out as a lump of shapeless sounds.

'Here,' the voice says. 'Let me help you wake up a little.'

Webber feels something touch the middle joint of his little finger and he lolls his head over to look just as a hammer strikes the top of a chisel, driving the angled blade right through his finger and into the wooden arm of the chair beneath.

The noise that comes out of him is from pure shock because he feels no pain – not yet at least. He stares wide-eyed at the chisel sticking up from the arm of the chair, the end of his little finger disappearing into the blade like some magic trick. His brain can't quite process what happened. He saw it but doesn't believe it and he continues to stare with numb detachment as a hand grips the handle of the chisel and wiggles it free, revealing the severed end of his finger lying in a spreading pool of blood.

In the same detached part of his brain that makes it feel like he's watching a video he wonders if the finger might be

re-attached, somehow, like maybe if he can pack it in ice and get to a hospital quickly they might be able to save it. He hears a static click and a low roar of flame and watches in the same detached, fascinated horror as the blue flame of a small blowtorch appears to his right and is held against the spot where his little finger used to be. He hears a sizzle, smells burning flesh – *then* he feels the pain.

It starts like a slow explosion, a low ache at the end of his finger that seems to double in size with every panicked breath, travelling up his arm and into the rest of his body. The flame is removed but the pain keeps growing, radiating and throbbing from the blackened, blistered spot where his finger had been.

He is fully awake now, dragged from his soft dreams of blissful nothingness into this sharp, damp, pain-filled nightmare. He bucks against the chair, every instinct telling him to get away, to run. But the chair doesn't move, and the straps don't give, no matter how much he thrashes, and he hyperventilates as he breathes in the smell of burnt flesh and piss.

He lifts his head, looks for a door, a window, any way out of this place. In the far corner of the room is a stall with what looks like a trapdoor set in the floor next to a large lever. Maybe that's the way in. Maybe he's on an upper floor and the way out is through there. But then he realizes that the sound of rushing water is coming from beneath it, so it can't be a way out, and he can't be on an upper floor. He takes another deep breath and lets out another long scream, this time the word clear and definite, sharpened by the pain still expanding inside him. 'HEEEEELP!!'

He screams until his lungs have no more air in them, then sucks in another big breath ready to shout again.

'Do that one more time and I'll take another finger.'

The voice is so close it silences him instantly. He clamps down on the shout, eyes wide. Holds his breath for a long moment before blowing it out. 'What do you want?' Webber

says, his voice unsteady and barely audible above the rush of water.

'Answers. I want you to tell me what you know about Operation Henry 8 and what happened to the diamonds.'

'The di—? I don't know.'

He senses movement to his right and looks across at the butcher's block in time to see a hand pick up the chisel. 'I swear to you, I don't know,' Webber says. 'I only dealt with the shipping side of things, made some calls, set a few things up.'

'Bullshit.' The blade of the chisel moves over his hand and Webber makes a fist to tuck his fingers away.

'I swear I had nothing to do with the finances. I never even saw any diamonds.'

'Open your fist or I'll take the whole hand.'

'No. Please. Don't do this. You don't need to do this. John Rees handled the diamonds. He handled everything. It was his operation. He set everything up. I only got involved to stay out of jail.'

'Open your hand.'

'I swear to you. I'd got myself in trouble, got caught, and John Rees offered me a way out. If I helped him with this I could walk. It was all him. He gave me the names of the people to contact, told me what to say. That's all he gave me.'

'So where did your money come from?'

'Everything I made, I made since then and it's all legit. I swear to you. I didn't get a penny from Rees. All I got was a clean slate and a fresh start.'

'Open your hand.'

'It's true. Jesus. Don't do this. You don't need to do this. I can prove it. I wrote a book about it. It tells you how I earned all the money.' The gloved hand places the chisel back down on the butcher's block and picks up a hatchet instead. 'Please. Don't do this.' Webber is sobbing now. 'I can give you money. We can sort something out. I know you went to prison, and that's a shitty deal, but I had nothing to do with it, I promise.

John Rees was behind everything, but I can help you out, give you the same fresh start I got. What do you need, give me a figure. Please!'

The hatchet moves over until the blade is hovering a few inches above his wrist.

'Finger or hand, your choice.'

'Oh Jesus.' Webber stares at the hatchet and tries to uncurl his hand but it refuses. 'I don't know anything else, I swear to you. Tell me what you want and we can figure something out.' His eyes are wide and fixed on the hatchet.

'What I want is the sixteen years that were taken from me. Can you figure that out?'

Webber continues to stare at the hatchet blade still hovering a few inches above his wrist, his mind scrabbling around for something to say, anything that might stop this nightmare from playing out. But his mind comes up blank and in the end it is the voice that speaks.

'You need to learn, my friend,' it says, close and intimate, 'some things, even money can't buy.'

Then the hatchet rises, so quick and sudden that no words or fresh bargains could ever come in time to stop it. It comes back down hard and fast, chopping straight through flesh and bone, severing the hand entirely as it bites into the wooden arm of the chair beneath.

53

Laughton can't sleep.

She lies on her back in her bed watching the dim lightshow of London playing out on the ceiling. She always sleeps with the blinds open, finding comfort in the movement of leaked light from outside. It shows her that other people are up too and she's not entirely alone.

She picks up her phone and checks the time.

A little after three.

Too late to fall asleep now and have anything approaching a full night, but still too early to get up and engage with the day. She looks over at the teetering pile of books by the bed but her head is buzzing too much to read. She gives in and gets up, slipping on a pair of tracksuit bottoms and a T-shirt before heading out into the dark flat.

She pads softly past Gracie's bedroom, hoping she at least is managing to sleep, then enters the third bedroom and closes the door behind her before turning on the light.

She narrows her eyes against the sudden brightness, opening them slowly again as they gradually adjust. The third bedroom is the only thing Laughton changed when she and Gracie moved in, removing the bed and built-in wardrobes and replacing them with weights, a running machine and two punching bags, one

heavy bag for kicks and combinations and a speed bag for timing, reflexes and stamina. Laughton does some stretches to limber up, the image of Shelby's ravaged body lying in the reeds flashing into her mind. She had no love for him in life but she feels a strange responsibility to him in death. She wants to find his killer. She wants to make him pay.

She moves over to the heavy bag and focuses on a well-worn, indented spot at around head height, picturing Billy Carver's face there remembered from the mug shot Tannahill shared with her earlier. She shifts her weight to the balls of her feet and stands side on, jinking from side to side and gradually building a rhythm until she launches herself at the bag, spinning on her left foot and driving up and forward with her right, straight into the spot where Carver's face would be. The contact makes a loud slap and the bag rattles on its chains, sounding way too loud for this time of the morning. Laughton turns to the door to check she closed it properly. She sound-proofed the room as part of the conversion but even so a full-on Muay Thai training session might still wake Gracie. She continues throwing punches and launching kicks at the bag for a few more minutes, being careful not to connect, but it feels weird and unsatisfying, so she leaves the room and heads to her office for a different kind of workout.

Her office is a mess, piles of books spilling off the shelves lining every wall, collecting in drifts around her desk and the purple velvet Chesterfield facing the wall of glass that looks out on to the river and the London skyline. Laughton sits at her desk, opens her laptop and stares into space for a moment.

She can't shift the feeling that history is repeating itself. She has become her father and Gracie is now her and she knows how that panned out last time. She thinks of Gracie, out on the streets, cold, hungry, scared, stupid, like she had once been. She imagines her meeting someone like Shelby and the thought makes her feel sick. She can't let that happen, can't let her present mistakes force Gracie into repeating her past ones. She

needs to take control of the situation by finding Billy Carver and making him pay for what he has done.

She taps her fingers on the edge of her laptop in patterns of three.

Thinks.

She needs to stop focusing on where Billy Carver has been and start thinking about where he is going next.

She opens her notes on Operation Henry 8 and updates her list of the six 'wives':

Catherine A	Billy Carver	???
Anne B	Malcolm 'Minty' Fowler	Dead
Jane	Shelby Facer	Dead
Anne C	Jimmy 'Mia' Farrow	Dead
Catherine H	Adrian Shanklin	Prison
Catherine P	Brendan Webber	???

Shelby had said Carver wanted to get even with everyone who had crossed him, and Shanklin and Webber are now the only two left standing. Tannahill was already on the case with Webber, and Shanklin is in maximum security, though Carver could still get to him. He could organize an accident, a fight in the lunch queue, an ambush in one of the blind spots every prison had. Life was cheap inside and people with nothing to lose could be bought for relatively little. But would Carver want to do it that way? It didn't seem his style. Not nearly personal or brutal enough, given what he had done to the others. There's something else preying on Laughton's mind, something Shelby had hinted at. Carver didn't just want revenge, he also wanted payback – literally. He wanted to be paid his share of the deal that had gone wrong, which meant he would be looking for the diamonds and the person who took them.

Laughton scrolls back through her notes and reads through what she knows about the diamonds: uncut, thirty million

pounds' worth. She didn't even know what thirty million pounds' worth of uncut diamonds might look like, or how you would go about converting them into cash. But as with many things criminal adjacent, she knows a man who does.

She does a hard-drive search for 'Solitaire Heist' and opens up the files from a case she had worked on a few years earlier, an armed robbery on a chain of jewellers where uncut diamonds had been the thieves' primary target. The investigating officers in that case had consulted with someone in Hatton Garden, the main diamond district in London, so there should be contact details for him in the list of expert witnesses. He had a peculiar name and worked in a building with a funny name too, the Bowery or the Bothy – something like that. She skims through the witness statements and sees it at the bottom of a PDF – the bourse. That was it, the diamond bourse in the heart of London, and the contact was a guy called Mr Max.

She copies the email address into a new message and writes:

Hi Mr Max,
My name is Dr Laughton Rees and I'm working with the Metropolitan Police on a case involving missing uncut diamonds. Would it be possible for me to talk to someone about this? It's an active homicide case so a quick response would be greatly appreciated.
Yours,
Dr Laughton Rees

She attaches her 'posh' signature at the end with all her academic letters after her name and the London Metro University seal to boost her credibility. She reads through it, thinks about deleting the last line in case it comes off as too pushy, but hits *Send* anyway. Everyone is a ghoul at heart so they're more likely to reply at the mention of 'active homicide case', even if it's only to pump her for details.

The whoosh of the email sounds in the quiet of the book-clogged office and Laughton stretches, arching her back to try and squeeze some of the tension out of it.

She looks up and catches her own faint reflection in the black mirror of the window. She looks pale and colourless, like the ghost of some poor, drowned waif floating high above the river that killed her. She gets up and walks to the window, her reflection advancing to meet her. She stops and regards herself for a moment then unlocks the door and slides it open, wiping her image away to be replaced by the restless night.

Like any large Western city, London never sleeps. There is always something going on in it somewhere, energy being expended, and Laughton feels connected to it because she is restless in the same way. She steps out on to the balcony and feels the chill of the night wrap itself around her. She can smell rain, damp and slightly chemical like wet pavements, but it's not raining yet. She looks down at the streetlights and the surface of the river, looking for raindrops, and freezes when she sees the man sitting on one of the benches that line the embankment. He has a folded newspaper in his lap and is facing out to the river, but his body is angled slightly towards the building, like he's been watching it. The rain comes, soft and gentle like mist falling out of the black sky and he moves slightly to turn up his collar and hug himself against the chill that comes with it.

Then he turns and looks directly at her.

54

Tannahill hears the sound of footsteps splashing closer and turns to find Laughton heading across the embankment holding an enormous umbrella above her head.

He squints at her from beneath the folded-up newspaper he is now using as a hat, smiling up as she stops in front of him. She stares down at him for a moment, her face unreadable as he blinks away the water dripping into his eyes.

'What are you doing here?' Laughton asks.

Tannahill looks around at the rain-soaked embankment as if he's just noticed where he is then shrugs. 'Getting wet.'

'Did you not check the weather before deciding to camp out in front of my flat for the night?'

'It was an impulse kind of deal; there wasn't much planning involved.'

'Have you not slept?'

Tannahill smiles, reaches behind him and produces a flask. 'Who needs sleep when you can have coffee? You want some? It's a bit old but it's still warm-ish.'

'How long have you been here?'

Tannahill shrugs. 'I don't know. A while.'

'Did you not go for cocktails with Evelyn Prior?'

He smiles and shakes his head. 'Here' – he gestures at the

bench beside him – 'take a seat.' He notices it's wet and uses his newspaper hat to blot the water away, newsprint bleeding through the picture of the Home Secretary on the cover as rain soaks through it.

Laughton sits down and holds the umbrella over them both as they stare out at the river, the soft percussion of rain on the tight material like a drumroll anticipating . . . something. They sit like this for a few moments before Laughton speaks.

'So, you turned down a date with a hot woman in order to sit out here in the cold.'

Tannahill nods. 'When you say it out loud like that it does sound pretty stupid.'

'Why though? Do you think Billy Carver might swing round and you were hoping to catch him?'

He shakes his head. 'No, because you're here and I wanted to make sure you were OK.'

'You don't think I can look after myself.'

Tannahill smiles. 'I *know* you can look after yourself. I actually wanted to keep the squad car here until we managed to track down Carver, but that didn't fly with the bean counters so' – he smiles and opens his hands – 'here I am. I couldn't sleep anyway so figured I could not sleep here just as well as in my flat.'

'Why didn't you buzz me?'

He shrugs. 'Wasn't sure I was welcome. Also, I didn't want to risk waking up Gracie. I'm not exactly in her good books at the best of times, and I'm guessing this is hardly one of those.' He looks back out at the river, the drumming of the rain filling the silence as he watches the black water sliding by and imagines Shelby's headless body floating past. He looks away. 'How is she?'

Laughton stares at the wet flagstones, cut from the same quarry as Tower Bridge, which is still lit up like a Christmas tree even at this late or early hour. 'She's still pretty mad at me. She thinks I didn't take him seriously and that's the reason he got murdered.'

'That's not why he got killed.'

'Isn't it? I didn't take him seriously, though. When I saw him outside my front door, all I could think of was getting rid of him as quickly as possible. I didn't really listen to what he was saying and I certainly didn't take anything he said to heart. If I'd been more sympathetic, if I'd let him in rather than locking him out, maybe he'd still be alive.'

'What about Malcolm Fowler; is it your fault he's dead too?'

'No, but . . .'

'No, but nothing. The reason Shelby Facer is dead is the same reason Malcolm Fowler is dead: they both mixed with the wrong person more than sixteen years ago and the chickens are coming home to roost. It's got nothing to do with you.'

'It does though. My dad was the one who orchestrated the whole thing. He's the one who made sure Shelby was recruited because he wanted to get him away from me and his as yet unborn granddaughter. And now that granddaughter is royally pissed off at me and I actually think she has good reason.'

Tannahill looks away and shakes his head. 'I don't understand why you're being so hard on yourself. Everything you've said only outlines exactly why none of this is your fault.'

'Not letting him in the other night was my fault.'

'Why? He turned up out of the blue after sixteen years, late at night, spouting some crazy story about a killer on his heels. Of course you were never going to let him in. You'd have been crazy if you had.'

Laughton shakes her head. 'I should have listened to him though. Gracie wanted me to hear him out and I should have done it for her.'

'But she's a fifteen-year-old girl; she probably doesn't know who her best friend is from one day to the next. You can't let a fifteen-year-old run your life. You need to remember that you're the parent and she's the child. In fact, you need to remind Gracie of that fact and tell her she needs to cut you some slack. Being a grown-up is hard. You made the right choice.'

Laughton shakes her head and continues to stare down at the wet ground. 'I don't think it's going to work out between us.'

'What!?' A frown flashes across Tannahill's face. 'What are you talking about? We're over now because your ex of sixteen years ago just got murdered?'

'I'm a nightmare, Tann. I'm never available, physically or emotionally. I've got a kid, I've got so much baggage that I literally discovered a secret storage unit filled with more of the stuff yesterday. You'd be way better off without me.'

'Why?'

She turns and looks at him, not quite understanding his question. 'Because of all the above. Look, I'm giving you an easy way out here – you should take it and run.'

'I don't want to.' He turns to her so he's fully facing her now. 'I like that you work all the time, because the work you do makes a difference and you're so gifted at it. I like that you're smarter than everyone else, including me, and I also like the way you don't use it like a stick to beat other people with. I like the fact that you have no idea how beautiful you are, and all those things you listed as problems I see as points of interest. With most people, life declines into boring function, but with you it will always be adventure. Why would I run from that?'

He continues looking at her, expecting her to shake her head, or look angry, or frustrated, or any number of standard, non-standard Laughton-type responses. But doesn't do any of these. Instead her eyes shine with what might be tears, though it's hard to tell in the darkness and the rain. She smiles and leans in, putting her hand on the side of his face. 'How can I let you go after you say something like that.'

Then she kisses him on the lips, softly and tenderly, like she really, really means it.

55

Gracie watches her mother with Tannahill from the kitchen balcony.

She'd been lying awake when she heard her sneaking out and had been watching them the whole time. The umbrella is hiding them from view but she knows what they're doing. She can see their backs, can see how close they are together, and it makes her want to scream. She grips the balcony rail and feels like ripping it off and hurling it down at them.

Her father is dead and they're behaving like it's prom night.

She can't believe her mother, already lining up the next daddy figure when the old one, her *real* one is barely cold and not even in the ground.

She turns away and storms back into the dark apartment, filled with the fury that had settled on her the moment her mother told her what had happened to her father. She needs to get away from here and has an idea, formed in the wakeful darkness, about where she might go.

She heads back into the chaotic mess of her bedroom, grabs her school bag and upends it on to her bed. Books and old snack wrappers tumble in a pile on to the crumpled covers, along with the stack of documents relating to her family tree. She pulls out the diagram of the tree itself and sits on her bed,

grabbing her phone from where it's charging on her bedside table and launches Google. She looks at the spots where her father had written the names of his parents, and copies them into the search field – *Graham and Iris Facer, Ravenfleet.*

The results she gets back are skimpy and chart small lives that made very little dent on the modern, online world. There's a mention of them on a golf club website, along with a list of other people who had taken part in a sponsored 24-hour game of golf to raise money for the Martlets Hospice. There's another mention of Graham Facer in a local news article about a campaign to put speed cameras up on a road through Ravenfleet. And there's a notice on a funeral home website recording the details of the funeral and remembrance service for Graham Facer, survived by his wife Iris with no mention of a son. There's no address either, so Gracie opens the phone directory, does a name search and discovers there are, surprisingly, three Iris Facers in Ravenfleet.

Gracie taps her fingers on the edge of her phone as she thinks, but stops herself when she realizes she's doing it. Tapping is something her mother does and at the moment she wants to put as much distance between herself and her mother as she can. She scrolls back through the results page and looks up the address of the golf club mentioned in the earlier article, cross referencing it with the three Iris Facers and finds only one who lives within walking distance of the club. They might have driven there from further afield, of course, but it's all she has to go on. She looks up the address on Google Maps and switches to Street View. The house is a brick box with a neat lawn in front of it and lace curtains hanging in all the windows that seem to hail from another time. It feels right. And even if it isn't, there are only two other options. She imagines herself walking up to the house, knocking on the door and waiting for her grandmother to open it. But what would she say to her?

Hi, I'm the granddaughter you probably didn't know you had – and by the way, your son's dead.

She saves the map, opens her contacts and scrolls down to the entry for 'D' that her dad had put in. She whispers his phone number as if it's some kind of spell, feeling unbearably sad that she never even got to call him or send him a message. She thinks about their conversation in the café earlier, how easy it had felt talking to him, and how she had never imagined it would be the only time they would ever get to do something like that. She tries to remember the last thing he had said to her but can't, not exactly. It was something about booking a table at the Ritz next time they met up because Gracie had said she'd pay. But there wasn't going to be a next time, and now she wished she'd said goodbye to him properly.

She types a message, reads it back then presses *send*, hoping that, wherever her father is now, he might somehow still get it.

56

The buzz of the phone cuts through the rushing sound of water.

Calais ties off the final knot then heads over to the shelf where Minty Fowler's burner phone is charging next to the other items he has taken from the men he killed. He adds Webber's wallet and his car keys to the collection then picks up the phone and reads the message.

Goodbye Dad. I'm so sorry about what happened to you. Wish we'd had more time together.

Calais reads it again – thinking.

He unplugs the phone and walks back over to the trapdoor where Webber's body lies ready for disposal, tied to the moped to help it sink. The sound of rushing water is getting louder now, telling him the tide is rising. He picks up Webber's hands and head, tosses them on to the trapdoor next to the rest of him, grabs the large lever to the side of the stall and hauls back on it. The sound of rushing water doubles in volume as the trapdoor releases and the bike with Webber tied to it slides into the channel and is instantly carried away. He releases the lever and the trapdoor closes again, locking back in place with a loud *thunk*, ready for the next load.

The sluice room had been something he'd discovered through Minty; a run-down, forgotten building that was falling apart and had no modern use because it was listed as being of historical importance. Back when the Thames had been little more than an open sewer, the building had been specifically designed and constructed to flush away the waste from the surrounding area, particularly nearby Hampton Court Palace, which, ironically, had been Henry VIII's main home. All the rubbish from the royal estate was collected during the day then brought here, dumped in the trapdoor stall and flushed into the river every time the tide turned and the waters flowed out to sea again, carrying all the crap with it. A deep channel under the floor diverted water from the river and narrowed beneath the trapdoor to make the water flow faster, creating a kind of super flush. It was ingenious and also a testament to the quality of Victorian engineering that the mechanism still worked.

He moves away from the trapdoor and stands by the pot-bellied stove, feeling the reassuring heat pushing back the damp as he re-reads the message from Gracie.

Gracie Rees, John Rees's granddaughter.

Rees had been behind everything, that's what Webber had confirmed. People tended to tell the truth when they were trying to save a hand from being chopped off. And though John Rees was dead, that didn't discharge his debt. In the world of street loans, debts never died with the debtor, they simply passed on to the next of kin.

Calais hits *Reply* and his fingers hover over the screen as he thinks about what bait he needs to lay in order to draw her in. In the end he keeps it simple because the simplest bait is always best. He types:

Hi!

Then:

Surprise!

Three dots appear, showing him someone is typing, then:

Dad?

Calais smiles.

Who else?

The three dots reappear, followed by:

I thought you were dead.

He taps a reply, the sound of rushing water drowning out the electronic clicks of the keyboard.

Not quite. Long story. Let's meet up and I'll tell you everything.

The three dots come back and his smile broadens when he sees her one-word reply.

Where?

57

Morning comes reluctantly to London.

The rain that started in the small hours drizzles on, drifting down from a sky the same flat grey as the city beneath.

In the early editions of the morning papers a new story about record hospital waiting lists has pushed Charles Nixon off the front page and shifted the uncomfortable spotlight on to a different government department and minister.

People rise, people get dressed, people go to work.

The river flows on in its timeless slow pulse, emptying again now and carrying away the night's secrets.

Beth Webber calls her husband again, leaving a message this time, wondering where he is and if everything's OK. Brendan has often come home late before but never not at all, and she wonders if this is the sign of a shift that he's becoming more cavalier and less bothered about keeping up appearances. She's suspected for a while her husband is not faithful, not because of any hard evidence, but because of a feeling and a certain evasiveness whenever she asks about his movements. She puts her phone down on the marble countertop and glances at it every few seconds as she makes breakfast smoothies for the kids, waiting for him to call or text her back.

In her own kitchen, Laughton pours hot water into the teapot and stares out at the grey, thinking about her early-morning conversation with Tannahill and wondering if he is up yet. She had reluctantly sent him home before dawn, wanting more than anything to invite him in but far too worried about how Gracie would react. There would be time for them, she believed that, but not yet, not now.

She picks up her phone as she waits for the tea to brew and sends him a text:

Call me when you're awake, I've had an idea.

The phone buzzes almost immediately and she smiles as she answers it.

'Did I wake you?'

'No,' Tannahill sounds fully awake, the traffic noise behind him suggesting he's already left home.

'Did you get any sleep?'

'Some. You?'

'Couple of hours.'

'Better than nothing. We can sleep when we're dead. What's your idea?'

Laughton lowers her voice and checks behind her before answering. 'I was thinking that Shelby must have been killed and dumped fairly soon after being released from Whitechapel.'

'Yes, within a few hours certainly.'

'But his manner of death and post-mortem injuries are exactly the same as the first body, so the killer most likely took him to the same quiet place where he killed Malcolm Fowler. Also, both bodies were found when the tide was going out, Fowler at low tide and Shelby when the tide was dropping.'

Laughton drifts over to the window and looks out at the grey vista and down at the river.

'So, if they were both killed and dumped at the same place, it must be somewhere upriver, somewhere in West London, but

definitely in London because of the small window of opportunity the killer would have had between Shelby being released and him washing up in the reeds by Kew Gardens.'

'Where though?'

Laughton stares into the grey-black water of the Thames, the waterline low again, revealing the wooden stubs of old piers poking up from the mud like vertebrae. She can see the water bunching up on one side of them, pushed by the current as it heads out to sea. She smiles.

'How would you like to go on a date?' she says.

'What, like now?'

'Yeah, like right now. Don't worry, it's work-related so you can square it with your boss. It's a very "us" kind of a date.' She hears a noise behind her and turns as Gracie shuffles into the kitchen, her eyes red and her skin blotchy, like she's been crying.

'I'll text you the address,' Laughton says, 'talk later.' She hangs up before Tannahill can reply and opens a cupboard filled with identical white, evenly spaced mugs. 'Morning,' she says, as brightly as she can. 'You want some tea?'

'No. Have they caught dad's killer yet?'

'Not yet.' Laughton takes a mug down for herself and starts filling it from the teapot. 'Listen, I think maybe you should stay off school today.' She turns back to her. 'You look like you haven't slept much, so I imagine your head's not really in the mood for maths, or geography, or whatever's on the menu today.'

Gracie nods. 'OK.' She goes to the fridge and opens the door to inspect the contents.

'I've got a couple of work things to do but I should be back by lunchtime,' Laughton says, joining her by the open fridge door and retrieving the milk. 'We can hang out together. Talk about things. Only if you want to, though.'

Gracie nods 'No, yeah that sounds good.' She grabs an Actimel and heads out of the kitchen without another word.

Laughton watches after her for a second, trying to fathom her mood. She seemed tired and wrung out, but her anger seemed to have blown itself out at least. She was grieving and grief was a process that couldn't be hurried, Laughton knew that well enough, so a day at home taking it easy was exactly what Gracie needed. It also meant she wouldn't have to worry about where she was.

She checks the time, still early enough for her to beat the worst of the traffic but only if she sets off now. She grabs a re-usable cup from the cupboard and decants her tea into it, then opens a new message to Tannahill and types:

Eel Pie Island, Twickenham.
Meet you there in an hour.

58

Kenwright gets into work early, hoping to get ahead of the news, and is relieved to see that his boss is no longer the lead story on all the early editions. Charlie is in too and he can see him in his office through the distorted glass panel by the door, pacing around, on the phone to Nigel again, still reassuring him, only with more conviction today. It'll be Health Secretary Chris Murphy's turn to fight for his job today.

Kenwright leans forward and looks down the length of the corridor, hoping to see the mail trolley trundling towards him with the bundle of morning papers. When it's not, he sits back and starts working through his inbox, deleting most things and flagging the few items that need attention. The request to reopen the case files for Operation Henry 8 is near the bottom. He stares at it for a moment, feeling irritated, then opens it and reads the email explaining why the request has been resubmitted. He drums his fingers on the surface of his desk for a moment, picks up his phone and scrolls back through the recently dialled numbers until he finds Brendan Webber's mobile number and calls it. It rings out and jumps to voicemail. Kenwright hangs up without leaving a message then looks back up at the blurred figure of his boss behind the frosted glass, no longer pacing so presumably off the phone. He rises from

his chair, checking down the corridor for the mail cart again as he heads over to the Home Secretary's closed door.

Kenwright knocks twice then opens the door without waiting for a response.

Nixon is sitting at his desk, scrolling through something on his laptop and looking much more chipper than he had done the previous day. He glances up at Kenwright and smiles. 'Have you seen the news, Tom?' He turns the laptop round to show him the BBC website. 'Thank God for whoever decided to leak those hospital waiting lists. We live to fight another day.'

'Yes.'

Nixon's smile falters slightly as he picks up on Kenwright's tone. 'Oh, come on, Tom, we dodged a bullet, you could at least pretend to be happy for five minutes. We should enjoy this moment of calm while we can because something else shitty is bound to come along sooner or later.' His expression darkens as something occurs to him. 'Or has it come along already?'

'No, nothing like that. It's that old case I told you about yesterday, the one Brendan was involved with.'

'What about it?'

'The request to declassify it has been resubmitted.'

'Well, deny it again.'

'The reason they resubmitted the request, sir, is because of another body that washed up. The victim appears to have also been involved in this case.'

Nixon nods. 'So, you think Brendan might be in trouble.'

'Maybe. I called him yesterday and told him to be cautious.'

'Did you tell him why?'

'No. But I called him again just now and he didn't answer.'

'Really?' Nixon checks the time on his gold Rolex. 'Maybe he's in a meeting or something.'

'Maybe. Still, I was wondering if, given that yesterday's storm seems to have passed, I should maybe grant this request to unlock the files? It might help the police catch whoever's going

293

around killing these people, and it does seem like Brendan might be on his hit list.'

Nixon looks back down at his laptop, mentally weighing up the benefits of helping a friend and campaign donor and preserving his own self-interest. He nods slowly as if coming to some momentous decision.

'I think we should leave it for now,' he says. 'No point chucking a cup of petrol on the fire now the flames are finally dying down. I'm sure Brendan will be fine. He's a big boy; he can look after himself.'

59

Gracie watches her mother from the balcony, walking swiftly away from the Brannigan building and heading in the direction of Tower Hill tube station. She waits until she has gone then hurries into her bedroom and pulls her school bag out from under her bed. She unplugs her phone charger and stuffs it inside, along with a grabbed selection of clothes and toiletries. She opens the drawer of her bedside table and takes out a small bundle of banknotes, all the babysitting money she's earned from the last few months. Using cash instead of cards will make it harder for her mother to trace her. She'll need to swap the SIM in her phone too, but she can do that later. Growing up with a criminologist had its benefits.

She hauls the bag up over her shoulder and heads into the kitchen to raid the cupboards for snacks and bottled water. She doesn't have much of a plan, might not even be away that long, but she wants to be prepared in case.

She takes one last look around, trying to think about what she might have forgotten then replies to the text she got earlier from her dad:

Leaving now. Should be there in about an hour.
Gx

60

The rain has thankfully stopped and Tannahill is already waiting for Laughton by the time she makes it to Eel Pie Island. He stands by the footbridge linking the island to the riverbank with a curious expression on his face.

'Why are we here exactly?' he asks the moment she's in earshot.

Laughton smiles and leans up to kiss him. 'Everyone should come to Eel Pie Island once in their lifetime,' she says, as if that explains everything, then she turns and heads away across the footbridge.

Tannahill follows, scanning the colourful jumble of buildings lining the bank of the island opposite. He can see the burned-out shell of what looks like an old art deco hotel further along the shore. 'And what exactly is Eel Pie Island?'

'An anomaly,' Laughton says, marching on, the sound of their footsteps reverberating on the metal bridge. 'A piece of prime Thames-front real-estate that's been protected from developers by the one thing that can't be bought or broken.' She pauses for a moment to give Tannahill the opportunity to guess what that might be before answering her own riddle. 'Community. There are about fifty homes on the island as well as artists' workshops, a recording studio, people living in houseboats.

They collectively own the island and there's no way any of them are ever selling. I mean, look at it. Why would you?'

Tannahill does look at it. It looks like a bunch of large garden sheds have been built along the shoreline then painted a multitude of colours that the weather has tried to batter back to grey. Strings of lights and bunting link the houses, flapping and sagging between roofs, and winding around posts and strange sculptures. One of the shack-like houses has an old car in front that looks like something from the 1930s and is the exact colour of rust.

Laughton reaches the end of the bridge and stops by a man standing by a bristling array of fishing rods. He doesn't look up, seemingly far more interested in threading something large and wriggling on to a fishhook.

'Any luck?' Tannahill asks.

The angler nods as he manages to spear the worm on to his hook.

'What's biting?'

'Eels mainly.' The angler nods at a small, hand-painted sign by the bridge saying WELCOME TO EEL PIE ISLAND. 'Clue's in the name.'

He turns and casts the still wriggling worm into the Thames with a *plop*.

'Come on,' Laughton says, marching on past a faded purple shack with solar panels on the roof and a small wind turbine spinning away in the breeze. 'I need to introduce you to Buddy.'

'Buddy!' Tannahill says, hurrying to keep up with her. 'Who's Buddy?'

'Someone I came across a couple of years ago while working on an old case. His full name is Budleigh Salterton, presumably after the place in Devon, but his friends call him Buddy.' She points at one of the larger buildings at the end of the row. 'That's his house there.'

Tannahill looks past her at a brick-and-wood structure that

appears to be a little more substantial than the other buildings, white-painted bricks forming a ground floor that supports a higgledy-piggledy upper floor made of wood, with over-hanging gables that give the impression that the house is looming.

'Buddy built it himself.' Laughton stops in front of a studded oak front door that looks like it might have been stolen from an old church, takes hold of the huge iron hoop hanging from the mouth of a lion and bangs it twice, the sound startling a seagull on the roof and sending it flapping away in noisy flight.

Tannahill looks back down the street. There are no cars here, no vehicles of any kind except for an old-fashioned bike propped up against one of the houses and a rotting boat filled with flowers and wispy clumps of grass. The whole place looks like a set for some post-apocalyptic drama where only the artists survived. The sharp noise of a latch being lifted makes him turn back around in time to see the ecclesiastical door swing open. It reveals a scarecrow of a man wearing a dark blue apron, with tufts of silvering red hair sticking out from his skull at all angles, like he might have recently electrocuted himself. He is tall but slightly stooped, like a man who has spent his life bent over in a workshop, his hunched posture accentuated by the way he is tilting his head down to peer at them over the top of his half-moon glasses.

'Dr Rees!' the man exclaims, the wrinkles around his eyes deepening as he smiles broadly in sudden recognition. 'How lovely. Come on in, no need to stand on ceremony. I was just prepping a body, you can help me finish up.'

He turns and lopes back into the cluttered depths of his house, moving swiftly and with a dancer's grace.

Tannahill leans into Laughton and murmurs. 'What does he mean "prepping a body"?'

Laughton smiles. 'You'll see.'

She steps into the house and follows Buddy down the hallway.

Tannahill follows, scanning the walls which are crammed from floor to ceiling with old charts and maps, the type with wonky outlines of barely recognizable countries and sea serpents snaking out of the oceans next to phrases like 'Beware all Seafarers' and 'Here be Monsters'. They pass through a kitchen that is warm and womblike and smells of sugar, then on through an industrial-looking sliding steel door into a surprisingly large, bright workshop. Light pours in from angled skylights illuminating the space below that looks as if a DIY enthusiast's shed had a love-child with a Victorian steamship.

Tools line up in serried ranks along every wall, held in place by magnetic strips, and shelves line the rest of the available space, crammed with well-thumbed books and old brass nautical instruments. A pot-bellied stove squats in one corner, with a small desk next to it on which a MacBook stands open, looking anachronistic. The back wall is all glass with French doors opening on to a jetty with a small sailing boat tied to it and a glorious view of the river. But it's not the million-dollar view that snags Tannahill's attention, it is the large, marble-topped island that occupies the centre of the room and the macabre object lying upon it.

'Isn't he a beauty?' Budleigh says, sweeping his hand over the object. 'I've got a contact in Smithfields who can get me one of these in any size, anytime I need it.'

The object Budleigh is so proud of is a full-sized pig, dead but with everything still attached – head, trotters, tail. The presence of the pig is in itself surprising, but what makes it more so is that it has been carefully dressed in human clothes. A T-shirt and jacket is stretched over its upper half, altered to accommodate the different proportions of the animal and stitched roughly back in place with thick black thread, giving the whole thing a vaguely Frankenstein-ish vibe. On the lower half the pig wears cargo shorts that have been similarly altered and stitched back together, leaving only a small area of flank exposed where a deep incision has been cut into the flesh.

'The clothes are necessary for drag, you see,' Budleigh explains, then explodes into laughter as he realizes something. 'Not drag as in ladies' clothes, of course, I mean drag as in friction – from the water.'

He turns back to the fully clothed pig and starts feeding something small and black with wires attached into the exposed wound.

Laughton looks over at Tannahill, a mischievous smile on her face, clearly enjoying the whole spectacle.

'What is this?' Tannahill mouths at her.

Over at the table, Budleigh snatches up a needle and starts stitching up the incision using the same thick black suture thread he used to mend the clothes. 'This is the GPS tracker,' he says, pointing at the electronic device he's stitching inside the pig. 'The water level is up because of all the recent storms and I wanted to see how that might affect the side currents in the Tideway.'

Tannahill stares down at the pig as he realizes what's happening here. 'You're going to dump this in the river?'

'Of course,' Budleigh replies. 'The size and density of pig's flesh is the closest thing to a human corpse, so it's by far the best thing to use for current-modelling exercises. Well, an actual human corpse would be the best thing, obviously . . .' He stares out of the window, a look of mournful disappointment on his face. 'Sadly, the authorities didn't really go for that idea – said it might frighten the tourists.' He looks back at Tannahill and brightens up. 'Still, a pig is almost as good.'

Tannahill looks back down at Frankenstein's pig in its T-shirt and shorts. 'Surely the sight of this thing floating past would be equally as alarming?'

'Oh no, I always wait until night-time to drop them in the drink, so there's hardly anyone around. I'm not a complete maniac.' He chuckles to himself and continues stitching the GPS tracker inside the body of the pig. 'So, what can I help you with, Dr Rees. Something juicy, I hope?'

'Two floaters,' Laughton says, 'both killed in the same way. We're assuming by the same person. Both had their heads and hands carefully removed post-mortem, so the killer must have access to somewhere private and out of the way, a place they could take their time and be sure they would not be discovered. Also somewhere near, or even on, the river.'

'You mean a place like this,' Budleigh says, with a twinkle in his eye.

'Yes, pretty much. Neither body was weighted down, so we're assuming that – coupled with the grisly nature of the murders – the killer wanted the bodies to be found. Also, neither body exhibited much in the way of post-mortem predation or decomposition.'

'Any signs of refrigeration?'

'No. We think they were killed, mutilated, then dumped in the river all within a few hours.'

'And you want me to help you figure out where they were dropped in the drink?'

'If you can.'

Buddy looks almost offended. 'Of course I can. What's more, it will be my absolute pleasure. Let's run your data through TiM and see what he says.' Buddy ties off the suture, snips it with an oversized pair of scissors then moves over to the laptop and starts closing windows and opening others.

'TiM stands for Tidal Modelling,' Laughton explains to Tannahill. 'It's a programme Buddy devised that takes all the tide and current data he's accumulated over the years and uses it to model and plot where an object in the water will end up at any given time. Only we're going to try and do it backwards.'

'Indeed we are,' Buddy says. 'Now where were the two bodies found?'

Laughton looks over at Tannahill.

'Oh, er, the first one was found the night before last by Tower Bridge.'

'Which side?'

'North bank.'

'Ahhhh, Dead Man's Hole.' Buddy turns back to the laptop and starts tapping away on his keyboard. 'Lots of things end up there. What time was this?'

'Around eight o'clock.'

'Eight p.m., night before last.' Buddy nods. 'Low tide, that's useful. And you say the bodies showed little sign of decomposition or predation?'

'Yes.'

'What about the second body?'

'That was found yesterday morning at around ten on the south bank by Kew Gardens.'

'I'm guessing the reed banks caught it?'

'Yes.'

Buddy nods. 'Course they did. Reed beds are natural filters – rubbish in, oxygen out, carbon capture in the middle, perfect and natural solution to CO_2 emissions. It's a shame there are so few reed beds left.' He checks a chart on the wall. 'Ten a.m. would mean the tide was heading out again, so I would say at a guess your killer's lair must be around here somewhere. Can't be too much further west as the river stops being tidal at Teddington Lock, so anything dumped further upstream would stay there. Were these bodies clothed or naked?'

'Both fully clothed, both between thirteen and fourteen stone, both around six feet tall – or at least they would have been before their heads were removed.'

Buddy's fingers tap away, transferring all the details into his database. 'OK,' he says finally. 'I think that should do it. Let's see what TiM says.' He hits *Return* with a flourish and the screen blinks, then a new window pops up showing a map of the Thames with several blue and red dots plotted on to it.

Buddy points at the dots. 'The red dots show the journey your first body would most likely have taken as it was carried

by the outgoing tide, given its size and condition. The blue dots track the second one. Now bear in mind that, despite all my years of research and data gathering, this is still a fairly inexact science as there are so many unknown variables at play in a body of water like the Thames – sewer overflow discharges, vehicle wake displacements and so on, all creating mini currents that would have an effect on a free-floating object in the water. Having said that, the twin facts that we have two very similar objects to track and we believe both originated at the same place, means we can aggregate the findings and at least narrow it down to a rough place of origin. Now let me see . . .' He clicks on the map and zooms in on the left-hand side of it where the river narrows and the blue and red dots are closer together. 'This area here looks like a good candidate.'

'Where is that?' Laughton leans in for a closer look at the screen.

'It's the Ham Lands Nature Reserve,' Buddy replies. 'It's about a kilometre upriver from where we are now. It's nice and remote, not many people there, but there are plenty of old, non-residential buildings on both sides of the river.'

A buzzing sounds in the room and Tannahill fumbles his phone from his pocket. 'Could you give us a printout of that?' he asks, nodding at the laptop.

'Er, normally yes,' Buddy replies, 'but unfortunately my printer is out of ink. One of the very few downsides of living here is that there are no local shops I can pop to.'

'Could you email me the results, then? It might be useful to have if I need a search warrant.'

'Of course,' Buddy turns back to the laptop and opens an email.

'Email them to me,' Laughton says. 'You already have my address and I can forward them on.'

Tannahill checks the caller ID and moves away when he sees that it's Baker.

'Morning,' he says, staring down at the dressed pig.

'There's been a development,' Baker replies, straight to business. 'We just got a call from a Mrs Elizabeth Webber, Brendan Webber's wife. She says she hasn't talked to him since yesterday evening and now he's not answering his phone.'

61

Gracie stops in front of the line of old red-brick buildings and checks the address on the text her father had sent her. She'd never been in this part of West London before and hadn't been too sure what to expect, but whatever she'd expected it hadn't been this.

She looks back up at the buildings, a long line of two-storey structures with tall windows covered with metal security grilles and weeds growing out of broken gutters. It looked like this had once been a factory or something, though whatever had been made here, they definitely didn't make them any more.

Gracie hits reply on the text with the address on it and types:

I'm here.

She stands, staring up at the building, unwilling to get any closer until she's absolutely sure she's in the right place.

Her phone shudders in her hand and she reads the reply:

Head round the right-hand side of the tallest building. There's a door by a parked car. It's unlocked.

305

Three dots appear showing he's typing something else:

Can't wait to see you.

Gracie looks back up at the row of buildings. The tallest one is to her left and almost completely hidden by trees. In fact, apart from this row of crumbling buildings, the whole place is covered with trees and bushes, so much so that it almost doesn't feel like she's in London at all.

She listens to the sound of birds and the rustle of the wind in the leaves, takes a breath and heads over to a small pathway between the tallest building and the trees littered with crushed beer cans and tissues. She picks her way through the litter as she rounds the edge of the outer wall and the greenery opens out into what looks like an old goods yard. Weeds grow tall from cracks in the concrete, and piles of rotting pallets are stacked over to one side. She can glimpse the river through a screen of reeds and weeds, which makes her feel more grounded. She can see the same river from her home, so its presence calms her a little. There is also a car parked in front of a metal security door, which suggests she must be in the right place.

Gracie emerges from the green and heads over to the car, also green but shiny and metallic, its modern newness in sharp contrast to the crumbling backdrop. She peers through the tinted windows as she walks past; there's nothing inside but an empty plastic water bottle.

She stops by the solid metal door and looks for a handle. A metal hasp on one side has a chain hanging from it with a padlock threaded through one of the links. It's unlocked, like the message said it would be.

She turns her head slightly and listens, hoping to hear comforting sounds, like music or conversation, but all she can hear is the burble of rushing water. She reaches out, opens the door slowly and the sound grows louder.

An old wooden door hangs open beyond the steel security

door, splintered and graffitied – DG ♡ CB, FULHAM FC, SKINZ. Beyond the broken door the building is almost completely dark apart from a weak orange light glowing in a stairwell over to her right. The light is coming from the basement and the thought of basements in creepy old buildings makes Gracie pause. She unlocks her phone to use the torch and the last message from her father pops up on the screen:

Can't wait to see you.

She turns on the torch and steps inside.

The light from her phone pushes back the darkness, illuminating the floor ahead. It is littered with vaguely disturbing rubbish: more crushed cans, broken glass, a few empty Nos canisters, a bent syringe, some rags with something dark on them that could be oil but probably wasn't. She sweeps the light in front of her, trying to see what else the building contains, but it's too big and too dark and the light only carries for a few feet. All she can see is that there's something huge in the centre of the room, her torch managing to pick out the outlines of thick pipes and a large wheel that reminds her of old-fashioned steam engines. Maybe this had been a pumping station before electric pumps did all the heavy lifting, the sound of rushing water would suggest so.

She sweeps the torch towards the lower stairwell, where both the light and the sound of water are coming from. She starts walking towards it, crunching pebbles of glass underfoot.

She doesn't see the wooden door swing shut behind her.

She doesn't see the figure with the bike helmet on, stepping out from behind it.

62

The morning traffic is maddeningly slow, even with the cab sliding down the bus lanes and avoiding the worst of it.

Tannahill is on the phone, Laughton stares ahead at the road, hating all the cars on it.

'We got a trace on Webber's mobile,' Tannahill says, covering the mouthpiece of his phone with his hand. 'It was in the city near Bank station between five fifteen yesterday evening and five forty-five this morning. It's been on the move again ever since, first slowly, going up and down all the streets like he might be walking or wandering about, but now he's picked up speed and is heading south. He's still not responding to calls or messages, though. Hang on.'

He uncovers the mouthpiece and frowns as he listens intently to whatever new information is being passed on to him.

Laughton stares ahead, weighing up the new information.

Static for twelve hours then mobile again but only at walking pace, up and down all the streets, all calls going unanswered.

ALL the streets? Why would he go up and down all the streets?

'He's heading somewhere south of the river,' Tannahill says, relaying the information as he gets it.

'Whereabouts south of the river?' Laughton asks.

'Not sure yet, somewhere south-east.'

Laughton nods as she joins the dots. 'I bet it's Bexley.'

'Could he be heading to Bexley?' Tannahill says to whoever's on the other end of the line. He waits for a response then nods. 'Yeah, he's heading in that direction, why?'

Laughton shakes her head. 'It's not him. Bexley is where the two main refuse collection points for London are based. Carver must have dumped his phone in a bin last night, which is why it didn't move until early this morning then went up and down every street at walking pace.'

Tannahill blows out a long breath of frustration. 'It was the binmen on their rounds.'

Laughton nods. 'If you go to Bexley you'll waste a lot of time and resources and all you'll end up finding is Webber's phone. Carver's pulling the same trick he did with the licence plate, wasting our time and making us look in the wrong place.'

Tannahill shakes his head. 'Did you get all that? Keep monitoring the cell towers until the signal stops moving. If it does end up in one of the dumps at Bexley we can send a uniform down to retrieve it. All other units stand down, I'm heading in now with a new lead about where Carver might be based.'

He hangs up and stares at his phone for a moment, scrolling through his morning messages and emails. 'Ah great!'

'What?'

'My request to open up the Operation Henry 8 files has been denied again.' He starts tapping out a reply.

'Are you telling them Webber is missing and asking them to reconsider?'

'Yeah. You would have thought that, with Webber being the Home Secretary's friend and everything, he might want to help us catch the killer before Webber ends up in the Thames like the others.'

'These are politicians you're talking about,' Laughton replies, 'a politician is someone who tells everyone he cares about them when the only one he really cares about is himself. Is it worth

sending a load of uniforms to the area Buddy identified upriver and doing a house-to-house?'

'Maybe. I'm not sure I'll get authorization though, and it's a hell of a big area to cover if we're having to patrol both sides of the river. How long do you think we have?'

'Probably until the next high tide. Carver obviously has to dump the bodies when the tide is going out to make sure they get carried away by the current. If he released them when the tide was coming in, they'd go upstream and get stuck at Teddington Lock, which is obviously too close to wherever he is based.'

Tannahill googles the Thames tide charts on his phone. 'Next high tide is three forty this afternoon. That gives us less than six hours to find him.'

Tannahill and Laughton stare out of their windows in silence for a moment, lost in their individual thoughts. They're close to the NoLMS HQ building now.

'I think if I could narrow it down a bit, I might be able to get a small search team together in time.' Tannahill turns to Laughton. 'When I went to Malcolm Fowler's address yesterday, the place Shelby had been staying, it seemed more like a rental than a home. Nothing personal there. Didn't feel very lived in. I'm thinking someone like Fowler had to have lots of addresses dotted around London, places for people to stay, places to stash things. If I can track down a list of those addresses and find one in West London close to the river, it might be the place Carver is using as a base. It might even have been the place Carver met with Fowler and killed him in the first place.'

Laughton nods. 'It's a good thought.'

'What you up to today, wanna help us out?'

'Yeah, of course. Any chance for us to spend some quality time together hunting down a killer.'

Tannahill smiles. 'Like I said – always adventure.'

Laughton thinks about Gracie safely at home and checks the time. 'I've got to go see someone first, but I can swing back

after if Gracie is OK. In fact I think helping you catch Shelby's killer and bringing him to justice would also help both of us with the current Gracie situation.'

'Can't hurt. Who you going to see?'

'A diamond expert.'

'Whoa, I know I said some things last night but it's still a bit soon to be shopping for rings.'

Laughton smiles. 'Don't get ahead of yourself, Romeo, I'm following the money. We know from Shelby's testimony that Carver's idea of payback isn't only about getting even with the people who crossed him, it's also about getting paid. And something must have happened to those uncut stones. I'm going to talk to someone who might know where they went or who handled them. If we can trace the money it might help us find Carver, because he'll be chasing it too.'

The cab pulls up in front of the ugly block of former insurance buildings and Tannahill turns to Laughton and puts his hand on her cheek. 'I hope this works out,' he says.

Laughton smiles. 'You mean us or the investigation?'

He leans in and kisses her. 'Both.'

63

The London Diamond Bourse occupies an angular, slightly dated white marble-clad building at 100 Hatton Garden, EC1. Hatton Garden, London's diamond district, has been the home of the bourse ever since the Nazis sent the diamond merchants fleeing from Antwerp in 1940 with their stock sewn into their clothes, or sometimes even swallowed to be retrieved later. Laughton learns all this from Maddox, the smart and eager young man who meets her at the front door at exactly the time prearranged on the prompt reply she got to her midnight email. He marches ahead of her now, leading her briskly down nondescript corridors lined with anonymous doors giving no clue as to the sparkling business being conducted behind them.

'The original bourse wasn't actually on Hatton Garden,' Maddox says as he unlocks another door using his thumbprint, 'it was just round the corner on Greville Street in a place called Mrs Cohen's Kosher Café. Diamonds were exchanged and traded there over coffee with little more than a handshake to seal the deal and nothing but trust to bind it.'

The door springs open and Maddox opens it for Laughton to pass through, then pulls it shut behind them before continuing deeper into the bowels of the building.

'And what is a bourse, exactly?' Laughton asks, feeling like

she's almost having to jog to keep up with his long-limbed pace.

'It's an exchange,' Maddox says, 'a marketplace really, somewhere things get bought and sold. No different from any other goods market, except the things we buy and sell have a little more glamour attached than most commodities.'

Maddox presses his thumb to another keypad and opens the door on to a neat and surprisingly small boardroom decorated with artfully lit black-and-white photos of cut diamonds. A long glass case against one wall displays an assortment of diamonds sparkling under hidden lights.

'Mr Max should be with you shortly,' Maddox says, pointing at a chair. 'Can I get you anything while you wait? Tea, coffee, water?'

'No, I'm fine. Thanks for the mini-tour.'

'Oh, that wasn't really a tour,' Maddox replies, flapping his hands in front of his face as if shooing a fly. 'No one ever gets a proper tour of the bourse. Far too much of a security risk.' He smiles. 'Mr Max shouldn't keep you long.'

He closes the door behind him, leaving Laughton alone in the cramped room. She looks around at the eight upholstered chairs pushed under a heavy, ugly, oval table that looks like it wasn't even stylish back in the eighties when this place was built. She moves away from the door and over to the display case where diamonds in a variety of cuts and sizes sparkle away. There are some uncut stones in there too, a small pile of white rocks about the same size and shape as the pebbles of glass you get when your windscreen shatters.

She'd never really understood the appeal of diamonds, never felt the magic or the mystery of them. They were bits of carbon with delusions of grandeur as far as she could see, useful for their hardness in various industrial applications, but with so much blood and bad karma attached to them it was hard to see past it.

The soft click of the door unlocking behind her makes her

turn as a very neat man in miniature steps into the boardroom. Laughton, not much more than five feet tall herself and allergic to wearing heels, is used to automatically looking up at the world and has to quickly adjust her sightlines down to meet the eyes of the man who has joined her in the room.

'Sorry to have kept you,' he says, his accent managing to sound both foreign and very London at the same time. 'Max,' he continues, holding out his hand.

She takes his hand – soft and warm – and shakes it. 'Laughton Rees. Thank you for seeing me at such short notice, Mr Max.'

'Oh, it's just Max,' he gestures at one of the ugly chairs for her to sit. 'My family name is Max and my parents, for some reason known only to them, decided to name me Maximilian, so my name is Max Max.' He smiles and his eyes sparkle like the diamonds he deals in. 'I think they must have had high expectations of the man I would become, but, as you can see' – he gestures at his small frame perfectly enrobed in a soft grey tailored suit so well-made it almost looks like it's been painted on – 'God had other ideas.'

Max waits for her to be seated then sits himself, a tiny gesture of courtesy that makes Laughton feel like she's been transported back to a time when people still had manners. 'You don't look much like your father,' he says, studying her with his bright eyes.

'You knew my father?'

Max smiles and opens his hands in an expansive, welcoming gesture. 'Why else do you think you managed to get this meeting so quickly? Your father was a good friend to the bourse in his day.'

'How so?'

Max studies her with a particular, amused look on his face that manages to be both open and wary at the same time. 'The bourse was built on trust and continues to operate on that reputation. If people don't trust us we have no business. Unfortunately, there have been times in the past when that

314

reputation has been threatened. Diamonds are a unique form of wealth, you see, very valuable, very portable, very hard to trace. At least, they used to be. That makes them a very attractive form of alternative currency for people who don't wish to conduct their financial affairs in a traditional or transparent way. Criminals, basically. As a result there have been times in our history when certain members of our organization got involved with, well . . . shall we just say the wrong people. Your father was that rare man who understood that a few bad apples did not mean the whole orchard was rotten. He worked with us to clean house from time to time and was always very discreet about it. He always treated us fairly, and I am now extending that same courtesy to you. So, Dr Rees – how can I help?'

'I would like to pick your brains, really, about how diamonds are bought and sold, particularly ones that maybe . . . aren't a hundred per cent above board.'

'You mean stolen diamonds.'

'Yes. Sixteen years ago a consignment of uncut diamonds went missing during an international sting operation. They had been seized by the police in another operation and were being used as bait to crack open an international drug-trafficking syndicate. The operation was compromised, the main culprits got away and the diamonds disappeared. No one seems to know what happened to them, but I imagine some of them might have come through here at some point?'

Max cocks his head to one side. 'Not necessarily. There are twenty-one other bourses around the world and your diamonds could have passed through any one of them, possibly even more than one. The fact that they were uncut also makes them very difficult, if not impossible, to trace. What quantity are we talking about?'

'Thirty million dollars' worth.'

Max raises his eyebrows. 'Quite a consignment. And depending on the size and type of diamond they will have more

than doubled in value by now. Of course, stolen diamonds rarely fetch top price because not many people are prepared to take the risk of buying them. Having said that, uncut stones are much easier to move because they can be altered before being offered for sale.'

'Altered how?'

Max leans forward, clearly warming to the subject of stolen gems. 'Whenever there's a large diamond theft we get notified by the police, who give us descriptions and sometimes images of the missing stones.'

'I'm presuming you keep records of all the transactions that take place here.'

'Of course, though I'm afraid I couldn't share them with you. We're a little bit like a Swiss bank: discretion is our middle name.'

'Could you at least tell me whether there was a large transaction of uncut gems about sixteen years ago, or possibly in the years following?'

'I can tell you that a consignment of this size would definitely have raised eyebrows if it had been brought to us and we would have checked with the police to make sure they were legitimate. The problem with uncut diamonds, and one of the main reasons they work so well as criminal currency, is that they can be altered relatively easily so that they don't look anything like the missing stones. They can be cleaved, which is when a rough diamond is split along its tetrahedral plane, its natural, weakest point. They can be sawed using either lasers or a phosphor-bronze blade, or they can be bruited to alter their shape by hand. Any decent cutter would be able to change the appearance of a rough diamond, given the right tools and enough time. The diamonds could then be sold directly to jewellers who would turn them into rings, earrings, necklaces, all the usual high street items. If that's what happened to your diamonds, they are unlikely to have even passed through these doors.'

'So you're saying you don't know if they did come through here?'

'I'm saying if they did, it wasn't as a job lot, and it's unlikely they would have remained in their uncut state. I'm sorry not to be more helpful.'

Laughton's phone buzzes in her pocket and she pulls it out then smiles an apology at Mr Max. 'Sorry,' she says, holding up her phone, 'I'm involved in a live homicide investigation, so I need to . . .'

Max waves away her explanation and she glances at the screen, expecting a message from Tannahill she can read quickly and reply to later, but instead there is a text message from an unknown number saying simply:

Your father took the diamonds.

She frowns at her phone, thinking this must be a joke or a wrong number, and slightly freaked out by the coincidence of someone messaging her about the diamonds at the exact same time she is discussing them.

Then another message comes in, this time with a photo attached, and Laughton feels like her body is being lifted up and slammed into the ground at the same time. The picture shows Gracie, bound and blindfolded, and tied to a chair in a room so dark it looks like a dungeon. Another message beneath it reads:

Will exchange your daughter for the diamonds.

Laughton stares at her phone, her mind screaming. She hits *reply*, her trembling fingers struggling to type out the letters of her message:

I don't have them.

'Are you all right?' Max leans forward across the table. 'You look like you've seen a ghost.'

Laughton can't summon a response. She glances up at him, shakes her head then stares back at her phone where three dots have now appeared, showing that Carver is typing.

You must have. Figure it out. You've got until the tide turns. Don't call anyone, and that includes your boyfriend. Tell me when you have them. Remember what happened to Henry's wives.

64

Laughton bursts out of the front door of the bourse like a swimmer breaking surface. She takes deep breaths and leans against the wall. Her instinct is to call Tannahill but she can't.

Don't call anyone, the message had said. She can't risk it.

The image of Gracie, gagged and bound, keeps flashing through her mind, making her want to scream, and cry, and break something.

She checks the time: 11:18.

High tide is at 3:40.

Just over four hours to fix this.

She thinks about the dingy room Gracie was in. Maybe Tannahill had made progress chasing down an address, but she can't call him to ask. He'd know something was wrong. She wouldn't be able to hide it from him. She had to fix this herself. Has to save Gracie on her own. But how?

Carver thought her father had the diamonds, but she knew that he didn't; she went through all his things when they moved into his flat and found nothing.

Actually, that wasn't true. Not any more. She hadn't searched *all* his things because there were some things she hadn't known about.

She steps into the road, prompting long leans on car horns,

and holds her hand up. About twenty feet up the road a cab with its light on eases through the traffic towards her and she sprints towards it. The driver winds his window down as she draws closer.

'I need to get to Bow,' Laughton says, opening the door and jumping inside before he has a chance to tell her he's not heading that way.

'Whereabouts in Bow, love?'

'Do you know the Big Yellow Storage Company?'

'Yeah, I know it.'

'Take me there, please, as fast as you can.'

65

Gracie is frightened, but also angry.

The room she is in is dark, the only light coming from an old-fashioned wood stove in the corner of the room that glows orange behind a partially opened door. She can't see much and all she can hear is the constant rush of water coming from somewhere beneath her.

She didn't see who grabbed her, didn't even hear them creep up behind her.

Stupid!

She had wandered into a derelict building as if she'd been walking into McDonald's to meet a friend, and now no one knew where she was. Part of her thinks she probably deserved to die for being such an idiot.

Only it would kill her mum if she did die like this, which was exactly why she can't let it happen.

She pulls on the straps on her wrists and ankles binding her to the heavy chair, working them backwards and forwards to loosen them, but all she succeeds in doing is rubbing the skin away until the pain makes her stop.

Her breathing is heavy from the effort and she tastes the dampness of the place in the back of her throat, along with something metallic, like iron, and the flannelly, cotton tang of

the gag in her mouth, forcing her mouth open and making her jaw ache. She thinks about screaming but doubts she will be able to make much of a sound. The noise of the rushing water would drown it out anyway.

She also doesn't know where *he* is. Probably behind her, though he might have gone off somewhere and left her here.

She tries to remember the name her dad had mentioned to her earlier, the guy who was looking for him. Billy Carter or something like that.

Maybe if she can remember his name she can use it to try and reason with him. Forge a relationship. Make him view her as a person and not just as . . . whatever he currently views her as.

There has to be a way out of this. Whoever pretended to be her dad to lure her here must have done it for a reason. If he'd wanted to kill her or do some other sick shit, he would have done it by now, wouldn't he? She needs to believe that the fact she's still alive and tied up like this is a good thing. She *has* to think that because thinking anything else is not going to help.

Tears leak from her eyes and she blinks them away.

She won't allow herself to cry.

Tears won't help either. If she'd been smart she never would have come here like this. She would have thought it through and at least have told Elodie or someone what she was doing, and where she was going. She should have told them to call her mum if anything happened to her. It was obvious now. Just because someone sent her a message using her dad's phone didn't mean it was her dad. Whoever killed him must have taken his phone.

Carver! That was his name. Billy Carver.

If she can only find a way to talk to him, find out what he wants, bargain with him, get him to drop his guard, *anything*, she will do whatever it takes to get out of this.

She *is* going to survive.

She *is* going to get out of this somehow and then she's going to tell her mum that she's sorry, and that she loves her, and

that she will never be a dick to her ever again. She promises it in her head to whoever might be listening.

The movement is sudden and makes Gracie's head flinch away from the thing that's appeared in front of her face. It's a bottle of water – open, held by a gloved hand. She feels tugging at the back of her head and the gag in her mouth slackens then falls around her neck.

'Drink,' a voice behind her says, sounding muffled and deep, like whoever is speaking is trying to lower their voice.

Gracie moves her aching jaw around but keeps her lips closed.

'Drink,' the voice says again.

'Why are you doing this?' Gracie asks, annoyed when she hears the slight waver in her voice.

The movement is fast and violent, a hand grabbing her forehead, yanking her head back so hard it bangs on the top of the chair. She lets out a cry of pain and the bottle is jammed in her open mouth, the hard edge of the plastic neck cutting into her gum as she clamps her teeth shut against it. The hand on her forehead slides down her face and pinches her nose so hard she cannot breathe. She bucks against the chair but the bindings hold her tight and she starts to struggle for air, tasting blood in her mouth.

She tries to turn her head away but the hand holding her is too strong so she holds her breath instead until her lungs are screaming and her mouth opens involuntarily to take a breath and she chokes on the water. She coughs and tries to take another breath but gulps and swallows instead. She carries on gulping, thinking maybe if she can drink all the water she'll at least be able to breathe again.

But everything starts going distant – the sound of rushing water, the feeling of panic. She drinks the water and everything goes out of focus, then she closes her eyes and the world falls away.

66

'Wait for me here.' Laughton jumps out of the cab and sprints across the car park and into the reception of the Big Yellow Storage facility. The man on reception looks up from his book and nods in recognition when he sees her.

Laughton ignores him, running straight across reception and barging through the doors leading to the lifts and the stairwell. She hits the call button but the lift isn't there so she carries on to the stairs, taking them two at a time all the way up to the third floor. Her shoes squeak on the polished concrete as she runs down the long corridor, her legs burning, her breathing heavy, but she powers on, thinking only of the tide steadily rising and time running out for her daughter.

Laughton rounds the corner, skids to a halt by the door to 301 then grabs the padlock, tears springing to her eyes as she taps in the code to unlock it: G-R-A-C-E.

The lock pops open and she yanks it free, pulling the door open so hard it clangs loudly against the wall as the lights *tink* to life inside the unit.

Laughton surges into the room, hustling past the green baize table and the shattered picture frame with the office chair still sticking out of it. She opens the wardrobe door and starts pulling her mother's clothes out by the armful.

It had come to her on the cab journey over, lighting up inside her head like a flash of lightning. Her father had left her more than the flat and a storage unit full of lost causes and personal memories. He had also left her one single book she had no memory of him reading to her when she was a child, a book about an ice kingdom reached through the back of a wardrobe.

She pulls the last of the clothes out and dumps them on the floor, feeling a rush of guilt as the vague scent of her mother hangs in the air, sparking confused emotions. She can't think about her mother now or the gentle preservation of her memory; she has to think about Gracie and preserving her.

She stares at the back of the wardrobe, looking for anything out of the ordinary – a hatch, a hinge – but can see nothing but panels of wood. She looks around for something heavy, a tool of some kind, but there's nothing here but the chair which is too unwieldy for what she has in mind. She thinks about the heavy padlock and hurries back to the door. She unhooks it from the metal hasp and hefts it in her hand, feeling the weight of it. It could work – not ideal, but it's the best thing she has. She turns to head back into the unit but spots something better hanging on the wall of the corridor under the security camera.

The wooden panel at the back of the wardrobe splinters the first time she hits it with the fire extinguisher. She pulls back and launches the heavy cylinder at the cracked wooden panel a second time and this time it gives, a large piece breaking off and falling into a narrow cavity at the back of the wardrobe. Laughton throws the fire extinguisher on to the pile of her mother's clothes and is on her knees, pulling at the splintered wood with her bare hands, yanking pieces free to reveal more of the hidden compartment. There is something there, something dark grey with a cable wrapped round it. She yanks at another section of broken wood, getting splinters in the palms of her hands as she makes the hole

325

bigger. Another piece of wood breaks free and she throws it to one side, then reaches into the narrow gap and pulls out the grey object.

It's a video camera, one of the old kinds with a tape instead of a memory card and a flip-out screen. She can see a tape inside but the battery is dead and she hasn't got time to plug it in and see what's on it. She lays it on her mother's clothes and reaches back into the gap, her hands feeling around for whatever else might be in there. Her fingers touch something soft and she pulls out a small cotton bag with a drawstring top. She can feel something loose and heavy inside and her heart races from more than exertion as her fingers fumble with the knot to open the neck of the bag.

Inside are maybe a couple of hundred or so white rocks, a variety of shapes and shades, ranging from clear white to dirty grey. They look like nothing at all, a handful of quartz or broken glass. They certainly don't look like they're worth millions, or a person's life.

Laughton pulls out her phone, opens the message from Carver, hits *reply*, then types with trembling fingers.

I have the diamonds

She stares at the screen, the only noise in the room the sound of her heavy breathing.

Three dots appear under her message, followed by:

Head to Richmond TW10, Riverside Drive. Message when you're there.

The three dots reappear and a second message pops up:

Come alone. Don't talk to anyone.

At the exact same time her phone buzzes in her hand with

an incoming call, almost like it's a test. She looks at the caller ID – Tannahill.

Apart from her daughter there's no one she would rather talk to right now. But she can't talk to him. She can't risk it.

She rejects the call and gets to her feet.

The only thing that matters right now is getting Gracie back safely.

67

Tannahill listens to Laughton's voicemail telling him to leave a message but hangs up before the beep. She never listens to her messages anyway. He drums his fingers on his desk and looks at the information on his computer monitor, the product of half an hour's worth of background checks on Malcolm 'Minty' Fowler. In that time he has managed to find twelve properties in and around London either owned by or linked to him through companies he's a director of. One is an old factory and pumping station in Richmond, close to Teddington Lock. It's by the river in the area Buddy identified and he'd love to go and take a look at it right now with a dozen armed officers at his back, but for that to happen he'll need proper authorization.

He looks across the room at the chief superintendent's office. The door is open and he can see someone inside but doesn't recognize Grieves' replacement. He gets up from his chair and threads his way through the desks and groups of officers, hoping that whoever the acting CS is will be overworked and under-prepared enough to rubber stamp any request that comes across his desk. He stops by the open door and raps on the door frame.

'Yes.' The acting CS doesn't even look up, his frowning attention fixed on the top sheet of a large stack of paperwork on his desk.

'Welcome to NoLMS, sir.'

'Thanks. I have to say I'm very much enjoying the welcome present Inspector Grieves left me.' He gestures at the stack of papers in front of him.

Tannahill smiles. Now he's up close he does vaguely recognize Grieves' stand-in, a ratty-looking guy from central division with a weak chin and receding hair brushed forward like a Roman senator. He tries to remember his name – Smith or Jones or something like that, generic and utterly forgettable.

'Can I help you with something?' the acting inspector pulls another document from the top of the pile and sets it on the desk in front of him, 'or are you the welcoming committee?'

'Actually, I was hoping I could get authorization for a search team.'

'On what case?'

'A double murder and possible missing person. Two bodies decapitated and dumped in the Thames over the last two days and a third potential victim missing. I've got a lead on an address that might be the place the suspect has been using as a killing room.'

Smith or Jones, or whatever his name is, looks up from his desk and seems to properly notice Tannahill for the first time. 'You're DCI Khan, aren't you.'

'Yes, sir.'

He nods. 'Grieves said you'd probably be the first person to come asking for something.' He opens the top drawer of his desk and pulls out an envelope with KHAN written on it. 'He told me to give you this.'

Tannahill takes the envelope and pulls a handwritten note from inside:

329

I may be on holiday but i'm still in charge. If you ask for any additional resources for anything to do with operation henry 8 while i'm away, consider it automatically denied.
D.G.

Tannahill looks back up at the acting CS, wishing he could remember his name so he could use it now. 'Sir, with respect, I think this note was written about something else. This is a new lead and time is a factor. I believe the missing person could well become the third victim unless we find him before the tide turns.'

'Before the tide turns! Who's your suspect, Captain Jack Sparrow?'

'Sir, we believe the killer is disposing of the bodies at high tide in order to utilize the current to carry them away from his base in West London, somewhere near Teddington Lock. I have found an address in that area linked to one of the victims and I'd like to check it out, preferably with a team in tow in case my killer does turn out to be there.'

The acting CS shakes his head wearily, a look of vexed annoyance on his narrow face. 'Can I see that note?'

Tannahill hands it to him and tries again to remember the guy's name as he reads it and hands it back without a word then turns his attention back to the paperwork. Tannahill stands there for a moment, not quite sure what he's meant to do. 'So, do I have authorization for a search team?'

'No, you don't,' the acting CS says, still frowning at the papers. 'I think Grieves made himself perfectly clear in his note, don't you? I'm keeping his chair warm while he's away so I'm not about to start by throwing my weight around and under-mining the direct recommendations of the man who's really in charge here. You cannot have any extra resources for this case. You'll just have to do what we all have to do, make do with what you have. Close the door on your way out, would you, I don't know how anyone gets anything done in this noisy zoo

you call an office.'

Tannahill stares down at the man, feeling a strong and instant dislike, not only of him but also his type.

Gray – that's it. He's called Stephen Gray. Gray by name, grey by nature. He's a company man, a safe but uninspiring pair of hands who's worked his way up mostly by not drawing attention to himself and by being careful not to offend anyone important. He's everything that's wrong with the current leadership within the Met, more interested in paperwork and stats and how things look, rather than how things actually are. But he is also senior to Tannahill, so there's nothing he can do about it.

'Thank you, sir,' Tannahill turns and leaves the office, mustering all his self-control to close the door behind him and not slam it.

He calls Laughton again on his way back to his desk. Again, it goes straight to voicemail.

Bob Chamberlain looks up from his monitor as he approaches. 'How did that go?'

'Grieves left me a note basically telling me to behave myself and stay in my lane.'

Chamberlain nods. 'Sounds like a Grieves thing to do.'

Tannahill perches on the edge of Chamberlain's desk and looks back across the room to where Gray is visible behind the stack of paperwork he is grinding his way through. 'Since when did policework become more about paperwork than catching criminals?'

'Since the internet came along, probably. Everything's shitter since the internet came along.'

Tannahill nods then turns to him. 'How do you fancy a trip out west?'

'You mean, will I give you a lift somewhere you've probably been told not to go?'

'Something like that, yes.'

Chamberlain shakes his head. 'After our little field trip

331

yesterday, I've got too much paperwork of my own to catch up on. Sorry. Blame the internet.'

Tannahill scans the room. 'When's Baker in?'

'Not until noon. He worked late last night on one of those other murder cases you don't seem to be that interested in.' Chamberlain regards Tannahill from over the top of his glasses. 'Maybe it's time to stop swimming against the current on this one and do what your "superiors" keep telling you to do.' He does air quotes around the word 'superiors' to show Tannahill he's still on his side. 'Work another case and give yourself a break. Give us all a break.'

Tannahill's phone buzzes in his hand and he looks at the screen, expecting Laughton but seeing a different name. He swipes to answer it. 'Good morning, Dr Prior.'

'Evelyn, please. I think we're beyond stuffy formalities now, don't you, although I am calling you in a professional capacity. I have news.'

'Is it good or bad?'

'I have no idea. All I can do is ascertain certain facts using my considerable skills and experience then hand them over to you. Whether those facts are good or bad is for you to decide.'

Tannahill senses an extra formality in her tone, despite the whole 'call me Evelyn' spiel, which is absolutely fine by him. 'So, what facts do you have for me?'

'Well, firstly, I have the fact that you were wrong.'

Tannahill waits for further explanation but clearly Evelyn Prior is going to make him work for it. 'What am I wrong about, exactly?'

'Many things,' Evelyn Prior says curtly, 'but in this particular case you are wrong about the identity of that second body you found in the river yesterday.'

Tannahill stiffens. 'Go on.'

'I did a DNA comparison against a swab we had on record for a . . .' Tannahill hears the sound of papers being rustled.

'Shelby Andrew Facer, and it's not a match, not even close.'

Tannahill looks up at the stained ceiling, lining up this new information with everything else he thought he knew.

'Aren't you going to ask?' Evelyn Prior's voice purrs down the line, reminding him she's still there.

'Ask what?'

'God, you really are a piss-poor detective, aren't you! Ask me who your DB actually is.'

'You know?'

'No, I'm just stringing you along – of course I know. Listen, you're really no fun at all and I'm actually glad now that I decided not to go for cocktails with you. There was a match on the database for your DB, an exact match with someone called Carver, William Carver. Does that name mean anything to you?'

68

The cab pulls over by a swathe of green and Laughton gets out, eyes wide, senses wired.

'You want me to hang around again?' the driver asks.

'No,' Laughton says, studying the wild meadowland dotted with clumps of bushes and trees. So many places someone could be watching her from.

She turns back to the cab and uses her phone to pay, then opens her messages and types: I'm here – as the cab drives off.

She studies the wall of green, waiting for a reply, looking for movement. It all seems so maddeningly peaceful, the sound of birdsong and the wind through the grass mingling with the distant, background hiss of London.

Her phone shudders in her hand with a new message:

Look for the chimney in the trees

She scans the tree canopy and sees the top of a brownish-red brick stack rising above a row of horse-chestnut trees. Another message buzzes in.

Head there and message me again

Laughton steps off the pavement and starts walking, picking her way through narrow tracks in the thick grass where animals have passed, her shoes and jeans quickly soaked by last night's rain.

She reaches the chestnut trees and passes under the lowest branches, shaking drips down on her as she enters the dark heart of the tree. She picks her way across damp leaf mulch and litter that suggests someone may have been living here fairly recently – food wrappers, an old shoe, scraps of clothing all grubby and twisted alongside a bedroll that has been pecked by unseen birds. Laughton moves past it all and emerges on the other side of the trees. The building the chimney is attached to is now visible behind a chain-link fence with 'KEEP OUT' signs and huge gaps in it, showing no one has taken any notice of the warnings.

Laughton heads for one of the larger gaps in the fence, scanning the building and the overgrown yard surrounding it. It looks like an old Victorian factory, judging by the vaguely ecclesiastical shape. Swap the chimney for a spire and it could easily pass for a church. Graffiti covers the lower walls, and the security panels fixed over every ground-floor window and door. Weeds choke the yard, sprouting from cracks in the bricks and the sagging gutters. Ivy is everywhere, spreading across the ground and up the fence and walls, like a wave of green water has broken against the building and been frozen in place.

There's more litter here too, crushed cans and shiny glass fragments gone cloudy with age. Laughton scans the upper windows, the ones not covered by security grilles, studying the darkness framed by the jagged edges of broken windowpanes in search of a figure or the face of the man who took her daughter.

Movement at the edge of her vision makes her head whip round to where a pigeon flaps out of the building and settles on the upper branches of a sycamore that has taken root by

the old gate. Beyond the gate she can see the river and something else, the back end of a car, its green metallic paint making it blend in with the ivy and the weeds. She moves across the overgrown yard towards it, trying to see if there's anyone inside, keeping out of view as she approaches in case it might give her some slight advantage. She reaches the corner of the building and peers round. She can see the whole of the car now but the windows are too dark to see if anyone is inside. She can see a metal security door too, standing open, darkness beyond.

She taps a message into her phone:

I'm here

The three dots appear again then her phone buzzes with a reply:

Find the door by the parked car and head to the basement

Laughton stares back at the thin column of dark at the door's edge. She feels scared and also angry. Her daughter is in this building, and Laughton is her only hope of getting out of it. She marches forward, phone in one hand, her other resting on the bag of diamonds in her jacket pocket. This is what he wants, and Gracie is what he'll give in return. And for now, that's all that matters. What comes after she can worry about once she has her daughter back.

She stops by the door, pulls it open and looks inside. The building is dark and cavernous and smells of old piss and damp. It's exactly the kind of place you never want to imagine your daughter in. She sees a stairwell over to her right and a faint glow of light coming from the lower level.

Head to the basement – the message had said.

Laughton steps into the building, her footsteps crunching over unseen rubble. She tries to soften her steps and walk slower but it's no use, everything echoes in the cavernous

building so she walks faster instead, making her footsteps louder so that at least her daughter and whoever has taken her might hear her coming.

The sound of running water grows louder as she descends, the flickering red light growing brighter too with each new step she takes. Both the light and the sound are coming from a door that stands open, directly opposite the foot of the stairs.

Gracie has to be in here, *has* to be, and Laughton heads straight to it, pushing the door wider as she steps into the room.

There is a fire in an old pot-bellied stove in one corner that sends wavering light into the rest of the room. A butcher's block stands in the middle of the floor with various tools lined up on it – a saw, some chisels and a hammer, a hatchet. Gracie is in the furthest corner, bound to a large wooden chair, her head slumped forward, her blonde hair covering her face.

Laughton rushes over, grabbing a chisel as she passes the butcher's block. She pushes the hair away from her daughter's face and checks her neck for a pulse. Gracie is unconscious but breathing. There is a thin streak of blood on her chin and Laughton's anger flares inside her when she sees it but she forces herself to focus. She places the blade of the chisel on the thick bindings on Gracie's wrist, her adrenaline-fried fingers trembling as they grab the handle and start rocking it back and forth to make the blade bite through the nylon.

The sound of a footstep crunching on the dusty ground behind her makes her head whip round, the chisel held out in front of her now and pointing at the figure who has joined them in the room.

He is standing between her and the open door, the light from the fire reflecting in the visor of the motorcycle helmet covering his face and making him appear inhuman and demonic. He has a gun in his hand, and it's pointed directly at her.

Laughton stares at the figure for a second, her eyes flicking between the gun and the visor, imagining the face behind it.

'I have the diamonds,' she says, reaching slowly into her pocket and pulling out the bag. 'Let us go and they're yours.'

The figure continues to stare at her for a long, uncomfortable moment then reaches up with one hand to unclip the chin strap.

'Deal's changed,' he says, in a muffled voice that sounds familiar.

He pulls off the helmet and lets it fall to the floor.

'Hello, Laughton,' Shelby says with a smile. 'Did you miss me?'

69

Laughton stares at Shelby, her mind trying to line up what she's seeing with what she thought she knew.

Shelby continues to smile at her, enjoying her confusion. He looks down at the chisel in her hand and his smile broadens. 'What's that line from the movie, about bringing a knife to a gunfight? Drop the shank, we're all friends here.'

Laughton holds up the chisel for a moment then lets it fall to the ground. 'Why are you doing this?' she asks.

Shelby pulls a face like it's the stupidest question he's ever heard. 'Why do you think? Why does anybody do anything?' He nods at the bag of diamonds in Laughton's hand. 'Money.'

'You killed all these people for money? You kidnapped and terrorized your own daughter for money?'

'Oh, come on, Laughton, it's not just a bit of money, it's a life-changing amount. You've got to remember I've spent the last sixteen years in a place where every single person would have done exactly what I did if they had the chance. Most of them would have done it for less.'

Laughton takes a step away from Gracie, moving to the side to draw Shelby's attention and the barrel of his gun away from her. She glances at it, trying to see what make it is. It looks like a Glock 19 but the light in the room is too dim to be sure.

It also looks scuffed around the muzzle. A street gun, probably. Which means it's unlikely to have been well-maintained.

'So, who was the body in the reeds?' Laughton asked.

Shelby smiles. 'You're smart, let's see if you can work it out.'

Laughton takes another slight step to her right. Webber is the third of the three missing 'wives', but he was last seen after the second body was found. Malcolm Fowler was the first, so the body in the reeds must be . . .

'Carver,' she says.

Shelby's smile grows wider, revealing the sharp edge of his broken front tooth. 'Bingo. Poor, dumb, violent and predictable Billy Carver,' Shelby says. 'The only decent thought he ever had was to get even with everyone once he got out and try and find the diamonds. I knew he'd probably come for me too so I suggested we meet to talk it out, see if we could track everyone down together. Just a friendly drink.'

'A friendly drink laced with fentanyl,' Laughton says, taking another small step away from Gracie. 'Why did you write my address on Fowler's arm after you killed him?' Laughton asks, glancing at the gun again. Definitely a Glock, which meant it had no safety.

Shelby smiles. 'That was a nice touch, wasn't it? I needed to get hold of the case files in order to find out the names of the other "wives" and figured a headless body with your address written on it would get your attention a lot faster than me turning up and spinning some story about scary old Billy Carver and his blood vendetta. I needed the names and I needed to know what happened to the diamonds and thought, seeing as your dear father set all this up to get rid of me, he must have kept copies of the files. So, I wrote your address on his arm to flush you out and get you worried. As soon as I knew the body had been found, I came round to see you to set the rest in motion. And what an eye-opener that was! The super-fancy apartment you live in, the private school that costs forty-five grand a year to send our dear daughter to. It got me thinking,

maybe there was another score to be had here, over and above the diamonds. You know Gracie and I had breakfast yesterday morning?' His smile broadens when he sees Laughton's surprise. 'Oh, yes, we had a lovely little catch-up. She showed me the family tree and how few names were on it, and that's what got me thinking. If you died, and she died, who would get that amazing apartment and whatever savings are paying for those ridiculous school fees?'

Laughton laughs. 'You really think if you kill us *you'll* inherit everything?'

Shelby shrugs. 'I am next of kin.'

Laughton shakes her head. 'You're deluded.'

'You have no idea what I am, or what I've become. I am not the man you knew. You don't even know my name. I can be whoever I want to be, even a grieving father.' He nods at the bag of diamonds in Laughton's hand. 'And I'll have enough money to hire the best lawyers to argue my case. That's something else I learned on my little holiday in Florida. Justice is like anything else, a thing that can be bought, so long as you can afford to pay the price.'

Laughton holds the bag up and opens the neck to reveal the rocks inside. 'Isn't this enough? These are worth tens of millions. Why don't you take them and go.'

The smile vanishes and Laughton sees the cold heart at the centre of him. 'You still don't get it, do you? It's not just about the money, it's about making people suffer as I have suffered. When everything has been taken from you, nothing will ever be enough to fill the gap left behind. I don't only want to have everything, I also want you to have nothing.'

'So, what? You're going to shoot us both? When was the last time you fired a gun, Shelby? They're not nearly as accurate as they appear on TV, and that piece of shit you're holding looks like it's been used as a football.'

He holds the gun up higher. 'I'll take my chances.'

'What about Gracie?' Laughton holds up the diamonds. 'Isn't

341

your daughter, your own flesh and blood, worth more than all this?'

The smile returns. 'You really don't know me, do you? If I'd found out you were knocked up back in the day, I would have done what I always did back then, slip you something to get rid of her and act like you had a miscarriage. You weren't the first little canary to fly into my cage. You were just the one that got away – and you only managed that because of Daddy.'

Laughton stares at him, feeling nothing but hate in this frozen moment. 'OK,' she says. 'If this is what you want. Have it.' She tosses the bag at him, the rocks spilling and scattering as it arcs high through the air. Shelby instinctively raises his hands to catch it, making the barrel of the gun shift upwards.

At the same time Laughton drops low, loading her legs with energy and launches forward, focusing all her anger on Shelby.

He sees the movement, sees her coming for him. Jerks the gun down.

Fires . . .

70

Tannahill has just passed through the gap in the fence and spotted the green Land Rover by the abandoned factory when he hears the gunshot.

He drops down to a crouching run and scampers over to the nearest wall, pulling his phone from his pocket and stabbing the screen to call Chamberlain. He clamps the phone to his ear and crabs along the graffitied brick towards the corner of the building closest to where the shot had come from. He peers around the edge and sees the metal security door hanging open by the parked car. The shot had sounded muffled, like it had come from inside the building.

Chamberlain's voice sounds in his ear as the phone connects. 'I told you already, I'm not—'

'Listen.' Tannahill cuts across him, his voice a low and urgent hiss. 'I'm already here and heard shots fired from inside the building. I need you to send an armed response team here right now, use my phone signal as a locator.'

He hangs up and listens for any further sounds as he scans the yard and the building for movement. Apart from the wind moving through the higher branches of the trees, everything is still.

He moves forward, sticking close to the wall as he makes

his way to the open door. He stops to the side of it, crouches down and slowly peers around the edge of the steel.

The building beyond is totally dark, the only light coming from the stairwell over to the right. He leans in slightly, opening his eyes wide to try and make out what the darkness contains. He can hear something, faint and indistinct coming from somewhere in the building. It sounds like scuffling then a crashing sound as something is knocked over. It could be an animal, only animals don't fire guns.

He checks the signal on his phone. Three bars – enough for the armed response team to follow. Chamberlain will have dispatched local cars too, which will probably get here sooner. You don't piss around with shots fired and an officer on scene.

He should wait for backup to arrive before going in, watch the door in case anyone tries to leave. That's protocol. That's the safest, most sensible thing to do.

But then he hears the scream from inside the building – a loud and anguished 'Noooo!' – and he's already running, through the door and into the darkness. Because even in the ragged, animal howl of that single word, he recognized Laughton's voice.

71

The bullet rips through Laughton's jacket, grazing her arm, but she doesn't even feel the pain. Her focus is all forward, her leg lashing out with speed and anger, her foot catching Shelby's wrist and snapping it back hard, making the gun fly from his hand and disappear into the darkness beyond the open door.

Shelby staggers, recovers, and scrabbles after the gun.

Laughton lands and sweeps her leg low, catching Shelby hard below the knee. His leg buckles and he collapses to the ground, arms flailing to try and stop himself. He knocks the butcher's block over, sending blades and saws clattering to the floor.

Laughton leaps over him into the pitch-black corridor and starts feeling around on the floor for the gun. Her hands bash against bottles and cans and other things she can't even iden-tify, but she can't find the gun. She pulls out her phone to use the torch, glancing behind her to make sure Shelby isn't there. But he isn't behind her at all, he's limping to the far side of the room, where Gracie is.

He looks over and smiles his broken smile when he sees Laughton staring at him. He reaches for the lever, pulls hard on it, and Gracie disappears beneath the floor where the sound of running water now rages.

'Noooo!' Laughton surges back into the room, eyes wide

and staring at the spot where Gracie had been. She stumbles forward, everything feeling way too slow, and grabs a chisel from the floor. Shelby's face shines with malevolent triumph as he lifts his hand and shows her the hatchet he's holding.

'Now you've brought a knife to an axe fight,' he says, taking a limping step towards her.

Laughton glares at him with utter hatred for a moment then jumps feet first into the open trapdoor and the churning water beneath.

The water is freezing, the sudden cold and heavy impact almost knocking the air from Laughton's lungs as the current grabs her and sucks her away into a slimy, pitch-dark chute.

She covers her head with her arms, making herself as small as she can as the roiling water carries her away to the river, bouncing her along the channel as if it was trying to drown her, or break her, or both.

She thinks of Gracie, just ahead of her in the dark, unconscious, and immobile, going through exactly the same thing as her. She will drown if Laughton doesn't get to her fast, die alone and in terror at the bottom of the river, weighed down by the chair she was strapped to.

Laughton holds on tightly to the chisel, clutching it to her chest, clenched against the awfulness of her situation, and focusing only on getting both of them out of it.

Her feet bang into something, the chair, most likely, heavier and slower than she is, then, as suddenly as everything went dark it goes light again, a dim muddy brown, and the rushing sound is gone as she is disgorged into the river. She reaches down to grab the chair and it drags her down until it hits the riverbed and jars free from her hand.

Laughton feels herself starting to rise and kicks against it. Gracie can't kick for the surface and grab a breath of air so neither will she. She swims back down, kicking for the bright halo of Gracie's hair dimly visible through the silt-churned water. The riverbed here is littered with rubbish, shopping

trolleys, road signs, a newish-looking moped with what looked like a bag of laundry tied to it. She ignores it all and kicks hard towards Gracie, grabbing on to the arm of the chair, anchoring her in place against the strengthening current, then twists around until she is level with her daughter's face, blonde hair swirling, her eyes wide open now and terrified, her mouth opening and closing as she fights desperately for breath.

72

Gracie stares at her mother.

She can't move, can't breathe.

In her panic she thinks she must be dreaming.

This can't be real. She can't be in the water with her mother floating in front of her.

She wants to breathe, tries to force herself to wake up gasping from this nightmare. She opens her mouth to take a breath but some physical instinct closes off her throat and her chest heaves but nothing happens.

Her mother holds a hand up in front of her face, like she's telling her to wait.

Wait for what?

Then her mother is gone and her panic explodes.

She looks down and can see her mother moving through the brown water. She wants to reach out and grab her to stop her from leaving but her hands won't move. Her mother tugs at the chair and she feels herself shunt forward a little. She does it again and again, like she is trying to drag her out of the river one inch at a time.

Gracie looks up, trying to see the surface, but all she sees is muddy water and the vague halo of the sun, way too far above her. There's no way her mother can save her like this.

Her chest is already burning with an overwhelming desire to breathe.

The chair shunts forward again and Gracie looks back down at her mother, floating next to what looks like an old motorbike.

She'd read once that if you died in your dream you died in real life too. And she was going to die in this dream, she knew that, and it wasn't so bad.

She wishes she could somehow tell her mother how sorry she is for all of this, tell her with her eyes if nothing else, but her mother is not looking at her, she's looking down at the riverbed instead, and feeling around in the mud for something.

73

Laughton can feel the cold sinking into her, making movement hard and her thoughts slow. Her lungs are almost exploding with the desire to breathe.

It's worse for Gracie – she repeats in her head.

However bad it feels for you, it's worse for Gracie.

Her hands continue to search through the slimy mud, kicking up silt as she feels around for something solid, a rock, a brick – anything. She grabs the frame of the dumped moped, using it as an anchor against the current and a scream robs her of air when she sees what is tied to it. The headless body is pinned beneath the twisted bike, bound to the metal, an arm trailing out to one side as if pointing downriver with its stump. Laughton looks away, forcing herself to focus. Her hand slides through the slimy mud and finally closes round a rock worn smooth by decades of tides. She snatches it up, then looks back at Gracie, mouth open, eyes unfocused. She looks dead but she can't be, she *can't*.

Laughton turns back and places the blade of the chisel against the rear tyre of the moped, ignoring the thing pinned beneath it as she raises the rock then bangs it down as hard as she can on the handle.

The water and the cold slow her effort and it strikes the

handle with a dull bang that does nothing. Her vision is starting to tunnel as her brain is increasingly starved of oxygen but she fixes her focus on the handle of the chisel and tries again, using all the strength she has left to strike it. The point of the blade bites into the rubber and she hits it again, her vision reduced now to a dwindling circle at the end of a lengthening tunnel.

A jet of bubbles springs from around the blade and she swims forward, moving down the tunnel of her own vision to clamp her mouth on the cut. She tastes rubber and mud and breathes in the rank but sweet air, filling her lungs and restoring her vision.

She turns to Gracie, her hair now covering her face like a small, silken shroud, bubbles leaking from her mouth as the last breath escapes from her. She reaches out, grabs her hair and pulls her head forward. She opens Gracie's lips with her fingers then pushes her mouth against the free-flowing jet of bubbles coming from the cut in the tyre.

74

Air rushes from the tyre, mixing with the water in Gracie's mouth and making her choke. She coughs and splutters but the hand continues to hold her head firm against the jet of air until her vision slowly returns and the rubber-tainted oxygen fills her lungs.

The coughing passes and she continues to breathe, blowing out gouts of bubbles then sucking in more air from the tyre.

Gracie feels the hand move away from the back of her head and experiences a moment of panic at the thought that her mother might be leaving again. She reaches out with her free hand to try and stop her, but she has already moved too far away, and she watches her stop at the other tyre and realizes what she is doing. She grabs the tyre with her free hand and holds it in place, feeling the jolts as her mother bashes the chisel against the other tyre until a second jet of bubbles appears. Her mother clamps her mouth over it, then looks across, their eyes meeting through the murk of the river as they fill their lungs with rubber-tainted air.

They stay like this for a moment, then Laughton moves again, down to one of the thick straps binding Gracie to the chair. She places the blade of the chisel on it, raises the rock and bangs it down until it cuts through the nylon and Gracie's other hand floats free.

75

Tannahill moves quickly down the stairs, listening for further sounds. He can hear rushing water but nothing else. It grows louder as he descends into the basement, masking the sound of his approach.

He reaches the bottom and moves across the dark corridor towards a door that opens on to a room bathed in weak, flickering firelight. The noise of the rushing water is loud and coming from the room.

He takes another step and kicks something in the darkness, making it skitter across the litter-strewn floor and into the dim spill of light.

Tannahill stares at the gun for a second then bends down and picks it up. He checks the magazine and pulls back the slide, trying to remember his firearms training. It's loaded and there doesn't seem to be a safety catch. He stands up, holds the gun in front of him, and steps into the room.

The sound of rushing water is almost deafening and the figure inside doesn't react when Tannahill steps into view behind him. He is on his knees, picking up what look like small pieces of glass from the dirty ground.

Tannahill scans the room quickly, looking for Laughton, but she's not here. He looks over at the open trapdoor, the noise

of the water roaring out of it and feels sick in his stomach.

'Police!' Tannahill shouts above the din. 'Hands in the air and turn around slowly.'

The figure freezes then straightens up. His hands rise slowly above his head, the left hand a fist holding the glass pebbles he was collecting. He gets to his feet, turns around slowly.

'Well, if it isn't the boyfriend come to save the day,' Shelby says with disdain. 'I know,' he says, catching Tannahill's confusion. 'You thought I was dead. I've been getting that a lot lately. Also,' he nods towards the open trapdoor where the sound of rushing water is coming from. 'I'm afraid you're too late to save your girlfriend. What's that line from *The Godfather*? Laughton Rees sleeps with the fishes. I sent her daughter down the chute and she jumped right in after her. Mother's love, eh?' He holds his hands up higher. 'So, you gonna shoot me or not?'

Tannahill raises the gun and adjusts his grip. The desire to pull the trigger and keep on pulling it until there are no bullets left is strong; but he can't do it, that's not who he is.

'I'm not going to shoot you,' Tannahill says, through gritted teeth. 'I'm going to arrest you.'

'And what if I don't want to be arrested?'

'You don't have a choice. There's an armed response team surrounding the building.'

Shelby looks past Tannahill's shoulder. 'I don't see anyone,' he says. 'And surely if there was a squadron of coppers out there they wouldn't send you in alone? That isn't even your gun.' He takes a step to his right. 'So you're not going to arrest me and you're not going to shoot me. either.' Shelby bends down slowly and picks up the hatchet from the ground. 'I just told you I killed your girlfriend and you're standing there feeling all confused about it. Truth is, you're not a cold-blooded killer.' He holds up the hatchet and inspects the blade. 'But I am.'

He limps towards Tannahill, raising the hatchet as he comes.

Tannahill takes a step backwards. 'Put down the weapon.'

'Or what?' Shelby says, limping closer. 'You gonna call on your imaginary SWAT team?'

Tannahill moves back into the dark of the corridor. 'Last chance.'

Shelby smirks. 'For you maybe.' He lifts the hatchet, ready to strike.

Light and sound explode in the corridor as Tannahill pulls the trigger. The bullet hits Shelby centre mass and knocks him backwards. He lands on his back and Tannahill moves forward, gun still pointed at Shelby, his ears ringing from the gunshot. The hatchet lies on the ground by Shelby's hand. Tannahill kicks it away and looks down at Shelby as his hands flutter to his chest, like two white birds that settle for a moment then fly away red. His breathing sounds grotesque and laboured, his chest wound foaming where air sucks in and out of the hole. The bullet must have clipped a lung; an artery too, judging by the amount of blood now spreading out from underneath him.

Shelby looks up at Tannahill, an expression of surprise and confusion on his face.

'You were right,' Tannahill says. 'I'm not a cold-blooded killer. Self-defence, though, that's a whole other story.'

He moves over to the trapdoor and stares down into the churning white water for a moment then turns and sprints from the room, taking the outside stairs three at a time.

He bursts out of the door and back into the daylight, narrowing his eyes against the sudden brightness as he runs towards the river. He pulls his phone from his pocket and scans the weeds ahead. He reaches the fence and squeezes through a ragged gap, glancing down at his phone long enough to call Chamberlain. He listens to it ringing as he starts running again, crashing through the long grass and low-hanging branches of the mature trees that grow thick along the riverbank.

'Armed Response is four minutes away,' Chamberlain says. 'A squad car should be with you any second.'

'I need the river police,' Tannahill says, bursting through a

screen of weeds and finally finding the river. 'Tell them to head to this location. Two people in the water. Send an ambulance too. It's Laughton Rees and her daughter. Tell them to hurry.'

He looks left and right, but the weeds and bushes along the bank are too thick to see very far. He scans the surface of the water, searching for bubbles, or eddies, or any sign at all of where the sluice might empty out. The tide has turned and the river is already lively. It could discharge anywhere. He sees a spot of dead water about twenty feet downriver and ten or so feet from the shore.

'LAUGHTON!' he calls out as loud as he can, but not nearly loud enough. He listens for a response, hears nothing but the whisper of the breeze through the branches overhead.

He steps back from the river's edge and starts battling his way through the vegetation, heading in the same direction as the current, yelling Laughton's name as he goes.

76

In the cold, murky depths of the river, Laughton grabs the tyre and takes another hit of stale, rubbery air. The air is almost out now and the current getting stronger. She has to jam herself against the bike to stop herself from being swept away and both the cold and the current are sapping what's left of her strength.

She fills her lungs then pulls herself back along the moped, hand over hand, to where the final strap is binding Gracie's foot to the chair. She lifts the chisel and holds the blade over the strap, forcing herself to focus, knowing the air must be low in the other tyre too. She won't have many more chances at this but she feels so cold, and so, so tired.

She picks up the rock, which seems ten times heavier than it did when she found it, and lines it up with the top of the chisel handle. Her fingers are struggling to grip now. She lifts the rock, ready to bang it on the end of the handle, but a sudden rush of current knocks it from her hand and sends it tumbling down to the riverbed where it vanishes in the muck.

Laughton grabs on to the leg of the chair to stop herself from being carried away and stares down at the spot where the rock disappeared. She hasn't got the strength to find it and try again. She feels if she lets go of the chair she will

be carried away and will not have enough strength to fight the current.

She wraps her arms around the chair leg and holds the chisel in place instead, rocking it back and forth to try and work the blade through the nylon strap.

She is so tired. Bone-weary, and so cold.

She looks up at Gracie, still clinging to the other tyre, a thin stream of bubbles rising from her mouth as she exhales, showing she is still OK at least.

She looks over at the other tyre, barely visible through the filthy water. There are no more bubbles coming from it now, her exertions having exhausted it long before her daughter's supply.

She looks back at the strap and saws the chisel blade back over it again. She has so little energy left that the idea of closing her eyes and drifting away is almost tempting. She bites on her lip, drawing blood and using the pain to focus her mind. She rocks the blade back and forth, pushing as hard as she can, her hands like claws now, so numb it's like they belong to someone else. It feels like she is doing nothing at all but one side of the strap suddenly pings apart and she rocks the blade over the section that still holds until it pops loose and the binding falls away.

In her relief she lets go of the chair leg and the current immediately pulls her away, too fast for her to react. She reaches out to try and catch the chair leg again but her hands grab at nothing but water and she sees Gracie slipping quickly from view into the thick murk of the river.

Laughton gives into the river, holding on to her last breath and praying that Gracie will leave her and swim to the surface to save herself.

But she doesn't.

She sees her growing closer again and realizes what she's doing. She is swimming after her, the current speeding her closer. She tries to shake her head, wants Gracie to leave her.

She knows Gracie won't have enough energy or breath to save them both. She wants her daughter to live and if she has to die to guarantee that then that's fine.

Laughton raises her hand to wave her away but then something else grabs her from above and she looks up. Tannahill is floating above her, holding her arm and swimming up.

The last thing she sees before she passes out is Gracie, right beside her, kicking for the surface and looking straight up at the light.

77

The story of Shelby Facer knocks everything else off the front page.

His victims are named and the connection between Brendan Webber and the Home Secretary are mentioned but not dwelt on. Kenwright manages to spin it so the press leaves Charlie Nixon alone while he grieves in private for the tragic loss of his dear friend, offering his support to Webber's widow and their two young children.

In the wake of this, the uniform scandal is largely forgotten, the news cycle moves on, and the PM's office issues a brief statement saying lessons have been learned and a more robust process will be implemented going forward. The directors of the company, the friends of Charlie Nixon who got the government contract to supply police uniforms without going through the proper tender process, somehow, incredibly, get to share the fifty-million-pound profit they made from the deal.

The public tut, but mostly people are far more interested in the other fifty million now dominating the news, the uncut diamonds at the heart of the Shelby Facer murders.

The rocks found at the crime scene where Shelby Facer died were fakes, nothing more than a handful of glass pebbles like you might find in the road after a car accident.

Online, all the true-crime enthusiasts and conspiracy theorists, including the woman who took the photo of the first body by Tower Bridge, start speculating about where the diamonds went. Laughton reads these stories with a kind of detached numbness as she lies in her hospital bed next to Gracie, as if everything described happened to someone else.

They had been brought here straight from the river, and pumped full of antibiotics to head off all the infections they'd been exposed to in the toxic waters of the River Thames. Gracie was also treated for secondary drowning, a condition Laughton hadn't even been aware of before today, an inflammation of the lungs that can prove fatal long after water has been aspirated. She looks at her daughter now, propped up slightly in bed as she sleeps, remembering another hospital bed and a different set of worries.

Laughton slips out of her own bed and pads silently over to the window, peering tentatively out at the night as if it was filled with hidden horrors.

Morning is still a few hours away.

When it comes she will have to make a statement and she is not yet sure what she will say – not entirely. She thinks about her father and all the work he'd done to remove Shelby from her life and how, in the end, all it had done was delay everything. Was she going to do the same? How much of what her father had done and, also, what he hadn't done, was she going to share?

'I'm sorry.'

The voice comes like a ragged whisper, making Laughton turn from the darkness beyond the window.

Gracie is looking up at her, her eyes soft with sorrow and pain.

'Hey,' Laughton says, moving over to her bed and stroking her hair from her face. 'You have nothing to be sorry about.'

Gracie closes her eyes and tears squeeze out. 'I do. I didn't listen to you. You said he was bad, and I didn't believe you. I didn't want to.'

'I know, I know, it's OK, shhh. Listen. You don't need to be sorry. I should be the one saying sorry. I pushed you towards him by not telling you about him sooner. It's perfectly reasonable to want to know about your own father, and I should have been more understanding. I mean, if I wasn't going to tell you what you wanted to know, who else were you going to talk to? But never forget it was him who did all this. He was the one who came to our home. He was the one who played on our good natures by pretending to be scared of some mindless killer when all the time it was him.'

'But it was me who went to find him. It was me who put myself in danger – you too.'

Laughton shakes her head. 'It wasn't your fault. You just walked into a trap he'd laid. I did exactly the same thing when I was your age. You can't blame the prey for the hunter's nature. All you can do is learn to recognize predators when they come along.'

Gracie nods and forces a weak smile. 'Is he definitely gone?'

Laughton thinks back to the crime scene photos she'd insisted Tannahill had shown her, Shelby lying on his back, eyes open but seeing nothing, a dark pool of his spilled life surrounding him.

'Yes,' Laughton murmurs. 'He's gone. Get some rest now, tomorrow is going to be an ordeal.'

78

Laughton squeaks to a halt in the neon brightness of the shiny yellow corridor, tucks the morning paper under her arm and taps the letters G-R-A-C-E into the lock. Lights flicker on as she pulls the door open and she stands for a moment, taking in the room she had run from in panic a few days earlier.

She takes a breath and steps inside, dropping the newspaper on the table before heading to the back of the room where the wardrobe stands empty, the back panel caved in and splintered. Her mother's clothes lie in a pile next to it, the video camera in the centre like some misshaped egg, wrapped in the black tendrils of the power cable. She picks it up and plugs it into the only socket in the room by the whiteboard, blowing out a small breath of relief when the red power button light blinks on, showing that it still works. The power cable is long enough to reach the table, so she places it on the green baize next to the newspaper. She pulls the chair free from the splintered frame of the film poster, wincing slightly at the tearing sound it makes, then wheels it over to the desk, sits down and closes her eyes. She sits like this for almost five minutes, enjoying the silence and peace after the chaos of the last few days, until a door bangs in the distance, followed by the squeak of approaching footsteps. Laughton opens her eyes, turns the chair

to face the door and smiles when Tannahill steps through it.

'Ah, Mr Khan,' she says, in her best Bond villain voice. 'I've been expecting you. Welcome to my dad's man cave where he kept all his cold case files, and also some personal stuff, which is the reason I asked you here.' She leans forward and flips out the screen on the camera. 'I have a horrible feeling there's a message from him on this, so I warn you I may dissolve into a puddle of snot and tears the moment I press play.'

'OK,' Tannahill says uncertainly.

Laughton pulls a pack of Kleenex from her pocket and looks up at Tannahill. 'You ready?'

He nods. 'Are you?'

'Not really.' She presses play anyway.

The screen blinks as the tape start and John Rees appears, sitting at the same table and in the same chair. 'Greetings from beyond the grave,' her father says, smiling at the camera.

Laughton smiles back and brushes a tear from her cheek with the back of her hand.

'I'm hoping this is my daughter I'm speaking to, but if not, this is your lucky day, or at least a day you will never forget, depending on what you decide to do with the information I'm about to give you. If this is Laughton I'm speaking to, however, then congratulations on figuring out *The Lion, the Witch, and the Wardrobe* clue I left for you, and though this place is hardly Narnia, in some ways it might prove to be every bit as magical.

'Along with this camera you will have found in the back of the wardrobe a bag of uncut diamonds. They were part of a sting operation I was in command of called Operation Henry 8 – you can find all the details of it in one of the boxes in this room. Long story short, it was a sting operation, a fake drug deal, and also the operation that sent Shelby Facer away for many, many years. I had my reasons for engineering this little intervention, not least because I suspected Shelby Facer was much more dangerous than he appeared.'

'He got that right,' Tannahill murmurs.

364

'Anyway,' her father continues, 'I don't want to waste time talking about him, I want to talk to you instead about the opportunity this room presents.

'When I was running Operation Henry 8, the Met was in a mess. There was so much corruption that I had to keep it hidden from the people who would happily sell us out to the very guys we were trying to catch. As part of the sting we needed bait to lure in the cartel reps, and I had recently seized the uncut diamonds in an arms deal bust. The guy in charge of that operation was on the take too, so I had not turned them in or reported them. Everyone had been killed in the bust anyway, so they were not required as evidence. I didn't really know what to do with them, to be honest, but I thought they'd be useful for Operation Henry 8 at least.

'I told my team I'd borrowed the uncut rocks from some contact in the diamond district who owed me a favour, and that they were strictly on loan. And it all worked perfectly, the diamonds lured in the cartel contacts, the rocks were authenticated by their guy, the real rocks were swapped for fakes and the sting went ahead. And when the dust settled, Shelby Facer was no longer in the picture and another guy went down too, a psychotic thug who was no great loss to society. The other four involved were window dressing really, useful pawns in setting up the sting but not worth reeling in afterwards, so I cut them loose. Shelby had always been the primary target.

'But when the dust settled and Shelby was safely locked away and no longer a danger to you, I still had the problem of what to do with the diamonds. I knew if I put them into evidence they'd either end up back on the streets funding more criminal activities, or they'd get "lost" along with everything else of value back then. So I decided the best thing to do was to keep them out of circulation. Officially, they didn't exist, so I chose to keep it that way until I could figure out what to do with them. Only I never did. And now you're listening to this,

it means the diamonds are your problem, and I'm sorry for leaving you this strange legacy.

'I always wanted to do some good with them but never quite figured out how, then life had other ideas and I ran out of time. But whatever you decide to do with them, I know it will be the right thing. Even if that turns out to be hiding them back in the wardrobe to keep them out of circulation.' He smiles. 'And if this is not my daughter I'm talking to, but just some random stranger who happened to find this, then please know that these diamonds are cursed and if you use them for anything other than good deeds your life will be blighted forever. Good luck.' He winks, leans forward and the picture cuts out.

Laughton stares at the blank screen and says nothing. It is Tannahill who eventually breaks the silence.

'But the diamonds we recovered from the pump house were fakes,' he says. 'We tested them and they were all just pieces of glass.'

Laughton rises from the chair and walks to the back of the unit where the broken picture frame is propped against a shelf. She bends down and scoops up a handful of the broken glass pebbles littering the floor, then carries them back to the table and tips them on to the green baize next to the newspaper. 'These aren't though. I swapped them for glass before I went to meet Shelby.'

Tannahill stares at her for a moment before picking up one of the rocks. It is small and white and looks like a piece of quartz. 'Why did you swap them?'

'Because I wanted some leverage. I wasn't going to go alone to some remote place to meet a killer and take all my cards with me. I figured leaving these here might work as an insurance policy. I needed something to bargain with, and holding back the location of the real diamonds in exchange for cutting me and Gracie loose was the best I could do.'

Tannahill nods. 'Smart.' He places the uncut diamond back

on the green baize next to the others. 'So, what are you going to do with them?'

Laughton stares down at the pile of white stones. 'Earlier today I went to see a diamond specialist to see if the diamonds had been fenced sixteen years ago. The guy I spoke to told me how easy it would be to cut and shape individual rough diamonds and sell them in the market one by one.'

'Whoa,' Tannahill says. 'You're not thinking of keeping them, are you?'

'I don't know,' She looks up at Tannahill. 'I'm not saying that I won't turn them in, but let's think it through for a second. If these do go into evidence they might not get pilfered like they would have done back in my dad's day, but they would still eventually get sold off in some government auction, and then what?' Laughton pulls the newspaper across the table towards her and opens it to the article about Charles Nixon and the police uniform procurement scandal. 'The money would still effectively vanish somewhere up the chain of command, get funnelled into some budget or other to plug a gap in funding, or be used in some grubby little backroom deal like this that would only enrich the friends of whichever weasel happened to be in power that day.' She shakes her head. 'If I knew the money would actually be spent on police work, then I'd hand it in, no question, explain where they came from and walk away." She turns to Tannahill. "How would you spend this money if it was down to you?"

'You mean apart from buy myself a really nice house?'

'Yeah, no houses, no holidays, just charitable stuff, something from your own direct experience that you know would tangibly make things better, something that would make a difference.'

Tannahill shrugs. 'I guess I'd use it to hire more police and make sure they were properly resourced. More uniformed officers on the beat, more backroom people to keep on top of the casework, maybe set up a couple of new labs dedicated to forensics.'

Laughton smiles and gets up from the chair. 'And that,' she says, putting her hands on either side of Tannahill's face, 'is why you and I are made for each other.' She kisses him hard on the lips then moves around the table and heads over to the first set of shelves. 'Take a guess how many boxes are in this room.' She lifts the lid off one and pulls something from inside.

Tannahill looks around the stuffed shelves. 'I don't know. A hundred?'

'More,' Laughton says. 'WAY more.' She fixes a photograph of a smiling young woman to the whiteboard.

'This is Alison Mainwaring. Twenty-three years old when she disappeared in Deptford on her way home from work, December ninth, 2004. Never found, case never solved, not enough resources or manpower available to properly review it subsequently. There are over four hundred cases like hers in these boxes – cold cases my dad worked on in his spare time because he knew if he didn't do it, no one else would.

'Now imagine if you used these diamonds to set up a dedicated team whose entire job was to review and investigate these cases and others like them, properly funded, no oversight, no chief inspector riding a desk with an eye on the budget and their own promotion telling you there wasn't enough money for lab fees, or a stakeout crew, or a ticket to Berlin so you can look a person of interest in the eye when you interview them. Independent autonomy funded by money confiscated from a criminal terrorist organization that no one else knows about and no one ever *needs* to know about. The diamond guy I spoke to earlier said this amount of uncut stones would be worth around fifty million.' She grabs the morning paper and holds it up. 'Fifty million is the same amount of money the Home Secretary, your boss, effectively gave away to his friends for a bunch of police uniforms that are not even fit for purpose and will be written off in the next budget review. So who would you rather this money went to?' She walks over to the whiteboard and slaps the paper against the wall so Charles Nixon

MP's worried face is lined up next to the smiling photo of the missing girl. 'Him or her?'

Tannahill studies the two photographs then shakes his head. 'Her obviously, but it doesn't matter what I think because it's not my decision to make. Those diamonds don't belong to me – they don't belong to you either.'

'They don't belong to anyone, though, that's the point. My dad said everyone was killed in the arms deal where they were seized. They were supposed to fund criminal activity but my dad took them and used them to help him do his job instead, by using the diamonds as bait money. All I'm saying is, why not take that idea to its logical conclusion? Keep using this money for good instead of bad. Think about it. How much time do you waste at work having to ask for more time or resources in order to do your job?'

'Too much.'

'Exactly, and how many times do you actually get what you need?'

Tannahill said nothing.

'Almost never, right? This kind of money could change that. It could be used to set up an independent support unit that you could call on whenever you needed, without having to run it by five different people in your department first – lab time, research work, phone bashing, whatever you needed could be yours.'

'Just like that?'

'Just like that. And you wouldn't even need to do anything different, you could stay exactly as you are and stay in your job, only I could help you do it now. I could give you the support to help solve the kind of crimes that would otherwise end up in boxes like these.'

'Like Robin to my Batman?'

'Exactly!'

Tannahill looks back at the photo of the smiling girl. 'Look, I know everything you say makes perfect sense, but much as

I'd love to be Batman, there is one major difference.' He turned to Laughton and smiled at her. 'I'm not Bruce Wayne.'

Laughton shakes her head, not sure of his meaning.

'Bruce Wayne is a billionaire,' Tannahill explains. 'All Batman's crime-fighting exploits are funded out of his own pocket. What you're proposing here is to steal tens of millions' worth of evidence.'

'OK, number one, like I said, it's not evidence,' Laughton says, her voice now edged with irritation. 'Operation Henry 8 is a closed case and Shelby Facer is dead, thank God – no trial pending, no evidence required. And, number two, the official record says the diamonds were fakes, so they don't officially exist. How can you steal something that doesn't exist?'

'But they do exist though, don't they.'

'Yes. They do. And so do all these unsolved cases.'

Tannahill looks around the room at all the boxes. He shakes his head. 'I'm sorry, it doesn't feel right to me.'

Laughton nods solemnly. 'Do you know what doesn't feel right?' She holds up the newspaper with the Home Secretary on the cover. '*This* doesn't feel right. Millions wasted and no accountability.' She drops the newspaper in the wastepaper basket then hauls a file box off the shelf and puts it down next to the small pile of rocks. 'Finding out what happened to this missing girl and giving some grieving family closure, that *does* feel right. So you can either help me or you can stand in my way. Your choice.'

Tannahill looks down at Laughton, her anger somehow managing to radiate from the back of her head as she pulls case files out of the box. He looks at the pile of diamonds, the smiling face of the missing girl, the crumpled-up newspaper in the waste bin. 'I'm not going to stand in your way,' he says. 'But I can't be a part of this either.'

He reaches out to touch Laughton but then stops, his hand hovering between the two of them for a second before dropping back to his side.

'Do whatever you think's best,' he says finally. 'This is your legacy, not mine.'

Then he walks past Laughton and out of the door, his footsteps squeaking away in the heavy silence of the vast building, filled with London's secrets.

Acknowledgments

Any book, despite having only one name on the cover, is a huge, collective endeavour, and so the person who gets the glory also has many people to thank.

Again, I owe a huge debt to my old school friend, Constable Peter Fairweather (ret), who read the first draft and helped me correct my numerous errors relating to police procedure: any mistakes that remain are mine and mine alone.

I am, as ever, encouraged, protected, supported by the editing genius of both Julia Wisdom at HarperCollins UK, Tessa James at Morrow US, and also by Alice Saunders at the Soho Agency – agent, friend, cheerleader, and occasional rocket-up-ass engineer.

To my family – Kathryn, Roxy, Stan, and Betsy – for all the love and support they give, even though I still lie around the house all day, talking to myself like a weirdo.

For all the other brilliant and talented people who helped turn an idea into the thing you are currently reading, they know who they are, and now you do too because they are listed in a rollcall of honour at the end of this book. Thank you. For everything.

And finally, I want to thank you, dear reader. I've said it before and it still holds true – without you I'm just a crazy person, sitting alone in a room, muttering to himself all day

long. And if you've read this far and feel like saying hello, please do. I can be found in all the usual online places – Instagram and Facebook mainly – and it's so lovely to hear from readers, especially happy ones.

Simon Toyne
Brighton – Sept 2024

HEMLOCK
PRESS

Hemlock Press would like to thank the following staff and contributors for their involvement in making this book a reality.

Editorial
Julia Wisdom
Lizz Burrell

Sales
Holly Martin
Harriet Williams
Angela Thomson
Ruth Burrow

Audio
Fionnuala Barrett
Sarah Allen-Sutter

Design
Sean Garrehy
Dean Russell

Production
Simon Moore

Operations
Melissa Okusanya
Hannah Stamp

Publicity
Maud Davies

Marketing
Vicky Joss